MALICE

Meddling mother Madge + dutiful daughter Alice =

MALICE

Liz Vincent

Matador
9 Priory Business Park
Kibworth Beauchamp
Leicestershire LE8 0RX, UK
Tel: (+44) 116 279 2299
Fax: (+44) 116 279 2277
Email: books@troubador.co.uk
Web: www.troubador.co.uk/matador

ISBN 978 1784620 769

British Library Cataloguing in Publication Data.
A catalogue record for this book is available from the British Library.

Typeset in Aldine by Troubador Publishing Ltd
Printed and bound by CPI Group (UK) Ltd, Croydon, CR0 4YY

Matador is an imprint of Troubador Publishing Ltd

*To my mother, whose funny little ways
inspired this story*

CHAPTER ONE

"I wanted to go to the Festival of Britain," Madge said to the midwife as her body was gripped by another contraction. "Aaagh. " She screamed in pain, which seemed to be getting worse by the second. "Will this take much longer?" she asked once it had eased off.

"Babies take their own time, Mrs. Harwood," the midwife answered, glancing at her assistant and rolling her eyes towards the ceiling. "It's the pain," she explained to the bemused nurse. "It makes them say strange things sometimes."

"It's coming, I can see the head."

Madge was overtaken by the mother of all contractions and she was urged to push with all her might. Tears ran down her face as she did so. There seemed to be a second's respite, then she fainted with exhaustion.

The midwife did her job, then laid the baby in the waiting cot.

"Let her sleep for a while, this was a long one. Then she can see her beautiful baby," she said as they both walked away.

Just before she slid into unconsciousness, Madge remembered the last time she had felt so much pain. It was in June 1939. She had been fourteen and the year was memorable for two reasons. The outbreak of World War Two and her accident. She had been playing tig in the school yard with her friends May and Doris when it had happened …

Running and getting up a good speed was no problem for Madge, who towered above most of her classmates due to her long legs. She was beating May easily when she realised that the classroom window was right in front of her and she couldn't stop in time. Instinctively she took a deep breath as she approached it at full pelt. She raised her left arm in a vain attempt to protect herself, then it went straight through the window with a glassy crash. There was blood everywhere and she fainted. As she did so, she heard Doris scream.

When she came to, Madge was lying on the ground. Doris and the teacher were gazing down at her. The teacher looked annoyed.

"Can you move your arm, Margaret? The left one?"

Madge didn't know. Now she felt the pain, but bravely looked across at her badly lacerated arm as she remembered what had happened. Using her right arm she struggled to push herself into a sitting position, shoving her gas mask in its box out of the way, then tried to move the injured arm with limited success.

"She's alright," said Doris breathlessly as she glanced at the teacher.

"Yes, nothing broken. Honestly Margaret, you always were a big, clumsy lummox. You'd better get off home, get that bandaged up."

Madge pushed her heavy brown hair out of her watering grey eyes. Everyone said the same about her, but it wasn't her fault she was so tall. She blamed her father. He was over six feet.

"Go with her, Doris," the teacher said over her shoulder as she walked back into the school.

"Yes, miss." Anger clouded Doris's clear blue eyes as she helped Madge get carefully to her feet. Then they began the slow walk back to the village.

Ingelfield was a small farming community in darkest Dorset where everybody knew everyone, their everyday lives and murky secrets intertwined in an inevitable sort of chaotic pattern. Madge lived in one of the new council houses on the far side of the village, and knew she was the envy of her friends because of this. Doris's dad had a tried farm cottage with less than primitive facilities, whereas Madge's father Albert had been lucky enough to qualify for one of the newer properties that had been built a couple of years ago. Madge could well remember their dreadful old house. If anything it was worse than Doris's.

Bert, as he was known, was a cowman. Anything and everything to do with cows and he knew it inside out. He had never done anything else in his hard working thirty-seven years. His wife, Eliza, was Ingelfield born and bred but they had met when she had been in service with a family near his home town of Devises. They had married, son Fred had arrived fairly quickly, followed two years later by Madge. Eliza had wanted to be near her mother and now things were going well for the Day family. Fred was working in a garage and Madge was due to go into service when she left school. The only cloud on the horizon was all this talk of a war coming. And the worst part about it was that no-one knew exactly when.

Doris opened the small wrought iron gate with Madge still leaning heavily on her shoulder, and led her up the path to the back door. The front door of the small three bedroomed semi was only ever opened for visitors and was largely ignored. The back door led into the kitchen and once she had got Madge through it, Doris stood to one side to watch the reaction of Eliza Day, a gentle kindly country woman with salt and pepper hair.

"Oh Lord," exclaimed Eliza, the blood draining from her face as she took in the sight of the sorry pair. "What happened?"

Doris explained while Madge sat down at the scrubbed kitchen table. She was feeling faint and sick. As her mother ran some water into a bowl, Madge glanced over at Doris, her best friend. Did she have to stand there looking so petite and pretty with her long blonde hair and bright blue eyes? She was everything Madge wasn't and sometimes, like right now, Madge hated her.

"Shall I go for the doctor, Mrs. Day?"

Madge's spirits lifted when she heard these words, then they sank again as her mother answered.

"We'll see, Doris. Wait till her dad gets home."

Madge sat miserably and made no objection as she saw the bottle of purple iodine come out of the cupboard. Doris helped her mother clean the wounds, then the whole arm was swathed in coarse white bandages. On the way home she had lost quite a lot of blood and now she felt light-headed. To her, getting the doctor seemed like a very good idea. The family paid their weekly subscription to the Ancient Order of Foresters but nobody liked to bother the doctor unless it was serious. To Madge this felt very serious indeed.

"She's been ever so brave." Doris smiled at her. "Hasn't cried or anything."

When Madge heard this her courage failed and she burst into tears. Quiet ones. She knew there was no use in making a fuss. Crying to get attention never worked.

"I should go home now Doris, or your mum'll be wondering where you are. Say hello for me."

"Yes, Mrs. Day."

"Now then Madge." Eliza turned to her as Doris left. "What are we going to do with you?"

"I feels bad," she blubbered.

"Of course you do, you's had a nasty shock. Go lie down for a while, I'll call you when tea's ready."

Madge nodded tearfully then walked slowly from the kitchen, through the spotless front room and up the steep stairs to the smallest bedroom on the back of the house. Her arm felt like a dead weight and was still smarting from the antiseptic iodine as she lay on her narrow bed and cried some more. She wasn't sorry when she eventually fell asleep.

Three days later it was her birthday. She had got to the ripe old age of fourteen without too much aggravation, and would soon have a long working life to look forward to. Madge actually wasn't looking forward to it at all. Her future had already been decided for her without so much as a by-your-leave. She had been put into service with the Carringtons, a rich family in a big house on the edge of the village, and was dreading it. It was bad enough she had to do chores for her mum without having to dress up like a penguin and wait on posh people hand and foot. She had even been told she would be expected to curtsey every now and then and Eliza had made her practice in the front room until the cows came home. Well, her dad anyway.

On the morning of her birthday her mum insisted on changing her bandages and Madge was both pleased and scared at the prospect. They weren't white any more and were beginning to smell. Eliza said she was worried about the wounds going bad ways and Madge made no reply, thinking her mother was quite right to be concerned. The grotty bandages came off, the iodine reappeared and the arm cleaned up painfully again.

Madge got through the morning somehow, helping her mum as best she could with only one useable arm. It was baking day, bread, cake and fruit pies made from rhubarb out of the garden. Madge managed to go and pull this and when she returned with a trug full of it, she was surprised to see a visitor standing awkwardly in the kitchen. Not any old visitor either. It was the rich lady from the big house where Eliza went cleaning four mornings a week.

"Ah, here she is," was the greeting Madge received from Mrs. Carrington. "How are you, Margaret?"

"I's alright," mumbled Madge nervously.

"Oh, what a beautiful basket." Mrs. Carrington enthused as Madge placed it on the kitchen table. "Wherever did you get it from?"

"My dad made it." Basket-making was one of Bert's hobbies in the limited spare time he had, and sometimes it supplemented his income. Madge took this, and a lot of other things, for granted.

"Did he really? How wonderful, I simply must have one exactly like it."

"I'll tell him," said Eliza quietly. "He'll make you one."

"Marvellous." Mrs. Carrington turned to go, then seemed to think better of it. "Oh yes, why I came, ha, ha, silly me." No-one answered. No-one dare. "Yes, Margaret, this injury. It's all very unfortunate …"

"She'll come to you as soon as she's better."

"Well you see, that's the thing." Mrs. Carrington smiled, far too brightly. "I'm afraid I really can't wait, I need someone now. I'm taking May Buckle. I believe she's a friend of yours, Margaret?"

"Yes." Madge was trying to fight back the enormous smile that was threatening to escape.

"May's a good girl," Eliza added.

"So I believe, so it's all worked out alright in the end. I'm really sorry, Eliza. I hope she can find a position when …" She waved perfunctorily towards the injured girl. No-one spoke. "Well, I must be off." Mrs. Carrington looked as though she couldn't get out of the small house quickly enough. "Oh, and don't forget the basket."

With that she was gone and both Days heaved a sigh of relief. Madge was still trying not to smile, while her mother seemed embarrassed and flustered by the brief encounter with her employer.

"So I's not going into service after all?"

"No," said Eliza firmly. "So some good's come out of it."

"I thought you wanted me to?"

"It wasn't my idea, Madge. I hate the idea of people like that walking all over us. Just 'cos they's got loads of money they think …" The sentence remained unfinished but Madge understood. Only too well. "Anyway, let's get this baking done, then we're off to see your grandma this afternoon."

"Oh." Madge was pleased. She liked her grandma.

"Two pies, we'll take one with us. She likes rhubarb."

Madge could believe this. Her dad always said her grandma had a sour face, one that could turn the milk. She never had much good to say about anybody either, yet Madge was drawn to her like a moth to a flame and hung on her every word. Eliza seemed to visit purely out of duty, and Bert didn't go at all if he could get out of it. Madge, on the other hand, would have been round there every day if she was allowed, which she wasn't. Her grandma was an old lady, she had been told, one who didn't need the exhausting company of a chattering girl like her. Madge didn't know how old she actually was but she appeared to be very. She was still wearing the long dresses and severe hairstyles from a bygone era. Victorian, Madge had heard.

The appointed time for the visit came round at last, after the pair had tucked into big chunks of warm bread to keep them going until teatime. A pot of stew was languishing on the gas stove for later when Dad would return from milking the cows. As well as doing this twice a day, he delivered milk on an old horse and trap with a large churn on the back, his half-pint measure ladling the liquid into whatever container his customer provided. All the dairy farms had their own milk rounds, usually twice a day, but recently there had been talk of putting it into glass bottles instead. Bert Day dismissed this suggestion as new-fangled twaddle. The day a bottling plant came to Ingelfield was the day he would eat his cap.

As they left the house, Madge held on tight to the rhubarb pie as she followed her mother down the path and out of the gate. She glanced across at Twenty Acres, a small arable farm that bordered Barnes Lane, the road she lived in. Often she would play there with Doris and May, but now they were to lose one of them to the big house. Madge didn't imagine May would enjoy being in service any more than she would have done, but knew she wouldn't have any say in the matter. If Mrs. Carrington said she wanted you, then you had to go.

None of this was really on Madge's mind as they walked to her grandma's large modern bungalow three streets away. Grandma Flossie had married well. In fact, she had done it three times and on each occasion had managed to find one with a few bob. Madge knew her grandfather had been killed in the Great War but didn't know much about the other two men. She had been told it was none of her business.

"Hello, you two." Flossie greeted them sternly as they walked through the open back door. As Madge glanced enviously around the huge airy kitchen she caught a glimpse of husband number three as he went past the window on his swift way to the potting shed.

"Hello, Mother." Eliza always seemed to be on edge in the presence of Flossie. That's how it seemed to Madge anyway. She seemed to know everything about everything and was never backward at coming forward to give advice on every subject under the sun, whether it was asked for or not. She had a reputation in the village for being something of an oracle, and never turned anyone away that needed help. And, as she had once laughingly confided to Madge, it was the best way to find out all the local gossip.

"Oh, what have you got there, dearie?" She turned her attention to the pie, eyeing it avariciously. "Is that for me?"

"Yes, Grandma," said Madge proudly. She was once again wondering what exactly her grandmother had done to end up in such a wonderful house. It was certainly much better than the previous two with their dark stained walls, infuriatingly fiddly gas mantles and old black range that had to be kept going even in the height of summer. Even the smelly oil lamp had been sold off to some unsuspecting poor soul.

"So, fourteen, all grown up and leaving school."

"She's already left," said Eliza. "Since her accident they said it's not worth her going back."

"Arm through the window, yes, I heard about that." Madge and Eliza exchanged glances. This came as no surprise. "Who bandaged her up?"

"I ..."

"It's all wrong, honestly Eliza, you're useless. How do you expect the girl to do anything with it all dangling like that? Come here, Madge, I'll sort it out for you. And you. " She turned to her daughter angrily. "You put the kettle on."

"Yes, Mum."

Madge took a deep breath as Flossie approached her, knowing from past experience that she was far from gentle at the best of times. The bandages were as good as ripped from her arm, but she daren't shout. Her grandmother didn't go in for tears and sympathy. Bingo and stout were more her style.

"Now then, soon have this all shipshape," said Flossie breezily as Madge fought back huge tears of pain. Eliza stood with her back to the pair doing the same. "Have you had iodine on it?" Madge nodded, biting her lip. "Good, at least your mother's done something right. Now then, bend it, go on, more. Ah, what's this?" Madge daren't look, but felt the woman tug at something. Then she realised she was holding a bloody shard of glass two inches long. "Better off without that, eh, Madge?"

Madge rocked backwards, convinced she was going to faint. The next few minutes were a blur of activity and agony, then Madge sat quietly, her arm now at right angles to her body in a makeshift sling. A cup of tea was placed in front of her by her redfaced mother, who didn't say anything. She didn't need to. Sorrow was written all over her.

"Take this to Bernard," ordered Flossie, holding out a bone china cup and saucer to Eliza. "Talk to him for a bit."

Eliza obeyed without a sound, looking glad of the escape. Then Flossie turned back to Madge.

"You've been very brave." Her voice was softer now. "That's good, you'll need to be for the things life'll throw at you. Remember that." Madge nodded, having no idea what she was talking about. "And don't ever tell no-one that arm was no accident. Told you it'd get you out of going into service, didn't I?"

"Yes, Grandma." Madge smiled happily.

"Whenever you got a problem, Madge, you just come to me. You listen to your wise old gran and you won't go far wrong."

Back in November 1951, Madge began to stir from her post-birth sleep. For a moment she didn't know where she was, then she saw the midwife smiling down at her.

"Everything's alright, Mrs. Harwood," she said, "although the doctor says you won't be able to have any more children. I'm so sorry."

"There's old damage, yes, I know. It's a miracle I had this one, but where is he? Is he alright?"

"She's fine, a lovely healthy baby girl."

Girl? Was Madge hearing right? She had been convinced she was going to have a boy. In fact, she had set her heart on it.

"What are you going to call her?" The midwife was still smiling.

"Alice." Madge's voice was dull with shock. "I suppose we'll have to call her Alice."

CHAPTER TWO

Alice grew into a fine, healthy girl, oblivious to her mother's increasing resentment of her. She wasn't particularly pretty, another thing that irked Madge. If she had to have a daughter, she could at least have the decency to be a looker. She was average at school as well, and Madge despaired of ever having anything to be proud of. Other people's children won prizes and competitions, did well in sports, or got gold stars for tests, but not Alice. She was just an ordinary little girl who didn't excel at anything but she was well behaved, obedient and good mannered, so at least she had managed to get something right.

Madge didn't go out to work, but her days were just as full as if she did. In fact, she had only had one job in her entire life, doing the bookwork in a garage in Ingelfield, and that had only lasted until she reached eighteen and joined the A.T.S. It was then that she had met Geoff, who was a clerk in the army, having previously been one in the hospital in Bath. He had been to grammar school and his parents were quite well off, so she couldn't let him get away. He was quiet and reserved while she was ambitious and bossy, so it wasn't difficult to steer him into matrimony. This was the only way Madge could get up the social ladder, so she took full advantage of the opportunity, took over as boss in the marriage and virtually told Geoff he had better do as he was told from now on. He raised no objections to this domineering behaviour, so Madge started as she meant to continue. By very firmly and very definitely wearing the trousers.

Now she had all her groceries delivered, had all the latest mod-cons to help her whizz through the housework, and had trained the pest of a daughter to make herself useful in the kitchen. Madge had more important things to do, like be a member of the Gardening Club, Treasurer of the Photographic Society, join the Women's Institute, the Young Mothers' Club, flower arranging, be on the church rota for fund-raising and coffee mornings, the Parent Teacher Association – and most importantly of all – organise a wives' club within the confines of the hospital where her husband worked and they lived. The house was much bigger than they needed and was draughty and cold, but Madge revelled in the size and opulence. There were Persian carpets in the hall and big old Victorian furniture in the drawing room. Alice had one huge empty room on the front as a playroom and spent many hours in there alone, tinkling on the out-of-tune piano, painting wistful pictures of a happier place or staring out of the enormous bay window. Madge left her to it and Geoff didn't bother with her either. He had been told she was perfectly happy, and wouldn't appreciate being disturbed by either of them.

Once she had got Alice off her hands and into school, she could concentrate on cultivating the other wives and getting in on their middle-class activities. She fancied the idea of morning coffee with the Group Secretary's wife, and dinner parties with the top surgeons who worked in private practice. This rarely happened. Madge might have the social pretensions, but she didn't have the skills to carry them off successfully. She never realised that she was regarded as something of a joke, but a few women tolerated her enough to pay lip service to her ambitions. Afternoon tea seemed to be one of their favourites, and they always came to Madge for her entertainment value and to save them the bother of doing it themselves. In any case, they were quite aware that their attention made Madge feel important, so they let her carry on with her delusions of grandeur while sniggering about it behind her back.

It was on one such occasion that Madge gave her fair-weather friends some information that delighted all of them. Geoff had won a promotion, and was moving to another hospital fifteen miles away in Lichfield to take up the job in a few months' time. Radiant smiles were exchanged all round, and Madge assumed they were happy for her, not glad to be seeing the back of her.

Someone cracked a rather intellectual joke that went straight over Madge's head just as Alice arrived home from school and walked into the sitting room. This only served to add to Madge's embarrassment. The last thing she needed was a nine year old prattling away and making her look even more stupid. She gave Alice one of her famous death stares and tried to wave her surreptitiously from the room. The child's face dropped immediately and she wasted no time in beating a hasty retreat. As Madge turned to one of her so-called friends with a bright fixed grin on her face, they all heard the playroom door slam. Madge gritted her teeth beneath the false smile as she reached for the cake stand to offer round homemade sweets. The child was developing a temper, she would have to do something about that.

Fortunately for Alice, Madge soon forgot all about the incident as she began making arrangements for the move. She got so wrapped up in all this that she neglected to even tell her daughter they were moving to another town to be nearer her father's job. She had so many things to do that were more important, and losing the big old house was one of her few regrets. It went with the job, and there was no such thing on offer at the newer hospital, so while Alice was safely tucked away at school, Madge and Geoff went house hunting. Madge didn't enjoy this. Every time she found something she liked Geoff winced and said they couldn't afford it, so she wasn't too impressed when they ended up settling for a standard three bedroom semi-detached in a quiet cul-de-sac on the edge of the small city. Madge, despite coming from a run-down council estate, had become accustomed to bigger and better things, and had no idea how she was going to get used to living in this sardine-can of a place.

She glossed over the details of the house to her friends, but had little cards printed up with their new address and phone number on to hand around to everyone she knew. Many empty promises were made to keep in touch and Madge left them with a warm glow in her stomach. It felt good to be so popular and well liked.

Two months before Alice's tenth birthday, the big removal van arrived and pulled up outside the heavy green front door. The child had recently been informed of what was happening, but she still looked confused as she clutched her teddy bear and was ushered unceremoniously into Geoff's car. She sat in the back staring out of the window as all her wordly possessions were loaded into the van, followed by those of her father. This didn't take long and they looked lost in the huge interior. Then came Madge, supervising their few bits of furniture and her clothes, which took quite a bit longer than anyone could even imagine.

"I really don't know where I'm going to put all these things," she fretted as she frowned at everyone around her. "I didn't realise there was so much."

"We've got three bedrooms," Geoff pointed out. "We can use one of them as a storeroom."

"Don't be ridiculous, we need a guest room for when my friends come to stay."

"Of course." Geoff smiled wanly. "Silly me."

When they got to the other end, the contents of the removal van suddenly looked as though they had bred on the journey. They were unloaded, taken into the house and were soon threatening to engulf the place. Madge shooed everyone out of her way as she fussed and faffed over every item that came out of the van.

"Alice, put the kettle on," she said to her young daughter. "I need a cup of tea after all this."

Alice did as she was told, and Geoff escaped the mayhem by going for a walk down the long garden. The garage was at the bottom of it, accessed by a lane that ran along the back of the houses, and it looked as though he had found himself a place to hide already.

They had time to settle in for a few weeks before Madge had the tiresome task of walking Alice to her new school. She had had trouble getting her in anywhere at such short notice, and the place that had accepted her wasn't the best school in town. It was little better than a collection of wooden huts, but it would have to do. It wouldn't be for long anyway, just until she could pass the eleven-plus and get into the girls' grammar school in the middle of Lichfield. This had a very good reputation indeed, especially for getting its pupils into some of the top universities. Madge sighed happily as they walked through one of the worst housing estates in the city to the dilapidated old school. She didn't see any of this, she was far too busy fantasising about Alice going to Oxford or Cambridge, thus giving her long-suffering mother something to brag about to her new friends. When she had made some, of course.

After the first week, she told Alice she could make her own way to school and back. She had organisations to join and help run, whether they wanted her to or not. She had a lot of experience in women's clubs and knew only too well how they could get bogged down in bitchiness, back biting and empire building. Madge herself was above all these things, of course, at least in her own opinion. Every gang of women had a bossy-boots with ideas above their station, but Madge didn't put herself into this category. Nor did she realise that everyone else did.

By the spring, this mission was accomplished to her smug satisfaction and she was feeling very pleased with herself. Geoff and Alice were largely ignored and left to their own devices, which was nothing unusual, then Alice came home with a school report and an invitation to the parents' evening. Madge was appalled. Her useless offspring had slid from her usual place in the middle of the class, which was bad enough, right down to the bottom. How dare she? What did she think she was playing at?

"That school isn't very good, you know," said Geoff when she showed him Alice's report. "I've been asking round. No-one's got much good to say about it."

"It's not the school, it's her. She isn't trying." Madge snapped back at him. "We've never had a report this bad before."

"When's the parents' evening? I think it's time we had a look at this place."

"I know it's not the best but it's only a primary school, they all teach the same things." Madge could feel some blame coming on for her having chosen the place. "The parents' evening is next week.

Do you know, they haven't even got a Parent Teacher Association. I think I should start one. Get them organised."

"Yes, dear," was Geoff's response. It was about the only one he ever made.

The parents' evening was not a great success. Not having any offers of a babysitter, they had to take Alice with them and she was less than helpful. She didn't seem to respond to any of the teachers, and even Madge could almost sympathise with her on this point. She didn't like the look of most of them herself. She was told that Alice wasn't any good at anything, didn't try and didn't pay attention. Just as Madge had suspected.

"She isn't very intelligent," was the parting shot from the last teacher, who taught most of the subjects to Alice's class.

"I know." Madge gave him one of her special looks as she dragged her daughter away.

The very next day, spurred on by these words, Madge caught the bus into town from the end of the cul-de-sac and marched through the quiet streets to the bookshop. She had to order what she wanted, and waited impatiently for the phone to ring to let her know when the volume had arrived. She was going to settle this once and for all. She was going to make Alice do some intelligence tests.

"I don't know why you're bothering," said Geoff when she told him she was now in possession of the necessary book. "It's obvious she isn't going to pass the eleven-plus."

"Of course she will." This option hadn't even occured to Madge in her worst nightmare. "You went to grammar school and I should have done. Of course she'll pass. How can she not do?"

"She's never done better than average at school," he said. "Perhaps she isn't very intelligent?"

"That's what I'm going to find out, but I don't believe she's not. She's our daughter, she must have inherited some brains from one of us. She's just lazy, that's her trouble and we've got to do something about it, before it's too late."

"Going to grammar isn't everything."

"It is to me."

"Yes, I know," Geoff murmured just before he buried his head in the newspaper. He was good at hiding behind broadsheets.

Come the weekend, Madge sat Alice down in the dining room on the front of the house with a notepad and a pencil. When she produced the book of intelligence tests, she ignored the puzzled look on the child's face and told her to begin working. She hovered over her for a while, like a circling vulture waiting to pounce on her smallest mistake, but eventually she gave in to the pleading looks, tutted, sighed heavily and informed Alice she had something to do in the kitchen.

Madge slowly peeled some potatoes, which was usually Alice's job, as she waited for the girl to finish the two pages of tests she had set her. After what seemed like an interminable amount of time, a tearful voice called to say she had finished. When Madge got back to the dining room it was empty and she heard hasty footsteps at the top of the stairs. She knew this could only mean one thing. The girl knew she had done badly.

One glance at the notebook confirmed Madge's suspicions. There were scribblings all over the place, with half-done sums and incomplete addings-up. The majority of the tests had involved numbers, and Madge had chosen these specifically because she was good at them. It had never occured to her that other people might have trouble with them.

"Alice!" she roared from the bottom of the stairs. "Get down here, now."

After a few seconds Alice meekly descended the stairs. Madge could see she had been crying, but ignored her red eyes and cheeks as she ordered her back into the dining room.

"Why have you made such a mess of these numbers?"

"I can't do sums, Mum."

"Don't talk such nonsense, everyone can do sums, they're the easiest thing in the world." Madge really couldn't understand what Alice was so upset about. "You just don't try, that's your problem. You'd better buck your ideas up, my girl, otherwise there's going to be trouble."

"Yes, Mum."

"Oh, get out of my sight." Madge despaired at the pathetic face looking at her with its quivering lip. "I'll call you when tea's ready."

Alice flew from the room and back upstairs to the sanctuary of the box room that was her bedroom. Madge made a funny sort of herumphing noise of frustration and stormed back into the kitchen to find something to take her temper out on. She had a short fuse at the best of times, and dealing with her daughter just seemed to make it worse. Geoff was nowhere in sight either, so she couldn't complain to him. She didn't know where he got to half the time. He seemed to have an awful lot of jobs to do in the garden or the garage. He was hardly ever indoors at the weekends.

Later she sent Alice to find him when dinner was nearly ready. She watched them walking up the path together, and felt a twinge of resentment. Geoff could make the girl smile, a thing she never managed to do, but he was far too soft with her anyway. She needed a firm hand and plenty of discipline and she wouldn't get that from Geoff, he was scared of his own shadow as well as his wife. She was going to have to keep them apart. Couldn't have him undermining all her efforts to whip the girl into shape and make something of her.

Time passed and Madge forgot all about the ordeal she had put her daughter through. She was Secretary of the Women's Institute now, and was pleased with herself for working her way up so quickly. Now she had her sights on the Gardening Club, where the Treasurer was making noises about leaving. Oh yes, she was enjoying this new town now and her circle of friends was growing week by week. She had even got used to living in the small house, although a lot of her clothes were now in the guest room wardrobe. None of her old friends had been in touch apart from the odd perfunctory phone call, and no-one had taken up her offer of coming to visit. They were all so busy, they said, and Madge could understand this. She hardly had time to entertain them anyway.

Then the letter arrived. Madge had almost forgotten about the results of the eleven-plus exam. Alice had admitted she hadn't done very well in the arithmetic section, but Madge dismissed her comments as irrelevant. What did children know about anything? For once she waited until Geoff was home from work to open the incriminating envelope and when she did, her face fell.

"Don't tell me," said Geoff. "She's failed."

"I don't understand it." Madge was dumbfounded. "There must be some mistake …"

"I told you you were pushing her too hard."

"Oh, you'd know a lot about it," Madge snapped at him. "You're never around when there's a problem. You don't know the half of it."

"You shut me out, that's why."

"Don't be so ridiculous, I don't do any such thing. I …"

The conversation soon degenerated into a full blown row and their voices got louder and louder. Madge enjoyed a good argument, it excited her and got the juices flowing. The making-up later was something to look forward to as well. It took quite a lot to get Geoff going, and it didn't happen often enough for her liking. Still, he had a good job which was steady and secure, she didn't have to work and could do anything she wanted, so shortage of intimacy seemed a small price to pay. She picked a fight with him at every available opportunity, not realising or even caring what kind of effect it might have on any other members of the family.

Alice seemed to know she was in disgrace without anyone saying anything to her. She made herself very scarce indeed over the next few days, until things had died down and Madge had found something else to worry about. Now a school had to be selected and when she began her enquiries into this, Madge was disgusted to find she had a choice of one. They lived in the catchment area for the Central school, as it was known, so Alice would be going there whether anyone liked it or not.

"The good thing is, they're building a new one," Geoff informed her when he had read the literature properly, unlike some people. "She'll only be at the Central for a year, then they move to a brand new building."

"Secondary school," Madge groaned. "I can't believe it. I had my heart set on the Priory."

"I know, but she isn't going there. It's not the end of the world. The main thing is that she be happy."

"Don't talk so stupid." Madge gave him one of her famous death stares. Happy indeed! What had that got to do with anything?

CHAPTER THREE

Starting at secondary school. The fateful day arrived and Alice made the thirty minute walk down into town alone wearing her new school uniform of grey skirt, blue blouse and navy blue blazer. She had a dark blue beret too, but this had come off her head and into her satchel once she had got round the corner out of sight of the house. She couldn't be doing with anything on her head. Every time Madge dragged her off to buy a new coat she made her have a hat to go with it, and Alice hated them. The more fuss she made, the more Madge insisted, so she had soon learned to keep quiet and find her own way around problems. It didn't pay to argue with Madge, she always came off second best.

She approached the school with a lump in her throat and her heart beating ten to the dozen. Not many of her classmates from the primary school were coming here yet, because her birthday was in November so she was a year behind everyone else. She knew she wasn't going to know a soul when she walked through the gates, but she also knew it was no good worrying about it. She didn't make friends easily anyway. She never knew what to say.

She clutched her satchel tightly as she walked onto the playground. She had never been here before. Madge had brought her once to show her where the place was but never inside. The single storey buildings looked old, dark and rather intimidating. Alice swallowed hard and tried not to look at them as she progressed across the tarmac.

"Hello, I'm Susan." A girl was suddenly standing in front of her. "What's your name?"

"Alice Harwood." The girl was about the same height as herself, and they both had medium brown hair. Alice's eyes were brown, the same as her father, but Susan's eyes were grey, reminding her of Madge. She seemed to sense Alice's uncertainty and smiled at her. Alice smiled back, her face feeling all funny. Smiling wasn't something she normally did much of.

The two girls weren't in the same class. Alice didn't know how these things were decided, but Susan was put into 1C and Alice into 1A.

"1A? That's good," said Madge when she got home. "And this friend you've made is in 1C?" Alice nodded. "She must be really stupid. You'd better make some friends in your own class instead."

"Yes, Mum," Alice replied dutifully, while secretly resolving to do nothing of the sort. She liked Susan and that was all that mattered.

The months went by quickly, and Alice and Susan became best friends. They went to each other's houses, and even Madge seemed to eventually accept that Susan was a nice girl and good enough for her daughter to play with. The fact that her dad was the manager of one of the best shops in town might have had something to do with it.

They were taken several times to look at the new school, and excitement grew as the move drew ever closer. They knew where their form room was going to be, on the top floor of three. The hall was huge with a modern, shiny wooden floor and there was a brand new gym. Alice wasn't too keen on the idea of this, she wasn't a sporty girl, but she was looking forward to going swimming once a week.

Once they got to the new school, Alice and Susan discovered they were in the same class. It had changed from a secondary modern into something called a comprehensive, but Alice didn't know what this meant. It was good to have her friend sitting next to her in lessons, that's all she knew or cared about.

Eventually the dreaded day came around when the school reports were issued. Alice took hers home in trepidation, not having a clue what it contained. Whatever it was, it wouldn't be good enough, she was quite sure about that.

"This is awful." Madge shouted at her after she had cast a cursory eye over it. "You go from bad to worse. Can't you do anything right?"

Alice sighed quietly but said nothing. She had no idea what the report contained.

"You're going to have to do better than this, you know, if you want to make something of yourself."

"Yes, Mum," was Alice's stock answer.

"We'll talk about this later when I've shown it to your father. Now go and do the vegetables. They're on the draining board."

"Yes, Mum."

After Alice had gone to bed, she heard voices getting louder downstairs, and knew her parents were arguing again. She wished they wouldn't do that, it upset her that people could shout at each other like that. She wondered if they were rowing over her, all her instincts were telling her that they were. If she had crept out onto the landing and hovered at the top of the stairs, like she sometimes did, she would have known that her dad was sticking up for her for once.

"It's not all bad," he was saying, just out of Alice's earshot. "She's third in the class at English and fifth in French."

"What about the rest of it? Twenty-second out of thirty in maths and all the other subjects are nearly as bad. She's useless. No good at anything and never will be."

Alice gathered her pillow up around her ears and bit her lip to fight back the tears. Why did the school have to send out reports? All they ever did was cause trouble.

After a few days Madge had calmed down. The report was filed away in Geoff's desk in the dining room and wasn't mentioned again. Life went on as usual. Geoff went to work at the hospital, where he ran all the administration staff, Madge went shopping and to meetings and Alice continued at her new school. She was good at English and French, found domestic science a breeze and enjoyed all the strange smells and experiments in chemistry. The rest of it was tedious, but had to be at least attempted. Maths was the worst, it was like learning Chinese as far as Alice was concerned. Numbers meant nothing to her and the whole subject just flew over her head. She knew she was never, ever going to get the hang of it.

When she got home that day, Madge had some news for her. As usual she didn't beat about the bush or try to prepare Alice for anything.

"You're joining the Girl Guides."

"Am I?" Alice said in surprise.

"Don't be cheeky," Madge snapped back. "Yes, you are. You start tonight."

"Where is it?"

"The Methodist church hall in town."

"I don't know where that is."

"Oh, you'll find it. Hurry up and help me with tea, then you can go off. Come on, chop, chop."

"But Mum …"

It was no use. Madge never listened to anything she had to say. Once Geoff came home, he did at least give her a few directions. Opposite the cinema was the most useful one, so an hour or so later Alice set off to walk back into town once again. The evening was chilly so she pulled her school mac closer to her slim body as she hurried down the long road. She found the hall and entered it, wondering if she would know anyone inside. She didn't.

The woman in charge looked at Alice then looked beyond her, as if searching for an accompanying parent. She seemed puzzled that Alice was on her own, but welcomed her kindly and put her in a group with some other girls, most of whom were older than her. The two hours went by quickly and Alice found she enjoyed the activities. The best thing about it was that Madge wasn't there. She had never even imagined life without her domineering mother, but now there seemed to be light at the end of the tunnel. Things were looking up.

Alice was even happier the next day when she called for Susan and they walked to school together. She told her friend about the events of the previous evening and Susan said she liked the sound of the Guides. The next week she joined too, and Alice thought she had never been happier. There was life outside the cul-de-sac.

Alice's fourteenth birthday came and went and her parents amazed her by buying her a record player. It was second-hand, but Alice didn't mind. Out of her meagre pocket money she had already managed to purchase a small and very tinny-sounding cheap radio and was discovering the delights of pirate radio and the top forty. Now she could buy records too, although not very often. The Beatles' latest was in her sights, and she had enough with her birthday money. Susan had asked if she was having a party, but Alice said no. She had never had one in her life, and didn't have enough friends to invite anyway.

Later in the school year, they began having lessons in the new language laboratory. Alice enjoyed these. She liked being confined in a booth repeating French phrases on the tape recorder in front of her. She was a natural mimic, and had Susan in stitches by imitating Madge's posh phone voice. Susan said Alice's mum was scary and all Alice could do was agree.

The French teacher seemed to like Alice as she praised her at every opportunity and told the rest of the class she was a shining example to them all. On her next school report this teacher wrote that Alice was a gifted pupil, but even this didn't impress Madge. All she was interested in was her maths result, which was pretty dire, as usual. Alice knew her mother was good with numbers, but she couldn't understand her obsession with them. Madge, for her part, couldn't see what use being good at French could be to anyone. She had enough trouble getting the hang of English.

It was the same teacher who, at the next class, asked if anyone would like a penfriend in a foreign country. Alice's hand shot into the air immediately. She had never been abroad and didn't imagine even in her wildest dreams that she ever would, but the idea appealed to her. She normally dreaded holidays. Madge always organised them, and dragged the three of them off to some godforsaken place in the middle of nowhere with absolutely nothing to do. She was expert at finding cottages in the wildest of Wales or caravans miles from any kind of civilisation. Back to nature, she called it. Alice could think of another, not quite so polite, definition but never dared voice it. That was more than her life would be worth.

The days went by as Alice waited impatiently for a reply to her letter to some unknown person overseas. Overseas. How wonderful that sounded. Exotic, romantic. Different sights and smells and foreign accents all around her. Alice dreamed and dreamed. Then the letter came.

She found out about it when she got home from school. She had made a detour through the town, as she often did, either with or without Susan. The record shop was her favourite. They had booths where people could listen to any record they wanted, which was useful when you didn't have much money and were trying to decide which long-playing record to buy. Alice spent many a distracting hour in the shop, and even Madge never complained when she was late home. She always said she didn't mind, so long as she knew where she was.

Alice walked through the back door, which had been left unlocked for her as Madge had never seen fit to let her have a key. They called hello to each other, then Madge informed her there was a letter on the hall table next to the phone. Alice's heart leapt at the thought of communicating with some foreign person and she hurried to open the letter and see what they had to say.

When she picked up the envelope, she frowned. It was already open. It was definitely addressed to Miss Alice Harwood but somebody else had opened it and no doubt read it. Alice glared towards the living room door.

Later, when she was helping her mother with the washing-up, Madge asked how she was getting on at school. Alice answered her mundane questions sullenly. She was still upset over the letter.

"What did your letter say?" Madge eventually asked.

"Someone opened it," said Alice quietly. "It was my letter, it was addressed to me."

"Ah." Madge hesitated. "Yes, well, I didn't think you'd mind."

"Well, I do. I …" Alice stopped as her mother had disappeared. That was strange, she was normally the one itching for a confrontation. Alice turned back and carried on at the sink. All she could do was hope it wouldn't happen again.

It did and it didn't. Alice sighed in despair when the next letter came and she turned it over to open it. The flap of the envelope was all crinkly and only half stuck down and Alice guessed what had happened. She could almost see Madge boiling the kettle to steam open the letter and have a nose inside. The good thing about it was that it was in half English and half French, the two penfriends had agreed on this to help each other with their languages. Madge hadn't got a clue about French, so at least Alice could get a bit of privacy.

This state of affairs continued for a while, and eventually the steaming stopped. The letters never contained anything out of the ordinary to interest a nosy mother, it was just two teenage girls telling each other about their lives. Alice was glad when she could be the first to read what was inside. It made it more exciting.

Before she knew it, Susan's fifteenth birthday had come round and she had somehow managed to persuade her parents to let her have a party. To add to the excitement, her mum and dad were going out on the evening concerned, and taking her pesky younger brother with them. Susan was bubbling over with enthusiasm for weeks running up to the date in August, and Alice caught party fever too. School had broken up and Alice and Susan spent most of their time together, usually round at Susan's house, in the park or around the town. Anything to stay out of Madge's clutches.

"Barry's coming to my party." Susan gave Alice a knowing glance.

"Barry who?" replied Alice, trying to appear nonchalant.

"Barry who." Susan laughed. "Don't give me that. I know you like him, you told me so."

"So what? You like John Reed but I don't go on about it."

"He's coming as well." Susan grinned. "I hope I can get a snog."

"Have you ever done that?"

"Yeah, once or twice."

"I haven't," said Alice quietly, not sure whether she wanted to or not.

"I know."

"You haven't said anything to Barry, have you?" From the look on Susan's face, Alice already knew the answer and was starting to feel embarrassed.

"Might have."

"Oh Sue." Alice put her hands to her face. Her cheeks were going red and she didn't know how to stop them. Susan just laughed.

When the evening of the party finally came round, Alice wasn't feeling her best. She had the raging stomach ache as she did every month, and even Madge's best headache tablets couldn't get rid of it. That was as much help as Alice had been offered. Her mother had told her that it was all part of being a woman, and she would just have to put up with it. Alice didn't feel the slightest bit like a woman, although she had no idea what that really entailed. A while back Madge had made a half-hearted attempt to explain the birds and the bees, as she put it, but Alice didn't understand the euphemism. She had learnt something about the facts of life from gossip at school and periods had been explained to her by Susan, who'd had the joy of them first. Alice was comforted by the fact that everyone else had them as well, it wasn't just her that had to suffer.

She got herself dressed in a nice blouse and skirt that didn't show off anything it shouldn't, which was one of her mother's sayings that Alice didn't really understand. She was developing a reasonable figure and was quite pleased that her chest was bigger than Susan's, but she wasn't aware of the real implications of this. She had never had anything to do with boys. They were a ruddy nuisance most of the time, but lately she had found herself looking at one or two of them without knowing why.

Alice called goodbye to Madge and Geoff and walked round to Susan's. She was the first guest to arrive. Susan was in the lounge, as it was called in her house, busy sorting through her records, so Alice helped her choose the best ones. After a while other people began to arrive, so Susan left her best friend by the record player while she welcomed them. Alice could hear them laughing and joking and felt uncomfortable. She had already decided that parties weren't her thing. A few people had brought bottles of cider and Alice decided she liked it. There wasn't enough for her to have much but at least it had been a new experience.

When Alice wanted the bathroom, she found Barry was on the stairs talking to his friends. He winked at her and a couple of his friends sniggered in typical schoolboy fashion.

"Come here, darling." Barry turned to face her. He looked strange, his face was bright red and his eyes were nearly closed. "Give us a snog."

Before Alice knew what was happening, he had her in a bear hug and had his tongue in her mouth. She began to panic, she could hardly breathe and was trying to pull herself away. Then he made it worse by groping at her left breast and grabbing it so tight it hurt. Alice squealed in protest and pain so Barry let her go, his friends falling about laughing all around him.

"Nice tits." Barry called after Alice as she fled through the hall towards the front door. This had been one new experience she could well do without!

As soon as Alice had left the house to go to the party, Madge had raided the cake tin, then picked up her knitting. Geoff was on the other side of the living room firmly installed behind the Daily Telegraph, and the only sounds were the ticking of the clock, the rustling of his pages and the clicking of her knitting needles. Madge had long since got used to the boredom of her marriage, but even so her mind slowly slid back over the years to her carefree adolescence. Sometimes she realised she was becoming jealous of Alice. It wasn't that she wanted to be like her, God forbid, it was the youth of her that irked Madge.

Oh yes, thought Madge dreamily, the needles flying through the wool of their own accord. When I was her age …

When Madge was not much older than Alice, she caught the eye of Tom Jury. She had no idea that Tom had caught the eye, and a few other things besides, of nearly every young girl in Ingelfield, him being a very handsome youth of seventeen.

For a few months now, every time Madge saw Tom she got a warm, damp feeling in a certain place. Sometimes her knees shook and she found herself lowering her eyes and flicking back her shoulder-length brown hair when she was in his presence. She had no idea why she did this, but when he asked her to go for a walk over Twenty Acres, she readily agreed. Her pulse was racing as Tom held open the gate for her at the bottom of Barnes Lane. Once they were on the track that ran at the side of the fields, he took her hand and pulled her towards him.

"Ever had a real kiss?" he asked cheekily.

"Dunno, don't think so."

The next thing she knew he had embraced her tightly and had his tongue in her mouth. At first she began to panic, then relaxed as she realised she liked what he was doing. One of his hands was reaching for the new lumpy things on her chest too. She knew they were called breasts and the purpose of them had been explained by Flossie, although at this precise moment in time Madge had absolutely no intention of ever having a baby.

By the end of that hot August afternoon she had almost changed her mind. Now she knew how babies were made and it hadn't taken her long to decide she liked that part. Tom had gone out of his way to assure her that she wouldn't fall pregnant on her first time and to make sure she understood, he had done it twice.

"I've wanted to do you for ages." Was as romantic as he got, but Madge thought his words were wonderful. She thought he was too.

When she next went to visit Flossie, she was bubbling over with happiness and it didn't take the old lady long to find out why. She told Madge off for not keeping her hand on her a'penny, an expression she often used and one Madge had never understood. Until now.

"Don't get involved with that family, Madge. The Jurys are rubbish, the lot of them. If you must go after a boy, then choose one with some prospects. Not that you're likely to find one round here. You needs to go to a bigger place. Dorchester maybe, or Yeovil."

"How do I do that?"

"When you gets to eighteen, you can join the A.T.S. Might as well, you won't find a decent husband round here."

"Mum did."

"He come from Devises and anyway, you needs to do better than a farm hand. I told your mother not to marry him, told her she'd never have no money if she did and I was right, wasn't I? Your ma was only seventeen when she married Bert, not much older than you are now. Mind you, that was her own fault, she never kept her hand on her a'penny either. Fred's proof of that."

"You mean …"

"Yes. I never would have agreed to it otherwise. Don't get yourself in that mess, Madge. Especially with the likes of Tom Jury."

"No, Grandma." Madge shuddered at the thought of babies.

Madge shivered as her mind came back to 1967, to the reality of boring Geoff and adolescent Alice, who ought to be home any time now.

She hadn't better be doing anything like that, Madge thought angrily, her thoughts still on the past. Maybe I should have told her to keep her hand on her a'penny!

CHAPTER FOUR

The next year or so sailed by on a sea of flower power, festivals and pyschodelia. Alice lost herself in the music of the time, and lamented that she couldn't buy enough of it. Her terrible sounding radio worked overtime, especially at the weekends when she was glued to Radio Luxembourg. Madge complained to her about the noise, despite the fact that Alice listened to it under the bedclothes half the time, and also moaned about the lack of help around the house. Alice did what she had to, then escaped to the sanctuary of her small bedroom as often as she could. Anything was better than sitting downstairs with those two. They hardly watched anything on the television apart from the news, and the rest of the evenings were spent with Madge knitting or crocheting and Geoff buried in either a medical journal or the Daily Telegraph. The art of conversation was virtually dead in the Harwood house, and the only time her parents really spoke to each other was then they argued. Alice had always wondered what the funny squeaking noise was that came from their bedroom later on and the truth of this was slowly beginning to dawn on her. Sometimes she watched films or other television programmes round at Susan's house, and had caught a glimpse or two of sex. It didn't look like it was anything worth bothering with and she was still haunted by the memory of Barry. He hadn't seemed to remember anything about the incident and Alice wished she could say the same. Susan had reckoned he was drunk, which was something else Alice didn't know anything about. Nothing like that happened in her house. Nothing much of anything did.

Another form of escape for Alice was the Girl Guides. She was a patrol leader now and Susan was her deputy, which seemed strange because Alice always let her lead the way in their friendship. They had been on several weekend camps, which Alice enjoyed a lot more than her friend. Susan wasn't really into roughing it or making do and mending, but Alice didn't mind that. It got her away from home, and anything that did that was alright in her book. Susan didn't comprehend Alice's aversion to being at home. She got on really well with her parents, and made Alice envious by telling her all about the things they did as a family. The only thing that annoyed Susan was her younger brother, who was always playing tricks on her and generally making a pest of himself.

During the school holidays, the Guides were going on a ten day camp, canoeing in the Wye Valley. Alice couldn't wait for this to come round but before she got to that, she had something else to do. The exams. Not any old exams. The exams, the O levels. Alice had been entered for the customary five, but was pretty sure she would fail maths and general science. The only ones she was sure about were French and English language. English literature usually left her a bit confused. She was never quite sure whether she was supposed to enjoy the stories or pull them to pieces.

Madge was bubbling over with enthusiasm as Alice settled down to some serious revision in the weeks running up to the exams. She was wittering on about Alice staying on to do A levels so that she could apply to go to university, and all Alice could do was give her a quizzical sideways glance and wonder what she was talking about.

"I don't understand my mum half the time," she said to Susan on the way home from school the next day. "She's always going on about how bad my reports are, then the next minute she's trying to get me to stop on. She wants me to go to university, but I don't want to go. I don't even know what I want to do when I leave school."

"I do," Susan replied firmly. "I'm going to be a nurse."

"I know," Alice said with a sigh. From the very first day she had met Susan, she had known this was her ambition. Alice wished she could say what her future held. She had thought about all sorts of jobs, but nothing really appealed to her. Even if she did go to university she wouldn't know which subjects to concentrate on, and her parents were no help in this. Geoff wasn't bothered either way, and Madge wasn't interested in minor details like choosing subjects. She just wanted something to brag about to her friends.

Alice was still puzzling over this conundrum when she got home. When she walked through the back door into the kitchen, she found potatoes on the draining board as usual, along with a note from her mother that read:

Cottage pie tonight, mince in the fridge. Gone to see Mrs. Croft.

Alice sighed and got on with preparing dinner. Mrs. Croft lived three doors away and was something of a recent acquisition. Alice didn't know where they had met, but it wasn't likely to have been in the street. Madge didn't have anything to do with the neighbours, looking down her nose at most of them, but this one was different. Mr. Croft had a good job in Birmingham and wasn't home much, and Alice suspected this was why her mother had cultivated the woman. This woud be another bit of social climbing that wasn't going to get her anywhere. Alice didn't know why she bothered with it. At least Mrs. Croft hadn't got some horrendous horsey daughter that she would be forced to associate with. She had a stuck-up son instead.

The exams came and went, then everyone could relax and look forward to leaving school. Alice still had no idea what she wanted to do, but she put this on hold as she prepared for the camping trip with the Guides. It was going to happen in August and would coincide with both the exam results and Susan's birthday, and Alice was glad. She had no doubt that the results envelope would be opened by her mother first, and it would give her a bit of time to calm down before she got home to face the music. Talking of which, Alice packed her tinny little radio into her rucksack. She couldn't miss the top forty show.

On the day she was leaving for camp, it was throwing it down with rain. Alice's heart sank when she drew back her curtains and saw what was going on outside. She didn't know if her rucksack was waterproof, and she knew full well that the chances of her dad giving her a lift down to the hall were slim if not inconceivable. He never took her to school when the weather was bad, even though he would have time to. It wasn't on his way, but it wasn't far out of it either.

Alice had her breakfast, glancing up every now and then while wondering if she dare ask him to drive her into town. She desperately wanted to, but was fairly certain she knew what his response was going to be. Madge was faffing about pouring everyone a second cup of tea when the phone rang. Alice froze as she wondered if the camp had been cancelled. Geoff carried on with his boiled egg, and Madge put down the teapot with a theatrical sigh.

"I suppose I'll have to get it," she said as she swept from the room.

"No-one else'd dare," Geoff muttered under his breath, and Alice suppressed a smile.

Madge was soon back and picked up Alice's empty plate. She was halfway out of the dining room door when she decided to relay the message.

"That was Susan. Her father's coming round to pick you up in fifteen minutes, although I'm sure I don't know why."

"I'll go and get ready." Alice's heart had just leapt six feet into the air.

"Hurry up then," said Madge as she disappeared into the kitchen.

They saw her off with barely a goodbye. Geoff told her to have a good time and Madge tutted. Alice hurried to the car, and forced herself to wave out of the back window as they drove away. Susan was in front of her, and Alice tapped her on the shoulder.

"Thank you so much for this."

"Well, I knew your dad wouldn't offer to take you."

"No, he never does," Alice muttered bitterly, barely able to see out of the window for driving rain.

Once they got to the church hall, Alice grabbed her rucksack and ran inside as quickly as she could. From the doorway she watched Susan and her dad as he got out of the car and put up a large umbrella. Then he went round to the other side like a knight in shining armour, opened the passenger door and Susan slid out of the car, looking every inch like a film star arriving at an awards ceremony. She hugged her father tightly and he kissed her on the cheek, before she too retrieved her rucksack from the floor of the car. Then he walked her to the door underneath the multicoloured protection and said a cheery goodbye. Alice had never seen anything like it and was amazed. Was that how normal people acted? No wonder Susan thought her parents were strange.

A while later, all the girls lined up in orderly fashion to get onto the bus that would take them to the start of the camp. They would spend the night there after cooking their evening meal, then they would set off down the River Wye, canoeing ten to fifteen miles a day, camping in fields along the way. Each canoe took two girls, so they were all divided up into pairs. Alice and Susan were together, of course, and found they had to share a tent with two other girls that they didn't know very well and didn't like much either. The feeling seemed to be mutual, so each pair kept to their own end of the small tent and had as little to do with each other as possible.

Alice took charge of the cooking as this was one thing she was good at. She had plenty of practice at home. She had virtually taught herself out of her mother's vast and expensive library of cook books. She never really understood why she had so many when she hated cooking, but it wasn't up to Alice to reason why. Her mother was always so busy doing other things, although she hadn't got a clue what half of them were. Alice enjoyed mooching through the books looking for different recipes, but her parents weren't very adventurous. Her suggestions of trying something Italian or Chinese had been met with outraged horror, so she stuck to basic, old-fashioned plain English food while fantasising that one day she might have a curry or a chow mein for a change.

The next morning everyone helped themselves out of a huge pot of porridge, which one of the supervisors had got up early to prepare. Then the girls packed up their things, which would be loaded into a Land Rover and taken to the next campsite along with the tents. Now the fun part could begin. The first ten miles of canoeing.

Alice went in the front and Susan was in the back to do the steering. They would take it in turns to paddle in this way, but today Alice could spend more time than her friend looking at the scenery and enjoying the view.

"Look." She pointed excitedly with her paddle as a flash of turquoise and orange zoomed through the trees on the near bank.

"What was it?"

"Kingfisher." Alice was still ecstatic. She had never seen one before.

"Oh," said Susan in total disinterest. "Is that all."

They both fell silent for a while as they concentrated on their canoeing. They were towards the back of the group; some of the other girls were more experienced than them and could go faster, but they didn't mind. They could hardly get lost.

Up ahead they could see that the other canoes were moving as far over to the right bank as they could, and when they got closer, they realised why. There were fishermen all along the river, there must have been thirty of them and they all seemed to be concentrating intently on what they were doing.

The line of canoes slid past them gently and nobody spoke. Alice and Susan had dropped right back so now they were last, and as they approached the fishermen, one of them reached into a paint container and pulled out a handful of something. He was looking at the procession that had already gone past as he raised his arm into the air and threw the mixture of ground bait and maggots into the water. Except it didn't land in the water. It went all over Susan.

When the screaming started Alice wondered what on earth was going on. Susan was behind her, so she hadn't seen what had happened, but it sounded as though she was being murdered or something from all the noise she was making. Susan's paddle was in the river, and when Alice looked over her shoulder all she could see were arms waving around, as her friend tried to get the fishing bait out of her hair.

The two man canoe rocked from side to side as Susan panicked and totally freaked out. There was nothing Alice could do to stop her, and out of the corner of her eye she could see several of the fishermen laughing. Her temper flared and she tried to steady the canoe with her paddle, while wishing she could get at the men and strangle them. Then the canoe capsized and all thoughts of this description vanished. Now they were both upside-down underneath the water, and all Alice could do was try to remember what they had been taught. She grasped the sides of the opening and pushed to release her legs from inside the boat. The water was dark and murky, but she could just about see that Susan had managed to do the same thing. They broke the surface of the water together, both gasping for air and wondering what the hell was going on.

"I can't feel the bottom!" Susan shrieked.

"Grab the canoe!" Alice shouted, seeing one of the paddles was within her grasp. She grabbed it and felt a little safer, then looked around for the other one, which was some distance away.

Susan took her advice and made for the boat. She had the presence of mind to kick and try to make for the riverbank while Alice retrieved the other paddle. She was the better swimmer of the two anyway. Alice was on her way back when Susan reached the grassy bank, and a couple of the fishermen had now decided to help instead of taking the mickey. One grabbed her hand and helped her out of the water, while the other grasped the end of the blue canoe and hauled it up onto the bank. They they waited for Alice to reach them.

"Which one of you stupid idiots threw maggots at me?" Susan demanded to know. "Of all the low down …"

"It was me," the one holding the canoe answered. "I'm sorry, I didn't see you."

"Didn't see me, didn't see me!" Susan continued her angry tirade but neither of the men were paying any attention. They were now both helping Alice out of the river. She lay on the grass to get her breath back, and one of them asked if she was alright. She just about managed to nod her head, still holding onto the two paddles.

The younger of the two, the object of Susan's fury, prised them out of Alice's hand then smiled at her as he asked how she was. That was fatal. Alice looked up into his sparkling hazel eyes and felt something she had never felt before. She hadn't got a clue what it was, but she liked it. She liked it very much indeed.

"I'm Joe," he said softly. He had a different accent from Alice, but she thought she had never heard anything so wonderful in her entire life.

"I'm Alice," she said breathlessly, and it hadn't got anything to do with being thrown into the river. "Thank you for helping."

"It was the least I could do, considering I caused you to capsize in the first place." He smiled again and his eyes crinkled up. Alice was convinced she had died and gone to heaven. She felt like she was melting and seeping into the ground, and all she wanted to do was continue to lie there looking up at him. "Where are you from?"

"Lichfield. We're in the Girl Guides, on holiday."

"Well, we'd better get you back to the others," Joe said as he and his friend turned the canoe back over for them.

"Yes. I suppose so."

"Hasn't anyone come back for us?" Susan had calmed down somewhat now. Now she was merely annoyed.

"Doesn't look like it." The other fisherman looked along the river. All the canoes were out of sight around a bend now.

"We'll have to try to catch them up," Susan decided. "I'm getting cold now."

"Some exercise will warm you up," Joe said as he helped them and the canoe back into the water. "Don't catch your deaths of anything."

Susan made a funny sort of herumphing noise as she got back into the canoe and took the paddle that was handed to her. Alice didn't know what to do. She was soaking wet, freezing cold and was beginning to smell unpleasant, but she didn't want to leave.

"Come on, Alice," Susan snapped at her. "We haven't got all day."

"Yes." Alice walked to the canoe now. Joe held the front of it steady for her as she got inside and paddled away. She daren't look back. Her heart felt as though it was being pulled back to the shore, where all the fishermen were now back to what they were doing before they were so rudely interrupted. Competing in a fishing contest.

When the girls caught up with the others, a great fuss was made of them. They were fetched out of their boat and wrapped in big blankets, after someone had found a phone box and telephoned ahead to tell what had happened. Alice and Susan were taken to a nearby farmhouse to change their clothes then went on to the evening campsite, while the others carried on paddling as if nothing had happened. They suffered no ill effects of their dunking in the river apart from catching a cold each, but Susan declared this was her last camp, and nothing Alice could say would change her mind. She knew she had never been very keen on them in the first place.

When Alice got home to the cul-de-sac, she didn't bother to tell her parents what had happened. She wouldn't get any sympathy from either of them if she did, and Madge would probably make some comment about such things being character building.

I should have the biggest character in the world, Alice thought as she unpacked her damp, smelly and rather muddy rucksack. So why do I feel so small?

She couldn't answer that one, and watched helplessly as Madge turned up her nose at her daughter's washing, then got tea ready as though Alice had never been away.

"Had a good time?" and "yes, thanks" were the sum of the conversation about her ten-day trip away. It was already as if it had never happened, and anyway, Madge had more important things to talk about.

"Your exam results have come."

"Oh." Alice's heart was beginning to travel towards her slippers, which were one thing she had missed over the last few days.

"Don't you want to know what they are?" Madge asked, her eyes flashing in annoyance.

"Yes." Alice glared at her briefly. Honestly, she never gave her a chance to say anything. "Where's the letter?"

"Don't use that tone of voice with me." Madge moved over to the sideboard. "Here." She held out the envelope. "You've passed three. Not very good."

Alice felt a bit better now, although she could pretty well guarantee that her mother's favourite subject wouldn't be one of them. She was right. She had failed maths and English literature, but the best thing about it was that her grades weren't good enough to put in for A levels. Well, two of them were, but Alice decided to keep quiet about this. She didn't want to go to university anyway.

"I don't know what we're going to do with you now." Madge sounded disgruntled. "You need five O levels to do any good."

"I'll get a job." Alice had already decided this weeks ago.

"Yes, I suppose you'll have to," Madge grudgingly agreed. "Just make sure it's something good."

CHAPTER FIVE

Something good. These words rolled around inside Alice's head, like renegade marbles bouncing in a pinball machine. What was her mother expecting? Brain surgeon? Rock star? Alice smiled at the last thought. Madge hated pop music with a vengeance, especially Procol Harem's Whiter Shade of Pale, which was one of Alice's latest acquisitions. The first time she had heard its cathedral-like tones emanating from Alice's bedroom she had gone bananas, accusing her daughter of blasphemy despite the fact that none of them ever went to church. Alice dutifully switched the record off, resolving to play it at a much lower volume next time. The radio went on instead, and Alice bopped around happily to the strains of the Kinks. She had to do this more or less on the spot; her bedroom wasn't very big.

After a while she lay on her bed, wondering what sort of a job she should get. She didn't fancy working in a factory, although she had never been inside one and didn't really know what they did. Make things, that was all she knew.

"Have a look through the paper," she decided, so went downstairs to fetch it. A few minutes later she realised this was futile. There was nothing an inexperienced girl like her could apply for. Alice sighed. She didn't know what to do now, and her mother would be badgering her before she was too much older. She groaned and turned over to bury her face in her pillow. Being a teenager felt like such hard work.

A few days later she walked into town to meet Susan. They did this nearly every day, and Alice was glad of an excuse to get out of the house. They never did anything very exciting but spent all afternoon doing it, and today was no exception. They went to the record shop, mooched around in Woolworths and went to the posh shop that Susan's dad managed to look wistfully through the windows at the very expensive clothes, draped over mannequins that had fixed expressions of vague surprise on their smooth faces.

"One day," Susan murmured.

"I'll need a really good job to be able to afford those." Alice laughed.

"Still no luck?"

"No. Everyone wants you to be sixteen yet have loads of experience. At least, that's how it seems. What are you going to do?"

"Well, I'm not old enough yet to start nursing, so I thought I might go to college and do a pre-nursing course."

"How long will that take?"

"Two years."

Alice whistled under her breath, that was a long time. If Susan did that and she got a job, they wouldn't see very much of each other in the future. Alice had never thought about this before, and only now did she begin to realise that things were going to change. She had got so used to having Susan by her side all the time that she didn't know what she was going to do without her.

They wandered aimlessly around the streets of the compact city until they found themselves in the centre. They were on the edge of the new pedestrian precinct that had only recently been finished, and they didn't usually venture into it. A lot of the units were offices, so there wasn't much to interest two sixteen-year-old girls.

"Look," said Susan, pointing to a notice on the door of an estate agents' window. "They want an office girl."

"Suit school leaver," Alice read.

The girls looked at each other, both thinking the same thought. "Should I?"

"Yes, go on," Susan urged.

Alice took a deep breath, then pushed the door open. She had never been inside one of these places before, but it didn't look too scary. There were pictures of houses in the window and all over the walls, and an officious looking woman was sitting at a big desk in the middle of the room. She did look scary. Very scary indeed.

"Can I help you?" She managed to look up at Alice and look down her nose at her both at the same time, and Alice wondered if she wouldn't be better off just turning round and running. Instead she explained why she was there and after she had, the dragon seemed to relent a little. She actually smiled as she reached for a very big book and arranged for Alice to attend for an interview. She left the estate agents' office feeling as if she was floating on cloud nine, and couldn't wait to rush to Susan to tell her the good news.

When she got home she gabbled out the information to her mother, who didn't seem as impressed as Susan had been. Something good, she had said, and Alice was sure nothing could be better than this. Madge didn't look convinced. She didn't appear to think it was anything good at all.

"Alice has got a job interview on Thursday," Madge said to Geoff when he came home from work. "At an estate agent."

"That sounds alright." Geoff smiled at his daughter. "Best of luck, Alice."

Thursday arrived at last, and Alice got ready for her interview. She had butterflies in her stomach, shaky knees and the start of a tension headache. By the time she had walked into town, most of these had gone, then she found herself sitting at a huge wooden desk in an upstairs office well out of the way of the dragon who had made the arrangements. The man seemed very large and pompous, asked her lots of questions which she managed to answer without stammering or stuttering, then dismissed her brusquely with the promise of a phone call. Alice didn't hold out a lot of hope, but the very next day a call came. She heard Madge answer it in her very best phone voice, then she called for her daughter.

"It's for you." Her face held a mixture of surprise and annoyance. Alice very rarely got phone calls.

She could feel her mother's eyes on her as she picked up the receiver. It was the dragon, but Alice's heart lifted as she told her they would like to offer her the job and could she start on Monday?

"Oh yes, I can." Alice's spirits soared. "Thank you very much."

"You got it?" Madge looked absolutely amazed. "Good grief."

Alice did her chores, doing her best to ignore Madge's inane chatter. She was going on about Mrs. Croft three doors away, what a good job her husband had and how well her son was doing. This was obviously Madge's latest obsession. She always had to have someone to suck up to, copy and emulate, as though their sophistication and good fortune would rub off on her. It never did.

For once, Alice couldn't wait for her dad to get home to tell him the news. She quite liked her father, anything was better than her mother, but he had always been a rather distant parent. His job was the most important thing in his life, he was married to the hospital, not to Madge, and Alice came even further down the list of priorities. He and Alice didn't have that much to do with each other, and when he was at home he spent most of his time down the garden or in the garage. When he had to be in the house, he hid inside a magazine or behind a large newspaper and Alice had never found him very approachable.

"Alice has some news." Madge got to him first as he came through the back door looking tense and harrassed. "She's got that job."

"Oh." He looked nearly as surprised as Madge had done. "How much are they paying?"

"Eight pounds a week," said Alice quietly. He didn't look very cheerful, whereas she was over the moon. There was no pleasing these two sometimes.

"Eight pounds!" Geoff nearly exploded. "You're not working for eight pounds, that's virtually slave labour. You ring them tomorrow and say you're not taking it."

"I can't do that, I start on Monday." All the colour drained from Alice's face and she felt sick. She couldn't believe what her father had just said.

"You are not. No daughter of mine is working anywhere for eight pounds a week. That's scandalous money."

"I thought it was quite good," said Alice, her heart sinking rapidly towards the floor.

"Good? It's pathetic." Geoff actually looked at her now as he tried to explain. "You don't know anything about these things, Alice. They're taking advantage of you and I can't allow that." He was calming down now. "We know what's best for you and we have to guide you in the right direction. You're not taking the job and that's final. You'll ring them up tomorrow and tell them so."

"But Dad ..." Alice had tears in her eyes now.

"No, Alice, no arguments. My mind is made up."

Alice disappeared to the sanctuary of her bedroom and cried and cried. For the first time in her life she felt as though she had achieved something, only to have it cruelly snatched away. And by her own father of all people.

The next day she kept out of the way, hoping he would forget all about it, but after lunch he marched her into the hall and stood over her as he sternly ordered her to make the phone call. Alice didn't know what to say, fumbled and stumbled over her words, then burst into tears as she replaced the receiver.

"It's for the best, Alice, really," Geoff wheedled. "You'll find something better."

Alice couldn't speak, she was so full of emotions, all different ones and none of them good. All she could do was go upstairs and sob in private, until her mother found her some jobs to do. Saturday was usually cake-making day, and Alice wondered if she could get out of it or talk Madge into letting her bake some bread instead. The kneading of the dough would give her something to take her distress out on. She was out of luck. Madge told her to make a fruit cake, which was her father's favourite, and this felt like adding insult to injury. Alice threw the ingredients together carelessly, her thoughts dark and angry. She daren't show this, of course, Madge would give her the rough edge of her tongue if she did. She didn't need much excuse at the best of times.

The only person she got any sympathy from was Susan. "Why don't you come to college with me?" she suggested. "If you're going to work in an office, then learning typing and shorthand would come in useful. Go on, what do you say?"

"I'll have to ask Mum and Dad," Alice sighed. "But they don't seem to want me to get a job. They might let me do it."

The more she thought about it, the more she liked the idea. All she had to do now was convince Madge and Geoff. This proved to be easier than she had thought.

"We were thinking of something along those lines," Madge said with a smarmy, superior look on her face.

"You mean you were," Geoff mumbled, through a forkful of steak and kidney pudding.

"I hear Tamworth is quite good. Stephen Croft went there."

He'd have to, wouldn't he, Alice thought to herself. She was getting fed up of hearing about Mrs. Croft's fantastic son. She was never going to be able to compete with him, and it was a waste of time Madge pushing her to do so. There was no way you could tell Madge that, though.

"Where is Susan going to college?" asked Geoff.

"Tamworth," said Alice with a hint of triumph in her voice.

"There you are then." It seemed Madge had made up her mind. "I told you it was good."

They had to hurry to get Alice enrolled, but enrolled she was and now couldn't wait for September to come round so that she could start. She and Susan caught the bus every day to travel the eight miles from city to town, and both of them soon got into the swing of their courses. They couldn't really compare notes as they were doing completely different subjects, and most evenings were taken up with homework, especially for Susan. The bus journeys and the occasional trip into Lichfield at the weekend became their only point of contact, and Alice was aware that they were growing apart. She was sad about this, Susan was the only friend she had ever had.

Then she met Matthew. He was on some sort of metal-working course and was a year older than Alice, and they started bumping into each other in the refectory and the common room. It was all very awkward and naive to begin with, but as they got to know each other things became more relaxed. Susan had taken up with a lad on her course named Graeme, so neither girl minded the other having a boyfriend. This meant that they saw even less of one another, but Alice was enjoying the attention. No-one had paid her any before. Matthew lived in Tamworth, not too far away from the college, so Alice started spending time at his house and catching a later bus back to Lichfield.

"Don't neglect your homework," said Madge in a very disapproving voice. "When are we going to meet this Matthew anyway?"

"He doesn't come over to Lichfield very often." Alice felt herself panicking. If anyone would put him off it would be Madge, and she had already decided to do her best to keep them apart.

"Is he taking you out for your birthday?" Madge wanted to know next.

"I don't know," Alice admitted. It was in just over a week's time. "I don't think he's got much money."

"Huh, doesn't sound like much of a boyfriend to me."

"He's alright," Alice replied quietly. The fact that her mother didn't have a good thing to say about him made him all the more attractive. Only now did Alice wonder about her birthday. She had never done anything special for any of them. It would make a nice change to do something different.

She reached the grand old age of seventeen with no bells or whistles, or anything else come to that. She spent an hour round at Matthew's house and he apologised for not buying her anything, but told her he had something to show her in his bedroom instead. Ever trusting, Alice followed him up the stairs. They were alone in the house but she felt no sense of danger. Really she didn't feel much of anything at all. When they got into his room he closed the door and led her over to the bed. The sat on it together, then kissed, as they had done before but never in such a provocative setting. Alice didn't mind snogging with Matthew. He was always gentle and never forced her to do anything she didn't want to. She felt comfortable with him, or at least, she usually did.

One hand was fumbling towards her left breast and suddenly she saw Barry's drunken face as she remembered Susan's party. She squeaked and pulled away from Matthew and he immediately asked her what was wrong.

"Nothing," she stuttered, then tried to smile. "It's just that, well, the thing is, I've never …"

"Neither have I," he admitted. "But I thought we might, well, you know, mess about a bit."

"Oh." Alice didn't really know what that entailed. "Okay."

Messing about proved to be not too unpleasant, and Alice didn't mind it at all. In fact, she was quite looking forward to messing about again. On the bus to college the next day she glanced sideways at Susan a few times, wondering whether she should mention it.

"What's up with you?" Susan asked with a smirk on her face.

"Nothing," Alice said, a little too quickly.

"I know you, come on, what is it?"

"Well …" Alice hesitated. Then she told Susan all about it.

"You mean you haven't done it yet?" Susan looked surprised.

"No." Alice shook her head firmly. "I don't want to."

"Alice, you can't keep saying no for ever," said Susan patiently. "He'll get fed up and find someone else. You don't want that, do you?"

"No." Alice shook her head again, then looked up somewhat fearfully. "Have you? Done it?"

"Oh yes, of course."

"Does it …" Alice lowered her voice. "Does it hurt?"

"Of course not, you are silly." Susan laughed. "It's nice, you'll love it."

Alice remembered Susan's words over the next few weeks as her relationship with Matthew progressed little by little. Eventually it got to the point where his parents were going away for the weekend, and Alice got up enough nerve to tell hers that she was staying at Susan's for the night. Susan was in on the deception and was encouraging Alice to 'go for it' as she put it.

Alice wasn't at all sure she was doing the right thing as she sat on the bus travelling towards Tamworth. She felt like the odd one out. It seemed everyone else in the college had 'done it' and she was the only one that hadn't. Even Susan had been making fun of her over it, but the real reason she was going through with it was because she didn't want to lose Matthew. She enjoyed his company and the attention he gave her, and she didn't want that to end.

He welcomed her into the house nervously, and asked her if she liked cider. She had only tried it once before and had liked it, so they had several glassfuls before moving upstairs, taking the rest of the bottle with them. Alice felt relaxed and a little bit tiddly but she didn't mind. She thought it might help her get through 'doing it'. Matthew wasted no time in getting all his clothes off, while Alice took her time. She glanced at his body anxiously, that thing looked awfully big but she couldn't back out now. She hurried to remove her underwear and slid under the sheet to join him, still not sure she was doing the right thing.

Twenty minutes later it was all over and Matthew was lying next to her with his back towards her. Alice didn't know how she felt. Was that it? She was sure there should have been more to it than that. Perhaps she hadn't done it right. She frowned as she pondered on this, and wondered how she could find out. She couldn't ask Susan. She would only make fun of her again.

Practice makes perfect. She remembered the old saying that a certain person in her household was fond of using. All Alice could do was try again.

Christmas came and went, then Easter and before she knew it, the end of the college year was looming. Susan had broken up with Graeme and was now going out with Peter, although she had recently admitted to Alice that she had her eye on Michael. Alice was still seeing Matthew, but even she had worked out that he wasn't as keen as he had once been. He was finishing his course soon and would be going off miles away to start at university, so she suspected she wouldn't be seeing or hearing from him as much. Alice had another year to do of her secretarial course, which was progressing well, and she had surprised herself by actually enjoying it. Madge approved of her boyfriend now, she would do, wouldn't she, just as things were cooling off and possibly coming to an end.

Through talking to Susan, Alice had worked out that her friend liked 'doing it' a lot more than she did. Alice was beginning to think there was something wrong with her, she had never reached the heights that Susan spoke of with such enthusiasm. Susan said they weren't doing it properly, but Alice didn't like to say anything to Matthew. She didn't want him to know they had been talking about him.

Finally term finished and Susan went off to drive around in Michael's car, probably to the golf course, which had a bit of a reputation for couples in backs of vehicles. Alice sighed heavily and walked to the bus station. She hadn't seen Matthew all day, and had the feeling he might be avoiding her. She could sense the end was near and was dreading it.

As she approached the bus stop, she could see him standing there. The strains of David Bowie's Space Oddity were wafting from a nearby radio, and Alice had a premonition that this song would for ever remind her of Matthew. He looked worried and nervous, as if he didn't know what to say. Alice's heart dropped. He looked how she felt.

"I'm sorry Alice, I can't see you any more," he eventually got round to saying as he saw the Lichfield bus coming towards them.

"I know," she said as she boarded it.

All the way home Alice felt numb. It was over, and now she didn't know what to do next. Only now did she realise she had never loved him, but it still hurt. It hurt more than anything she had ever felt before.

CHAPTER SIX

Back home in the cul-de-sac, Madge had no idea what Alice was going through and cared even less. She had her own problems to worry over. When the girl came home she went straight up to her room, which was nothing new, although Madge did shout after her about the dinner needing cooking later. About all she got in response was a grunt, which didn't please her any, so she took herself off into the living room with the cake tin for a well earned sulk and another foray into the past. When she was seventeen in 1942.

Eliza had been out on this particular afternoon, and Madge was in charge of cooking tea. Madge hated cooking. She didn't mind doing cakes because she liked eating them, but they had become less lately due to the rationing of sugar and fat. Rationing was a ruddy nuisance. Good job they had a big garden to grow lots of vegetables. Recently there had been talk of them keeping chickens and pigs, but this had come to nothing and Madge was glad. She had quite enough to do as it was.

She set about peeling potatoes, to go with the bully beef she had collected from the village butcher a few days before. The meat ration was small, but Madge had worked out that if you had enough money you could get extras. She had seen it going on as Mr. Moore wrapped unseen items in white paper, before handing them over with a cheeky wink at his affluent customer. If only her mother could get more friendly with Mrs. Carrington. Then they might get more than a few fatty lamb chops and two tins of corned beef to last the four of them the week.

Madge sighed as she put the potatoes in a saucepan and covered them with cold water. She debated whether to make some gravy, but soon decided against it. Her attempts at things that ambitious usually ended in disaster and complaints. Then she thought about Flossie and realised she had left it too late to go round, as evenings were out of bounds. "Must spend some time with Bernard," she had been told firmly. She knew they went to the club several times a week, sometimes for bingo or a whist drive but mainly for a bottle or two of milk stout. Madge couldn't understand the attraction of the club. Every time she walked past it there seemed to be a smell of yeasty beer, old sweat and stale cigarette smoke. Madge couldn't imagine what went on inside there, but if it produced smells like that it couldn't be anything very healthy. No thanks, she would stick to running around over on Twenty Acres and trying to get Tom to 'do' her again. She couldn't get the experience out of her mind and desperately wanted it to happen again. And again.

Tom, it seemed, had other ideas. Whenever Madge saw him now he did nothing more than give her a cheeky knowing grin and walk on by. Madge felt stupid and disgruntled by his attitude. Had she done something wrong? Wasn't she any good at it? It was all so confusing.

A few days later it was the weekend. Madge and Eliza were in the kitchen brewing up some of the endless tea that went on in the Day household. Madge kept glancing at her mother, trying to picture her when she was seventeen and doing things she wasn't supposed to. Since her talk with Flossie on the subject she had wondered whether to tell Eliza about Tom, but had decided against it. There was obviously a lot about her mother that she didn't know, so she could have some secrets as well. Added to this, she knew Flossie was right about the Jury family. The rumour was that Tom's dad was selling things on the black market, and seeing as hardly anyone in Barnes Lane could afford to buy anything, no-one approved of his activities. Spiv, Madge had heard him called, which made him as good as a social outcast.

The tea was mashing away nicely when the back door opened. Madge nearly gasped when she saw who it was: Mrs. Carrington, proudly holding a paper bag.

"Eliza, my dear, I've caught you in," she said in that horribly false cheerful voice of hers. She was older than Eliza by only a few years, but her greying hair was coloured yellow and permed in such a way that it looked like it belonged to someone else and had been plonked on her head by a person with a very bad aim. Madge had to suppress a giggle every time she saw it.

"Oh, Mrs. Carrington." Eliza was immediately flustered and looked as though she didn't know where to put herself. "What brings you here?"

"I've brought you a little present."

"Present?" Eliza repeated, unable to contain her amazement.

"Yes, I thought these would be useful to you." She held out the paper bag and Eliza took it automatically. "In these hard times every little helps. Just a few bread crusts for you. You know, for making croutons."

Madge sat quietly wondering what on earth croutons were when they were at home. Eliza suddenly had a face like thunder, and even Mrs. Carrington flinched a little when she noticed it.

"Thank you very much," said Eliza stiffly. "Most kind of you."

"Well, I try to look after my employees. That reminds me. May has a day off tomorrow, she'd like to see Margaret."

"Thank you, Mrs. Carrington." Madge felt cheerful now. She hadn't seen May for ages, because she only had a day off occasionally and usually spent them with her family. "Is it alright if I come to the house to meet her?"

"I have no objection to that, as long as you go round the back," replied Mrs. Carrington with her nose in the air. "Well, must be off. Parker's outside with the engine running. Next stop the butcher."

With that she was gone. As soon as the back door clicked shut, Eliza thrust the offending paper bag into the bin under the sink with a frustrated grunt.

"Croutons indeed, I'll give her bloody croutons." Madge said nothing, she was still looking forward to seeing May. "And she's off to the butcher's. She won't be fobbed off with a few chops or bully beef. It'll be the best steak, no doubt, or a joint of pork. They don't stint themselves in that house."

"No." Madge could well believe this. "I don't suppose they do."

The next day she set out early to walk to the Carrington house to meet May. She had met her mother out of work a few times, so knew the procedure. The main entrance wasn't for the likes of them. That had been made abundantly clear to her years ago.

May was just leaving by the back door of the servants' kitchen when she arrived. Madge looked up at the imposing house, trying to imagine how many rooms it must have. She knew they did a lot of entertaining. The Colonel had important and influential friends in London, wherever that was. Madge had never been out of Ingelfield, so London could have been on the moon for all she knew.

The two girls chatted happily as they began to walk away from the big house towards the stables, where several people were talking and laughing while the stable boy struggled to get a saddle onto a huge brown horse.

"See that blond one?" May said quietly. Madge nodded, he was difficult to miss. Tall, slim and very good looking. "That's Russell Carrington, the son."

"Mmm." Madge tried to steer May closer so she could get a better look. She was remembering what her grandmother had said about money and prospects. If only she could get him to look at her …

Then he did. He raised an eyebrow and smiled at her.

"Who's your friend, May?" he called over.

"I'm Madge Day." Madge surprised herself by speaking in a much more refined voice than usual.

"I'm here at this time every day," he replied. "If you ever fancy a horse ride."

"Thank you," said Madge as they walked away.

"Don't you dare," muttered May. "Or if you do, be careful."

"Oh, I will." Madge laughed happily. "I'll be very careful."

Madge actually put a lot of care into her next move. Russell lived in a completely different world from her, one that she wanted to experience and be a part of. Suddenly she wanted to learn about which knife and fork to use, and other things she had heard mention of when overhearing snippets of conversation between the grown-ups. Now she was heading towards being a grown-up herself and was beginning to realise just how little she knew about the world. Time to educate herself, she decided. Learn about the finer things in life.

Flossie turned out to be a great help in this mission. She gave Madge an old book on etiquette, which she studied avidly over the next few days. In her bedroom she practised in front of the peeling mirror, making her mouth into the shape of a letter O and trying to speak properly. Eventually bath day came round and then Madge felt ready, confident enough to walk up to the Carrington house and hang around the stables in the best clothes she had.

She didn't have to wait long. Russell emerged from the stables, leading the splendid brown horse she had seen the other day. He raised his eyebrows when he saw her, then smiled and called her over.

"Do you ride?" he asked in a very plummy voice.

"I've never been on a horse," she answered, surprising herself at how different she sounded.

"First time for everything."

He helped her mount the horse, then swung up behind her. As the animal walked slowly away Madge tugged at her skirt, which was now up way past her knees. She was embarrassed, she was way out of her depth here. Russell steered the horse away from the house, and Madge was convinced she was going to fall off the damned thing as it rocked from side to side. She was very glad when, fifteen minutes later, it stopped in a field a good way away. Madge knew where she was, halfway between Ingelfield and the neighbouring village of Hinton.

"Had enough of that?" Russell breathed hotly in her ear.

"Yes," admitted Madge. "Can I get down now?"

"Certainly," he purred. "Lie on the grass for a while."

Madge did so in relief. She had never had her legs so far apart before and feeling something moving between them like that had quite got her going. So that's why people rode horses. She had learnt something about posh people already. She lay on the grass in the warm sunshine with her eyes closed, but saw the shadow go over them as Russell joined her on the ground.

"No, don't open your eyes," he murmured as his lips brushed against her cheek. Then his mouth found hers. He wasn't as rough as Tom had been, and took his time over everything he did. And he did everything.

When it was all over, Madge was convinced she had died and gone to heaven. She sighed in complete happiness and Russell chuckled.

"Oh, I can see I'm going to be able to teach you so many things," he whispered in her ear.

"Oooh, yes please." Madge giggled, remembering Flossie's book.

Russell did indeed teach Madge an awful lot, but most of it was nothing to do with etiquette. Madge thought he was being romantic when he bought her presents every now and then. The new coat was most appreciated, as were the pieces of paste jewellery that she thought were real. Madge felt like a princess who had found her knight in shining armour, and the situation lasted for some time. She studied her book with a growing understanding, and her strong Dorset accent had all but disappeared. Nobody made any comment on this, except Flossie had given her a knowing wink. She was the only one who knew what was going on.

Then Eliza gave her some news that made her mouth drop open in shock. She was expecting another baby. Madge couldn't believe it, her mother, pregnant? Surely she was far too old to be doing that! Madge didn't realise that Eliza was actually only thirty-six, in her prime and at her best. It was the years of hard work and deprivation that made her look a lot older.

Madge had hardly got over the horrified realisation that she was going to have a baby brother or sister when she had a nasty shock of her own. The curse hadn't arrived for three months, but she had been so busy enjoying herself that she had hardly noticed.

"Madge Carrington," she said in front of the new mirror Russell had got for her. "Oh yes, I can see it now. Wheeling a Windridge around the estate. Dinner parties with mother and the Colonel. Oh yes, I am so ready for that."

Russell, it transpired, didn't think so at all. Madge had fully expected him to do the honourable thing, but instead he looked annoyed and said he would sort it out.

"But …" Madge began.

"But what? You didn't honestly think I'd marry you, did you? Madge, your mother is our cleaner, for heaven's sake. I can't marry a village girl. Mother would never hear of it."

Madge had no choice but to put her clothes back on and walk home. She could hardly believe his reaction. So after all this time, it turned out she just wasn't good enough for him. A village girl. That's exactly what she was, she couldn't deny it. Merely a simple country bumpkin.

She would have been even more upset if she could have heard Mrs. Carrington's reaction to the bad news. It was just as well she was miles away in her bedroom at the time.

"Oh, Russell, not again, what have I told you about village girls? Here, take this money and get her to the woman as quickly as you can. And don't let it happen again."

Madge was given the money and the address of the woman who did these illegal abortions. She was also told by Russell that he didn't want to see her again. He told her she had just been a plaything. Something to see him through the afternoons, a boredom reliever. Madge held in all her emotions and maintained a very stiff upper lip throughout. Until she got back home and went round to see her grandma.

"Typical of his breed," Flossie didn't help by saying. "Only out for what they can get. I did warn you, girl, not to set too much store by him."

"Yes," blubbered Madge. "You did."

"I'll come with you to see this woman, I know who she is." This came as no surprise. Flossie knew everyone. "And afterwards you can come and stay with me for a while. There'll be pain and mess, and your mother doesn't need to know."

"What will I tell her?"

"That I need you to help me, that's all you have to say."

"She's still working, but she's tired all the time."

"That Carrington woman'll work her into the ground, she's got no heart." Madge thought Flossie ought to know, as she didn't seem to have one either. "And I should know." Madge nodded dutifully. "I've known her for years, long before she married the Colonel. Now she thinks she's Lady Muck."

"She is Lady Muck."

"All those airs and graces." It was as though Flossie hadn't heard Madge's very accurate comment. Everything went quiet and Madge found herself wondering what exactly it was that her grandmother knew and why she hadn't mentioned it before. Still, it had come too late for Madge to be able to use the information.

"Anyway." Flossie eventually awoke from her reverie. "How's that brother of yours doing?"

"Alright." Madge nodded. "We don't hear from him much, but he seems to be enjoying the Merchant Navy. Dad says it'll do him good. Keep him out of trouble."

"Was he in any?"

"Think so. Dunno really, they don't tell me anything."

"Well, two can play at that game. You don't tell your ma about what we're doing. It's our secret, right?"

Eliza accepted the weak explanation without a murmur. She had enough problems of her own to be worrying about Madge, and for once Madge was grateful. The procedure was done and Grandma's prediction proved to be accurate. It did result in pain and mess. Lots of it.

Madge, being young and strong, soon recovered. Flossie had seen these sorts of things before, and now recognised that her young granddaughter needed something to take her mind off things. There was no future in her moping around wallowing in self pity, so Flossie wangled her a job at the garage where Fred used to work. She had influence in this village, and hardly ever passed up an opportunity to use it. Madge didn't argue and Eliza said it was a good idea, some extra money coming in wouldn't go amiss. Soon Madge was in the thick of it, sitting in the office overlooking the workshop. She had always been good with numbers, so keeping the books straight and doing the wages was child's play for her. It also had the desired effect. Soon Russell and the baby had faded away into the background. The only reminder she now had of the Carringtons was May.

It turned out that while Madge had been enjoying herself in Russell's company, Doris had gained a reputation for being friendly with the boys, and May had got engaged to local boy Sam Hames. Now the news came that they had set a wedding date, so May would have to leave the big house. Madge had panicked when she first heard this, having visions of being summoned to the Carrington estate to be May's replacement. Flossie told her not to be so stupid. She was getting too long in the tooth now to go into service and anyway, she had a job. Flossie mentioned the A.T.S. again, and Madge said she'd think about it. She wasn't sure she fancied going in the army. Boys had to go into the Forces, and she knew Fred had only gone into the Merchant Navy to avoid the call-up.

"You needs to go to a town to better yourself," Flossie reminded her. "You should have gone to grammar school, you passed the exam."

"I know," Madge sighed. "But they couldn't afford the uniform or the books, and they've still got no money."

"They'll manage." Flossie was totally unsympathetic as usual. "Things are tight, but they'll survive. You think on about the A.T.S. You've done well in improving yourself but now you needs to work on it by seeing more of the world. You won't do no good in Ingelfield. You's got too big for it now."

Madge mulled over these words and decided Flossie was right, so began making enquiries. Doris was thinking along the same lines, which pleased Madge no end. If they joined together, then Madge wouldn't have to cope with unknown Bournemouth on her own.

Then something happened that brought back unwelcome memories and made her want to leave home. Eliza had her baby. It was born six weeks early, a little girl, and weighed as much as a bag of sugar. Madge could hardly bear to look at her baby sister. Tears prickled at her eyes, but she couldn't explain to her exhausted mother. June was so tiny and helpless, and Madge felt exactly like the big, clumsy lummox she had been called at school. If anything she was even bigger now. Five feet nine tall with size eight feet.

Four days after she had been born, June died. Now Madge could give vent to her feelings and Eliza did the same. For a very short time mother and daughter were united in grief. All Flossie had to say was "it's probably for the best." When she had got over the shock, Madge found herself agreeing with her grandma, but she didn't say anything to Eliza. They didn't really need another mouth to feed, even though Fred had left home and Madge was bringing some money in. The war in Europe was still raging. The Americans had recently joined it but it all seemed so very far away. Reports of town bombings came through on the radio, but Madge didn't know where any of the places were. London, Birmingham and Coventry were a mystery to her. Flossie's words kept coming back to her and she realised that yes, she did need to see more of the world. There must be life outside Ingelfield.

And so Madge took the plunge and joined the Auxilliary Territorial Service. Doris did the same, so they went off on the train to Bournemouth together, catching up on all the news on the way. It seemed Doris had been very busy indeed, especially around the local boys. Tom Jury was mentioned, but Madge gave no reaction.

"I've heard there are Americans in Bournemouth," Doris enthused when they had run out of Ingelfield gossip. "Hope we get to meet some of them."

"Who wants to talk to foreigners?"

"They say they're ever so well paid, and can get hold of all kinds of things. Real stockings, chocolate, all sorts."

"Real stockings," said Madge dreamily. "I've never seen real stockings." The nearest she got was to rub damp sand on her legs then paint a line up the back with whatever she could get her hands on.

"Mind you." Doris laughed. "I think you might have to do more than just talk to them to get anything."

"I don't mind that," said Madge. Russell Carrington was a distant memory now. "I wonder what Bournemouth is like?"

"I dunno," replied Doris quietly. "I ain't never been to a town."

"Neither have I." Madge was looking forward to seeing both the town and the Americans. Little did she know that looking for them would lead her to meeting Geoff …

CHAPTER SEVEN

Alice's hurt went on and on all through the summer of 1969. She took a temporary job in a supermarket stacking shelves, to take her mind off Matthew and give herself some pocket money. Madge had got the job for her without consulting her first, but for once Alice didn't mind her interfering. She hadn't told Madge about her split up with Matthew yet. Sometimes she wandered through the park alone going over the events of the past year, or other times she and Susan went to town in the evenings just to spend some time together. Alice didn't want her mother knowing what her every move was, and Susan agreed with her. Her mother didn't know the half of what she got up to, which was just as well. She would probably never let her out of the house again if she did.

"Be back at college soon," said Susan as they crossed the market square for the third time.

"Yes." Alice nodded. "It'll get me out of Mum's way all day. The worst thing about holidays is having to be at home."

"I dunno how you put up with your mum."

"Haven't got a lot of choice, have I?" Alice sighed. "I only hope I can get a decent job at the end of all this. I don't want to live there for ever."

"I don't mind being at home. But then my mum isn't as scary as yours."

"I know, your mum's lovely," said Alice wistfully. They had reached Woolworth's now. It looked totally different when it was closed. They sauntered up Market Street, heading towards a couple of pubs. Chatter and laughter was oozing out of the windows and front door.

"Ever been in a pub?" Susan suddenly asked.

"No, I'm not old enough."

"What's that got to do with anything?" Susan laughed. "I've been in a few, depends which boy I'm with at the time."

"Mmm." Alice didn't want to comment on her friend's morals, or lack of them. "Haven't got any money anyway."

"What about your job?" They were walking past the small supermarket in question now, and Alice shuddered. The job was alright, but she wasn't very keen on the other people that worked there. They seemed short on manners and weren't very nice to her. One of them had even accused her of being stuck-up, and that worried Alice. Maybe she was more like Madge than she had imagined.

"Mum takes most of the money off me. Bit of a waste of time really."

"What a cow, what's she doing that for?" Susan looked amazed.

"She says I have to pay board," said Alice quietly. "It does seem a bit unfair. I've only got the job for six weeks."

"I wouldn't bother going if my mum did that to me."

They were nearing the end of Market Street now, and were turning right into Bird Street. They were on their slow way home and the smell of the fish and chip shop was just reaching their nostrils. They looked at each other, read one another's minds, then laughed as they went to join the queue. A bag of chips each to eat while wandering up the road home was just what they needed.

The greasy aroma from the chip shop was competing with the Indian restaurant a few doors away. Susan said it smelt disgusting, but Alice loved the smell of curry. She still hadn't tried any foreign food. Madge wouldn't have it in the house, but she lived in hope. Walking slowly past the Indus and drinking in the sights and smells was the nearest she could get. She had been hoping to save enough money and talk Susan round to going in, but she wasn't doing very well on either score.

As they waited their turn in the Golden Griddle, both girls looked out of the large plate glass window to see what was going on in the street outside. There was a group of young men, three or four, and suddenly Susan grabbed Alice's arm.

"Him." She pointed. "Look, it's the one that threw maggots all over me."

The man in the queue in front of them turned around to give them a quizzical look, as though he couldn't make up his mind whether they were drunk or just mad. Alice stared. She remembered the incident, and thought about it every now and then with a warm glow in her stomach.

"You're right." Her heart was doing the most enormous somersault. "It is him. Joe his name is."

"You like him." Susan looked at the dreamy look on her face and her flushed cheeks that had nothing to do with the heat of the chip shop. "I'll go and get him for you."

"Sue, no!"

She was gone before Alice had a chance to stop her. She stood where she was while the man in front got served, gave her a dirty look, then left. Alice asked for two portions of chips, her pulse racing and her heart hammering against her chest as she wondered what Susan was saying to him. It was bound to be something embarrassing. She left the chip shop with a bag in each hand and found Susan standing outside the door of the Indus. As she handed her the chips, Susan explained.

"He's gone in there." She jabbed a thumb backwards over her shoulder. "I'm not going in that smelly place."

"Thank God for that," Alice muttered under her breath.

"You going to find him?"

"No, of course not."

"No wonder you never get any boyfriends. If you see something you like, go after it, that's what I do."

"I know." Alice walked away, eating her chips. That was the end of the conversation as far as she was concerned, but Susan had other ideas.

"Didn't think much of his mates." She hurried to catch her up. "He's not bad though. Bit old, mind.'"

"I never noticed," Alice said truthfully.

"He must be at least twenty."

"Suppose so."

"Wonder what he's doing here?"

"He doesn't come from round here, he talks different."

"Oh, so you did notice some things then."

"He's got a nice smile." Alice remembered. Suddenly she was back on the river bank gazing up into his hazel eyes and feeling all melty and gooey inside. Then Susan brought her back to reality.

"There's more to it than a smile," she said. "There's ..."

"Yes, Sue, I know, you've told me. I have had sex, you know."

"Yeah, okay." For once Susan knew when to stop. She knew Alice was still getting over Matthew. "I forgot."

"S'alright," Alice said with her mouth full, something her mother would tell her off for. If she could hear some of their conversations she would go bonkers and ban the girls from ever seeing each other again. Alice was never going to get past the age of twelve in her parents' eyes.

Susan and Alice went back to college the next week, and the year sped by in a blur. The work was harder in the second year, but Alice had mastered a good speed in typing and a reasonable one in shorthand, and Susan was doing well in biology and human anatomy. Both thought the other's courses were boring, so didn't discuss them much. Christmas came and went, with Alice having a dose of Asian flu, then Easter slid by and the summer was approaching. The pop music was still good and whenever she could, Alice bought a new record and played it over and over on her old red and cream Dansette. She was into Simon and Garfunkel and the Beachboys as well as Roy Orbison and the Beatles. Madge said it all sounded the same and Alice meekly agreed with her, while privately wondering how she could be so stupid.

You wouldn't say that about Jimi Hendrix, Alice thought to herself. Even I don't like him.

End of term was approaching and with it exams. Alice didn't enjoy exams, but knew she had to do them, and do as well as she could if she wanted any peace at home. She was already beginning to worry that she wouldn't be able to find a job. She was nearly nineteen now, a bit old for an office junior. She couldn't explain this to Madge, of course. She had already made plans for her and got her life organised for about the next five years down the line.

Alice ploughed through the exams one by one, and finally they were over. Susan was having the same problem, and they hadn't seen much of each other lately as her exams were at different times and on separate days. Alice was almost getting used to catching buses and walking through the town on her own. As it was a nice sunny day, she decided not to catch the bus at the bus station as she usually did, but to walk to the stop on the edge of town. That way she could go past the Slow Boat Chinese restaurant and read the menu again. It sounded so wonderfully exotic, although she didn't know what half of it meant, and she once again wondered if she could get up the nerve to go in. She wouldn't know what to order, and although that was half the attraction, she didn't want to make a fool of herself.

She hoisted her bag onto her shoulder and set off through the small town. Soon she was approaching the Slow Boat, which was up a wide flight of red carpeted stairs. The menu was on the door at the bottom and Alice began to read it, knowing that she wouldn't be disturbed by any of the staff. Chow mein, chop suey, oyster and black bean sauce. How very foreign it all sounded.

Suddenly she was aware of a presence behind her, and felt awkward. She stepped aside so the other person could read the menu too, then thought maybe she should leave. It seemed as though the lunchtime rush was about to start. As she turned she caught sight of the person's face, and could hardly believe her eyes as she recognised him.

"Joe!" His name was out of her mouth before she realised what she was doing, then she felt herself blushing at the look of surprise on his face. "River Wye," she stammered. "We capsized."

"Of course." The penny had dropped now. "Alice, isn't it?"

"Yes." She nodded, far too enthusiastically. She was delighted that he had remembered, it had been nearly two years ago.

"Are you going in?" He waved towards the stairs.

"Oh, I, er ..." Alice floundered as her eyes flashed this way and that in alarm and embarrassment. She was blushing again, and trying to tell herself not to be so stupid. Words wouldn't come, and she didn't know what to do with herself.

"Come on," Joe said quietly as though he understood. "I don't like having lunch on my own. Please say you'll join me. We can celebrate meeting up again, it isn't every day I fish a girl out of the river."

He smiled at her and her knees went weak. He had one of those smiles that could make a girl do anything he said, no matter how ridiculous or outrageous it was. But having lunch with him was surely neither of those things. What harm could there be in that?

"Alright," she heard herself saying.

They walked up the stairs together, and Alice felt as though she was entering a completely new world. Joe opened the door for her and ushered her inside, and her eyes widened at the huge pictures and the red and gold Chinese lanterns. She had never seen anything like it, and couldn't get over how different it was. She glanced at her companion, who seemed perfectly at home in this alien setting, and wondered if she should make a run for it. She wasn't going to know how to cope with this.

"Table for two?" an immaculately dressed waiter inquired. Joe nodded and they were shown to a table in the window, where they could see what was going on in the street outside.

"I'm having the businessman's special," said Joe. "They only do it at lunchtimes."

He handed Alice the printed card with the details on. It was as if he knew she had never been in one of these places before, but that might have something to do with the way she kept looking around the room, trying to memorise every aspect of it. She had wanted to do this for so long it wasn't true, and she could hardly believe she was actually here.

"I'll have the same," she decided. She had noticed the price on the bottom of the card and knew she had enough. In fact it was a lot cheaper than she had imagined, especially for three courses.

"Soup or orange juice?"

Alice was tempted to play safe and have the juice, then told herself off. There was no point coming into a Chinese restaurant and having something she could have at home.

"Soup," she said in a determined sort of voice. Now came the tricky choice, the main course, so she decided to come clean, hoping he wouldn't laugh at her. "I've never had Chinese food before," she said in a hushed tone.

"I'd go for the chop suey then" he said, equally quietly. "It's not that foreign tasting."

"Okay, thanks."

Joe chose the other option which was beef in oyster sauce, then gave the order for both of them. He had a beer while Alice just had water. They both sipped their drinks while they waited for the first course to arrive, Alice eyeing the pair of chopsticks by the side of her plate in semi-panic.

"So," Joe began, maybe to take her mind off them. "Do you live in Tamworth, Alice?"

She loved the way he said her name, then told herself to behave and answer his question. "No, I'm at college here, well, I've just done my exams so I'll be leaving soon. I live in Lichfield."

"I work in Tamworth but I come from Walsall," he said. "I quite often come here for lunch, it's good value and it's quick."

The soup had arrived now, and Alice recognised some of the things in it. There was shredded chicken and bits of sweetcorn, but it tasted quite bland.

"It's not as different as I thought it was going to be," she confessed.

"Some of their food is quite boring." Joe laughed. "But some of it's alright. I prefer Indian actually, but that's better at night after several pints of beer."

"We saw you a while back in Lichfield," Alice said, then

immediately wished she hadn't. It sounded as though she was stalking him. "Outside the Indian," she added lamely.

"Yes, I go to Lichfield sometimes for a change," he said. "We? Do you have a boyfriend?"

"Oh no, nothing like that." Alice laughed now. "Me and my friend Susan. She was the one you threw maggots at."

"Oh yes, she wasn't too pleased about that, was she?" He grinned and Alice's knees started shaking. "I didn't see you, I thought all the canoes had gone past."

"What were you doing all the way down there?"

"Taking part in a contest. I was concentrating so hard on catching fish, I wasn't taking much notice of anything else. But one thing came out of it, I won. You must have brought me luck."

"Oh." Alice could feel herself blushing again as the waiter removed the soup dish, and replaced it with a bowl of rice and a plate covered in chicken and vegetables in a light brown sauce. She looked at the chopsticks again, and wondered if she was brave enough to pick them up.

"You can ask for a fork, they won't mind."

"Are you using them?" she asked unneccessarily. He was already taking them out of their paper packet.

"Yes, all it takes is a bit of practice." He snapped them apart. "I'll show you if you like."

"Alright. Thanks."

Joe showed her how to position each chopstick, then she copied what he did with the food, placing some on top of the bowl of rice and eating from there. She was only semi-successful, and after a few minutes the waiter took pity on her and brought a fork and a spoon. Alice finished her meal with these, but was glad she had at least tried with the chopsticks. They wouldn't seem so scary in future.

"They'd be quite fun once you've got the hang of them," she decided out loud. "And you obviously have."

"I've been eating Chinese food since the fifties," he said, expertly manipulating his own pair of chopsticks.

"I was only born in nineteen fifty-one." Alice laughed. "You must be a bit older than me."

"I'm thirty-three," he said and Alice's heart nearly stopped. "Almost thirty-four, my birthday is next week."

"Oh." Alice didn't know what to say. She had thought he was just a few years older than herself, he certainly didn't look thirty-four. "I'm eighteen. And a half."

"So you're just finishing college?" He seemed to sense her disquiet. "The one in town?" She nodded. "So what will you do next?"

"I don't know really," she admitted. She hadn't really thought about it in any great depth. "Get a job in an office, I suppose. I've been doing a secretarial course." She looked up at him now. "What do you do?"

"I'm a metallurgist, mainly involved with steel," he answered. It all sounded rather grand and way over Alice's head. "I work for Stefoco, it's on the edge of town. We sell products to steelworks and foundries."

"Oh. That sounds …"

"Very boring, I expect." He laughed. "But I enjoy it."

Suddenly a waiter was at their table, looking very apologetic.

"Mr. Lange?" he asked in his curious Chinese accent. When Joe said he was, the waiter continued. "Phone call for you."

Joe looked both puzzled and worried as he excused himself and went to the front of the restaurant to answer it. He was back within a couple of minutes, and by the time he had returned, Alice had finished her chop suey.

"I'm really sorry, but I've got to go," he said, his forehead lined with anxiety. "Emergency at work, I'll have to get back."

He grabbed his jacket from the back of the chair and left. Alice didn't know what to do. All of a sudden she felt stupid and out of place in this strange environment. Before she knew it the icecream was brought that she had selected, and Joe's place was cleared away. Alice ate the icecream slowly, wondering what she was going to do about the bill. Up to this point she had been enjoying the experience, but now everything had fallen flat. She had liked the food and his company, although his revelation about his age had come as a bit of a shock.

Eventually Alice knew she couldn't put it off for any longer, and the next bus to Lichfield was due in ten minutes. She got up from the table, knowing she hadn't got enough money and went to find the waiter. He looked surprised to see her walking towards him with her purse in her hand.

"Bill paid," he said with a slight bow in her direction. "Gentleman pay before he left."

"Oh." Alice was both pleased and relieved. She was escorted to the door and very politely shown out of the restaurant.

As she stood at the bus stop, she looked up at the window and could see where they had been sitting. She smiled as she relived their chance meeting and remembered the taste and texture of the bean sprouts, bamboo shoots and water chestnuts. What a peculiar and lovely day this had been.

I haven't got his address, she thought as the bus sped down the road towards her. Or his phone number. Oh hell. Her heart dropped like a stone. I'm never going to see him again.

CHAPTER EIGHT

Madge glanced up at the clock on the mantlepiece, tutted, then put down her embroidery. It was a special piece for the Women's Institute Craft Show, and she had been working on it for days. Now her eyes were aching, her fingers were stiff and Alice was late. She had been expecting her home hours ago.

"That girl's been having too much freedom," Madge grumbled to the empty room as she pushed herself out of her comfortable armchair. "Out there enjoying herself doing heaven only knows what. She needs bringing into line. Oh yes, my girl, you just wait. Things are going to change around here."

Madge moved from the living room to the kitchen, stood by the sink and filled the kettle with water. The garden was looking particularly lovely, she thought, the result of a lot of her handiwork. Geoff was in charge of the boring things, like digging and planting vegetables, while Madge did the fun bits, hanging baskets, tubs and flower beds. And a very good job she thought she made of them too.

As she was waiting for the kettle to boil, Madge wondered what they should have for tea tonight. It would have to be something quick now that Alice had decided to be two hours late. She was probably wasting time in the record shop again. Madge couldn't understand why she spent so much time in there, it wasn't as if she ever bought anything half the time.

As if she knew she was being thought about, Alice suddenly appeared after pushing the back door open. Madge whirled round in preparation for the interrogation.

"Where have you been till this hour? Have you any idea what

time it is?" Alice began to push up her sleeve to look at her watch and Madge's nostrils flared. She'd teach her to make fun of her mother. "Never mind, where have you been?"

"I had lunch in a Chinese restaurant with ever such a nice man." Alice had a big daft grin on her face, and Madge's first instinct was to slap her.

"And where did you meet this man?" asked Madge, not believing a word.

"Ages ago, when I went canoeing with Susan in the Wye Valley."

Madge put her hands on her hips and glared at her daughter for several seconds before answering. "I really don't know how you keep managing to think up such lies," she began. "One after another spill out of your mouth. First all that fuss over Matthew and now this. I know what your problem is, you can't get a real boy to look at you, can you? I'm not surprised, I suppose it's not your fault you're nothing to look at, but I really do wish you'd stop making all these things up. You're making yourself look very silly."

"Yes, Mum."

"There's no need to sound so sullen, I'm only pointing out the truth. Now make me a cup of tea and we'll see about food. I don't know what we're going to have, now you've finally decided to roll in at this hour." Madge hesitated, waiting for Alice to answer, but no sound came. She watched her as she made a pot of tea, and didn't know whether to smack her with the frying pan or strangle her with the teatowel. Alice poured out two cups, glanced at her mother, looking as though she was about to say something and then changed her mind.

"Just going to put my things away."

"Hurry up. Your father will want his tea when he gets in."

"Yes, Mum."

Madge watched Alice walk from the kitchen into the hall and turn to go up the stairs, the teacup rattling in the saucer as she went.

"I'll give you yes Mum," she muttered through gritted teeth. "Cheeky young wippersnapper."

Madge took her tea into the living room and sat back in the

armchair, a disgruntled sort of sensation sweeping over her. She hadn't been feeling herself lately: her moods were even more irrational than normal and she kept having hot flushes all the time. She had been forty-five in June, which was only a month ago, and considered herself far too young to be going through the menopause. She had toyed with the idea of going to the doctor, but had dismissed the notion nearly as soon as it had occured to her. Even if he confirmed that she was going through the change of life, what could he do about it? She didn't hold with pills and potions, you never knew what they were going to do to you, and she had one friend in the Photography Club who had been addicted to tranquilisers for years.

She finished her tea, fetched herself a refill and drank that as well. She had always been fond of the beverage, although she had never got Alice to do it properly. Maid's water, Geoff called her brew, he liked it so that you could stand your spoon up in it, and Madge had got used to drinking it like that too. Second cup was always the best, much stronger with all that lovely tannin. The way Alice made tea seemed to suit her temperament, as far as Madge could make out. Weak and wishy-washy.

"Far too much like her father for my liking," Madge muttered as she picked up her embroidery again. "Still, at least that makes her easy to control."

The next day the local paper came sliding through the letterbox, and Madge heard Alice's footsteps running down the stairs. She stood with her ear to the living room door, and heard the pages turning as she wondered what she was looking for. Then she heard her dialling the phone, and decided it was time to see what was going on.

"Who are you ringing?" she demanded to know as she marched out into the hall. The newspaper was spread across the telephone table with some of the pages out of place and half hanging over the edge. "And what's all this mess?"

"I'm ringing after a job," replied Alice. "It says to ring for an interview."

"What a way to go about things. Whatever happened to writing letters?"

"This is quicker."

Madge didn't like the tone of her voice. The way she said the few words was as if that should have been obvious. This girl was getting too cheeky by far, and it was about time something was done about it.

"I suppose next you'll be saying it's cheaper too."

"It is." Alice nodded. "And soon we'll be doing it on computers. You'll be able to see the person you're talking to, as well as hear them."

Madge put her hands on her hips for the second time in as many days. She always did this when she was annoyed.

"There you go again," she said. "Where do you get all these crazy ideas from? I think we'll have to stop you watching that Doctor Who. I always said it was a load of rubbish anyway."

"Yes, Mum."

"Don't keep saying yes Mum!" Madge roared. She was losing her grip on reality now, she could feel her sanity slipping. "Can't you think of anything else to say?"

Alice didn't answer. She stared at the telephone instead. Madge didn't know what to do, the child wouldn't even look at her now. After a few seconds she decided this confrontation was useless. If Alice wouldn't react, then she had nothing to fire back at her. The girl was hopeless, she coudn't even conduct a decent argument.

"Use the phone then if you must," she eventually said. "And don't take all day over it."

Alice didn't do anything straight away, so Madge gave up and stormed off. She went back into the living room and slammed the door behind her. Then she flopped down into her armchair and picked up a magazine, as though she was grabbing hold of a rabbit by the scruff of its neck. She flicked through a few pages but couldn't concentrate on anything. Her nerves were jangling and her emotions were all over the place. She didn't know how she felt or why, and she didn't know what to do about it either. She strangled the rolled-up magazine with a shriek of frustration, then threw it across the room as she burst into unexpected and uncontrollable tears.

"What's happening to me?"

Madge put her head into her hands and sobbed. She didn't think she had ever felt so peculiar in all her life.

This state of affairs went on for several weeks, with Alice looking for jobs and Madge feeling more disorientated by the day. Geoff made no comment about either situation but then again, nobody really thought he would. He floated in and out of their lives like some vague, disembodied spirit, his presence never having any kind of effect on either his wife or his daughter. He left the parenting duties to the woman of the house, little realising that there were now two of them. Not that either of them regarded Alice as a woman. She was still their little girl as far as they were concerned.

After two months, Madge was at the end of her tether. Alice was still hanging about the house, and all she seemed to do lately was run up the phone bill. She had gone after every job she could, but everyone had given her the same answer. At nearly nineteen she was too old for an office junior, and had no experience for other positions. Madge continually told her she was wasting her time, although she secretly wished she'd hurry up and find something to get out from under her feet. Not that they had that much to do with each other. The child spent most of her time lurking in her bedroom listening to some God awful caterwauling noise that she had the nerve to call music. Really, Madge didn't know what the youth of this country were coming to. Bone idle long haired Yetis, she called most of them.

Then Alice amazed her completely by actually getting an interview. While she panicked and searched through her small wardrobe for something suitable to wear, Madge sent up a silent thank you to somebody. At last she was going to have the house to herself again.

She hummed tunelessly as Alice left the house, forgetting to wish her luck, while not thinking she needed it. Then again, the child did have a tendency to muck things up, her exam results were proof of that. The fact that she had done well in typing and shorthand was completely overlooked. They weren't proper subjects anyway, in Madge's book.

She had just settled down in her favourite armchair with her weekly women's magazine when the phone rang. With a tut and a sigh she let it ring a few times, before hauling herself out of her comfortable position and walkihg into the hall.

I hope it's somebody important, she thought on her way to the hall table next to the front door. The Treasurer of the Women's Institute maybe?

She picked up the receiver, and listened to the person on the other end with a frown on her face. She didn't recognise the voice, but after a few seconds realised it was Susan, the only friend her antisocial daughter had.

"No, I'm afraid Alice isn't here at the moment." She didn't bother putting on her phone voice. It was only Susan. "In fact, she isn't around much at all lately, she keeps herself very busy, you know. Yes, I'll tell her you called. Yes, I expect she'll ring you back."

With that, Madge hung up.

"Huh." She glared at the instrument as if it had just done something very wicked indeed. "I'll do nothing of the kind, she's used the telephone quite enough as it is lately."

When Alice returned home Madge said nothing about the phone call, and was disgruntled to learn that they both had to wait to find out if the girl had got the job or not. Madge didn't hold out a lot of hope. From the little Alice had told her, it didn't sound as though the interview had gone very well.

Two days later a letter came addressed to Alice, and Madge had to use all the restraint she could muster not to rip the thing open to find out what was inside. Alice had taken to getting up late recently, much to Madge's disgust. A daily shouting at and regular use of the hoover on the landing were having little effect, she was going to have to think of something else. Unless the letter conveyed good news.

Madge made sure she was in the room when the envelope was opened, and could tell what it contained by the way Alice's face fell as she read it.

"I didn't get the job," she said with the beginnings of tears in her eyes.

"Well, I didn't really think you would," said Madge. "I mean, you haven't got much to offer, have you? You're too mousy, Alice, you should smarten yourself up a bit. And let's face it, you're not too strong in the personality department either, are you? Just like your father, it's a shame really, I know you can't help it but ..."

Alice had gone. Disappeared upstairs at the speed of light.

"Strange," Madge muttered, then remembered her tirade and shouted up the stairs. "Come back here, I haven't finished with you yet. No manners, these youngsters."

She was still lamenting this fact, and quite a few others, when she went round to Mrs. Croft's for coffee a few days later. Not that she was going to say too much against Alice to her. The girl didn't seem capable of finding herself a boyfriend, so it fell to Madge to do it for her. Stephen Croft was the ideal choice, he was young, slim, reasonably good looking, good enough for Alice anyway, and he had a well paid job with prospects in a bank. What more could the girl ask for? He was about the right age too, five years older. Just the right sort of time to get married, and Madge had made up her mind to steer him into it. That way she would kill two birds with one stone, get Alice off her hands and have something to brag about to her friends in the various clubs. It was about time Alice did something to make her parents proud of her.

Doreen Croft's house was a semi the same as Madge's, but it appeared that very little had been done to modernise it since it had been built just after the Second World War. Coal fires were used in both the living and dining rooms, picture rails still adorned the walls and the kitchen, well, Madge wouldn't have put up with it. Old-fashioned was hardly the word.

She waited patiently in the dining room while Mrs. Croft brewed a large pot of coffee, put biscuits onto a bone china plate on top of a paper doily, then carried everything in on an ornate wooden tray to begin their weekly session of putting the world to rights.

"That was a good speaker we had at the Institute last week," Mrs. Croft began.

"Wasn't it?" Madge agreed. She always agreed with everything Doreen said, whether she actually did or not. "Very professional, I thought."

"Yes, there isn't much of that around any more. Biscuit?"

"Thank you so much. Oh, home-made."

"Yes, they're so much nicer than shop bought, don't you think?"

"Oh, absolutely." Madge took a small bite. Doreen never put enough sugar in things for her liking.

"So." Doreen sipped her coffee without appearing to even get her lips wet. "How are things with you?"

"Oh, not so bad you know." Madge lied through her almost gritted teeth. "Apart from Alice. I really don't know what we're going to do with that girl."

"Is she still talking about getting a job?"

"Yes. I blame the schools you know, giving all this advice on careers, it's enough to get them confused." Madge flashed her one of her special smiles. "All she really needs is a little something to keep her occupied until the right boy comes along, stop her becoming aimless."

"Children are such a problem these days." Doreen sighed. "But I've been very lucky with my Stephen. He got the first job he applied for but then again, I think my husband pulled a few strings behind his back."

Both women laughed, each with their own private thoughts. Madge was suddenly thinking that maybe she should have a quiet word in Geoff's shell-like. There must be some sort of little office job going somewhere within the hospital group.

"After all, there's no point in educating girls and encouraging them to have careers when all they're going to do is go off, get married and have children, is there?" Mrs. Croft continued.

"Oh, I quite agree." Madge was trying not to remember her own ambitions of going to grammar school. She had only got married to Geoff because it had been the easiest option.

"My Stephen says he'll never let any wife of his go out to work, he's quite adamant about that." Mrs. Croft looked like she was pretty determined about it too. "A woman's place is in the home."

"Oh, absolutely." Madge couldn't argue with that, considering that was all she had ever done throughout her married life. "That's one good thing about Alice, she makes herself useful around the house."

"I'm sure you've taught her well," Mrs. Croft said, in a rather condescending tone, Madge thought.

"Oh yes. She's an excellent cook, better than me actually. I shall miss her when she goes." Madge forced herself to laugh.

"Cooking is probably the most useful skill a girl can have." Mrs. Croft nodded approvingly. "After all, it's right what they say, the way to a man's heart is through his stomach."

"Yes." Madge was seeing Geoff's submissive face in her mind's eye. "I'm sure." Then she remembered where she was, and flashed Mrs. Croft a big smile that was a little too jaunty and bright. "Alice is a good girl, always does as she's told. She'll make someone a lovely dutiful wife."

Doreen and Madge looked at each other sideways, and Madge wondered if they were both thinking the same thing. Mrs. Croft smiled a little enigmatically and Madge was sure they were both visualising the wedding between Alice and Stephen. She felt very pleased with herself, today was turning into one of her better ones. She had sown the seeds in Doreen's mind, and now had to leave them to sprout and grow. Oh yes, she'd make something of Alice if it killed her.

A little while later Madge took her leave of Mrs. Croft, with her coffee percolator and bone china tea set, and went back to her own house. Alice was busy in the kitchen chopping potatoes to go with the casserole she had prepared earlier. This was languishing in the oven on a low heat and smelled absolutely delicious. For once Madge couldn't wait for Geoff to get home so they could eat. Oh yes, and she had something she wanted to talk to him about.

Later in the evening, after they had eaten and Alice had washed up then gone up to her room, Madge eyed Geoff carefully, trying to judge his mood. He was stuck in a copy of the Lancet, which was nothing new, and Madge wondered how to attract his attention. In the end she decided to just come straight out with it.

"I went round to Mrs. Croft's today."

"Oh yes?" Geoff sounded totally indifferent.

"Yes, we had a good chat and she told me something rather interesting."

"Oh yes?" He sounded somewhat suspicious now.

"Apparently Mr. Croft helped Stephen get his job. Pulled some strings behind the scenes."

"Oh yes?" Geoff was almost smiling now, as if he knew what was coming next.

"Yes, I just wondered …"

"Mmm?"

"If there were any little office jobs within the hospital group that might suit Alice? It doesn't have to be anything much, just something to keep her occupied. It's driving me mad having her around the house all the while."

"Okay." Geoff turned the page of his magazine with a wry smile on his face. "I'll see what I can do."

CHAPTER NINE

Geoff was as good as his word. Three days later they all sat down to the dinner table at five forty-five exactly. Geoff was a stickler for punctuality and ate the meal Alice had prepared in complete silence. Dinner, or rather tea as Madge always called it, was for eating not talking through. Nobody looked at each other, yet Alice had the distinct impression that her mother was trying to catch her father's eye, which was strange. They usually had very little to say to each other. The meal was concluded and Madge got quickly to her feet.

"Tea anyone?" she asked brightly.

"Er, yes," answered Alice, and Geoff nodded. Madge collected up the empty plates, told Alice to stay put, then swept from the room theatrically. Alice was puzzled. They always had a cuppa after dinner, so she couldn't understand the reason for the question. What was going on here?

"I've got something to show you, Alice," Geoff suddenly said, as he reached behind him for his briefcase which he had placed on one of the chairs in the window. Alice sat quietly as he opened it, sifted through some papers, then took one out. "Here." He handed it to her. "This might interest you."

It was a job description all neatly typed out, with an application form attached with a staple. Alice didn't understand. Where had he got this from?

"It's in Walsall, I'm afraid." Geoff almost sounded apologetic, but not quite. "That's all we've got going at the moment. It's at the General Hospital."

The penny was beginning to drop. Then Alice remembered his first comment.

"Walsall?"

"Yes, it's a bit of a way to go but it might be worth you trying for it. They don't need anyone with any experience."

Alice was heading swiftly towards cloud nine. The mention of the town some ten miles away had brought Joe's face floating into her mind's eye, and now she felt all warm and glowy inside.

"That's alright." She was fighting down the biggest grin that had ever tried to escape from her body. "I don't mind travelling."

"I'll leave it with you then." Geoff looked satisfied that he had done his duty. "You can post the form back when you've filled it in."

"Yes." Alice still had it in her hand. "Thanks, Dad."

Geoff tried to smile kindly, failed miserably, cleared his throat in discomfort and went back to his briefcase. Alice almost felt sorry for him and to save him any further embarrassment, she studied the two pieces of paper in her hand. The duties didn't sound too complicated, doing the post, answering the phone and bits of typing for whoever needed it. She could manage that, and it was a job. A real job!

As soon as she possibly could, she went to hide in her room, lie on the bed and daydream about Joe. She thought about him quite often, as she liked the way the thoughts made her feel. She had relived the afternoon in the Chinese restaurant countless times, and wished they had exchanged phone numbers so they could keep in touch. That reminded her, she hadn't heard from Susan for ages. She was probably somewhere training to be a nurse now. Wouldn't it be a turn up for the books if she happened to be in Walsall?

I suppose that's too much to hope for, Alice thought as she settled down to fill in the application form.

Once it had gone in the post, all she could do was wait. It seemed to take for ever to get a reply, but eventually she did. She was invited to go for an interview, so she set off early. She had never been to Walsall and had no idea where the hospital was. Madge dismissively told her she would be fine, and Alice meekly agreed.

At least it wasn't raining, as it appeared she might have quite a bit of walking to do.

Walsall was a bigger town than Lichfield, and had a different feel to it. People were milling about everywhere, and they all seemed to be in a rush to get where they were going. The market was on, which made it even busier than usual, but Alice walked calmly through the main streets and up the hill to the hospital. It was well signposted, which was fortunate as Alice didn't really fancy stopping any of the frantic shoppers to ask them the way.

The interview was with a man who reminded her very much of her father, and Alice didn't know whether it was going well or not. She didn't have much experience of interviews. She was expecting to be told she would be informed of the outcome by letter, then the man surprised her completely by offering her the job there and then.

"Can you start on Monday?"

"Yes. Thank you very much."

Alice was floating on air as she walked back into town and up to the bus station. So this was the town where Joe lived. It had a bit of a hard-nosed feel to it, there was more industry here than she was used to. She decided she would have to explore the shops when she got a chance, they were bigger and better than most of the ones in Lichfield. She couldn't wait to see the look on Madge's face when she told her the good news, although she was going to have to ask for money for bus fares to last her through the first month.

Oh blimey, Alice thought in dismay as she boarded the bus back to Lichfield. Mum's not very good at giving me money.

Monday came round very quickly, and Alice was dispatched down to the bus station with enough money to last the first week, and some sandwiches wrapped up in a bit of tin foil. At least she knew where she had to go this time, and was welcomed at the door of the general office by a middle-aged kindly looking woman with permed hair and huge glasses.

"I'm Mrs. Roberts,"she said. "Your desk is opposite mine, although you'll probably spend most of your time in the front office answering the phone. We do the post in there too. I do all the requests for surgical appliances, built-up shoes, trusses, neck braces, all that sort of thing. Just settle in and find your way around, then at break time I'll show you where the canteen is."

"Thank you." Alice felt a little overwhelmed by all these new things as she sat at her desk and examined the old typewriter. Then she told herself sternly that she could cope. She would be alright after a week or two.

A few days later Mrs. Roberts called her over. They didn't talk much, they had little in common, but the woman was helpful towards Alice. She was a similar age to Madge, but a lot more supportive and sympathetic than the monster from the black lagoon.

"Now then, I want you to take these papers down to the Physiotherapy Department. You'll do this every week, they're the requests for assessments for appliances. Ask for Pamela and give them to her, then she'll give you some papers for me. Got that?"

"Yes," said Alice confidently. She was finding her feet a bit now.

She felt like she was going off on some great adventure as she left the general office. The only other places she had been to so far were the canteen and the toilets, which were quite close together. She followed her instructions and found the department easily. The General wasn't a huge hospital, it would be difficult to get lost.

Pamela turned out to be a pleasant girl several years older than herself, and Alice realised they had seen each other around the corridors and in the canteen. Over the next few weeks she was sent on other little errands, and got to know Maureen in X-ray and June in Casualty as well. She settled into the routine of work easily and happily, and the best thing about it was that Madge had to take over the cooking. Alice didn't get home until after six o'clock.

"You can do it at the weekends," she was told. "Don't pull a face like that, it's not as if I ask you to do much around the place."

"Yes, Mum." Alice groaned under her breath. Her mother had got a very short memory when it suited her.

So it was that Alice fell into a new routine at home. Saturday was always fish and chips and Sunday a roast beef dinner. She wasn't allowed to deviate from the menu, so didn't bother to try after a while. Susan still hadn't been in touch as Madge had told her she promised she would, and Alice didn't like to bother her parents to find out where she was. The message Alice had received through Madge was that Susan was moving around a lot, and would get in touch when she was settled somewhere. They had seen very little of each other over the last six months, and Alice missed her friend, but slowly she was coming to terms with life without her. She had been hoping to make some new friends at the hospital, but this wasn't really working out. She spent most of her time in the front office on her own manning the phone, occasionally handing out hearing-aid batteries and doing the post. When she wasn't doing this, she was in the other room with Mrs. Roberts. She was a nice woman but over twice Alice's age, so they didn't have a lot to talk about. Mrs. Roberts seemed to realise this and they both did their work in silence most of the time, she sorting out requests and requisitions for surgical appliances and Alice getting on with the few bits of typing she was given now and then. Mrs. Robert's job seemed really boring as far as Alice could make out, and the things she typed weren't much better. Then again, it was better than being at home. Anything was better than that. The best thing about it was that she was managing to save a little as well, but she daren't mention this to her mother for fear she would ask for more board money.

Every day one of the seven medical secretaries came down from their office upstairs with the post. They had the largest amount, although other bits came in from different departments slowly throughout the day. Alice enjoyed sorting all this out, then putting it through the franking machine ready to be transported off to other hospitals, general practitioners and patients. This was her last job of the day, then she could hurry down the hill to the bus station to catch the five thirty-five back to Lichfield.

She was just preparing to do exactly that on the following Friday when she noticed a car pull up on the drive outside the door. Parking in this area wasn't really allowed as Casualty was nearby, but sometimes people did pull up there to drop off or pick up. Vague curiosity crept over Alice, so she hesitated just inside the doorway.

Then her heart leapt and her stomach turned over as the driver opened his door, got out and stood looking directly at her. He couldn't see her, the window blind was obscuring his view.

"Joe!" Alice breathed.

Her joy was short lived. Her acquaintance from Physio, Pamela, rushed up behind her, called a cheery goodnight, then breezed through the door as if she was in a tearing hurry. She got into Joe's car as though she had done it a thousand times before, and Alice's heart sank. Pamela had mentioned a boyfriend, and had even told Alice that they were going away for the weekend to visit his parents. As she watched them drive away, Alice felt despondant. She should have known a nice, good looking man like him would have a girlfriend.

How she got to the bus station that night she would never know. She did the journey home like a zombie, going over and over in her mind every time she had seen Joe. Only now did she realise that she liked him a lot more than she had ever dreamed possible, but he was spoken for. Now she would have nothing to fantasise about during the long, lonely hours in her bedroom.

"Oh, Joe," she whispered as she got off the bus, tears prickling at her eyes.

As she approached the cul-de-sac, she tried to banish all thoughts of Joe from her mind as if that would block out the hurt and disappointment. At least Madge didn't know anything about it, so she wouldn't be making any sarcastic comments or poking fun at the situation. Alice really didn't know how her father put up with her mother, as she treated him in exactly the same way. He seemed to be able to shrug it off, but Alice couldn't do that. Every nasty remark cut like a knife, and each cruel put-down made her feel stupid and inadequate. Madge was forever telling her she was useless, and at the moment that's just how she felt. Maybe her mother was right. She couldn't make friends and she didn't have a boyfriend. As she walked into the back door of the house, Alice decided she had never felt so miserable in all her life.

Over the weekend things didn't improve much. Alice cried

herself to sleep as quietly as she could, she didn't want any unwelcome questions from either of her parents. On Saturday she got up late, after trying to ignore the vacuum cleaner that Madge had left running outside her bedroom door, had a bacon sandwich, then did her best to summon up enough enthusiasm to make Geoff a fruit cake, before grinding up baked crusts of bread to coat the three pieces of cod that were languishing in the fridge.

She got through the long afternoon somehow, with Madge only disturbing her once by shouting from the living room to tell her to make a pot of strong tea. Alice sighed, but did as she was told. She didn't know how they could drink it like that, and made sure she poured her own out long before the other two got to it.

During tea she chased the last few peas around her plate before finally giving up and squashing them. Madge had been wittering on about Mrs. Croft's new three-piece suite, and Alice and Geoff had actually exchanged glances and known what the other was thinking. Geoff even risked a wink at his daughter and she had suppressed a smile. Taking the mickey in the Harwood house was very much a one-sided affair.

"How's the job going, Alice?" Geoff asked, when he could get a word in. "You haven't mentioned it for a while."

"Fine thanks, Dad."

"The travelling's not getting you down?"

"No." Until a couple of days ago this had been true, but now Alice wasn't so sure.

"What do you do all day?" Geoff persisted. It seemed he wanted to keep Madge quiet on the subject of Mrs. Croft. Probably every other subject too.

"A bit of typing, the post and answering the phone." Alice nearly laughed. "Some of that's a bit strange."

"Oh?"

"The funniest one is having to give out the measurements to the funeral people." Madge was staring at her wide-eyed now. "You know, for the coffins."

"Oh yes," replied Geoff. "Length, width and depth. Mmm, I'd forgotten about that."

"You have to do what?" Madge exploded in horror.

"The man from the mortuary brings them to the office," Alice explained as she continued this rare conversation with her father. "Tom his name is, nice man, but I try not to think about what he has to do in his job."

As Geoff nodded in agreement, Madge was still protesting.

"I can't believe they make you do something so morbid. I thought office jobs were just bits of typing and filing."

"I do that as well. It's no big deal, Mum, it's only measurements."

"It's got to be done, Madge. All coffins are different sizes."

"It's not something I care to think about, thank you very much." She got to her feet and began piling up the empty plates. "I don't know what Mrs. Croft is going to say when I tell her."

With that she swept from the room in an outraged huff, and went to deposit the plates in the kitchen and fetch the bowls of tinned peaches that Alice had put out earlier.

"One of the medical secretaries is leaving," Alice told her father, seeing as he seemed to be in an interested mood today. "I thought I might apply for it."

"Oh, are you sure, Alice?" He looked concerned now. "That's quite difficult work, you know, you need to know a lot of medical terminology."

"She said I could learn as I go along. It's orthopaedic and ear, nose and throat, not the really hard stuff."

"What's she going on about now?" Madge wanted to know when she came back with the puddings on a tray.

"Applying for the job of medical secretary. I've told her I don't think it's a good idea."

"Of course not." Madge agreed. "You don't want anything like that. You've only got the job in the first place to tide you over until you get married."

"Yes, Mum," Alice answered and that was the end of that.

She thought about the job over the rest of the weekend and

wondered if it would be too difficult for her. Then she reasoned the girl wouldn't have mentioned it to her if she didn't think she could do it. When she got to work on Monday and was out on one of her errands, she went to see her to discuss it. They went through the correct channels, and Alice accompanied the secretary to a few clinics over the next couple of weeks. She soon discovered that the work wasn't over her head at all, and had no trouble in plucking up the courage to go to see the necessary person to apply for the job properly. Needless to say, she didn't say anything about it to her parents.

A few weeks later, she said goodbye to Mrs. Roberts and moved upstairs into the medical secretaries' office. She had a big desk opposite Patricia who worked for the Consultant Physician, and her own telephone. There were seven of them in the office, and it got a bit noisy at times, but they all attended their various clinics to take dictation and Alice was very glad to be using her shorthand skills at last. The time flew by and she loved every minute of it. Her pay had increased too, which was another reason not to say anything to Madge. She had been making noises about putting her board up anyway.

"I'm going to save up for a car," Alice told herself happily, "and get myself some driving lessons."

Alice settled into her new job and situation quickly. She didn't really pal up with any of the other girls, a couple of them were married and as the others all lived in and around Walsall and she lived in Lichfield, it wasn't easy to do things together. Once a month they all went to a Chinese restaurant just down the road and had the businessman's lunch. Alice enjoyed this and had amazed everyone by opting to use chopsticks, but the outings were always tinged with a hint of sadness. Chinese restaurants would always remind her of Joe.

She didn't see so much of Pamela these days, although two of her weekly clinics were conducted in the Physiotherapy Department. The only time they really had any contact was once a week, when Alice had to go round most of the departments with a list of people who were having operations that week. She didn't mind this task, which got her out of the office for a few minutes to walk around the hospital, although she wasn't keen on going to theatre. Sometimes she caught a glimpse of someone unconscious on a trolley, or a trayful of nasty looking implements, and the theatre sister was a bit fierce as well. Alice took comfort in the fact that none of the other secretaries liked going there either.

Most days she took sandwiches to work with her, and ate them in the office before going down to the canteen for a cup of tea to wash them down with. Once a week she treated herself to a dinner, the meals in the staff canteen were excellent. She always tried not to sit with the nurses, as a lot of their subjects of conversation were stomach churning. Alice realised that a certain amount of detachment was necessary to work in a hospital, but some of the nurses took it a little too far. She couldn't always avoid them though, particularly when it was busy.

Occasionally she got a table all to herself, but not very often. She didn't mind sharing, it was another way to get to know people, but she still found herself wondering about Susan. She wished she would get in touch, she had no-one to go out with now. She still went for a walk around Lichfield sometimes, but it wasn't the same and she wouldn't go out in the evenings on her own. Madge had declared that she was becoming antisocial, but Alice couldn't make her understand that she didn't want to go out alone at night. She felt stupid enough in the daytime.

Alice was lost in dark thoughts about her mother and wistful ones about Susan, when Pamela suddenly appeared and sat down opposite her. Alice gave her a weak smile and tried to behave normally. Pamela wasn't to know that Alice's heart was wrenched into pieces every time she thought about her and Joe.

"I've got engaged." She wasted no time in telling Alice with a radiant look about her. "Look." She flashed the engagement ring into Alice's face.

"Congratulations," said Alice stiffly. "I hope you and Joe will be very happy."

"Joe?" Pamela looked puzzled. "No Alice, my boyfriend is called Nick. Joe? Oh heavens, no. Joe's my brother."

Alice looked up at Pamela as her heart soared, then she smiled at her. Brother not boyfriend, oh, thank the Lord for that!

CHAPTER TEN

Alice's world had just improved by leaps and bounds. How was she to even guess Joe was Pamela's brother, when they looked nothing like each other? Alice explained to Pamela how they had met, but she didn't say anything to her about the way she felt about him. He might very well have a girlfriend, after all, he was fifteen years older than her. This fact didn't bother her in the slightest, it was completely irrelevant as far as she was concerned. The day ended in total joy for Alice when Pamela told her she would tell Joe that Alice was now working at the hospital. Maybe they would get in touch again, Alice could only live in hope. Now the monthly visit to the Chinese restaurant had taken on a whole new meaning and Alice could fantasise about Joe once more. Oh yes, things were looking up and this weekend she was having her first driving lesson.

The news of these had a mixed reception in the Harwood house. Geoff conceded that being able to drive might be useful one day, but Madge declared it to be a complete and utter waste of time and money. They already had one car cluttering up the place, there wasn't room for another. And anyway, what was wrong with the bus? Alice said nothing, it was usually the easiest way, but she wondered whether her mother's reaction would have been the same if she was the one hanging around in the cold and rain waiting for them. Alice had just survived her first winter of travelling to Walsall by buying a heavy coat and a pair of boots, and was glad it was now over. Spring had arrived, bringing with it sunshine, leaves on trees and new hope for the future. This was Alice's view of it anyway. Her father was complaining that now he would have to start cutting the grass again.

The driving lesson went reasonably well so she booked one for the following Sunday too. No-one asked how she had got on, which didn't surprise her, but Madge told her to put the kettle on then go and find her father.

"He's disappeared down the garden again," said Madge grumpily. "I really don't know what he finds to do down there."

Alice had a fair idea that he was just keeping out of the way, but didn't dare say so to Madge. Instead, just as soon as she possibly could, she escaped to her own hiding place upstairs.

Monday morning brought the busy fracture clinic in a small room next to Casualty. People on crutches were hobbling about, and others were sitting patiently with their arms in slings or calming fractious children. Alice enjoyed this clinic. It was fast and furious, and she didn't have time to think about anything else but her work. Mr. Barton was the orthopaedic surgeon, and Alice loved him. He had a wonderful sense of humour and they got on really well, not even needing to speak to each other half the time. She had never had such a good rapport with anyone before, and looked forward to his clinics three times a week. The other consultant she worked for was a rather dreamy and distant figure, they couldn't have been more different.

Before she knew it, the middle of the week had arrived and she was hard at work in the office typing up the clinic letters from Tuesday. Every now and then the phone rang and disturbed her concentration, and when it went off again she tutted as she picked up the receiver.

"Medical secretaries."

"Can I speak to Alice, please?"

"Speaking." Alice frowned. The voice was vaguely familiar.

"Hello. It's Joe." She froze as he continued speaking. "I'm coming over to Lichfield on Friday and I wondered if you'd like to meet me for a drink and maybe a curry later?"

Alice didn't know what to do. Her mind was thinking three million things at once and her hands were shaking.

"Alice?"

"Oh yes, I mean yes, that'd be lovely."

"Good. I'll meet you, uh, where? Do you know the King's Head?"

"Yes." Alice knew where it was although she had never been in there.

"Seven-thirty okay?"

"Yes." She didn't know what else to say.

"I'll look forward to it. See you on Friday then."

"Yes."

The phone went dead, but Alice continued to sit with the receiver in her hand. Now her mind had stalled completely, and a warm treacley glow was seeping all through her body. She was going out with Joe. A real date. What was she going to wear? And what was her mother going to say?

"Alice?" Patricia was looking at her a bit old-fashioned from across their double desk. "Are you alright?"

"Uh?" Alice abruptly woke up from her amazing dream and realised where she was. As she put the phone back on the hook, she continued. "Oh yes, I'm fine. Absolutely wonderful."

When she got home, she wondered what to tell Madge. She ate her dinner alone in the dining room, trying to think up a story that her mother would believe. Usually the truth was met with derision and all sorts of outlandish accusations.

I could tell her I'm meeting Susan, she suddenly realised. Yes, that's what I'll do.

And so it was that the deception was arranged. She was told to be in before midnight, then went out to catch the bus into town from the stop at the end of the road. She had her own doorkey now. Once she had started work they had finally agreed to let her have one, but only for the back door. She despaired of ever getting one to the front.

She got off at the bus station, and walked slowly back through the town to the pub where they had arranged to meet. She was a quarter of an hour early, so didn't rush her steps as she speculated on what the evening was going to hold. What was she going to say to him? She had been all teenagy and tongue-tied on the phone, how was she going to cope with seeing him in the flesh? And what would she do if he didn't turn up?

At two minutes past seven-thirty, Alice took a deep breath and entered the pub. She had never been inside one before, but doing unknown things on her own didn't frighten her, she had been doing that for most of her life. She looked around anxiously, there were quite a lot of people around, but there he was, standing at the bar with a pint of bitter on the counter in front of him. Alice's knees went weak. She had dreamed about this moment for so long. All she hoped now was that she wasn't about to make a complete idiot of herself. He smiled at her as she walked over to him, said hello, then asked her what she wanted to drink.

"Oh, er, orange juice, please."

They stayed standing at the bar as most of the seats were already taken. Alice had no idea where the time went as they talked and talked, and caught up with what the other had been doing since they had last met.

"We go to the Chinese once a month from work." Alice laughed. "I've got half of them into using chopsticks."

"I suppose I'm going to get the blame for that." Joe laughed too. Alice loved it when he did. He had the most alluring smile she had ever seen in her life. "Are your parents still dead against foreign food?"

"Oh yes, even worse than ever if anything."

"So, have you ever had a curry?"

"No, but I've wanted one for ages," she admitted. "The smell when I walk past drives me mad. I'm dying to try one."

"That's settled then, we'll go to the Indus."

"Great."

"Another orange juice, or will you try something else?"

"Ooh, a cider, please. Haven't had any of that for ages."

"Coming right up."

After two ciders they moved the short distance to the Indian restaurant. This time Alice had no trouble not gawping around herself in a strange situation, she only had eyes for Joe. She let him take the lead, as a very smartly dressed and polite Indian waiter showed them to a table and helped them make themselves comfortable. Then he brought poppodums and pickles and two halves of lager and left them alone for a while at Joe's request.

"Try them all," he said as he saw Alice eyeing each pickle in turn. "Some are sweet, others hot. You decide which you like best."

Alice watched what he did, then followed suit. She found the mango chutney too sweet, liked the onion and tomato salad and said she couldn't quite make up her mind about the lime pickle. She went back to it several times and quickly developed a bit of a love-hate affair with it.

"So," Joe said a few minutes later, "shall I order?"

"I don't know what to have," Alice confessed. "You choose something for me."

"Do you like onions?" Joe's eyes twinkled mischievously as though he already had something in mind. Alice nodded. She was still having trouble believing she was here with him, she was expecting to pinch herself and wake up somewhere else any second. "Right then, it's chicken dupiaza for you, I think, and I'll have a madras. That's quite hot so you can try it and see if you fancy it next time."

Next time, he was talking about next time! Alice half held her breath and willed this evening to never end. She snook a glance at her watch and winced a little. It was eleven o'clock already.

She told herself not to panic as Joe ordered the two curries, then they finished their drinks and nibbles. Then came the moment of truth as the food arrived. Alice had been looking forward to this for such a long time, and now the moment had finally come. She was convinced she was going to like it, and she wasn't disappointed. The meat was moist and tender and the sauce was divine. She soon decided that she had never tasted anything so good in her entire life, and from the look of things, he might be bringing her here for another one. If she wasn't late home and got banned from going out ever again.

All these thoughts flew from her mind as she ate, looking up at Joe every now and then. He had introduced her to two new experiences now, and she allowed herself to wonder how many others there would be in the future. She hoped there would be lots. He had mentioned that he went abroad with his work every now and then, and Alice fantasised about going with him to far flung places. Then she told herself to be sensible, her imagination was running away with her. Oh, but the thoughts felt good.

"Would you like to try some of this madras sauce?" he interrupted her dream by asking. "It's quite different from what you've got."

"Yes, please." Alice was thoroughly enjoying trying new things. "Wow!" was her verdict when she tasted it. "I like that too."

"Indian has long since been my favourite food, there's so much variety," he said. "Seems like you think the same."

"That curry I had was absolutely gorgeous." Alice was trying to look at her watch again without him seeing her but wasn't having a whole lot of success. He was studying her with a quizzical look, as if he knew what the problem was.

"Have you got to be in by a particular time?"

"Yes, midnight. My parents are a bit strict, they still think I'm about twelve."

"Better that than not give a damn." Joe smiled, then looked at his own watch. "Ten to twelve. Come on, I'll run you home."

As he called the waiter over and paid the bill, Alice fought down her panic. When he had said what the time was she had nearly died with shock, thinking she had got a twenty minute walk home. It was good of him to offer to take her in his car, she wasn't used to having lifts.

Joe's car was parked just around the corner, and as Alice slid into the passenger seat she felt like a film star. She gave him directions to the cul-de-sac and they pulled up at the end of the road.

"Are you doing anything tomorrow evening?" he asked.

"No," said Alice breathlessly.

"Shall I pick you up at the same time? We can go for a ride out and have a drink, if you like."

"That'd be lovely, Joe." She was reaching for the door handle.

"Until tomorrow then." He was out of the car and coming round to open her door. As he stood there holding it and Alice got out of the car, she was aware of just how close he was to her.

"I've really enjoyed tonight," she said quietly.

"So have I." He kissed her gently on the cheek. "Goodnight, Alice."

She had to wrench herself away, still feeling his lips on her face all the way down the avenue, through the gate and up the path to the back door. She found her key quickly, let herself in as quietly as she could and went through the kitchen and into the hall in total darkness, half afraid to even breathe. She slipped off her shoes at the bottom of the stairs then crept up them one by one, willing none of them to creak. She made it to the top without the slightest sound, now all she had to do was tiptoe along the landing to her room.

"You're late." Madge's disembodied voice came from their bedroom. "I'll speak to you tomorrow."

Alice winced and carried on into her room. Once the door was closed behind her, she switched on the light and checked her watch. It was seven minutes past twelve but she hardly cared. Not even her mother was going to spoil what had happened tonight. She was going to remember this evening for the rest of her life.

The next morning brought a telling-off and the usual interrogation. Alice told the truth about what she had done in all except one thing. She was still leading her mother to believe it was Susan she had been out with. She wasn't sure she was ready to hear about a boyfriend yet. Once the Spanish Inquisition was over, she told Madge she was going out again tonight and wasn't the slightest bit surprised by her reaction.

"Again? Good grief, I hope you're not spending all your wages on drink and eating out."

"Oh Mum, you're always moaning I never go out."

"Two nights running, it's a bit much."

"It's the weekend."

"Oh, I suppose so." Madge sounded sullen. "Just don't be late again."

At half past seven Alice left the house and was sure she could see the net curtains twitching in the dining room. She had to walk past Mrs. Croft's house too, and could imagine the same thing happening there as well. She and her mother were as thick as thieves lately, but at least it seemed to be taking Madge's attention off Alice a bit. She hadn't been getting on to her quite as much lately, maybe she was mellowing in her old age.

Joe drove out of Lichfield to a small village a few miles away, and found an olde worlde pub. Alice had never explored any of the villages and hamlets around the city, and found the place quite charming.

"I've always lived in towns, but I like being out in the countryside," said Joe. "Suppose it comes from the fishing."

"Are you still doing that?" Alice remembered only too well that was how they had first met.

"Not so much now, I don't have time. My work keeps me pretty busy."

"What do you do when you go abroad?"

"Solve other people's problems most of the time." He smiled wryly. "Or I'm selling technology. I'm not a salesman, I'm a technical man, but they send me 'cos I know the products inside out and backwards."

"You must have been to some interesting places." Alice was fascinated by all this.

"Mmm, all over Europe and America," he answered. "Now they're talking about getting into China, but I've told them there are two places I've never had any desire to visit. One of them's the moon and the other one is China. Bet I end up going there though."

"Isn't there anyone else they can send?"

"Yes, and I hope they do."

"So that's why you've got into foreign food, is it?"

"Not really, I was eating Chinese and Indian long before that." He smiled. "It helps though."

"Well, thanks to you I've tried them both now. Thank you Joe. If it'd been down to my parents I'd never have done that. They won't ever try anything new."

"Some people are like that, stick to what they're used to."

"What about your parents?"

"My dad died a few years ago but Mum'll try new things. She works in a school canteen and she's got the kids onto curry. They love it."

"Does she live in Walsall?"

"Yes, we all do. Down the Mellish Road."

"Oh, I've heard it's quite nice down there."

"Yes. The house is quite big, too big really. Mum's on about moving to something smaller when Pamela gets married, and I suppose it's about time I got my own place. It's easier to stay at home though, especially with all this travelling about."

"I suppose so." Alice hesitated, then voiced a thought that had been on her mind for a while now. "I've been thinking about leaving home, maybe getting a little flat nearer to work."

"Don't you like Lichfield?"

"Yes." She tried to laugh. "But it's my parents. They just won't let me grow up."

"It's probably because you're an only child."

"I don't know what it is, but they don't seem to realise I'm nearly twenty. I feel as though I need to get away and be myself. If I ever find out what that is."

"I've just had a thought." Joe put down his pint after taking a sip. "There's an old school in our road that's being converted into flats. They're not finished yet, but there might be something there that might suit you."

"Oh Joe, that's a wonderful idea." Alice could hardly believe her ears. Things seemed to be going from best to better since she had met up with him again.

"I'll see what I can find out, shall I?" he asked and Alice nodded.

The next few weeks sped by. The weather was improving and Alice was floating on air most of the time. Her mother managed to break her good mood and deflate her every chance she got, but this was nothing new. Lately there had been sarcastic remarks about Susan owning a car, and Alice knew it wouldn't be long before she had to own up and admit she had a boyfriend. She didn't want to give her mother the chance to spoil things, as she was pretty certain she would do so just for the fun of it. She had that sort of sense of humour.

Once every few weeks, Alice had to work a Saturday morning. The secretaries took it in turns to do this, in case of emergency correspondence, of which there was little, and it gave them a chance to catch up on their normal work. Sometimes after this Alice caught the bus into Birmingham for a look around the shops, although she was still expected to do her chores when she got home. She had got into peeling the potatoes the night before to save time, as her father insisted on having his meal at the same time every night.

On her next working Saturday, she met the postman by the gate as she was leaving the house. They knew each other, so he handed her a letter with a French stamp on it. Alice cheerfully shoved it into her bag as she glanced back, glad Madge hadn't got to it first, although she had long since given up steaming them open. She didn't understand French.

Once Alice was safely installed on the bus to Walsall, she pulled the letter out of her bag and ripped open the envelope. The contents of it made her frown, so she checked her handbag again. She had two letters, one from France and this other one, which she now realised was addressed to Mrs. Harwood. Alice began to put it back into the envelope, then her curiosity got the better of her. She flicked through it, and saw it was to Madge, signed Mum and Dad. Alice's brain nearly stalled. Grandparents had never been mentioned to her, why had she not met them? And where did they live?

The letter gave her the answer to the last question. Somewhere in Dorset called Ingelfield. Someone called Flossie was ill, but all Alice could feel was confusion. All this time and she had never known of their existence. Anger began to rise within her, and she made up her mind she would write to these people. Behind her mother's back. Why not? Madge had obviously been going behind hers for years.

Work was quiet, so Alice composed a draft letter to her unknown grandmother which she would perfect later in the safety of her room. Before that though, she was meeting Joe outside the office at lunchtime so they could spend a couple of hours together. Joe had got the details of some of the flats for her, and today she was going to look at two of them. Both of them were easily in her price range and Joe was coming with her, although they had agreed she was taking the flat on her own. No sense rushing into anything.

Alice liked both the flats but chose the least expensive one, it was plenty big enough for one person. She left the building and walked to Joe's car in seventh heaven. She was almost free. Now all she had to do was tell Madge.

CHAPTER ELEVEN

Alice got Joe to drop her at the bus station, then caught the twenty to four back to Lichfield. This and the walk back to the cul-de-sac gave her some time to think and try to figure out how she was going to tell her parents she was leaving home. She knew they weren't going to like the idea, especially her mother. She couldn't make Madge out half the time. She didn't want her, yet she didn't want to let her go either. It was as if she was a pawn in some sort of surreal chess game that was never going to end. Ever.

This thought was plagueing Alice as she walked home slowly. She imagined herself cowering on a huge chessboard with an enormous hand hovering overhead as the person it belonged to debated on which piece to pick up. Alice hid behind the bishop and then …

Stop being so stupid, she told herself as she stopped to cross the road at the top of the hill. The driver of the car waiting to turn into town waved her across, so she put her hand up to thank him as she went on her way. Another ten minutes and she would be home, but she wouldn't be doing that for much longer. She brightened as she remembered the flat and pretended it was already hers. It wouldn't be ready for several weeks but Alice was looking forward to saving both time and money by living closer to her work. And then there was Joe, that was something else she was going to have to tell her parents about.

Not yet, she thought. Don't want to give them a chance to spoil it.

She was feeling a litle better by the time she got home and

pushed open the back door. The kitchen was empty, although the ingredients for cake making were lined up on the worktop. Alice's heart sank, she had been hoping to get out of it this week. She went through to the hall to hang her coat up, hearing the radio in the living room as she went past.

"Is that you, Alice?" Madge's voice drifted out into the hall.

"Yes," replied Alice. Who else did she think it was going to be?

"Oh, be a good girl and put the kettle on."

"Yes, Mum."

Alice did as she was told and while she was waiting for the kettle to boil, began weighing out the flour for the cake. As she was sieving it, Madge suddenly appeared behind her and made her jump.

"We've got a new recipe," she said, thrusting it into Alice's hand. "There's the fruit." She pointed to the bag with a label on it that Alice had never seen before. "It's a different mix. I'm sure your dad'll like it."

"Where is he anyway?" Alice asked, expecting the answer that came. She hadn't seen any sign of him on her way in.

"Oh, I expect he's doing something in the garage again, he usually is."

"Will he want a cup of tea?"

"It's up to you. I wouldn't bother if he can't be in the house."

"Okay."

The water boiled and Alice made the tea as though she was on automatic pilot. She put out three cups, reconsidered, then put one of them back into the cupboard above the fridge before reaching inside it for the milk. Then Geoff appeared, as if by magic. It was as though he could smell the teapot.

"Don't pour mine out yet," was his greeting.

"No, Dad." Alice sighed and got on with her chores.

Later, during dinner, which was fish and chips and frozen peas as usual, Alice glanced from Madge to Geoff and back again, while wondering when to broach the subject of the flat. Nobody spoke as they ate, which was the normal procedure. Madge took food very seriously, which probably explained why she was on a half-hearted diet most of the time. Meals were to be savoured and devoured, and conversation was all but banned. Alice had never known any different until she ate in other places, such as at Susan's house or with the Guides. Only then did she realise just how peculiar her home life was.

I shall let people talk as much as they want, she decided, very much to herself. When they come to my place to eat.

Suddenly she noticed her mother was staring at her. It was one of those stares. The 'I'm going to find out everything that's going on' type of look.

"What are you looking so happy about?"

"Nothing." Alice gulped. "Just thinking."

She put her head down over her plate, realising she had just missed her chance to say something. She cursed herself for being such a coward and knew she was going to have to pluck up the courage to tell them. She had better do it soon too. The longer she left it, the more difficult it was going to be.

"Alice has made you a cake," Madge announced to Geoff with no warning. "Isn't she a good girl?"

Geoff murmured something unintelligible, and Alice went back to finishing the last of her chips. She hadn't liked the look of the cake mix when she put it into the tin, there were some very strange ingredients in it that she had never used before. She was dreading his reaction to it, as she was pretty sure she knew what it was going to be.

"This is …" he said after he had taken a bite, "different." He chewed his mouthful slowly, his eyes moving this way and that, then he swallowed and put the rest of the piece of cake back onto his plate. "It's horrible. I don't like it."

"Oh, but I got the recipe from Mrs. Croft. It's her husband's favourite, and Stephen likes it too."

Alice's plate was empty now, so she stood up and took it into the kitchen. She hovered there, as she didn't want another lecture all about how well Stephen was doing and why couldn't she be more like him. She hardly knew him anyway, they had gone to different schools and he was older than her. They had barely even said hello to each other in the last two or three years, yet Madge took every opportunity to bang on about him as if he was the best thing since sliced bread. Alice knew the reason, but she was more than convinced she could find her own boyfriends, after all, she was going out with Joe. She debated yet again whether she should tell Madge about him, it would put a stop to all these comments about Stephen.

The weekend dragged on endlessly, as they always did in the Harwood house, until it came time for Sunday tea. This involved sandwiches and cake, and was served up at five forty-five or Geoff would want to know the reason why. Lunch had been at one o'clock on the dot and had been roast beef, as it was every week. Alice longed to cook lamb in rosemary or pork with apricots, but knew her chances were about as good as a snowflake's in hell. She would have to wait until she moved into her flat, then she could invite Joe round, maybe Pamela and their mother as well. Alice had only met her once and that had been briefly. Perhaps when she was living in Walsall she could get to know the family better, she would look forward to that.

The offending fruit cake from yesterday was still lurking in the tin, where it had been deposited by Madge after Geoff's rejection of it. There was a bought sponge cake, which was Madge's favourite, so Alice put some of this onto a plate and carried it into the living room. The occasional table was now groaning with food, but there was just room for the tray containing three cups and saucers and the teapot. As there was every week.

"No fruit cake?" Geoff frowned as he looked at what was on offer. He didn't look very impressed with what he saw.

"Only that from yesterday," said Madge through a mouthful of corned beef sandwich.

"Yes, and you know what you can do with that," Geoff answered. "And don't get any more recipes from Mrs. Croft."

"Well someone's got to eat it, I'm not throwing it away." Madge turned to her usual victim. "Alice can have it."

"I don't like fruit cake."

"Don't talk silly, of course you do. You can take some to work with you. You need building up anyway, just look at you, all skin and bone."

"Yes, Mum," Alice muttered bitterly. She would be consigning the cake to the nearest bin once she got it out of the house.

"How's work, Alice?" Geoff asked this question nearly every week.

"Good," Alice replied, then took a deep breath. "I went to look at a flat yesterday. It's in the Mellish Road, it's a good area and it's not far from the hospital."

Geoff stared at her in disbelief, and Madge's hand, containing sponge cake, stopped in mid-air halfway between the teaplate and her mouth. They stayed transfixed for what seemed like an eternity, then Geoff cleared his throat, as he always did when he had something important to say.

"Do you really think that's such a good idea, Alice?" he said. "It's a big step to take."

"I know Dad, but I think I'm ready."

"Leave home?" Madge all but squeaked. "No, you can't, it's impossible."

Alice sighed wearily, she had been expecting something like this. Still, the subject had been broached now, the worst part was over. Or was it just beginning?

"Well." Geoff reached for his tea. "It's a bit of a shock, Alice, and I'm still not sure it's the right thing to do. You'll have to look after yourself and pay bills, and then there's the safety aspect. You'll be all alone, you know."

"I know Dad, but I've got friends in Walsall."

"Walsall," Madge herumphed. "What kind of a place is that to live in."

"It's alright," Alice said, not really knowing what her mother meant. She doubted if she had ever been to Walsall.

"Well, I think it's a ridiculous idea," Madge continued. "You haven't thought it through at all, I can see that. You'll never cope on your own, you haven't got what it takes."

"Your mother's right, you know." Geoff backed her up for once. "She knows what's best for you. We both do."

"Oh well, the flat won't be ready for a few weeks anyway," Alice sighed. Maybe that would give them time to get used to the idea.

"Good." Madge looked happier now. "It's not too late then. There's still time."

"For what?"

"To talk you out of this stupid idea," Madge threw back at her. "Leave home indeed, the very idea."

"I'm nearly twenty, Mum."

"You're still a child."

"Yeah, always will be as far as you're concerned," muttered Alice sullenly.

"Another year or so and you'll be getting married." Geoff put his two penn'orth in for good measure. "It isn't worth setting yourself up in a new place just to move again."

"Oh, one minute I'm a child and the next I'm getting married, I wish you'd make your minds up!"

"Don't shout at me, I'm your mother."

"Don't I know it. You're always trying to run my life for me and tell me what to do. I'm quite capable of doing things myself, you know."

"Oh yes, you've made a wonderful job of it so far," Madge snapped at her. "You wouldn't even have that job if it wasn't for your father, and as for the rest of it, well, you've got no friends and you can't even get yourself a boyfriend."

"I have got a boyfriend, his name's Joe."

"Ah." Madge raised a triumphant index finger into the air. "Now we're getting to the truth." She whirled round to face Geoff. "She's moving in with some fellow we've never even clapped eyes on, that's what this is all about."

"It is not, he's just a friend."

"I thought there was something going on." Madge was still talking to her husband. "Cars at the end of the street and all sorts of comings and goings. I knew it wasn't Susan you were going out with. Mrs. Croft's seen this boyfriend. Well, only through the car window."

"How long has this been going on, Alice?" Geoff asked. "Is it someone from work?"

"No, yes, sort of." Alice felt flustered. "His sister works in Physio."

"I knew we shouldn't have let her get a job in a strange town. We should have known something like this was going to happen."

"I thought you wanted me to get a boyfriend?"

"Not like this." Madge looked horrified. "Not someone we don't know."

"Are his intentions honourable?" Geoff wanted to know.

"Eh?" Alice wondered what century he had been born in, or which one he should have belonged to.

"What your father means," Madge glared at him for reasons known only to herself. "Is, er, um …"

"You mean is he a nice man?" Alice smiled now. "Yes he is. Very nice."

"Man?" Geoff looked alarmed.

"Don't worry, Geoff, she isn't capable of attracting a real man," said Madge. "It'll be some gangly youth covered in spots, that's all."

"Well, he's got a car by the sound of it." Geoff didn't sound so sure. "What sort of car is it, Alice?"

"A Corsair, I think. It's a nice car."

"You're telling me." Geoff looked alarmed. "It's better than the one I've got. I think we should meet this – what did you say his name was?"

"Joe," said Alice quietly. "Joe Lange."

"Yes," Madge decided immediately. "That's the first sensible thing anyone's said this afternoon. Bring him home, Alice. I want to have a look at his man of yours."

Alice didn't react as her mother put a strong derisory emphasis on the word man. Events would speak for themselves, but she wasn't looking forward to informing Joe that he had been issued with the royal command. She had been dreading this day, and was quite certain that Madge was going to come out with something to cause her excruciating embarrassment. All she could do was warn him and hope he wouldn't be too upset by the visit. And get it over with as quickly as possible.

A couple of days later Joe rang her at work during her lunch hour, and Alice told him about the confrontation.

"They want to meet you," she ended by saying.

"I supopose they do," he said calmly. "When?"

"Can you come on Saturday afternoon?"

"Of course. Don't worry, Alice, it'll be fine." He sounded very relaxed and lighthearted. "They don't bite, do they?"

"Mum might." Alice laughed, then they got onto a lighter subject. She never knew where the time went when she was around Joe, it was the complete opposite to being at home where every minute dragged by in intermidable boredom.

On Saturday morning she had a driving lesson, but couldn't concentrate on what she was doing. Twice the instructor asked her what was wrong, so she told him she'd had a row with her parents and then he left her alone. For once she was overjoyed to get back home and found Madge dusting the living room and moving all the furniture in readiness for 'the visit'. The best china had been got out and given a wash, and there was a tablecloth on the occasional table where the tray of tea would be deposited. Alice hadn't got the heart to tell her that Joe rarely drank tea, and didn't dare suggest she offer him a beer instead. She would have him down as a raving drunkard if she did that.

Two o'clock came around at last, and the doorbell rang at exactly the appointed hour. Geoff looked impressed, he was a great one for punctuality. Alice flew to the front door and ushered Joe inside nervously. He smiled at her reassuringly and followed her in the living room. Into the lion's den.

"Good afternoon, Mr. Harwood." Joe sounded so mature and confident as he held out his hand to Geoff, who shook it automatically and didn't have time to say anything as Joe turned to Madge. "Mrs. Harwood."

As Madge took Joe's hand, Alice held her breath as she watched her face. Gangly youth covered in spots, eh? Madge smiled in a girly simpering sort of way, and Alice could have sworn she saw her eyelashes flutter. There was no doubt that Joe was a good looking man, not at all what Madge would have been expecting. Alice willed him to smile and he soon did. That seemed to seal his fate. He had one of those smiles that could melt the hardest of hearts. Even Madge's.

"Please Joe, do sit down." Madge was halfway into her posh phone voice and Alice winced. Still, it looked as though she liked Joe. So far anyway. "Alice, go and put the kettle on."

"Yes, Mum."

On her way into the kitchen, which was next door, Alice deliberately left the door ajar so she could hear what was going on. While the kettle boiled noisily, she stood as near to the living room as she could and listened.

"So Joe, you live in Walsall." Geoff began the interrogation. "Alone?"

"No, with my mother and sister. My father died some years ago, so I'm sort of the man of the house now. My mother relies on me."

"There aren't many young men who would take care of their mothers like that." Geoff sounded approving. "Very commendable."

"So you're not planning to leave home?" Madge started now.

"Not just yet, I have no plans to anyway."

Alice heaved a sigh of relief, that was one problem out of the way.

"So, what do you do, Joe?" Geoff took over again.

"I'm a metallurgist, in the steel industry. I work for Stefoco in Tamworth."

"Oh, I've heard of them." Geoff surprised everyone by saying. "Good reputable firm," he informed Madge sideways.

"Yes. I joined them after I'd done my apprenticeship and been to university. I'm Technical Manager now."

"Oh." Madge sounded suitably impressed. "You've been to university."

Oh hell, Alice thought as she heard the kettle switch off. Here we go.

"Technical Manager?" Geoff had picked up on the other piece of information they had been given. "Aren't you a bit young for that?"

"Not really." Joe still sounded very casual. "I'm thirty-four."

Oh no! Alice panicked as she rushed over to the teapot. That's torn it.

There was an ominous silence for several seconds, and Alice could imagine their shocked faces looking at each other in disbelief. Joe didn't look much older than twenty something, and she knew they weren't going to like what they had just heard. Eventually one of them cracked.

"Alice!" Madge roared. "Where's that tea?"

The rest of the visit was conducted in a polite but strained atmosphere. Joe and Alice exchanged one anxious glance, but didn't have a chance to speak to each other privately until she saw him to the front door an hour or so later. There was one brief panic for Alice when Joe and Madge were left alone together for a few minutes. Geoff had excused himself to pop upstairs, and no sooner had he gone than the doorbell rang. Madge glared at her daughter, then ordered her to go and see who it was. Alice went reluctantly to find it was a charity collection, and as she searched on the hall table for some loose change, she wondered what poison her mother was feeding to Joe. When she returned to the living room there was a distinct silence, then Joe smiled at her fondly and said it was time he was leaving. Relief flooded through Alice as she walked with him to his escape route, wishing beyond wishes that she could go with him. She apologised profusely for her parents' behaviour and although Joe told her emphatically not to worry about it, Alice had an ominous feeling that things were never going to be quite the same ever again.

CHAPTER TWELVE

The next morning Madge got up later than her customary six-thirty. She had always been an early morning person, quite unlike her husband and daughter, and declared to them, and anyone else who was willing to listen, that this was by far the best part of the day. However, the previous night hadn't brought her much sleep, and now she was lying quietly in bed trying to do two things at once. Think and ignore Geoff's snoring.

The meeting with Alice's boyfriend yesterday had been very unsettling. He wasn't at all what Madge had been expecting, but it didn't matter how responsible and mature he was. Joe didn't fit into her plans, so therefore he needed to be got rid of. Quickly too, before the stupid girl got attached to him, or God forbid, decided to fall in love with him. This was Madge's dilemma, how was she going to do it? She had to break them up in a totally convincing way. She needed to think up something Alice wouldn't suspect or question.

Eventually she gave up and got out of bed, throwing a death stare at the lifeless but very noisy figure under the covers. Not for the first time she reassured herself that once Alice was safely married off and out of the way, they were going to have separate bedrooms. Peace and quiet at last.

Actually peace and quiet were the last things on Madge's mind today. Her brain was working overtime and going ten to the dozen as she mulled over the problem and tried to decide what to do. She needed information, the more the better, so after lunch she offered to help Alice with the washing-up.

"I'm glad you brought Joe round yesterday," she said kindly. It was no good shouting at the girl if she wanted to get something out of her. "Did you say he lives in a good part of Walsall?"

"Yes, Mellish Road," Alice replied as she grasped a handful of cutlery and plonked it in the sink.

"Nice house, is it?" Madge probed.

"Yes." Alice nodded. "I"ve only been there once. It's on the left with a big cherry tree in the front garden. Joe says the dining room looks all pink when it's in blossom."

Madge wasn't the slightest bit interested in cherry blossom, especially not in a place like Walsall, but it was looking as though a visit to the awful place was going to be necessary.

"He's got a good job." Madge persisted. Might as well find out what she could.

"Yes, and they send him off abroad quite a lot too. He has to go and sort out other people's problems. He's off to America soon." Alice reached for the saucepans. "He'll be gone for nearly a month."

"Oh." This was music to Madge's ears. "What a shame for you."

"You almost sound as though you like him." Alice seemed surprised.

"He seems nice enough." Madge was preparing for phase two of her plan. "But don't you think he's rather old for you?"

"No," said Alice. "I've never even thought about it."

"Well, maybe you should, dear. I mean, fifteen years is an awful lot and let's face it, why do you think he's interested in you? A man like that, that sort of age, he'll only be after one thing. That's why he's taken up with you, a young, naive girl." Madge took a deep breath. "Or it is already too late?"

"No, Mum," said Alice quietly. "He's always a perfect gentleman, he hasn't laid a finger on me."

"Oh good." Madge heaved a sign of relief. The girl was still intact, thank heavens for that. She could never have faced Mrs. Croft if it had turned out otherwise. Then she thought about what Alice had said. "Not at all, nothing?"

"Nothing," answered Alice, turning away as she did so. She

seemed embarrassed for some reason that Madge couldn't understand. "Can we talk about something else?"

"We only want what's best for you, you know." Madge forced her flaring temper under control as she spoke as sweetly as she could. "And we have had a little more experience with the world than you have."

"Yes, Mum." Alice sighed, as if she was bored with the conversation. That made two of them, so Madge finished drying the saucepans then made for the living room and her notepad. She was quite pleased with the way the dialogue had gone, she had managed to sow some seeds of doubt in the stupid girl's head. Now all they had to do was germinate. Madge was good at this sort of thing, at least in her own opinion, but hadn't had much practice for a while. The last time she had really been on a mission like this was when she had met Geoff. In 1943.

When Madge and Doris had joined the A.T.S. in Bournemouth, their billet had been on the edge of town, so they didn't get to see much of it for a while. Eventually they got some leave and went to explore together. That had been the first time Madge saw the sea, and it frightened her to death. All that water! It was enormous and seemed to go on for ever, and she had decided there and then never to go to the beach again. It was all too much to comprehend. Doris didn't agree. She thought the moving waves were fascinating.

Madge loved the town centre, there was so much to do. Ingelfield had a handful of shops, but they only sold the basics and essentials. Here she saw shops selling brand new things, not that she had enough money or coupons to buy them. She browsed around the chemist, savouring the various strange aromas it was giving out. She hovered by a display of female sanitary items, most of which she had never seen before. What exactly was a tampon anyway? She picked up the box and read the label, then, having decided she simply must have them, searched her purse for the right money.

They'll never call me smelly again now, she thought happily as she left the shop.

Basic training came and went, and Madge settled into a routine along with Doris and the rest of the girls, most of whom were a similar age to herself. Some Saturday nights there was a dance, and the men from the nearby army base were invited. Madge and Doris always attended in the hope of meeting some Americans, so far without success. However, tonight it seemed their luck had changed. Well, for Doris anyway.

Madge suddenly found herself alone, as Doris went off dancing with a tall gorgeous Yank with a New York drawl and the smartest army uniform she had ever seen. Some of them had looked Madge up and down, but they obviously didn't like what they saw. They seemed to prefer the small blonde ones like Doris. Once again Madge seethed. There were times when she hated pretty little Doris.

She was so busy feeling jealous that she didn't really notice a small figure in a khaki uniform coming nervously towards her.

"Hello," it said. "Would you like to dance?"

"I can't dance," she hated to admit.

"Neither can I," he said seriously.

"So why did you ask me?"

"Well." He hesitated. "My mates dared me to, they said you'd never say yes."

Madge drew herself up to her full height, then realised her mistake. In her heels she was a lot taller than this bloke. He was a bit of a weedy effort, about five foot six, and his chest must have been all of thirty-four inches. How on earth did he get into the army? Then she remembered. The boys had no choice. They were called up at eighteen.

"In that case, I'd love to dance." She smiled at him, wondering if she could actually reach any parts of him. "We can shuffle around the floor or something."

He agreed and off they went. It turned out his name was Geoff and he came from Bath. Madge knew Bath was regarded as a posh place, so decided this Geoff wasn't so bad after all. She was as nice to him as she could possibly be, and by the end of the evening they had arranged to meet again. Doris and the American had disappeared, so Madge wasn't too surprised when she showed her a packet of real nylons a few days later. Madge had nothing to show for her efforts. Nothing had happened anyway.

When she saw Geoff again, she determined to find out more about him and his family. He was nearly twenty-one, she learned, had been to grammar school and had a diploma. In what she didn't like to ask, but it sounded impressive. It seemed his family had a bit of money, so when he asked about hers, she glossed things over and said as little as she could.

And so it was that Madge convinced Geoff that she was his social equal and was worth taking seriously. She was sure Flossie would approve of him, so when she got a forty-eight hour pass she went home for the weekend to tell her grandma all about him.

The weekend she had off was going to be a busy one and the only thing that marred it was the absence of Doris, who hadn't been granted any leave. May was getting married and Madge was invited. She was a little annoyed that she hadn't been chosen as bridesmaid but she supposed nobody wanted her towering above the bride. She tried not to think about this as she got off the bus and walked to Flossie's bungalow.

"Look at you, all posh in your uniform," Flossie commented as they waited for the tea to mash. "You getting on alright?"

"Yes, I'm loving it. You were right, I did need to go to a town and Bournemouth's lovely."

"There are better places."

"Are there?" Madge was amazed to hear this. "What's Bath like? I've met this boy ..."

"From Bath?" Grandma seemed to sit up straight and take notice so Madge nodded. "What's he like? His family got money?"

"I think so," said Madge slowly. "He's twenty-one and was training to work in a hospital. In the office. He's in the Pay Corps."

"So he won't get sent anywhere to get shot at, that's good."

"He's a bit weedy, shorter than me. Not very exciting."

"Have you kept your hand on your a'penny?"

"Oh yes, no problem there. He says he doesn't believe in sex

118

before marriage, which is boring. He's quite boring all round actually."

"That's good." Flossie nodded. "That means you'll be able to mould him into what you want him to be. Keep hold of him, Madge. Don't think you'll do any better."

"Doris is seeing an American," said Madge, sullenness creeping into her voice.

"There'll be no future in that, bunch of fly-by-nights from what I've heard. Only out for what they can get."

"She's had loads of presents."

"I daresay, but that's all she's likely to end up with. You had one that gave you presents, remember?"

"Yes." Madge could have done without the reminder.

"So you knows what I mean. This boy, what's his name?"

"Geoffrey Harwood."

"You work on getting to be Madge Harwood. Got a good ring to it, eh?"

"Yes." Madge suddenly realised. "It does."

"Anyway, you go and enjoy May's wedding and tell this Geoff all about it when you gets back. Put the idea in his head."

"Yes, Grandma. I will."

So May married Sam Hames, and looked lovely in her silk wedding dress made from an old parachute as everyone wished her well. Especially Madge, who now had her sights on marriage. She didn't really have any feelings for Geoff, but he had prospects and seemed to be fond of her. Anyway, if she did marry him it would mean going to live in Bath, and then she wouldn't have to come back to Ingelfield. Ever again.

After a few months of working on him, Geoff suggested they get engaged and go to meet his parents. They managed to get leave at the same time, and went off the Bath together on the train. The journey was long and slow, and they had the compartment to themselves as the steam train chugged and clickity-clacked its way along the track. Madge managed to get him to kiss her a few times and hold her tightly to him. Once she reached for his groin and was pleased to find a hard lump there, but he brushed her hand away in embarrassment.

"We can't," he whispered. "Not yet."

"Alright." She admitted defeat. "But you do want to?"

"Of course I do, I'm a man."

Madge nearly laughed but told herself to behave. Up to now he had done very little to prove he was a man. All he had shown her was that he was every inch an office clerk. Just as she had been at the garage. It didn't seem much of a job for a real man.

The visit to Bath went well. Madge was impressed with the Harwood house. It was privately owned and well furnished and Geoff's parents were pleasant to her. His mother was well spoken and had obviously never worked in her life, and his father worked for the Council. Madge didn't like Geoff's father. He was a dour sort of character and she could see a lot of Geoff in him. Still, Geoff was young and malleable and she was sure she could turn him into something more interesting and vibrant, like his mother. Madge put on her best posh voice all through the visit, and Geoff made no comment. It was as though he hadn't noticed.

They only stayed for a couple of hours, then went back to the railway station to wait for a return train. Geoff was very quiet, which was nothing new, and Madge's head was full of thoughts about the afternoon. She was hoping she had made a good impression.

"They like you," he eventually said. "Mother said it's about time I had a girlfriend."

Madge had already guessed that he hadn't had one before, but made no comment. She was delighted the day had gone well, but now she was going to have to take him to Ingelfield to meet her parents. All she could do was take a deep breath and hope that everyone would behave themselves. Particularly Flossie. It was Flossie Madge wrote to asking her to make the arrangements, and she was waiting in the front room of Bert and Eliza's house when the engaged couple arrived.

The front door was ceremoniously opened, cracking the layer of paint on the inside, then Eliza greeted Geoff politely and respectfully, just as Madge had hoped she would. She was also pleased to see that everyone was wearing their best clothes. Geoff entered the tiny hall which led straight up the stairs and through the door into the living room with wide eyes, seeming overwhelmed by the three people inside waiting to meet him. Madge wasted no time in introducing him to her father, who shook him warmly by the hand and Flossie, who nodded towards him with an approving little smile.

"I'll put the kettle on," she said.

"Sit down, Geoff, make yourself comfortable," Eliza added. She looked nearly as nervous as he did.

"Thank you," he muttered, looking grateful for a sit down.

Madge faffed and waffled on about nothing in particular until Flossie came back with the tea tray, which didn't see the light of day very often. It was unusual for her to stir herself to make a brew as well, so everyone, except Geoff, recognised this as a special occasion.

"Lovely tea," was his verdict when he tasted it. "I like it strong."

"Grandma always makes it so that you can stand your spoon up in it." Madge was pleased. So far this was going very well.

"And we have some cake," said Eliza proudly. "I hear you like fruit cake, Geoff."

"Oh, you haven't used all the ration on that, have you?" Madge couldn't hide her annoyance. She hated fruit cake. All those bits that got in your teeth.

"There wasn't enough to make a sponge as well," Eliza tried to explain. She cast her grown-up nineteen year old daughter a pleading glance. Flossie kept her face straight, and Bert accepted a chunk of cake and ate it slowly. He seemed to prefer to eat than talk.

Geoff's eyes nearly fell out of his head when he tasted Eliza's excellent cake. He chomped his way through it happily, slurped his tea quietly, then sat back on the sofa looking mighty satisfied.

"That was the best cake I've ever tasted," he declared. "I hope you've got the recipe, Madge."

"There isn't any recipe," she said sharply. "We just throw it together."

"How clever you all are." He smiled.

"So Geoff," began Flossie. "What do you do when you're not in the army?"

"I was training to be a hospital administrator," he said. "I still try to do a bit of studying when I get time."

Flossie looked impressed, Madge noticed. It looked as though she approved of her fiancé, which was good. She wouldn't have liked to think she had done all that work on him for nothing.

Another hour or so went by amicably and with no mishaps, then Madge thought she could safely steer Geoff away. The women seemed loathe to let him go while Bert shook his hand again and wished him well. Then they began the short walk back to the bus stop.

"What a lovely family you've got." Geoff surprised her by saying. "Warm and friendly, nothing like mine. You've got real people, you're so lucky."

"What do yours do then?" Madge asked, wondering why he was coming out with all this drivel.

"Father just goes to work and all Mother does is go to clubs and meetings. I never get home-made cake."

Madge nodded as she took this in, and stored the knowledge away for future reference. Now she knew what was expected of her as an administrator's wife.

The bus took them into the nearest town towards the railway station, then they began the long journey back to Bournemouth and their barracks. It was beginning to get dark when they returned, but Madge didn't care. Today had gone well and she was happy. As they walked back to their respective billets, she tried to get Geoff to laugh. He hardly ever did. He didn't seem to possess a sense of humour, either that or he kept it very well hidden. Office clerk he definitely was, and being in the Pay Corps suited his personality down to the ground. He would have made a first class accountant.

Madge thought seriously about performing a cartwheel, something she had been very good at as a child. She hadn't done one for years now, and wasn't sure what Geoff's reaction would be to it. Besides, they were both in uniform and there might be regulations against that sort of thing. Madge wouldn't have been surprised. Instead she began to do an impression of a girl she had been at school with who had been a bit simple. She waved her arms around in an approximate guesture of a demented chimpanzee, laughing as she did so. Geoff just stared at her.

The upshot of all this frenetic activity was that her left hand caught the edge of his army cap, and it flew from his head into the long grass at the side of the narrow street. He tutted, said she was too silly for words, then went to retrieve it.

"Where's my badge?" he asked, his voice high in abject panic. "My hat badge has gone. Madge, you've lost it."

"Oh, it'll be around here somewhere, it has to be." She might have known he wouldn't find her actions funny. He never did.

They both searched and searched, but Geoff's precious badge was nowhere to be found.

"How can I go back to barracks without it?" he fretted. "I'll be on a charge and it's all your fault."

They searched some more amongst the grass but twilight had now turned to night and they could hardly see each other, never mind what was on the ground. Madge was trying not to laugh. He really was so funny, behaving like a spoilt little boy. In the dim light she couldn't see how worried he looked.

"That's it then," he finally said as he stood up and straightened his jacket back into place. "I'll walk you back to your billet but after that, it's over. You're far too irresponsible, Madge, it's never going to work. The wedding's off!"

CHAPTER THIRTEEN

Madge hardly slept a wink that night. It couldn't be over, she wouldn't allow it. She had worked so hard on Geoff, and she was damned if she was going to let him get away now. As soon as it got light, Madge slipped quietly out of the billet and went back to the scene of the crime. She just had to find that badge and get it back to Geoff.

In full daylight it took her no time at all to find the badge. Now all she had to do was get it to him as soon as she could, and hope he would forgive her. After she had put on her best apologetic act and added some pathetic wheedling, he gave her a kiss and the relationship was back on, although Madge found herself wondering what she was getting into. Was he always going to be so boring?

Madge and Geoff got married just before the war ended, and May was bridesmaid. Doris's American was sent home and she went with him, and Madge never saw or heard from her again. Many years later she heard she had returned to Ingelfield with a child, but she didn't make any effort to get in touch. The village was behind her now. She wouldn't go back there if she could avoid it.

The newly married couple moved to Bath, and bought an old house in which to begin their new life. Suddenly Madge was back to cooking on an old range and fiddling with gas lights. Sometimes Geoff studied by candlelight, he was aiming for another diploma. Madge was despairing of him already. He seemed to prefer work to anything she had to offer, but she knew another diploma would mean more money coming in, so she didn't complain. Sometimes she lay awake at night after his short and rather unenthusiastic attempts at making love. She was very rarely satisfied, and all the things she had learned in that department had been met with either shock or rejection. Yes, Geoff was boring indeed, in everything he did. Not that he did much apart from work. He was useless around the house, he didn't even know how to change a fuse.

A couple of years went by and they were able to make improvements to the house. Madge organised them and Geoff paid the bills. Sometimes she thought about Flossie, and wondered if she had been right to set so much store by what she said. She had taken every word of her advice to heart, but what had it got her? True, she had what she wanted, a meek and mild husband with a good job with prospects so she would be comfortably off for the rest of her life, but where was the spontaneity, the fun, the romance? Was this the price she had to pay for stability? Madge felt old before her time.

Despite Geoff's apparent low sex drive they made love regularly, but there were no signs of Madge becoming pregnant. Maybe that operation she had when she was seventeen had done some damage, and she rather panicked at the thought. How would she explain that to Geoff? He would be mortified if he ever found out she had been through an abortion.

Then he came home with some news that raised her spirits. A job had come up that meant promotion, and he was wondering whether to apply for it.

"It'll mean leaving Bath," he said. "It's in the Midlands. In Staffordshire."

Madge hardly had any idea where Staffordshire was, but she was assured that it was a long way away. This delighted her, she remembered the last time she had moved to where no-one knew her. She had been able to reinvent herself, and it felt like time to do it again.

"Go for it, Geoff," she urged. "There's nothing really keeping us here and if you can advance yourself, then do. You owe it to yourself." She was tempted to add 'and me' but resisted the urge. She was still pretending to be the obedient, dutiful housewife.

Geoff got the job and they moved to the Midlands in 1950.

Madge enjoyed the big house that went with the new position. It was in the grounds of the hospital and had a big living room and a huge kitchen. She had all her groceries delivered and spent her days making cakes and looking for clubs to join. Her excuse was that she didn't know anyone and needed to meet new people, but they had to be the right people. Other women she could climb the social ladder with. She was middle-class now.

The next year Madge got pregnant and everyone was pleased. Except her. Having babies was expected of her, but she wasn't very keen on the idea. Still, as long as it was a boy everything would be alright. She was really looking forward to having a son. Something to be proud of and show off.

Then in November 1951, Madge gave birth. To a daughter. She was devastated, but Geoff was over the moon with his baby girl. She was healthy, he said, that was all that mattered. She was healthy alright, she never seemed to stop crying. They called her Alice, which was Flossie's middle name. Madge wrote to everyone in Ingelfield to tell them of the new arrival, and promised to visit in the spring.

At the appointed time, Madge made preparations to travel to Dorset by train and bus. Geoff had got a driving licence in the army but still didn't own a car, so that was something else she was going to have to work on. Honestly, her life was so busy. She hardly had time to look after a child. Geoff insisted he was far too busy to have time off work, so Madge sighed and went off on her own. Work always came first with Geoff, it was as though he was married to his job instead of her.

Eliza went into raptures over Alice, saying she had never seen anything so beautiful. Madge just tutted, it was only a baby. They were put into Fred's old room, which was bigger than Madge's, with the news that Fred had got married several years before but hadn't invited any of the family to the wedding. He was still in the Merchant Navy, working on large luxury cruise liners, and was living in Southampton. He wasn't home much, Madge gathered, and no-one saw him when he was. Totally selfish, Madge decided, without ever stopping to consider that she was exactly the same.

When Madge got fed up of Eliza cooing over Alice, she took her daughter round to see Flossie, who wanted a full update on the situation.

"He's boring." There was nothing else to say really.

"Most men are," replied Flossie. "Bernard's boring."

"Russell Carrington wasn't boring."

"And look where that got you. Nowhere. Still," she chuckled, "you've got a child, that'll keep him happy. Maybe you'll have a boy next time."

"There won't be a next time. I can't have any more because of …"

"Ah, shame, they like to have boys. Still, you've done well for yourself even if it isn't very exciting. Being married isn't about that."

"Or being happy?"

"Happy? Good Lord, where did you get that idea from?" Flossie roared with laughter as Madge glared at her, deciding on the spot that she was never going to visit her ever again. "Oh, you'll get used to it, Madge, it won't be so bad. You can do what you want, can't you? And you's alright for money? What more do you want?"

"I don't know," said Madge quietly. "But it feels like something."

As Madge's mind came back to the present, she found tears rolling down both cheeks. She wiped them away roughly as she picked up the notepad and read what she had written. Mellish Road, Walsall. Tomorrow she would go to the unknown town and find this house with the cherry tree in the front garden.

The next day she did just that, wondering where the bus was taking her. Madge had never been to Walsall, when she wanted more variety of shops she caught the train into Birmingham. It never occured to her to go anywhere else, and she wouldn't be doing so now if she didn't have a good reason.

The bus ride took about half an hour, and stopped every few minutes to allow people with strange sounding accents to board. At least Alice had found one that didn't sound as bad as some of these, but he wasn't Stephen Croft, and Madge had fully made up her mind now that nobody else would do. This thought reminded her of why she was taking this horrendous journey today, so at the next stop she moved down to the front of the bus to speak to the middle-aged driver, who looked like a cross between a scout tent and a beer barrel. They bred them big round here.

"Do you stop near Mellish Road?" Madge asked in her very best phone voice.

"Ar, I do. D'ya want me t' shout yow?"

"Er, yes please."

She had lost her seat now so had no choice but to stand for the rest of the way. How awful! It was bad enough being surrounded by all these peculiar sounds, without having to look at the people as well. Still, it gave her a chance to look down her nose at them and think herself lucky she didn't live amongst them.

The bus rocked and jolted its way along, getting busier and more crowded at every stop. Now the whole aisle was filled with people standing, and Madge was feeling definitely claustrophobic. No wonder they used a double decker on this route. She couldn't wait to get off the thing and get a breath of fresh air.

"Mellish Roe-ud," the driver called out a few minutes later and Madge fought her way past two gossiping women to get to the front. How Alice did this journey every day she would never know, but then again, she was nearly as dim and stupid as these people appeared to be.

She needs saving from herself, Madge thought very firmly as she finally escaped, not even thinking to thank the driver on her way out. She watched the big grey and blue bus disappear towards the arboretum with a sense of disgust, her nose crinkling up as though she had a nasty smell under it. Alice knows nothing about the world and even less about men, her thoughts continued.

Madge never stopped to even consider that this might be her fault, as she walked quickly along the pavement towards the next turning. When she entered the wide road and sauntered along it, she felt herself becoming rather impressed. It seemed Alice had been right, there were some very nice houses along here.

"I suppose even a place like this can have a posh area," Madge

128

conceded reluctantly. "Now, where's the one with the cherry tree?"

A few minutes later she found it and walked past it very slowly, trying to fight down the rising tide of jealousy. It made the semi she lived in look absolutely ridiculous, she had never been happy with the way Geoff had insisted on buying it. She was sure they could have afforded something better.

The next thing she knew, Madge was several hundred yards further down the road, her mind clouded with dark thoughts about her dozy husband and even dopier daughter. Why was she surrounded by such morons? The fact that she had chosen Geoff because he was so submissive didn't come into it. Neither did the one that she was a manipulative control freak, who always wanted her own way and wasn't too fussy about what she had to do to get it.

Found out what I wanted to know, she told herself. Let's get out of here and back to civilisation.

When she got back to the cul-de-sac, it was lunchtime. She made a pot of tea then raided the cake and biscuit tin, completely ignoring another fact. She was supposed to be on a diet. She lay back in her armchair tucking into a huge slice of sponge cake and thought over the events of the morning. Now she had Joe's address, and a warm glow of satisfaction spread through her body. All she had to do now was write two letters, one for him and one for Alice, then chat up Mrs. Croft. There was an old typewriter in her dining room.

It was several days before Madge was ready for the next part of her plan. She took her time over the letters, not wanting them to be too long and rambling. Concise and to the point was what she was aiming for, a short sharp shock that would hit home with the force of a sledgehammer. By the time she had finished she was pleased with the outcome. She had taken a bit more notice lately of how Alice spoke, so she could put her 'thoughts' down on paper. They had been involved in several conversations, and Madge had to fight hard to resist the usual temptation to make derisory comments and generally put her daughter down. Being nice to her brought much better results, but Madge found it difficult. It was much easier to mock her, after all, she had been doing it for nearly twenty years.

By the time she took herself and her two dishonourable pieces of paper round to Doreen's, she had found out something else that was useful to her. Joe was going off to America in three days time and would be gone for over three weeks. The timing was perfect, now all Madge had to do was get the letters typed and posted off. Gleefully she followed Doreen into her dining room and waited there while she made the coffee and called to her from the short distance away in the kitchen.

"How's Stephen?" asked Madge as she eyed up the typewriter in the corner. She had never used one, but Alice did it all the time so it couldn't be that demanding.

"He's up for promotion." Mrs. Croft's voice drifted in through the open door. "That'll mean a rise and other things too, like doing socialising and entertaining. I've told him that'll be difficult on his own, and that it's about time he thought about getting a wife."

"What did he say to that?"

"He agreed with me, but he says he doesn't know any girls. I told him the ideal candidate is right under his nose, three doors down, in fact."

"And what was his reaction to that?" Madge half held her breath. If it was negative, then all her hard work could have been for nothing.

"Actually I was quite surprised." Doreen joined her now, carrying in a plate of biscuits. Madge was pleased to see they weren't her usual low sugar home-made ones. "Sorry about these, I just haven't had time to make any. I've been so busy lately, I just don't know where the time goes." She put down the plate and Madge noted the paper doily again. She kept meaning to buy some, but kept forgetting.

"You were saying about Stephen?" Madge nudged her back towards the point.

"Oh yes." Doreen simpered. "Just fetch the coffee."

Madge sighed impatiently. Sometimes this woman drove her mad, but she couldn't say anything. She was Chairwoman of the Women's Institute and Madge was only Secretary, so she daren't do anything to upset her. She was a fussy little woman who annoyed Madge intensely, but she was about the best friend she had. She was the only one she regularly had coffee with. Nobody else ever invited her.

Finally Doreen came back with everything else on the very ornate tray that Madge had long since admired. Mrs. Croft had some nice things, somebody had very good taste in this household.

"Now then." She sat down opposite Madge. "Stephen. Yes, I was quite surprised. He said he'd had his eye on Alice for a while, and had just been about to ask her out when he saw her getting into a car at the end of the street. Is that still going on?"

"Not for much longer." Madge waved the letters.

"Oooh, what've you got there?" Mrs. Croft looked intrigued.

"Take a look." Madge handed them to her. "They'd look better typed."

Mrs. Croft read both of them slowly, her mouth twitching every now and then as she absorbed every word. She always took her time over documents, that was another thing that irritated Madge. She generally wanted to do things at a hundred miles an hour.

"They should do the trick." She eventually gave her verdict. "But I don't agree they should be typed. Too impersonal. I'll write the one out to Alice if you like. Don't want her recognising your handwriting, do we?"

"Definitely not." Madge shuddered at the mere thought.

"Let's have our coffee, then we can sort that out." Doreen took charge as though they were at an Institute meeting. "Where does this Joe live?"

"In Walsall. I mean, I ask you."

"You'll have to go over there to post his, it'll look a bit suspicious if it comes with a Lichfield postmark."

"I suppose so." Madge's heart sank at the thought of having to do that horrendous bus ride again. "I hadn't thought of that."

"Details are very important." Doreen sounded serious. "We'll only get one chance at this, must do it properly."

131

"Yes, of course." Madge instantly realised that she was right. She was further away from the problem, so could see things more clearly. "Ah ha." She forced herself to laugh. "What would I do without you?"

"We help each other." Doreen looked nearly as false as Madge felt. "That's what friends are for."

The next fifteen minutes felt like an eternity as the two women sipped their coffee and ate biscuits. Mrs. Croft nibbled genteely at hers, while Madge demolished them as quickly as she could. Well, the first two. After that she made an effort to behave like her friend, delicate and refined. It wasn't easy though, her natural greed kept coming to the fore.

When the niceties had been properly observed, they could get down to business. Doreen rewrote the letter to Alice, while Madge did the same with the one to Joe. Doreen provided very plain white paper that could have been bought anywhere. She said it was important that nothing be traced back to either of them. She was obviously much better at conspiracies than Madge, and this reminded her of one of the reasons for being friends with this woman.

"Make sure you post them both on the same day." Doreen warned just before Madge took her leave. "It'll be much better if they arrive after he's gone away. Just in case."

"Yes. It'd be just like Alice to try and ring him." Madge could see the sense of this. "I'll go to Walsall tomorrow."

And so it was. Now all Madge had to do was wait for the fateful rattle of the letterbox, and keep a straight face when Alice revealed what had been sent to her. She couldn't wait to see the look on her face, and hoped she would believe the lies that she had gone to a lot of trouble to create. Time would tell, Madge told herself, as she willed the hours to go by until the letter arrived.

It came on the Friday, as Madge had planned, although this was the day Joe was due to fly to America. Hopefully he would leave for the airport before the post arrived but in any case, Madge couldn't see him cancelling a work trip over something as insignificant as this. She had to bide her time and curb her impatience until Alice came home from work. She ate her tea then reluctantly washed up the dishes, revealing to Madge that she'd had a hard week and was feeling tired.

"There's a letter in the hall for you," Madge finally got round to telling her as she dried up the cutlery. "That should cheer you up."

"Oh, is it from France?"

"I didn't look," Madge lied. She had almost forgotten that the penfriend thing was still going on. Why was anyone's guess, and she still couldn't see any point in learning a language that was never going to be used.

Alice finished in the kitchen and headed upstairs, as was her usual routine. Madge glanced at her as she made her own way back into the living room and smiled maliciously as she saw her stop by the hall table to pick up the letter before taking herself off to her room. Madge went to her comfortable armchair, sat down and picked up her knitting. Geoff was buried in the newspaper again, making small grunts and huhs every now and then. That was as much conversation as she was likely to get out of him this evening, or any other evening come to that. Most of the time they behaved like strangers.

She looked up to the ceiling a few times, waiting for the scream that never came. Alice was taking it very well, Madge had been expecting some vocal weeping and wailing. This could only mean that she wasn't really too bothered about this Joe person, and Madge was pleased. That meant steering her in the direction of Stephen Croft shouldn't be too difficult. Oh yes, there was going to be a huge wedding soon. And Madge was going to be instrumental in organising it. She couldn't wait.

As the time dragged by between Madge and Geoff, she thought over the events of the last week. She had been very busy indeed, but was well delighted with the outcome of her efforts. Several times during the evening she thought about the letter she had so cleverly constructed. She could still remember every word, and her only regret was that she hadn't been able to be present when Alice opened it and read what it said.

Dear Alice,

I'm sorry to be writing to you like this, I know I should speak to you in person but I haven't got the courage. I've enjoyed being with you more than you could ever know and I feel like I'm starting to fall in love with you. That's the problem. It won't work. Alice, I'm so much older than you. I was a fool to think we could have any kind of future together, the age gap is just too wide. I don't want to make you old before your time so I must let you go. Please don't argue with me, Alice, or try to contact me about this. I've made my decision and I know I'm doing the right thing. I'm very fond of you and I couldn't bear to hurt you any more than I have already. Please forgive me, Alice, and forget all about me and I hope that one day you'll find someone of your own age and be happy with him.

Thank you for the time we've spent together. I only wish things could have been different.

Joe.

CHAPTER FOURTEEN

Joe was in the airport, his travelling bag at his feet and a cup of black coffee in his hand. He was on his way to Cleveland, Ohio to visit the steelworks there, review their working practices and sort out any problems. He knew there would be some, they had recently installed a new casting system that he had helped to develop, and the plant back home had experienced some teething troubles. Still, he enjoyed being a technical sleuth, and anything that took him out of the office was also a bonus. If he could wangle a day or two to explore New York or Washington on the way back, he would, he usually managed to fit in a little sightseeing at the end of his working trips. The air ticket was already paid for by the company, so he didn't mind using his holiday and paying for his hotel rooms on the way home. Fortunately he liked travelling, and it seemed the firm knew this and took full advantage of the fact.

Joe was always meticulous with his travel details, so when he had finished his coffee, he reached into his bag to check the times of the flights and make sure he had got everything. This bag also contained his electric razor and two changes of clothes, he had been caught out several times by flight delays or cancellations. Hopefully nothing like that was going to happen today, but you never knew with air travel. It had a habit of being unpredictable. He pulled out his literature, then frowned as he noticed a letter in amongst it. His mother must have hastily stuffed it into his bag while she was seeing him off and telling him to take care of himself.

"Oh Mum, what've you done that for?" he murmured to himself in dismay. If it was something connected with work that needed a reply, then he was stuck. It would just have to wait until he could get access to an office at the other end.

Hoping it wasn't anything important, Joe ripped open the envelope and pulled out the single sheet of paper. He scanned his eyes over it quickly, not taking in the words, then they widened as some sort of sense came out of them. Then he went back to the beginning and read the letter properly.

Dear Joe,

I'm sorry to be writing to you like this, I know I should speak to you in person but I haven't got the courage. I really don't know how to tell you this, Joe. I've enjoyed being with you and hearing all about your life and travelling with your job, but now I have to end it, it wouldn't be fair not to. I thought it best to tell you now before we got too attached to each other.

I know I should have told you before that I'm very friendly with the boy from three doors away. We've sort of grown up together, and I never really thought too much about it until I met you. Now I realise what he means to me and he says he feels the same, and yesterday he asked me to marry him and I said yes. I'm really sorry to have to tell you it like this, I know I'm a coward and that you'll never forgive me.

I hope you can forgive me one day, and that you'll wish me well in my new life. I'm so sorry Joe, I only wish things could have been different.

Alice.

Joe continued to stare at the paper for several minutes, his eyes unseeing and his mind completely numb. Then he calmly folded the letter and put it back into the envelope. His flight was being called, it was time to go.

On the way across the Atlantic, he tried to make sense of what he had read. He just couldn't believe it. Alice, his Alice, was off and marrying someone else. It wasn't true, it couldn't be! Joe closed his eyes, then reached into his pocket for his handkerchief. Tears were threatening, and this was hardly the time or place. He sniffed hard and tried not to think about the letter. His heart was disintegrating and breaking into a thousand pieces. It had happened again. What was it about him and women?

Joe hadn't got into girls very early. He had attended a boys only grammar school until he was sixteen, then had gone as an apprentice in a laboratory because he had always enjoyed chemistry. He had done all sorts of jobs in the lab, had been very good at all of them and was going to college one full day and two evenings a week as well to study metallurgy. He was an able student and did well in his exams, so much so that the company provided a bursary for him to go to university to study for a degree. He had had a fleeting girlfriend at the company, but once he went off to university this ended amicably and he threw himself into his studies.

The next four years passed quickly and happily. The work was hard but rewarding, and he had some mates to go for a drink with in the evenings when they all had enough money. He liked living away from home, although he missed his family at times. They were close to each other and helped one another out whenever they could, but up to this point his sister Pamela was about the only female he had ever had anything to do with.

At the end of his university days, he left with the best degree they had given out in the last fourteen years. His parents were so proud of him, and he was very pleased with the results he had achieved. Then he resumed his employment at the company and soon began working his way up.

Then he met Pauline and everything changed. Everybody said she was the one, that they looked really good together. They had so much in common and Joe had never been happier. They went out together for a couple of years, and he was even thinking about asking her to marry him. He was Chief Metallurgist now, earning a reasonable wage and for the first time in his life he felt ready to settle down. All he had to do now was pop the question.

After a while he decided that the only way to do this was to go round to her house and surprise her. She lived with her parents on the other side of town, so one Saturday afternoon he drove over to her home, with an engagement ring in its box hidden safely in the depths of his suit pocket. He had butterflies in his stomach and a lump of expectation in his throat as he turned into the street where Pauline lived and prepared to pull up outside, the all important question playing cheerfully about his lips.

As he approached the house, he frowned as he saw there was already someone on the doorstep. He didn't recognise the man, but when the door opened Pauline kissed the visitor passionately then followed him to his car. Joe hung back, puzzled at what he had just seen. The couple got into the old banger and drove away speedily. Joe went after them.

He followed them for several miles until they turned down a quiet country lane and parked in a secluded gateway. Joe left his car further back and walked the rest of the way, using trees and bushes to hide him from view. The windows of the banger started to steam up, then the car began to rock from side to side. He could even hear some of the noises they were making as they made wild and abandoned love in the back of the car. Joe turned away, his fingers reaching for the ring he had been about to slip on his true love's finger. Now he would have to take it back and try to explain to everyone why it was all over. Pauline had told him emphatically that she didn't believe in sex before marriage, and yet he had caught her doing this. He was soon glad he had. If he couldn't trust her now, there was no sense in marrying her, and he would rather be made a fool of sooner than later. Next time he saw her he told her it was over and he told her why. She made no attempt to defend herself, saying it was good while it lasted, but now she was on to pastures new. Joe realised he had been used and felt a complete fool, but tried not to show it and it was a long time before he got involved with anyone again. And when he did, he kept it casual.

Then, when he was in his late twenties, his beloved father died. This was the greatest shock Joe had ever received, and for a long time he couldn't think about anything else. His mother had been devastated, and it took a long time for all of them to come to terms with the loss, then Pamela went to work at the hospital and Joe began travelling with his job. It helped take his mind off his family problems and gave him something to focus on. Then he was promoted to Technical Manager, which meant even more work and even more travelling.

All these thoughts of the past plagued him on the uneventful flight from England to America. He tried to read a magazine, but couldn't concentrate on anything. His mind kept drifting into the past. The business with Pauline had been bad enough and he thought he had become quite a good judge of character, but he was obviously wrong. He remembered, with slivers of bright pain stabbing into his heart, the first time he had laid eyes on Alice. He had been the cause of the two man kayak's capsize, their eyes had met and Joe had lost his heart. He had never believed in love at first sight, dismissing the notion as romantic twaddle but that was before he saw Alice. After she and her friend had paddled away, he had never expected to see her again, but it seemed that fate had intervened and thrown them together again once more, at the Chinese restaurant and later at the hospital, and Joe had been over the moon. Alice was so different from any girl he had ever met, or so he had thought. There was a charm and naivety, an all embracing innocence, or so he had thought. Now he really didn't know what to think. He was obviously good at picking deceitful women.

"Work," he told himself sternly as he got off the plane at the other end. "And plenty of it. That's all there is left now."

From the airport he took a cab to his hotel, left his things there and went out to find somewhere to have a few beers then a meal. Next day he would begin work at the Cleveland company, the main American offshoot of Stefoco, which had its head office all the way across the ocean in 'liddle ol' Great Britain' as the Yanks were so fond of putting it. Joe had a sneaking suspicion they were actually more than a tad jealous of the success in Tamworth. They hadn't come close to repeating it in Ohio, and now they had to put up with some interfering Limey visitor who was coming to tell them all where they were going wrong. Joe had been to this steelworks before, and wasn't too fond of the huge gorilla of a man that ran it.

Dick Vogel was his name, and Joe never enjoyed dealing with him. It usually came down to a slanging match or a drinking contest, and Joe was quite capable of winning both of these things. Sometimes it was a bit like a pub landlord challenging his best customer to a game of pool then deliberately letting him win to keep him on side. Joe was a good diplomat, he generally knew when to win and when to play the customer game.

Dick Vogel welcomed him loudly and enthusiastically into his enormous office with windows down to the floor, offered whisky, which Joe politely refused, then poured a large one for himself.

"Later for me," said Joe. "I'm still working on UK time." Sometimes he was a good fibber as well.

"How are things in the old country?" Dick asked, his tone creeping towards being patronising already.

"Fine," said Joe smoothly. He knew how to out bullshit a bullshitter. "And here?"

"Yeah, well ..." Dick looked annoyed that Joe had got to the point so quickly. "We've had one or two problems. Only small ones though, and it is a new system."

"I know," Joe said dryly. "I helped develop it."

"Yeah," Dick mumbled. "I know."

"So, shall we have a look around and you can tell me what's wrong?"

"I guess so." Dick got to his feet rather unsteadily. "And I hope you're gonna let me take you out to dinner tonight?"

"Certainly." Joe smiled. He could feel another drinking contest coming on.

The tour of the steelworks took most of the rest of the day. Joe and Dick argued a lot, called each other quite a few rude names then agreed to differ, call it quits and buy each other a drink in the works social club. Several beers were followed by two or three vicious games of pool, all of which Joe won easily. He tried not to make this too obvious though.

"You don't play half bad for a Limey." Dick slapped him roughly on the back, nearly knocking Joe over. He had hands like shovels.

"I practice in the Tamworth Social Club." Joe laughed, not adding that he didn't need any practice to beat Dick. He was so fat he could hardly lean over the table, and when he did it took him all his time to pot a ball. He was a guest in this man's country, there was no point in upsetting him any more than he had to.

An hour or so later, Dick decided it was time they went to eat. He drove the two of them in his car, which was nearly as big as the famous Greyhound bus, to a steak house that he told Joe he often used.

"Best ribs in town, man," Dick promised as they parked up then walked towards the restaurant. "You just wait and see."

Joe felt a little bemused as they entered the steak house to find it full of diners and waiters alike. All the waiters were black men dressed in smart black trousers, white shirts and red jackets, who were transporting the biggest plates Joe thought he had ever seen containing even bigger steaks and beef ribs. Dick waved towards the open kitchen and smiled at the look on Joe's face as he took in the sight of half a cow being turned over on a spit roast and basted regularly by one of the chefs. Joe took in the size of the lumps of meat on the ribs, not taking any time at all to decide he couldn't eat one of those in a month of Sundays. Actually, that was about how long one of these meals would last him.

Once they got established at a table, Joe perused the menu, looking for the smallest steak he could order. He had been brought up with food rationing during the war and hated wasting food. He had just decided on his order when Dick insisted he must try the ribs because they were "the best in town!" Joe quickly moved to plan B and ordered the lady's portion of ribs. He had been to America before, and knew this would be a smaller meal. When it came he began to wonder. The beef chop on his plate was two inches thick, and was big enough to feed a hungry family of four.

"Excuse me." He detained the red coated waiter who was just trying to move away. "I ordered the lady's portion."

"Man," he said patiently. "That is the lady's portion. Normally they cut them two ribs thick."

"Oh," was all Joe could find to say. Dick laughed heartily then told him to tuck in and enjoy. Joe had no choice and the meat was very good, but he didn't finish the meal, as he had known he wouldn't be able to.

Dick ordered another bottle of wine without consulting anyone and Joe let him drink most of it, knowing from past experience what a greedy so-and-so he was. They left the restaurant some considerable time later, Dick being completely pie-eyed, wobbling when he walked and slurring his words.

"Let's go find some pussy, man," he just about managed to say when he got back to his car.

"I don't think either of us is in any fit state …"

"You speak for yourself, Limey." Dick suddenly looked a whole lot more sober. "I can manage two. Both at the same time."

Joe sighed quietly. Not only was this man roaring drunk but he had a lovely wife and two teenage daughters at home waiting for him. Joe was rather old-fashioned about these things and couldn't bring himself to condone what Dick was proposing to do.

"Tell you what," Dick came up with another suggestion. "Let's take a cab to the Blue Note Club. You like jazz, don't you?"

"Very much," Joe answered truthfully.

"Okay then, let's go." Dick staggered towards the taxi rank. "Might pick up some pussy on the way."

They did indeed, as they headed into what looked like the more dubious side of town. Every time the taxi slowed up at a junction or a traffic light, a woman, sometimes two, would wrench open the door of the cab and jump inside. Dick sat half reclined laughing at the situation, while Joe shooed them away. All Dick was likely to pull tonight was a muscle, and the only relief he was liable to receive was having his wallet stolen. There was no telling him this though, his befuddled mind was firmly fixed on sex, and all Joe could do was try to steer him in the opposite direction. A music club seemed like a good idea.

Once inside the club, which was on the edge of town and very, very dark indeed, Dick got himself onto Martinis, a favourite

American drink of the time. Joe joined him in a few of these as he couldn't stand the tasteless maid's water they had the nerve to serve up as beer. Joe was lucky in that he seemed to have a cast iron metabolism that could cope with anything and everything he threw at it. Including Martinis, which consisted of quite a lot of neat gin, a very small dash of Vermouth and an olive. That on top of everything else he had drunk tonight.

An hour or so later he tried to make a move by asking Dick how he was going to get home.

"By cab, of course." Dick looked at him as though he was totally stupid. "Why?"

"Want to go yet?"

"No way, man, I'm just getting started."

"In that case I'll see you tomorrow," Joe said as he got to his feet.

"Yeah, okay," Dick said, then laughed as he fired one parting shot at him. "Lightweight."

Joe ignored the taunting jibe and left the club in search of his own taxi. Back to the hotel for a good sleep seemed like the best thing now.

By the end of the week all the problems at the Cleveland plant were solved, and it was on to Chicago to see what was wrong there. Joe knew he was in for more of the same treatment, but all he did at the thought was sigh. He was developing the handy-lad syndrome, and his firm knew it and used it to their advantage every chance they got. Whatever the problem was Joe could fix it, and he knew that because of this, there was likely to be a lot more troubleshooting trips around the world in future.

Eventually his visit to the United States came to an end, and he packed up his suitcase and headed for the airport. He had paid the necessary fee of a few pounds to divert his flight to Bermuda, where he was going to spend a few days relaxing on the way home. He felt he had earned it.

Bermuda turned out to be the prettiest place Joe had ever seen or even imagined. The sand was pink, the sea varying gorgeous shades of turquoise and the buildings calming pastel colours with white rooves. Joe felt instantly relaxed, the stresses and strains of Cleveland and Chicago dissipating into the complimentary rum swizzle on arrival at his hotel. He had three days here and intended to make full use of the time, looking around the capital, Hamilton, the quaint toytown settlement of St. George's and all the bays and coves in between.

It was as he was standing on a deserted beach watching the sun go down through an archway of pink and grey rock that his mind suddenly turned to romance. Wasn't this just the ideal place for a honeymoon? Thoughts of Alice plagued him as her face swam before his eyes. If only. If only …

CHAPTER FIFTEEN

It had been a week since Alice received the letter from Joe, and she was still in a state of total shock. If anything she was worse now than she had been in the beginning and neither she, nor her parents, had any realisation that she was slipping into depression at a rate of knots. Everything she did was as if her body and mind were on automatic pilot, it was the only way she could operate. Work came and went unseen and unfelt, the bus rides were the same as usual and the chores at home just got done. The evenings were the worst, when she was alone in her bedroom. Every song she played somehow seemed to remind her of Joe, and she couldn't concentrate on a book to take her mind off it. After only a few paragraphs her thoughts began to wander and huge tears wet the pages. Alice didn't know what she was going to do. She didn't believe she had ever felt so wretched in her entire life.

Saturday came round at last. Alice had been dreading the weekend, that was the time she was normally out somewhere enjoying Joe's company. Now all she had was Madge, so she did her usual trick and hid in her room. She had thought about going down into town for a wander around but what was the point? She couldn't think of anything else but her heartbreak, and as she was peeling the potatoes, the tears started again and dripped into the water in the bowl. Alice took a deep, shuddering breath as she wondered where they all came from. And whether they would ever stop.

She jumped as she heard a sound behind her, and automatically tried to pull herself together. Nothing had been said about what had happened, but she was waiting for it. The fact she had been at home all afternoon was giving the game away. No doubt her mother was going to have a field day with this one, and Alice didn't want to give her any help. It was going to be bad enough as it was.

"Oh, here you are," said Madge totally unneccessarily. "Shall we have a cuppa?"

"If you want." Alice carried on with the potatoes while Madge faffed about behind her. She didn't know what she wanted apart from Joe. He was still uppermost in her thoughts and she didn't think she was ever going to get over it. Right at this precise moment in time, she didn't even want to.

A few minutes later a cup and saucer were placed on the draining board close to Alice's elbow. She glanced down at it, then looked up and stared out of the kitchen window. Autumn was in full swing and soon she would be twenty. Twenty. It felt more like a hundred and forty-nine. She felt very old and very tired and more miserable than she could ever had believed possible, and now her mother was standing behind her preparing to stick the knife in. Get on with it, Alice willed her, let's get it over with.

"So. Is it all over with Joe?"

"Yes." Alice nearly choked on the single word.

"I thought so," said Madge quietly. "What a shame." She slurped her tea noisily. "But I did try to warn you. I had a feeling it was all going to end in tears."

"Yes, Mum."

"Would you like to talk about it, dear?"

"No, Mum."

"No, I suppose not." Madge put down her empty cup with a sigh. "How's the cake coming along?"

"Should be nearly ready," Alice guessed. She really had no idea. "I'll have a look in a minute."

"Yes." Madge moved towards the door, then hesitated. "You will get over it, you know."

"Yes, Mum."

Then she was gone and Alice could cry anew. Maybe she was right and she would get over it, but it didn't feel like it at the moment. It felt like a huge gaping hole that she was falling headlong into. A bottomless pit that was sucking her deeper and deeper down. A quicksand of raw emotions that wouldn't let her go and it went on and on into eternity. And beyond.

She got through the rest of the day somehow, went to bed early but didn't sleep. She got up as late as she could on Sunday, having no reason to rush. She had cancelled her driving lessons until further notice, after mounting the kerb last time then nearly running over a child on a zebra crossing. The instructor had been alarmed at her lack of concentration and offhand behaviour, and hadn't objected at all when she said she didn't think she wanted to do this any more. They had parted, each feeling a huge sense of relief, and now Alice had one less thing to worry about. She knew she was a menace behind the wheel at the moment.

She prepared Sunday lunch and just before it was due to be served up, she went down the garden to find her father. He had been busy digging over part of the vegetable patch this morning, she had caught several glimpses of him while she was doing the dinner. He always managed to keep his distance and stay out of things, and today Alice envied him enormously. Maybe she should take a leaf out of his book and try to be more like him. Perhaps that way she wouldn't get hurt again.

I won't get hurt again, she told herself sternly as she walked down the concrete path. 'Cos I'm never going to love anyone again. I can't. It hurts too much.

When she got to the bottom of the garden, Geoff was nowhere in sight. She looked in the garage, which was mainly filled with his car, but there was no sign of him there either. That only left the shed and she knew this was a particular favourite of his. Anything seemed to be better than sitting in the house with Madge, at least that was one thing they both secretly agreed on.

"Alice." He suddenly appeared by her side. "Crikey, is it that time already?"

"Yes, lunch is ready."

"Alice." He put his hand on her arm gently. "Mum's told me

what's happened. I'm so sorry. Then again, he was a lot older than you."

"I know. But it didn't matter."

"Maybe not now, but it's an awfully big age gap. It would've caused problems, Alice."

"Yes, Dad." She couldn't be bothered to argue.

"You don't believe me, I can tell. Never mind, it doesn't matter now."

"It does to me." Alice couldn't help it. She burst into tears again. "You don't understand how I feel. Mum's …"

"Yes, your mother isn't the most understanding person." Geoff sympathised for once. "I know she comes over as a cold fish, but she can't help it. She isn't very good at showing her emotions."

"I can't stop with mine," Alice sobbed.

"It's better that way," Geoff assured her. "Crying's good. It gets it all out of you. Cry as much as you can, Alice, it'll help. Really, it will."

"Yes, Dad."

"Come on, dry your eyes now." He reached into the depths of his gardening trouser pocket and pulled out a grubby handkerchief. "Let's go and have lunch. You always make a wonderful job of it."

"Thank you," she said, not really knowing why she should. She never had any choice in cooking at the weekends.

"You're not still thinking of moving to Walsall, are you?" he asked as they approached the back door of the house.

"I suppose not." Alice hadn't given it any thought at all in the last week. The flat was in Mellish Road, the very road Joe resided in. How could she go to live there now? That would only break her heart even further. "No, I won't. No point now."

"Oh good," Geoff sounded extremely relieved. "I know you're good at cooking, but I don't really think you could have coped on your own. It's a big step to take, leaving home and you're not ready yet. I think you can see that now, can't you?"

"Yes," Alice answered truthfully. "I can."

She pondered on this all through lunch. There was no

conversation to break her train of thought as she wondered if there really was such a thing as fate, and whether it was trying to tell her something. She had thought she and Joe were meant to be for ever and ever, but obviously they weren't, otherwise why would this have happened? Perhaps she wasn't ready to live on her own yet, although a few weeks ago she had been convinced she was. Maybe her parents really did know what was best for her. So ran her thoughts as she ate her roast beef, yorkshire pudding, roast potatoes and boiled vegetables. She had forgotten the sage and onion stuffing today, but no-one had commented on it. They both seemed to be being really kind to her at the moment, and she wasn't used to that. It was all rather unnerving.

The next day she went to work in the fracture clinic, which lasted all morning. Alice had always enjoyed this clinic, it was by far and away her favourite and was a good way to start the week. Today she got completely lost in the speed of the dictation and the seemingly endless procession of wounded patients hobbling in and out of the treatment room. She didn't think about Joe once, she didn't have time, and found herself wishing all her work could be this fast and furious. She didn't want to think at all, it was all far too distressing.

The week didn't continue as it had started. By Wednesday she was sliding into daydreams again, and this earned her a severe telling off from the fearsome theatre sister for being late in delivering Mr. Barton's operating list. She was shaking by the time she came away from her small office. Nobody messed with the theatre sister if they knew what was good for them.

The week ended, then another couple crawled by, and Alice's demeamour hadn't improved any. She had thought about going to see Joe's mother, but decided against it. She had only met her once, so didn't know her well enough to cry on her shoulder and anyway, what would it achieve? All she would do is make herself look a fool. She couldn't talk to Pamela either. She had been deliberately avoiding going too far into Physio and now she discovered that Pamela had left on the previous Friday. She must be getting married soon, she had told Alice that was the plan. This thought only made Alice even more depressed, and over the weekend she went through the bathroom cabinet. There was a bottle of nearly a hundred aspirin in there. All she needed now was the nerve and the opportunity to take them.

"What are you doing, Alice?" Suddenly her father was in the bathroom doorway. "Have you got a headache?"

Alice was still staring at the bottle in her hand with unseeing eyes, then she sighed and put it back into the cabinet.

"No, Dad," she replied quietly before she walked past him and into her room. Before she had even closed the door, she heard him open the cabinet and remove the bottle of tablets. She could hear them rattling as he carried them into the main bedroom, no doubt to hide them somewhere out of her reach.

At dinner that evening the atmosphere was tense, and Alice guessed that Geoff had told her mother what had happened. They glanced at each other a few times during the meal, and when it had finished Madge shot to her feet to collect up the plates. She came back a few minutes later with a trayful of tea, and placed it in the middle of the dining table.

"Isn't this nice?" she said as she poured milk into the cups.

No-one answered. It was as if they both knew some sort of announcement was on the way.

"And how's Alice these days?"

"Okay," Alice mumbled.

"No you're not," Geoff piped up, quite sternly, Alice thought. "Far from it, I'd say."

"Yes." Madge supported him. "We know you've had an upset, dear, but you really should try to do something to forget about it. You can't mope around over him for ever."

"No, Mum."

"I agree with your mother," Geoff added. "You need to find another interest or something. Go out and meet new people."

"I can't go out on my own," Alice protested. They were ganging up on her again.

"We've been through all this before," Madge pointed out. "You've got to do something, Alice. You won't get over it by locking yourself in your bedroom for the rest of your life. Join a club, there's plenty of them around. You can come to the Women's Institute with me, for instance."

Alice stared at her mother open-mouthed. Was she serious? What could Alice possibly have in common with a bunch of middle-aged women? And if even half of them were anything like Madge that would be a fate worse than death.

"I don't think I'd like it, Mum."

"You won't know unless you try." Madge was completely unforgiving, as usual. "That's your trouble, Alice, you'll never try new things. You could be missing out on a whole new world."

"Yes, Mum."

"It's no good keep saying 'yes mum', you know I'm right." Madge sighed. "I don't know, here you are pining away over some man twice your age that doesn't even want you, when there's a perfectly respectable boy a few doors away that's just itching to take you out."

"Oh, not Stephen Croft again," Alice groaned. "I hardly even know him."

"All the more reason to go out with him. Oh Alice, really. What have you got to lose?"

"I don't like him."

"How can you say that, you've already said you hardly know him. I'm sure he's a very nice boy. He must be, his parents are."

"Yes, Mum," Alice muttered sullenly. Oooh, she wished they would just leave her alone.

"Good. I'll tell Mrs. Croft you've agreed and we'll organise a date. I'm sure he'll take you somewhere wonderful."

"Mum, I never …"

Madge was gone, teatray and all. Geoff flashed Alice a nervous little smile, then picked up the newspaper. He always bought the Daily Telegraph, and Alice was sure he did it because it was big enough to hide behind, for hours at a time sometimes. He was going to be no help at all on this one, he was doing his usual trick of keeping well out of things. This was between mother and daughter.

A couple of days went by with no mention of either Stephen Croft or his saintly mother, and Alice was beginning to get her hopes up that it had all been forgotten. Until she came home from work on Wednesday to find Madge all bright-eyed and fired up.

"He's taking you out on Saturday, isn't it wonderful?" She paused as she waited for a response, that came in the form of a slight grimace and a shrug of the shoulders. "Oh, it's only to the new French restaurant in town. You're such a lucky girl, Alice, I wish I was going."

"You can if you want," Alice muttered under her breath.

"Now then." If Madge had heard her, she ignored it. "What are you going to wear? You need something special for a place like that."

"I'll sort something out."

"I went through your wardrobe this afternoon, as soon as I heard where you were going," Madge rushed on apace. "You haven't got anything suitable at all. I don't know, what are we going to do with you?"

"I'll wear my blue dress, that's alright." Alice was bored with this conversation but as usual, once Madge had got the bit between her teeth, there was no stopping her.

"I've told you, how many times, you should buy a little black dress. That would have been perfect for this, you can wear a little black dress anywhere. Anyway, problem solved." She reached behind her to pick something up. "You can wear my dark green dress, I'll alter it for you."

Alice stared at what she was holding up in front of her in total disbelief. The dress was heavy, lacey and sequiny and would come down to Alice's ankles as Madge was a fair bit taller than her.

"No Mum, I can't wear that. It's your favourite dress, I'll ruin it."

"Nonsense dear, it's the least I can do. Come on, try it on then I can see where it needs taking in."

"Oh alright." Alice still sounded unwilling, but now an idea was coming to her. Maybe this was the ideal way to frighten Stephen away. One look at her in this awful nineteen fifties' creation would be likely to put him off for ever, then she wouldn't have to go out with him again. Anyway, she had never been to a French restaurant, she might even be able to get to use her French language. She still had her penfriend in Lille, and now always wrote to her completely in French to keep in practice. She was also regularly writing to her grandmother, although she had these letters delivered to the hospital for safety reasons.

"I'm not having snails or frogs legs." She found herself speaking aloud. Those were the only French foods she had heard of.

"I'm sure they eat other things as well." Madge glossed over the comment while pulling a face. "And you seem to like eating foreign food for some unknown reason."

"Yes, Mum."

"Now hold still while I go and fetch the pins. We'll soon have you looking like a film star."

"Yes, Mum."

Once the dress was altered it looked even more ungainly than it had to start with, but secretly Alice was pleased with the dreadful results. All she had to do, she was sure, was act naturally, and by the end of Saturday evening Stephen would be running off screaming and would never want to see her again, and that would put an end to her mother's pesky matchmaking.

Saturday came around all too soon, but Alice was ready. She wore very little make-up at the best of times, having never really learned how to use it properly, but tonight she wasn't wearing any at all. Not even a smudge of lipstick. She put on the dress, looked at herself in the mirror and suppressed a smile. This was sure to work. There was no way he could possibly fancy her looking like this.

At seven-thirty she and Madge were waiting in the dining room, and exchanged glances as they heard the squeak of the garden gate being opened. Madge immediately panicked and shooed Alice towards the front door. She went calmly to open it, almost looking forward to this date now.

"Alice, there you are," said Stephen as the door swung inwards. "My word, you do look lovely."

153

"Thank you," she said, while thinking, yeah, right.

"Well, if you're ready." He offered her his arm. She didn't know what else to do but take it, then turned to say goodbye to her mother, who was standing in the hall looking all dewey-eyed. "Off we go."

Gordon Bennett, Alice thought, is he always like this?

Stephen led her to a small car, opened the front passenger door for her then ushered her inside. Alice was impressed by his manners, but very little else as he started the engine and pulled out of the cul-de-sac. He drove into Lichfield, and it crossed her mind that he seemed nervous, while she was perfectly calm. She felt in total control of the situation, while he was acting as if he had never been out with a girl before. Alice smiled at this thought. If that was the case, it shouldn't be too difficult to scare him off.

He chatted inanely, but Alice didn't take any notice as they walked the short distance to the restaurant then took their places at the table Stephen had reserved. When the pompous waiter, who looked as though he had a stick up his behind as well as a very nasty smell under his nose, handed them fancy printed menus, Alice noticed Stephen's eyes widen in alarm.

"Oh, it's in French," she realised. "No problem, I was good at French."

"Wonderful." Stephen looked mightily relieved. "Drink?"

All through the evening Alice had the impression that she was supposed to be overawed by the occasion, the restaurant and Stephen but she wasn't. Going out with Joe had taught her to take these things in her stride without her even realising it, and as she glanced across the table at her very attentive companion, she found herself wishing he was someone else. No-one would ever take Joe's place in her heart. Certainly not this Stephen Croft.

CHAPTER SIXTEEN

Madge had been unsettled all evening, waiting for Alice to come in. Geoff had watched the news and Panorama on television, then buried himself in the financial section of the Daily Telegraph for the remainder of the duration. Not for the first time in her life, Madge wondered why on earth she had married him. It certainly wasn't for his scintillating personality or his riveting conversation. No, it had been for money and security, and sex, of course. Mind you, the latter hadn't lasted long, the novelty had soon worn off as far as Geoff was concerned. Once Alice had been born it had gone on ration, and now the only time she got it was after they had one of their blazing rows. That reminded her, they hadn't had one of those for ages and they were in the house alone. Madge glanced up at the clock on the mantlepiece. No, there wasn't time to do it properly, she didn't want the cause of her deprivation walking in on them halfway through.

I hope that's not what she's doing. This unnerving thought suddenly occured to Madge. It was nearly half past ten, bedtime as far as she was concerned. No, Stephen isn't like that, I'm sure. Certainly not on the first date.

Her friend Doreen had assured her that her darling son emphatically didn't believe in sex before marriage, and Madge had reciprocated by guaranteeing that her pesky daughter was a virgin. Mrs. Croft was extremely straight-laced and Madge could imagine that Stephen was the same. Then again, he was young and Madge remembered only too well what young men could be like. She only wished she could get hold of one now, she was fed up with being a middle-aged housewife who spent all her time being ignored by her husband.

Still, she assured herself for the forty-millionth time, I don't have to work and we've never had any trouble paying the bills. If it's good enough for me, then it's good enough for Alice. Why should she be happy if I'm not?

The newspaper rustled as Geoff folded it up with a sigh.

"Time for bed, don't you think?"

"You go up. I'm going to wait up for Alice."

"Why? You know where she is and who she's with."

"I want to know how she got on, silly."

"She's gone out for a meal, what do you expect her to say?"

"Oh, you men are useless," Madge tutted. "Go to bed out of the way."

"Yes, dear."

After he had gone, Madge installed herself behind the net curtains in the dining room. It was getting late but maybe that was a good sign, that they were having a good time. Madge hoped beyond hope that Alice wouldn't do anything to put him off, she wouldn't put it past her to completely mess up all her well-laid plans on the first attempt at getting them together.

After what seemed like an eternity but was in reality only about ten minutes, she saw the headlights of a car as it turned into the cul-de-sac. It pulled up outside Doreen's, then Stephen and Alice got out, and Madge watched with bated breath as he walked her to the gate. There was a short conversation, she saw Alice nod, then her heart soared as she saw Stephen kiss her daughter gently on the cheek. Oh, the joys of having a streetlight right outside the front gate.

It seemed the first date had gone well, so Madge relented and decided to let her daughter off the hook, at least for tonight. She rushed up the stairs as she heard the key rattle in the back door, then listened as Alice hurried up the stairs and into her room. Hopefully they were going to go out again, and Madge would have to curb her impatience until tomorrow to find out.

While Alice was preparing the vegetables the next morning, Madge joined her in the small kitchen, using making a cup of tea as an excuse to begin a conversation. She put the cups, saucers, milk jug and sugar bowl onto the tray in readiness then waited for the kettle to boil.

"So," she said. "Did you have a good time last night?"

"It was alright."

"What was the food like?"

"Quite good, but I'd rather have Indian." She sounded more interested now, although Madge crinkled up her nose as the mere mention of curry. Alice always reeked of it when she had eaten it. "I had coq au vin, it was very nice. Stephen had something else that was full of butter and cream. He said it was good, but I'm glad I didn't have it. I'd soon get fat eating stuff like that."

"A bit of extra weight wouldn't hurt you." Madge defended her own situation. It wasn't her fault she only had to look at cake and biscuits to pile on the pounds. "You've always been skinny."

"I'm not skinny Mum, I'm slim."

"Same thing. I've seen more meat on a butcher's apron."

"Yes, Mum."

"Anyway." They were drifting from the point. "Has he asked you out again?"

"Yes, we're going to the cinema next Saturday."

"You don't sound very keen," Madge noticed. Alice didn't answer and now the water was boiling. Madge made the tea while wondering what was wrong with her offspring. "He's a nice boy though, isn't he?"

"He's alright, I suppose."

"Oh, Alice, really." Madge tutted as she manhandled the tea cosy onto the teapot. She had knitted this herself many years ago and was sure it had shrunk recently. "You don't know anything about these things. I keep telling you we know what's best for you but you never listen, do you?"

There was no answer apart from the sound of the knife against the carrot. Madge couldn't see Alice's face, but she could imagine her beginning to blubber. That was all she ever seemed to do lately, and it was time she snapped out of it. Madge didn't believe in depression, it was merely weakness and laziness as far as she was concerned. It didn't fit in at all with her concept of the stiff upper lip, digging for victory and British bulldog fighting spirit. Nostalgia and romance didn't come into it, these were notions that Madge had never encountered or understood. And she didn't see why anyone else should either.

"So Stephen's alright, is he?" she continued angrily. "Your trouble is you don't know when you're well off, my girl. What other sort of man do you think you're going to attract, you aren't even pretty, never have been. Be realistic, Alice, Stephen is the best you're ever going to do. He's got a good job with prospects, you'll never be short of money, and before you say anything yes, that is important. It's much more important than wasting your life pining over some man twice your age that's thrown you over. That would never have worked, Alice, you're far too inexperienced and immature to keep a man like that. It's about time you realised that and grew up."

There was still no sound coming from the figure in front of her, so Madge growled irritably, picked up the tea tray and carried it into the living room. Geoff was nowhere in sight as usual so she poured out his tea, took it back into the kitchen and placed it on top of the fridge.

"Take this to your father."

As Madge was leaving the kitchen for the second time, she thought she heard a quiet strangled sob emanate from her daughter. Honestly, the girl was so stupid, she just couldn't have any sympathy for her. Here she was with the ideal candidate for a husband being handed to her on a plate, and all she could say was "he's alright, I suppose." Madge despaired once again, Alice was just like her father.

A day or two later, Madge went round to Mrs. Croft's for coffee in an extremely good mood. For two nights running she had managed to engineer an argument with Geoff, and was sure that Doreen would give her enough ammunition for another one.

Madge enjoyed the stimulus of a blazing row. It was the only thing that made her feel alive these days.

While she sat in Doreen's dining room waiting for her to come back with the coffee and biscuits, Madge glanced around the walls at the photographs there. One was a very good one of Doreen and her husband, whom Madge had never met, but all the others were of Stephen. He didn't really look like either of his parents, but they were obviously very proud of him. There was one of him in his university robes and mortar board, another standing by his car and one holding his banking diploma. This was the most recent one, yet it looked old somehow. After a minute or two Madge realised why, it was the way he was dressed. She wondered for a second whether Stephen had borrowed his father's old blazer, that was what it looked like.

As Doreen pushed open the dining room door and placed the tray of goodies on the table, Madge noticed her clothes were rather outdated too. Madge was no fashion aficionada herself but she did have Woman's Own every week. Doreen evidently didn't take any women's magazines.

"Cake this week," Doreen announced as she poured the coffee from the percolator into bone china cups. "I got the recipe from a book out of the library."

"Oh, what a good idea."

"I do it all the time." Doreen laughed. "No sense in buying a book when you can borrow one."

"Oh, absolutely." Madge agreed, although this thought had never actually occured to her. She had quite an extensive collection of cookery books herself. Still, Geoff earned a good wage. One thing she had never had to think about was money.

Doreen handed her the coffee then offered the cake plate. Madge took a small slice tentatively, as her friend's cake-making attempts tended to be a bit hit and miss. At least she tried, which was more than Madge could get Alice to do. All she wanted to cook were these awful new-fangled foreign things instead of sticking to plain old-fashioned British food. Never mind, Stephen would no doubt make her see how silly she was and get her back on the straight and narrow.

"I hear the date went quite well," said Madge, vowing not to reveal Alice's reticence on the subject.

"Oh yes, it did indeed." Doreen sounded extremely pleased and was even blushing. "Stephen is quite taken with your Alice, he says she's a lovely girl, quiet, reserved and so well mannered."

"Thank you." Madge felt a bit embarrassed herself now.

"You've obviously done a good job of bringing her up. You must be so proud of her."

"Of course," Madge lied through semi-gritted teeth and one of the bright, false smiles she was so good at. "She's always been a good girl."

"And they're going out again this Saturday."

"Yes, to the pictures, I believe."

"That's right. Stephen's made the good first impression by taking her to a posh restaurant, but he won't be doing that too often. No sense wasting money on meals out when he can eat just as well at home."

"Oh, absolutely." This was one thing Madge did agree on.

"Alice won't be expecting him to spend a lot of money on her, will she?" Doreen looked a little anxious now.

"Oh no. She hasn't really had a proper boyfriend before, she's quite an innocent in the ways of the world."

"Oh good." Doreen sounded relieved. "I think she's just what Stephen needs, he's never had a girlfriend at all."

"Really?" Madge tried to sound surprised despite the fact she wasn't at all. Secretly she found Stephen somewhat effeminate, although Doreen insisted he was sensitive. Madge wasn't really bothered anyway, she wasn't the one that was going to have to live with him.

"I think we'll soon be able to start planning the wedding," Doreen said in a hushed tone.

"Mmm." Madge grinned at her carefully through a mouthful of cake which was surprisingly good this time. She would have another piece, and maybe one more after that. Just as she had been thinking of starting another diet too.

The weeks went by quickly, and Madge worked on Alice every chance she got to convince her to keep seeing Stephen. Eventually the girl seemed to give up resisting and went along with whatever Madge suggested, much to her delight. No-one even suspected that Alice might be in a deep depression, certainly not her mother. As far as she was concerned, Alice was behaving herself for once and doing as she was told. Weeks turned into months and before anyone knew it, a year had gone by in a blur. Then Alice finally came home with the news that everyone had been waiting for.

"Stephen has asked me to marry him."

"And you said yes, of course?"

"I haven't said anything yet."

"Quite right, Alice." Geoff nodded. "Keep him dangling a bit. Don't let him take you for granted."

"Oh, be quiet, you," Madge snapped at him. "I didn't keep you dangling, did I?"

"No." Geoff only uttered one word but he made it sound as though it was the biggest regret of his life. Madge glared at him, willing him to remain silent, which he did, of course. He always knew when to stop, never when he was ahead, usually when he was threatening to break even.

"When are you seeing him again?" Madge wanted to know.

"I'm going round to his house tomorrow." Alice looked totally resigned to whatever was going to happen to her now, but Madge took this for enthusiasm. "I said I'd give him an answer then."

"There's only one answer you can possibly give him. Don't you dare let him get away. You'll never find another one as good as him."

"Yes, Mum."

"That's a good girl." Madge beamed at her. Her conduct had been much better lately, no sulks or answering back. "Now go and put the kettle on."

"Yes, Mum."

Madge watched her go with a wry smile on her face. They were nearly there now and she couldn't wait to see Doreen to get the well-laid wedding plans into operation. Between them they had already sorted out most of the details, all they needed now was a date and a couple of venues.

"I wonder if the cathedral will be free?" Madge mused aloud.

"Huh!" came from the Lancet in the corner. After a minute it got put down and Geoff spoke again. "If Alice and Stephen get married, will you invite our relatives? I haven't seen my parents for years, could be dead for all I know."

"There's nothing stopping you from going to see them. It's just you can never have time off to go. If you were that concerned, you would."

"Work needs me. It's important."

"As for my lot," Madge chose to ignore his last comment. "They're too old and decrepit to come up here. They don't even know Alice anyway."

"Don't you think it's time they did?"

"It's a bit late for that, don't you think? Ingelfield's too far away to bother with. We've all got another life now."

Alice returned with the tea tray, and that's when Madge realised that the living room door had been left open. A shaft of fear stabbed at her heart. How much of the conversation had Alice heard? The pregnant pause was about to give birth, so there was only one thing to be done. Quickly change the subject.

"So, Alice." She tried to smile at her. "You are going to say yes to Stephen?"

"I don't know. I don't have any feelings for him."

"Oh, don't worry about that." Madge waved a dismissive hand. "That'll come later. When you've lived with him for a while."

"I suppose so." Alice poured her own tea and left the rest to brew. "He wants me to give up my job."

"I should think so too." Madge tutted at the thought that she could even object to the suggestion. "How would it look, eh? Him with such a good job and you having to go out to work? What would people think?"

"I like my job."

"Oh Alice, you know full well that was only to give you something to do until you got married. You can't honestly tell me you enjoy going to Walsall every day."

"It does get to be a bit of a drag sometimes," Alice admitted.

"Well, there you are then, you've answered it yourself. It's only a little office job anyway, nothing much to give up."

"Yes, Mum."

The next few months went by in a complete blur of activity for Madge. The date was set, the church booked, the wedding reception arranged in a local hotel and best of all, Alice hadn't mentioned anything about distant relatives attending. Madge spared no expense, insisting on the best of everything. This was the only wedding she was ever going to have to arrange, and Mrs. Croft had the same attitude, so Madge put all her efforts into it and pulled out all the stops. The fact that neither Alice nor Stephen wanted all this fuss had got nothing to do with it. They were shouted down time after time, and about all it served to do was unite them, which suited Madge and Doreen anyway.

Geoff, despite being the person who was paying for most of this, had no say in the matter either. All he could do was look on helplessly as Madge booked the most expensive photographer she could find, rented a Rolls Royce to take him and Alice to the church, and chose tiger prawns and caviar for the reception just because they were the most costly things she could think of. When it came down to selecting the champagne he gave up completely. Might as well let her get on with it. There wasn't anything else he could do.

Eventually the date in September came around and Madge's head was in a spin. She had been looking forward to this for so long that now she couldn't think straight. Her outfit had cost nearly as much as Alice's wedding dress, but she didn't care. The fact that she would probably never wear it again didn't weigh too heavily on her either. This was her day. At last she had something to be proud of. Her daughter had made a good match, and now Madge wouldn't have to worry about her any more. She was free. Now she could reorganise the house, turn Alice's bedroom into a storeroom and kick Geoff out into the spare room. She had had quite enough of his snoring.

All these thoughts were buzzing around Madge's head as she sat quietly in the church waiting for Geoff and Alice to arrive. She was a little miffed that she hadn't been able to travel there in the Rolls, she had had to make do with a Mercedes. She smiled across the church to Doreen, who gave her a discreet little wave back. Stephen's father was sitting next to her, staring straight ahead as if he was wishing he was somewhere else entirely. Doreen had told her he was an uncommunicative sort of man.

The wedding march struck up, and all heads turned to look at Alice. Her dress was wonderful, all lacey and floaty, and her face was hidden by a small veil. Her hair was intertwined with ribbons and Madge thought she had never seen her look so beautiful. Her face was covered up for one thing, that could only improve matters.

Stephen was just in front of her, staring at the vicar, so Madge couldn't see the expression on his face. Slowly the bride and her father progressed down the aisle until they drew level with Stephen. As he turned to glance at Alice, Madge could see tears in his eyes. He looked so happy, and Madge wondered what was going on underneath the veil. If ever she backed out …

Madge held her breath as the ceremony commenced, but Alice didn't budge. She was half expecting her to turn and run, but she hadn't better. Madge had worked hard for this day, she wasn't about to be cheated out of what was rightfully hers.

The service ended with the couple being pronounced man and wife, then Alice lifted the veil so that Stephen could kiss her. Madge was delighted with what she saw. Although Alice looked far from happy, she also had tears in her eyes.

CHAPTER SEVENTEEN

Alice and Stephen left the church amid a cacophony of people patting them on the back and congratulating them. Most of the guests were friends of their mothers' and Alice's one regret was that she hadn't been able to get in touch with Susan. Her parents had moved, she had discovered, and no-one knew their new address. She had invited Eliza and Bert, but they had declined. In a way Alice was glad. She could imagine Madge's face, but she would have loved to meet them at long last.

Stephen led her, beaming from ear to ear, to the car that would take them to the reception for a few hours. Then they were off on their honeymoon. Alice didn't know where they were going, she had been promised a surprise but she just knew it was going to be somewhere in France. They had talked about France quite a lot, although Stephen admitted that he had never been there. He liked the food, but they had only been to the restaurant a few times as well. High days and holidays, he had told Alice. She would get spoilt if she went there too often.

Something else she hadn't been able to persuade him to do was go for a curry. He flatly refused to go anywhere near an Indian restaurant, and Alice despaired of ever getting him to relent. She had gone for one last Chinese meal with the girls from work just before leaving them for ever. One thing Madge had been right about, and that was catching the bus to Walsall every day. She was well fed up with it, especially in the winter, and Mr. Barton was retiring soon anyway. Walsall had lost its charm since the business with Joe. Joe, oh Joe. If only it had been him she had married instead.

Alice had thought about him a lot lately. Stephen was nothing like as relaxed and entertaining as Joe, but Alice knew that her mother had been right about one thing, he probably was the best she was going to do. She never went anywhere to meet any other men anyway. Alice had no feelings for Stephen, apart from feeling sorry for him every now and then. His mother fussed and fawned over him as though he was a prize poodle at Crufts, but Stephen didn't so much as show the slightest bit of annoyance. However, he had admitted to Alice recently that he would be glad to get away from home, and all she could do was confess to a similar wish. Getting her own place had fallen through, and now this seemed like the next best option, and being married was better than being alone. That's what she told herself anyway.

Two hours into the reception and Alice had had enough. Mrs. Croft had buttonholed Stephen and was giving him last minute advice on every subject under the sun, and Madge was mingling. She was doing it quite loudly, and with yet another glass of gin and tonic in her hand. Alice had never seen her mother like this before, and suspected she was getting drunk. She only hoped she could leave before she really got going, she had made a beeline for one of Mr. Croft's young colleagues twice already.

Eventually Stephen got away from his mother, and made straight for Alice with a look of relief on his face. His curly blond hair was tousled from Doreen running her hands through it every few minutes, and his forehead was crinkled with lines at all the conflicting things he had been told.

"Shall we be making a move?"

"Yes," said Alice without hesitation. "I'll just go and get changed."

At least she had been able to choose the going-away outfit herself, and had caught the train into Birmingham to go and fetch it. It was quite trendy and up to the minute, and Alice was pleased with herself for actually managing to like something that was in fashion, she normally missed it by at least six months. She had selected a turquoise trouser suit, the jacket having short sleeves and the trousers big, baggy flares. A plain white top and a pair of white platform shoes finished off the outfit, and when Alice looked at herself in the mirror of the hotel bedroom, she hardly recognised the person who was looking back at her.

"Knock 'em dead," she said to her reflection just before she left to go back downstairs.

The reaction she got wasn't quite what she was expecting, and certainly not what she wanted. The room went quiet for a few seconds and Alice caught some of the looks of horror as she walked through the open doorway. It crossed her mind that most of the guests were middle-aged and didn't understand seventies' fashion, but even Stephen's face had fallen as he had seen her.

Oh no, Alice thought with a groan of despair. I've got it wrong again.

"Alice." Stephen looked as though he was wearing one of Madge's well practiced bright smiles. "There you are."

Alice didn't answer. What was wrong with him?

"You look awful." Madge didn't beat about the bush when the happy couple came to tell her they were leaving. "What on earth possessed you to buy that?"

"The fashion fairy," said Alice quickly. "Goodbye, Mum."

She walked away briskly before Madge had a chance to make any further derogatory comments, and waited in the foyer for Stephen to say goodbye to his parents and join her. To her great surprise, Geoff followed her then gathered her up in his arms into a big hug. She could smell something on his breath that she didn't recognise, but maybe he should indulge in whatever it was more often. At the moment he was actually behaving like a normal human being.

"Oh Alice," he murmured into her hair. "My little girl. Married and leaving home, I can hardly believe it."

"Neither can I," Alice muttered.

Geoff gave her a sloppy wet kiss on the forehead then disappeared back into the main room with tears in his eyes. Alice rubbed away the wetness irritably, and wondered where Stephen had got to. Everyone else was enjoying the proceedings and having a good time, but she hadn't even been allowed one drink. Now the wedding night was on her mind, and she wished she could be half drunk to get through it. Stephen hadn't so much as laid a finger on her so far and Alice was quite happy to keep it that way, but she knew there wasn't much chance of that now they were married. She remembered her experiences with Matthew and grimaced a little. They hadn't been anything to write home about either.

Stephen finally escaped and joined Alice by the hotel reception desk.

"Shall we go?" he said quietly, eyeing her up and down again and apparently not liking what he saw.

"Yes." Alice had no choice but to follow him, but instead of going towards the hotel car park he headed off into town.

"I parked my car round the corner," he explained. "Didn't want ribbons and old tin cans all over it."

"Oh," said Alice. She thought that was all part of getting married.

"Can you walk alright in those shoes?"

"Yes, of course. Why?"

"They look awful. I don't know why you bought them, Alice, you're taller than me in them."

"Oh." Alice understood now. Stephen was only five foot five.

"I don't like your outfit either. Can you take it back and get your money back?"

"What's wrong with it?"

"It's far too modern. I thought you were an old-fashioned girl, Alice. That's the one I like much better."

Oh great, Alice thought violently. And after I went to all that trouble.

The rest of the evening didn't go much better. Stephen drove to a hotel on the outskirts of Birmingham, they had a meal and Alice finally got the drinks she was after. Later she felt a bit more relaxed and when he announced it was bedtime, she took a deep breath and told herself she was ready.

They went up to the room and Alice eyed the double bed as they entered. Stephen went into the bathroom and was gone for some time and when he returned, Alice smirked and had to fight quite hard not to burst out laughing at his flannelette pyjamas. She made an excuse and went to the bathroom herself to look at her reflection in the mirror and wonder what on earth she had married. Stephen was twenty-six, so why was he behaving like a pensioner?

When she went back to him all the lights were out, except the one on his side of the bed. Once she had got between the sheets this went off too and then the fumbling started. Alice's mirth was bubbling up again but she fought it down as best she could. At least she couldn't see his face, that was one good thing. Doing it in the pitch darkness, how more Victorian could you get?

The entire business only took a few minutes, and Alice realised this must be Stephen's first time. He obviously hadn't heard of foreplay or even snogging but she didn't mind. Getting it over with as quickly as possible was what she had been hoping for anyway.

"I didn't hurt you, did I?" His voice came out of the darkness.

"No."

"Oh good."

Within seconds he was snoring loudly into her right ear, so all she could do was turn her back on him and try to get to sleep herself. Alice had never slept all night with anyone before, apart from the one time with Matthew, but he hadn't snored and whistled all night. She was going to have to buy earplugs if this kept up.

The next morning they awoke early and Alice got out of bed quickly, in case he fancied a repeat performance. When she came out of the bathroom, having had a long, hot shower, she found him standing at the side of the bed. The sheets were pulled back and he was staring into the bed as if he was looking for something.

"What's the matter?" she asked.

He waved towards the bed, puzzlement all over his face. "Where's the? I thought ... Wasn't last night your first time?"

"Well actually ..." Alice hesitated. They had never talked about things like this, and she felt embarrassed. She took a deep breath before she continued. "No, it wasn't."

"Oh, this is terrible." He put his hand to his forehead. "I was assured you were a virgin. Oh heavens, what am I going to do?"

"Stephen," said Alice patiently. "You never mentioned this before. What made you so sure I was a virgin?"

"Your mother promised my mother that you were. Oh Alice, I'm so disappointed."

"My mother? Your mother?" Alice could hardly believe her ears. "They've been talking about? Things like this?"

Stephen was crying and Alice didn't know what to do. She was shocked that such a thing could be discussed and by her own mother of all people. Was nothing sacred?

After a while Stephen pulled himself together and they went to breakfast. Alice was wondering how long they would be staying here before they went off to France, then she was informed they were staying in England.

"The weekend is in this hotel," Stephen told her. "I can't be away from work at the moment, there's too much going on."

"Oh." Alice felt totally deflated. So far this marriage hadn't got off to the best of starts, and she was beginning to dread what the future was going to hold.

After breakfast Stephen said he had a special treat in store, and told Alice to put on some sensible shoes. In her small suitcase she had summer clothes, her bikini and sandals but now it seemed as though she wouldn't be needing any of these things. She had assumed they were going to the continent for a few days and now told herself never to take anything for granted again. Already Stephen seemed like a different person from the one she had got to know over the last year or so, and she liked this new one even less. Alice hadn't really thought much past the actual wedding ceremony. That was what everyone, including herself, had been focused on for many months.

The special treat turned out to be an afternoon in the Science Museum which, while it was all very interesting, wasn't what Alice had been expecting to do on her honeymoon. She despaired of finding even one ounce of romance in Stephen, and told herself this was how it was going to be from now on. Secure but boring.

At eight o'clock on Monday they left the hotel, after having had an early breakfast. Three months ago they had bought a large house just a few streets away from the cul-de-sac, and had clashed a lot over how it should be decorated and furnished. Now Stephen dropped Alice off here before he went to work at the bank in town. Alice sighed as she entered her new home, which didn't look that much different from her previous one. Stephen liked the old style of furnishings, so now they had dark Victorian wardrobes in the bedroom, a double bed with both a headboard and a footboard, burgundy patterned carpet in the lounge, a big heavy three-piece suite and a dining table that could seat six people. Alice had been informed that she would be expected to do a certain amount of entertaining, but this didn't particularly worry her. Stephen could do all the talking while she concentrated on the cooking.

The day was long and not very interesting, as Alice wasn't used to being at home all day. Going round to see Madge crossed her mind, but the idea didn't hang around for long. The main reason she had married Stephen in the first place was to get away from her and her snidey comments. Alice had never been able to do anything right as far as her mother was concerned, and now it looked as though her new husband had a similar attitude. Maybe she should have taken the flat in Walsall after all and taken her chances alone.

By the end of the week she was nearly tearing her hair out with boredom and frustration. She missed her job and the company of the other girls more than she would ever had believed possible, and now began to understand why Madge belonged to so many clubs. The only thing Alice had ever joined was the Girl Guides and that hadn't been her idea. Something deep within her was screaming 'no!' at the notion of joining a women's club. She didn't want to end up like her mother, that was a fate worse than death.

Alice had been looking forward to the weekend but when it arrived, she changed her mind. She had thought that maybe she and Stephen might have a drive out somewhere, go for a drink perhaps, or to the cinema. They had gone out somewhere every Saturday since they had met, but now suddenly this was at an end. Alice's heart sank down to somewhere beyond her feet as Stephen picked up the Daily Telegraph and proceeded to bury himself in its pages for several hours. A nasty sort of déja vu was creeping over her.

Sundays turned out to be the worst day of the week, as this was the time Stephen had allocated for sex. Not that it ever lasted long. It was all very cold and clinical, like it was something that had to be got out of the way as quickly as possible.

"We'll have one child," Stephen informed her after a few months. "Then we won't need to do this any more. We got married under false pretences, but all we can do now is make the best of it. I suppose it's not your fault you're a strumpet, no wonder your mother was so keen to get you married off. I've been duped, Alice, by both you and your family, but I won't be made a fool of in public. We'll keep quiet about your past and present ourselves to the world as the perfect couple." He turned to glare at her. "Won't we?"

Alice swallowed hard. There was something in his eyes that she didn't like the look of at all and it killed her rising outrage immediately.

"Yes, Stephen," she gulped.

"I had such high hopes for you, Alice." He sounded sad now. "It's such a shame you've let me down. All you can do to redeem yourself is be a good wife, and I know you'll be able to manage that. You are at least obedient."

"Yes, Stephen," she mumbled, hardly able to believe what she was hearing. This man had certainly been born in the wrong century.

"While we're on the subject." Of what, Alice couldn't be sure. "I've got a very influential couple coming to dinner tomorrow. Cook something good for them, will you? Three courses. Oh, I thought beef wellington might go down well, it's all the rage, you know."

"Tomorrow!" Alice was aghast.

"That's not a problem, is it?" He was looking down his nose at her in a very supercilious way, and she was damned if he was going to get the better of her.

"Not at all," she replied, managing to sound relaxed and haughty both at the same time.

"Oh." He had been leaving the room, but now turned back as another thought occured to him. "Being as this is your first dinner party, I've asked your mother to come round to help you."

"Oh, great." Alice groaned but Stephen was gone.

This Monday was anything but boring. In the morning, after Stephen had gone off to work, Alice went into town to buy the food she needed. She had planned a menu out the previous evening, and had decided to go along with the other things that seemed to be trendy at the moment, prawn cocktail and black forest gateau. Madge could do the latter, she was only any good at puddings.

The beef wellington that Stephen had suggested in a 'don't you dare cook anything else' demanding sort of way was a new one on Alice. She was willing to admit to herself that she didn't know the first thing about it, but not to her husband. He became more bossy and picky as each month went by, and Alice could rarely do anything right. She was determined this evening was going to be a success, even if he hadn't given her any time to prepare for it. The shopping was done, the starter prepared and placed in the fridge and the table laid. Alice grabbed a quick bite to eat for late lunch, then waited for Madge to arrive. She didn't really need her prattling company but maybe she did need her help.

Madge duly arrived at three o'clock, weighed down by several of her large, expensive cookery books.

"I bought fillet steak," Alice informed her. "I don't know if that's right but if it's a posh dish, I suppose it would be."

"I would have bought brisket," said Madge in one of her superior tones. "I like brisket."

"Yes, Mum." Alice sighed.

"Anyway, you get on with that and I'll start on the cake."

"Okay." Alice was relieved. The kitchen was quite big so she could escape up to the other end of it and try to find a recipe for beef wellington.

It was half past four when she finally found one, then realised she hadn't got any paté. She asked Madge to make some pastry for her, then flew into town, wondering where on earth she could buy paté at this time of day. When she returned, the oven was on and Alice panicked. What was Madge playing at?

"The book says to pre-cook the meat a bit." Madge explained when Alice squeaked at her unintelligably.

"That's fine." Alice heaved a sigh of relief. Time was getting on now. "All I've got to do is spread it with paté, wrap it in pastry and cook it."

"I've done the cake." Madge waved to the masterpiece on the table. When Alice looked at it she was pleased she had shunted the job of preparing the dessert off onto her, she had made a wonderful job of it.

"That's lovely Mum, thank you so much."

"Right, everything else seems to be under control." Madge took off her apron with a smile that actually looked genuine for once. "I'll leave you to it."

Once Madge had left the house, everything went wrong. Alice didn't know she was supposed to leave the meat to cool before wrapping it in the pastry. Once she began to put the wellington together the paté melted and oozed everywhere and the pastry went soggy and broke up. After ten minutes Alice burst into tears and by the time Stephen came home she was in a hysterical state.

She got through the evening somehow. The guests were very polite and complimented her on the food, especially the fillet steaks which she had served up with perfectly cooked and presented seasonal vegetables. Stephen spent all evening glaring at her, and once the guests had gone he tore her off a strip then banished her to the spare bedroom. This had been the best bit of the whole proceedings.

Once in the bed alone, Alice could cry to her heart's content. What on earth had she done marrying this monster? How could she get out of it? What was she going to do?

CHAPTER EIGHTEEN

"Alice is doing very well, thankyou."

This was Madge's response to the query from one of her friends in the Gardening Club that she hadn't seen for a while. Most of the club had now boarded the coach that was taking them on a day trip to Trentham Gardens, some thirty miles away. It was late summer, and Madge was enjoying the weather. She was also thoroughly relishing ushering everyone to their seats, choosing to ignore the tuts of irritation and dirty looks that were coming from some of them. She had organised this excursion, along with several others earlier in the year. They had been to the bulb fields, the lupin growers and the bluebell woods but this was the biggie. Not only a coach outing but a guided walk as well. Madge had excelled herself this time, it was a shame that the majority of her fellow travellers didn't seem to agree.

Not wishing to dwell on their lack of appreciation, Madge took her seat near the front of the bus, next to the poor unfortunate woman who had made the mistake of mentioning 'the daughter'. Now she was to be regaled with all her exploits, whether she liked it or not. The rest of the coach sympathised with her plight, while at the same time thanking their lucky stars it wasn't them sitting next to the Treasurer of the Gardening Club, little miss bossy-boots and all round pain in the behind.

"They've just had the living room decorated," Madge continued to bore her friend senseless. "And they're talking about having a greenhouse put up in the garden. They have a little man come to do the garden, you know. Stephen says Alice isn't strong enough to do all that digging and things, and I quite agree. That isn't a woman's job, is it?"

"Er no." The hapless victim looked around, but couldn't see a lot due to the fact she was sitting by the window. She couldn't escape either, Madge had made quite sure of that.

"They're off on holiday soon as well." Madge laughed. "I don't know, it's all go for these young folks. Did I tell you my son-in-law works in a bank? I …"

Madge prattled on and on, not noticing, or even caring, whether her unwilling companion was listening or not. She loved nothing better than an audience, and a captive one was even better. The whole bus heard all about Alice's life for the thirty-ninth time, and there was a silent wish that this coach would get to its destination as soon as possible if not quicker.

"Why do we put up with her?" someone murmured when they got to the other end and disembarked from the bus.

"Because she's Treasurer and no-one else wants the job," was the quite logical answer.

Madge raised herself above all this, of course. She had detected complaints before and not just in this club, but what all these people didn't realise was the enormity of what she had taken on. She was on the committee of every organisation she belonged to, and that brought so much work and pressure. She knew most of them were reluctant to do what she did, and the majority of them wouldn't be capable either, so all she could do was ignore their mutterings and put it down to ignorance. They just got the fun bits, she had all the stress.

Everyone enjoyed the gardens and the walk. Madge lagged behind the main group, wielding her huge camera with its zoom lens, snapping away at nearly every flower in the place. A competition was coming up at the Photography Group, and she was determined to win it this year. She had been runner-up twice and was convinced she had been cheated out of first prize last time.

Madge got so far behind everyone else that in the end she had to run to catch them up. They were all chatting and laughing, but this died down as she got nearer. She tutted to herself at their reactions, really, some people were so ungrateful. She didn't know why she bothered half the time, her efforts were hardly appreciated at all.

Things didn't improve much on the way home either, and by the time she got back to the cul-de-sac, Madge was in a foul mood. This continued into the next day. Alice had promised faithfully to come round for coffee at three o'clock and she was late. Madge sighed as she looked at the clock again. Honestly, anyone would think she had nothing better to do than hang around waiting for her stupid daughter to turn up. The only reason she had her round in the first place was to keep tabs on her fantastic life. It was no good having all these friends in high places if she couldn't keep up with them on the social front. Alice and Stephen had recently returned from Scotland, where they had been on a hiking holiday, and Madge couldn't wait to hear all about it. She had never been to Scotland and wanted to know if the place was worth a visit. She could see herself now, standing in the doorway of a crofter's cottage, the wind blowing through her hair and some rugged Highlander in a kilt beckoning to her in the distance ...

The doorbell rang at last and Madge hurried to answer it. Alice was ten minutes late now, which was virtually unforgiveable.

"Sorry I'm late, Mum and I can't stop long." Alice looked harrassed and suddenly very old today. "Stephen's been on the phone, he wants me to go and meet him out of work."

"Oh, some sort of emergency?" Madge's spirits lifted and her eyes lit up.

"No, a client." Alice sounded sullen now. "We're always having to suck up to his customers, I'm sick of it."

"It's all part of his job, Alice, you have to accept that."

"I know." She sighed. "But I don't have to like it. They always make me feel so stupid."

"Well ..."

"Most of them have been all over the world and I haven't been anywhere. Stephen won't go abroad at all."

"A lot of people haven't, Alice." Madge should know, she was one of them. "There are lots of lovely places to visit in the British Isles."

"Are there?" Alice was looking at her now as if she was wondering where they were and why she hadn't been to any of them. Madge cleared her throat slightly as she remembered some of the far from successful holidays she had organised for the family when Alice was younger, then decided it was time she changed the subject.

"So, what time have you got to meet him?"

"Half past four at the bank. There isn't a bus at that time so I'll have to walk into town." Alice sighed. "I was going to start up my driving lessons again but Stephen won't let me. He says it's a waste of money."

"I suppose it is." Madge wasn't quite sure she agreed with that, but there was no way she was going to admit this to Alice. "You've got all day to do things."

"I did have," Alice said enigmatically. "Things are going to change in about six months time. I'm expecting a baby, Mum, next June."

"Oh." Madge didn't know what to say. For once in her life she was genuinely dumbstruck. "So soon."

"We've been married for two years, it's not that soon."

"Two years. It doesn't seem like five minutes."

"It does to me," Alice muttered gloomily, but Madge heard her. "You are happy with him?"

"Not really." Alice looked up now, the beginnings of tears in her eyes. "He's like an old man, he won't do anything or go anywhere. We haven't been out on a Saturday hardly since we got married, he's really bossy and wants everything just so. Oh, I don't know, he just makes me feel awkward and totally inadequate."

"Well …" Madge began, then hesitated. She had been about to say that Alice was awkward and inadequate, always had been as far as she could make out, but now she was pregnant. Madge hadn't anywhere near got her head round that idea. She was going to be a grandmother, how was she going to cope with that? "That's all part of being married, Alice," she said instead. "It's not all roses round the door."

"You're telling me."

"Oh, it's not that bad. It's you, you never were much good at relating to other people. Cheer up, Alice, and don't be so silly. Look on the bright side, you really have got it made, you know. Lots of girls would love to be in your position."

"Really?"

"Of course. Think about it, you don't have to go out to work, you've got plenty of money, Stephen has a good job and he's just been promoted, hasn't he?" Alice nodded, still looking three shades of miserable more than she should do. "You've got a nice house and now you're having a baby. What more could you ask for?"

"I don't know." Alice sighed wearily. "I just thought … I thought it would be different."

"You'll be alright when the baby comes along. Then you won't have time to dwell on silly thoughts like this. Marriage is all about give and take, Alice, just remember that."

"Yes, Mum."

"There's a good girl." Madge beamed at her, doing her best to ignore her unhappy face and slightly quivering lip. "Let's have a cup of coffee. You stay there while I go and make it."

She went into the kitchen, leaving Alice to pull herself together in the dining room. Honestly, she didn't know what she was going to do with her, she was always moaning about something or other. She seemed to have this weird romantic notion that marriage was supposed to be something people enjoyed. Madge couldn't imagine where she'd got this idea from, it certainly wasn't from her.

They had a quick cup of coffee and Madge had a slice of cake. It was rather a large slice, she noticed, but she had a puddled daughter to deal with. She had thought she had got her off her hands to everyone's satisfaction but she kept coming back with problems. They weren't real problems, of course, just Alice's imagination running away with her.

After Alice had left to walk into town, Madge thought she might as well be hung for a sheep as a lamb and had another piece of cake. Victoria sponge was one of her favourites and was only very light anyway. She tucked into it with large ungainly bites, determined not to think about calories and trying to ignore a saying she had heard recently. A moment on the lips, a lifetime on the hips.

Eventually she tore herself away from the cake tin, replaced its lid with a scene of a thatched cottage in Devon with an old English garden, then put it back in the pantry. As she did so, she tried to remember when she had been to Devon and failed miserably. It obviously hadn't been much of a holiday. None of them ever were, she had noticed over the years, and Geoff always said he didn't know why they bothered. He would say that though. Madge knew full well that he never wanted to go anywhere anyway, he was more than happy to sit in his armchair in the corner of the living room.

"Suppose I'd better get something for tea." Madge sighed as she caught sight of the clock. "I really can't be bothered, wonder what's in the freezer?"

Madge was really proud of her chest freezer that she had insisted on buying a year or so ago. It made life so much easier, and avoided the need to cook every day. Not many of her friends and colleagues had one, so yet again she had beaten them all to it. She had done the same with the colour television and full central heating, telling Geoff that they must have these things regardless of the cost. She hated cooking anyway unless it was a cake or a fruit pie, so batch cooking suited her down to the ground. She found a cottage pie from a few weeks ago and shoved it unceremoniously into the oven. That would do, with a few frozen peas.

She waited until later in the evening to tell Geoff the news. She let him watch television for a while, and bided her time as he sat engrossed in some deep political discussion that went way over her head. Once he switched the set off and reached for the Telegraph, she cleared her throat slightly.

"Alice came round this afternoon."

"Oh yes?" He didn't sound interested. "How is she?"

"Pregnant." Madge didn't see any point in beating about the bush. It had never got her anywhere so far.

Geoff sat rigid for a few seconds, the unopened newpaper suspended in mid-air before he spoke.

"Good grief."

"That's what I thought but she's managed to do it," said Madge grumpily. "I don't know whether I'm ready to be a grandmother, it's not something I'd even thought about."

"Well, I suppose it had to happen sooner or later." Geoff frowned. "I can't believe it, our little girl expecting a baby. It hardly seems five minutes since she was one herself."

"It's been a very long time, Geoff." Madge pointed out. "You only don't think so because you were hardly involved in bringing her up. You left all the hard work to me, as usual."

"I work hard as well. I …"

A row was brewing and Madge relished the thought. Maybe later she would let him into her double bed for a while before banishing him back to the single bed in the spare room, which was where he now spent all his nights. The box room had been fitted out with wall to wall cupboards to house all Madge's junk as Geoff called it, but she had let this comment go. All it meant was that there was no way Alice could come back home. Madge had more than a sneaking suspicion sometimes that she might like to, but there was no way on the planet she was going to allow that. She'd worked really hard to get her daughter where she was, so she could damned well stay there now. Madge had had her fill of let-downs from that girl, she was determined there wouldn't be any more.

Before anyone knew it, Christmas had come round. Madge and Doreen took it in turns to invite Alice and Stephen round on Christmas Day, and Boxing Day was always spent with the six of them round at the detached house a few streets away where the happy couple lived. Madge was still coming to terms with what the approaching year of 1975 was going to bring, and she hadn't yet warmed to the idea of becoming a granny. She had had enough of children with the one of her own.

Doreen, on the other hand, was over the moon and couldn't wait for the baby to arrive. She had got the knitting needles out as soon as she had heard the news, so Madge had felt obliged to follow suit. Between them they now had quite a supply of clothes and there was still over five months to go. Madge watched as Doreen fussed over Alice with half a sneer on her face. No wonder the girl was such a nervous wreck, but she couldn't say anything to Doreen, she still pulled rank on her within the Women's Institute and Madge wasn't about to rock the boat. Certainly not over anything as insignificant as Alice.

"Have you decided on names yet?" Doreen wanted to know as Alice poured her the tiniest glass of wine in the universe. Doreen wasn't a drinker.

Madge noticed the way Alice threw a disapproving glare at her husband but made no comment. She was going to have to have serious words with this daughter of hers. Who did she think she was?

"Stephen and Doreen," replied Stephen sternly. "What else would they be?"

"Well …" Doreen hesitated. "I thought maybe Henry, after your father."

Alice looked aghast at this suggestion, then turned her back on everyone as Stephen gave her a warning glance.

"What an excellent idea," Madge added fuel to the fire by declaring. An argument on Boxing Day, how wonderful. "Or Geoffrey, after Alice's father."

"I think the young people should find their own names," Mr. Croft put in for good measure. "I don't think there are too many Henrys around at the moment and I've never liked the name."

"Henry!" Doreen looked and sounded shocked to the core. "How can you say that?"

"Because it's true," he said calmly. "Is there any wine left in that bottle, Alice?"

"Yes, Mr. Croft," she said quietly, pouring what was left of it into his glass. Madge noticed the look that went between them, as though they understood the other's situation and sympathised. It seemed Alice had found an ally, that was a little worrying. Still, she wasn't likely to see much of her father-in-law, he worked away from home a lot of the time so wouldn't be around to provide a shoulder to cry on. Just as well really.

"I suppose the other names are worthy of consideration," said Stephen. "We could use ours as middle names."

"It'll be a little girl anyway," said Doreen dreamily. "I always wanted a little girl."

"You've got one now," said Madge, watching Alice as she placed a can of beer on the table in front of Geoff. It was his third, and she was imagining all sorts of problems with him when she got him back home. Then again, it might loosen him up a bit.

"We'll have to wait and see what it is," said Alice calmly. "I'm not bothered one way or the other."

"You mean, you don't mind," Stephen corrected her.

"That's what I said."

Madge frowned to herself. Alice was getting into answering back and that was unusual. She had never stood up for herself before. Madge resolved to have a word with Doreen about it before she was too much older. Find out what was going on, and put a stop to it.

Christmas was concluded and soon they were into the New Year, then before anyone knew what was happening, the news came that Alice had gone into hospital. Doreen came round to tell Madge the good news, then promptly proceeded to go into a complete tizzy over it. Madge tried to calm her down with a pot of strong tea and a mega-sized slice of Geoff's fruit cake, which did slow her down somewhat.

"How long do these things normally take?" She wondered as she sat half slumped in her armchair in the dining room window. "I can't remember."

"Alice took a long time." Madge remembered only too well.

"Oh, I hope she's alright."

"Of course she is, she's in hospital," Madge almost snapped. She just wished Alice would get on with it, instead of keeping everyone hanging around waiting. Madge was hoping beyond all things on the planet that she had a boy. Doreen's words on Boxing Day had reawakened emotions within her, and she recalled how disappointed she had been when Alice was born a girl. She had never had the son she so desperately wanted, but maybe she would get a substitute now. Either way, one of the mothers-in-law would be happy.

It was the next day before anyone got a phone call to say Alice had given birth. She seemed to have taken even longer over it than Madge had, and Stephen had mentioned something about complications.

"What is is?" was all that Madge wanted to know.

"A boy," Stephen said, very calmly and proudly. "Seven pounds two, very healthy and his name is Harry Stephen."

"When can I see him?" Madge was so excited she almost thought she was going to wet herself.

"Leave it until tomorrow," Stephen advised. "Alice is a bit out of it at the moment."

"Stuff Alice," Madge muttered to herself as she hung up the phone. "I just want to see my darling grandson."

CHAPTER NINETEEN

Just under a week later Alice and the baby were allowed to go home, but she couldn't summon up any enthusiasm to call him anything and certainly not darling. It was strange, from the moment of his birth she had felt absolutely nothing for him, although Madge and Doreen had fawned over him. All the other new mothers' faces had lit up when they saw their babies, and they couldn't wait to hold them, feed them and bath them but it didn't happen to Alice. She hadn't said anything to anyone, she didn't want to be singled out for special treatment and she put it down to being in hospital. Despite having worked in one, she didn't enjoy her stay on the maternity ward. Being a patient was a lot different from working in the office and she couldn't wait to get home to have a decent night's sleep. Maybe when she got back things with Harry would improve, once she was in her own house, in an environment that suited her better.

When she got home she placed Harry in his crib and walked around the four-bedroomed detached house slowly, room by room, as if she was seeing it for the first time.

"It's horrible," she muttered. "How can I live here?"

Alice herself had had very little say in the decoration of the house, her comments being dismissed as juvenile irrelevances. Stephen and his mother had taken care of most of it, ably assisted by Meddling Madge, which was Alice's latest secret nickname. The outcome of this meant that her home looked like an amalgum of Mrs. Croft's and her mother's, with not a jot of modernity in it anywhere, apart from the colour television, which Madge had bought as a wedding present. Alice was seeing this now, the dark furniture, the heavy curtains and the dull patterned carpets that 'wouldn't show the dirt'. This wasn't the house a twenty-four year old mother and her baby should be living in. Maybe it would look better with a few toys about the place. If Stephen would allow them any.

When he came home from work, Stephen looked surprised to see her.

"I thought you were coming tomorrow," he said. "How did you get home?"

"I had a taxi."

"Taxi? That was a bit extravagant. Why didn't you get the bus?"

Alice didn't answer, he sounded just like Geoff. Instead she took him to see his baby son. She noticed how his face softened when he looked at him, and was pleased. At least one of his parents could feel something for him.

It'll come, she told herself. I'll get used to being a mum.

Alice fed Harry while their own dinner was cooking, then put him back in the crib, hoping he would sleep through until the morning while very much doubting it. The smallest bedroom had been got ready for his arrival, with plain white walls, a white cot and all the usual things that surrounded infants but no fuss or palaver. Alice had wanted wallpaper with fluffy bunnies on it but had been sternly voted down. It was as though she was going to give birth to a fully grown adult, not a helpless baby.

"You've done me proud, Alice," Stephen said later as they both looked down on a peacefully sleeping Harry. They were on their separate ways to different beds. "You've given me a son, thank you."

Alice didn't know what to say, so just brushed a stray strand of hair back out of her eyes. What Stephen said next nearly floored her.

"If he wakes tonight I know it'll be a struggle for you but don't worry. Ulrika arrives tomorrow and she'll take over Harry for you."

"Ulrika?" Alice repeated.

"The au pair. She's here to look after Harry."

"But I'm his mother, he's my child."

"No, Alice," said Stephen firmly. "He's my child. Your side of the bargain has been kept. We agreed one child and present a united front to the world, beyond that I don't really care what you do. Ulrika will look after Harry and you'll run the house."

"But Stephen …"

"Oh Alice, I know you mean well but let's face it. You're not capable of raising a child, I can't trust you with an infant. Forget about him, Alice, he's not your responsibility. A boy needs a firm hand, and you can't provide that."

"You're not even giving me a chance!"

"Look." Stephen pointed at her threateningly. "I got sucked into this marriage under false pretences, and now all I can do is make the best of it. I don't want my son being influenced by the likes of you, or your family. When we take him to see your parents, you tell them nothing about this. All we can do is try to hide your problem, alright?"

"Yes, Stephen," Alice sighed. What else could she say? He really was never going to forgive her for not being a virgin on their wedding night, and he never passed up an opportunity to comment on it. She left the nursery quietly, went to bed and lay there for most of the night mulling over what he had said. Incapable of raising a child. Untrustworthy. Bad influence. Perhaps that was why she felt nothing for Harry. Maybe Stephen was right.

The German au pair arrived the next morning, and was installed in the guest bedroom as a permanent fixture. All Alice could do was go along with it, once again her life was being ruled by other people. In the privacy of her own room she cried and cried, quietly so Ulrika wouldn't hear her. At first she had tried to be friendly to the girl, who wasn't much older than herself, but she didn't want to know. Mister's instructions was about all she could get out of her.

Weeks turned into months and Harry was growing fast. Alice had very little contact with him, the fierce and very Germanic Ulrika saw to that. It seemed Stephen had chosen well. A snowflake in hell would have a better chance than Alice. Once a week she was allowed to take him to see Madge and Doreen, one in the morning and the other in the afternoon, to allow Ulrika to have a day off. Her presence had been explained to the grandparents as giving Alice a little help. The uncomfortable truth was well and truly concealed.

"You look peaky," Madge commented on the next visit.

"I don't feel right," Alice admitted, recognising the understatement of the year. Anyway, even if she told the truth she knew she would get no sympathy from Madge. She would more than likely side with Stephen.

"It might be this post-natal depression I've been reading up about," said Madge in a typically superior way.

"Maybe." Alice had heard of it but hadn't discussed it with anyone. She felt enough of a freak as it was. Now she was almost beginnning to understand Madge's indifference to her. Perhaps the same thing had happened to her. "If it is, what can they do about it?"

"Oh nothing," said Madge dismissively, as if she was an expert on the subject. "It only lasts for a short time, you'll snap out of it." She turned to look at her now, Harry gurgling happily in her large cardiganed arms. "It's quite normal apparently, I shouldn't worry about it, Alice."

Later, as Alice took the baby home, her mother's words were still fresh in her mind, and she decided she might actually be right for once. Ever since she had received that letter from Joe she had felt down, and the only thing that cheered her up were occasional letters from France and other ones from her grandparents in Dorset, which were now coming to her own house instead of the hospital. The hospital, one of the few good things that had happened to her. Now it all felt like a million years ago.

Alice, ever the dutiful wife, cooked dinner for everyone and tried to pretend Ulrika didn't exist as she ate hers in the lounge away from the happy couple. Alice pushed the food into her mouth as if on automatic pilot, which was how she got through most of her days.

"Do you think I'm depressed?" she ventured to ask when Stephen had finished.

"Of course not." He looked surprised that she had even mentioned it. "You're just quiet, always have been. Why?"

"Oh nothing. It was just something Mum said."

"Well, you should listen to your mother, Alice, they always know best."

"Yeah, right," she muttered.

"It's true." He reached for the newspaper, which signalled the end of the conversation. "And so is the other famous saying. Your mother is the best friend you'll ever have."

Ye Gods, Alice thought in horror as he disappeared into the pages of the Daily Telegraph. With friends like that, I'll never need any enemies!

Harry's first birthday soon came round, although Alice hardly noticed as she wasn't involved in buying any presents or putting candles on the cake Madge had made. Ulrika drifted in and out of her life, always with Harry in tow, and Alice slowly learnt to ignore them and all the snubs she received. She spent her days keeping out of the way, cooking, reading and going for walks like a zombie with no aim in life other than to survive. Her evenings were partly spent sitting on the opposite side of the lounge to Stephen, sometimes watching a documentary on television and always the news. As soon as she could, she always escaped to the sanctuary of her room, to listen, very quietly, to the radio or her tape recorder. It was like being back in the cul-de-sac with her parents. Only worse.

A few years dragged by and suddenly Alice realised she was thirty. What had happened to her youth? It had just disappeared somewhere. Her birthday came and went with no recognition from anyone, apart from a card sent to her by Eliza and Bert. She longed to go and visit them, but daren't mention it to Stephen. He was bound to tell his mother, who would impart the knowledge on to Madge. She had tried to ask Madge about her family, only to be brusquely told that she didn't have any. Alice wished she could say the same.

Then something happened that lifted Alice's spirits. Harry was sent away to boarding school and Ulrika left Stephen's employ. At last, Alice had the house to herself. She could have the radio on all day and the music made her feel a little better. Occasionally she would stand in front of the mirror and ask herself who that person was that she was looking at. She was a stranger. A sad, lonely, downtrodden housewife with a supercilious husband who put her down all the time. Why did she stay with him? Because she had no money and nowhere to go.

Thoughts of leaving had been on her mind for some time, but she had no idea how to go about it. She wondered about getting a job, then remembered how difficult it had been when she was nineteen and now she was thirty. Geoff wasn't around to help her this time. In fact, she hardly saw him at all now. She kept up the pretence by going to see Madge for coffee once a week, and Doreen, when Stephen reminded her. Occasionally very short letters came from Harry at his posh school, but Alice was never invited to read them. It was as though she didn't exist.

When Stephen deigned to ask her what she did all day, she lied and said she had joined some women's clubs. This seemed to make him happy, although he never asked for details, so Alice was able to keep this charade going as well. Her days weren't actually that exciting. Mornings involved housework, and afternoons were spent either listening to music, doing something in the garden, or going into town for a walk around. Just like in the old days, except now she had to do it on her own. She had got well used to doing things on her own. She felt like she had been doing it all her life.

Lichfield had changed a little over the years. The record shop was still there, although they had long since removed the listening booths. Woolworths was still going strong, but the shop that Susan's dad had managed had changed into a bank. Alice had no idea where either Susan or her parents were now, she had completely lost touch with them.

Alice wandered around all their old haunts, W.H. Smith, Boots and the snack bar where they had sometimes indulged in a very American bottle of Coca Cola. This place had now gone upmarket and was called something half French, but Alice smiled as she looked through the window and remembered her adolescence. It had seemed pretty awful at the time, but it was better than what she was enduring now. Then she had only had Madge to contend with.

Alice turned and looked across at the building that used to be a cinema but was now a hardware store. There were a couple of cleaning items she could do with, so she walked to the kerb and waited for two cars to go past so that she could cross the road.

"Hello Alice." A female voice came from in front of her.

"Susan!" She could hardly believe her eyes. Her old best friend from years ago was coming out of the shop with a carrier bag over her arm. She had on a navy blue and white nurse's uniform and her hair was shorter, but otherwise her appearance had hardly changed in the ten years or so since Alice had last seen her. They met in the middle of the road, stared at each other, then fell about laughing like the two carefree teenagers they once were.

"Shall we have a coffee?" Susan pointed towards the revamped snack bar. "I know it's changed but we can pretend."

"Why not?" Alice smiled, suddenly feeling happier than she had for a very long time. "Come on, let's go and catch up on all the gossip. I want to know everything you've been doing."

"You must have some news too."

"Only boring stuff, like getting married and having kids. I'd much rather hear about you."

They walked into the cafe and Alice was immediately transported back to the sixties by the smell of the coffee machine and the faint aroma of cooking burgers. She hadn't been into one of these places for years, and now asked herself why. She was always watching the pennies, something ingrained into her by Madge and strongly reinforced by Stephen, but the price of a coffee and cake wouldn't break the bank.

Susan was ordering just that for the two of them as Alice came back to the present and realised she was sitting in the window with her friend, just as they had done so long ago in the past.

"Where have all those years gone?" Alice wondered aloud. "What have you been doing? Where did you go when we left college?"

"Birmingham mostly, at the big training hospital, I thought you knew." She frowned. "I rang your house several times but I always got your mum. I left my number with her to pass on to you."

"Did you?" Alice said in surprise. "I never got it."

"You mean …"

"She deliberately held it back," Alice realised. "That's typical of my mum. Always had to spoil things for me." Suddenly, completely unbidden, an image of Joe's face flashed into Alice's mind. Had Madge something to do with that too? "I wonder …"

"I'm working at the hospital in Lichfield at the moment," Susan was saying. "I've got a six month placement there, I've only been back a few weeks."

"Your parents moved, didn't they?"

"Yes, I'll give you the address. Yours still in the same place?"

"Certainly are." Alice sighed. "Haven't changed much either."

"Your mum still as scary?"

"More if anything. She isn't showing any signs of mellowing with age. Godzilla, I call her."

"So, who did you marry in the end?" Susan's eyes were twinkling mischievously.

"Stephen Croft," said Alice as quietly as she could.

"Oh no." Susan burst out laughing. "How did that happen?"

"Do you know, I really don't know. I just got sort of railroaded into it."

"By your mother, no doubt."

"Yes." Alice wanted to get off this subject. "How about you?"

"No commitments, I'm enjoying myself too much. How is marriage, can you recommend it?"

"Definitely not," said Alice firmly. "Stupidest thing I ever did and now I'm trapped. We have a son but that's a whole other story. I had a smashing job until I married him but he made me give it up. Now I've got nothing."

"How long have you been with him?" Susan sounded serious now.

"Nine years," Alice answered with a heavy sigh. "Feels like a million."

"Leave him then."

"It's not that easy. We're not short of money but Stephen accounts for every penny. I can't put any away to escape with."

"Oh Alice, you never did do things by halves." Alice had expected Susan to laugh again but she didn't. "You know, I reckon you're depressed. Have you been to the doctor about it?"

"I don't want a load of tablets that send you to sleep." Alice was horrified at the mere idea. "I've heard about people getting addicted to them."

"There are other treatments too," said Susan gently. "Like counselling."

"I know what my problem is, I don't see how counselling can help. I need to change my life and that's down to me. I just don't know how to go about it, that's all."

"Maybe I can help," said Susan. "Why don't you become a volunteer at the hospital? Give yourself something else to think about. You never know, a paying job might come out of it."

"Stephen'd go mad."

"So don't tell him." Susan leaned forward and took her hand like she used to when they were younger. "Come on, Alice, where's the old fighting spirit?"

Alice looked into her friend's very concerned grey eyes and remembered the old days. She had survived all Madge's attempts to put her down and undermine her fragile self-confidence, only to allow Stephen Croft to do exactly the same thing.

"What sort of things do volunteers do?" she asked anxiously.

"Oh, all sorts," replied Susan. "Talk to patients, some of them never get any visitors, you know. Take the tea trolley round, there's a library trolley too. Run errands, buy newspapers. I caught one of them trying to bring in four cans of lager the other day." She laughed. "I mean, I had to draw the line at that, it's not a hotel."

"What did you do with them?"

"I had to get rid of the evidence." Susan winked at her. "Drank 'em myself. When I was off duty, of course."

"Good for you." Alice chuckled.

"So what do you think? About being a volunteer?"

"Oh, I dunno … I don't know whether I can do it."

"Alice, of course you can. You were always the one who'd go off and do things on your own. You were never frightened to have a go. That's why I liked you so much."

"Really?"

"Really. I know your mum pushed you into a lot of it, but at least you'd do it. I was always too scared of new things. Like the thing with the chopsticks, I'd never have done that."

"That was fun," replied Alice dreamily, her mind going back in time and entering the Slow Boat restaurant.

"See? That's what I mean."

"Okay, I'll try it," Alice promised as she looked her full in the eyes. Yes, she was going to do it. At last Alice was beginning to see light at the end of a very long tunnel.

CHAPTER TWENTY

A couple of days later Alice and Susan met up again, at the same cafe in Lichfield. This time they didn't stay for a coffee, but walked the half a mile or so to the hospital which was just off the main road that led towards Birmingham. Susan was going to introduce her to the person who dealt with the voluntary helpers. They didn't have all that many and a lot of them didn't stick it for long, but Alice had experience with the sights and smells of places like this, and wasn't put off by them as some people might be.

"I'll be in the canteen at one o'clock," Susan told her just before she left her in Mrs. Smith's capable hands. "It's down there." She pointed. As she did so a door opened and two junior nurses emerged, all smiles. Alice caught a quick blast of chatter and chinking cutlery before the door swung shut again.

"So, Mrs. Croft ..."

"Alice, please." She fought back a shudder at the mention of the name. She hadn't enjoyed being a Harwood either, but it had been better than this.

"Alice." Mrs. Smith smiled kindly, then glanced at her watch. "It's just gone eleven and I was just about to go round with the library. Would you like to come with me? Get a feel for the place?"

"Yes, please." Alice swallowed hard, wondering what it was she would have to do. She hoped she wasn't about to make a pig's ear of things. It had been a long time since she had had to think for herself.

"We don't have any set hours," Mrs. Smith continued. "So if you want to stop and chat with anyone, that's fine. Some of them enjoy someone new to talk to, and a lot of them are very lonely on the quiet."

"I can identify with that," said Alice quietly. She had been lonely for a lot of her life, and especially now. Meeting up with Susan again had given her an enormous lift, like a huge weight had been taken from her. She felt that perhaps now things were maybe going to improve. Someone had heard her tearful prayers after all.

Mrs. Smith collected the library trolley then led Alice to the male surgical ward, which was full of men of varying ages recovering from all sorts of operations. Most of them were cheerful, and Alice just followed her new colleague to see what she would do. She felt a little overwhelmed by all these people, and only now did she realise just how isolated she had become. Her universe consisted of Stephen, Harry, Madge and Doreen and she didn't see that much of any of them. She was more alone now than she had ever been. She was finding this morning quite frightening, but remembered what Susan had said yesterday. Alice summoned up all the fighting spirit she could muster, and determined to make a go of this. She desperately needed something new in her life to make it feel worthwhile.

She lingered on the female ward to talk to an old lady who had clung onto her hand and didn't seem to want to let go. Alice didn't mind, she knew exactly how the woman felt, there had been times when she would have killed for a bit of company.

By the time they had finished their conversation, Mrs. Smith was long gone. Alice panicked slightly then looked at her watch. It was ten to one, so she decided to make for the canteen to find Susan. She looked at the identity badge around her neck, and wondered if she would get an official one with her photograph on as she had been promised.

As she walked through the main corridor of the small hospital where she had given birth to her son all those unhappy years ago, Alice saw Mrs. Smith again. She now had on her outdoor coat and looked as though she was leaving.

"Alice, there you are. I've just left a message for you with Susan," she said. "Would you like to come again?"

"Oh yes." Alice nodded enthusiastically.

"Very well." Mrs. Smith looked pleased. "Ten o'clock on Friday."

"Look forward to it," said Alice as she waved goodbye. Then she carried on to the staff canteen to see what was on offer for lunch. All of a sudden she realised she was starving and couldn't remember the last time she had been even interested in food. Her life must have become very boring indeed.

Alice entered the canteen and looked around for Susan, but there was no sign of her. She knew she was a few minutes early, so went to the counter to see what she could have to eat. There were sandwiches and cakes, then Alice spotted a notice advertising jacket potatoes. She opted for one with cheese and beans. She hadn't had anything so fantastically ordinary for ages.

The potato was placed onto a tray along with a cup of tea, then she paid a ridiculously low amount and looked around for somewhere to sit. Susan had now arrived and was at the back of the queue, so Alice nodded and smiled at her. Susan replied by pointing to a table in the far corner where a woman of around their age was sitting. As she noticed the exchange, she smiled and beckoned Alice over.

"You must be Alice," she said as she approached, tray in hand. "I'm Fran, I work in admin upstairs."

"Pleased to meet you." Alice put down the tray and organised its contents onto the table.

"I nearly always have lunch with Susan. We used to live in the same road."

"Oh, I see." Alice sat down now. "We were best friends all through school, then we lost touch. I'm really glad we met up again."

"Susan's talked about you quite a lot," Fran revealed. "I think she's missed you."

"Oh." Alice was both pleased and flattered. It was nice to know there was someone in the world that actually cared. Alice picked up her fork and began on her lunch, glancing at Fran and taking in her appearance. She was blonde with large green eyes and a ready smile, and Alice liked her already.

"Have you done volunteer work before?" Fran was asking.

"No but I used to work at Walsall General before I got married and had my son. This was Susan's idea, I'd never have thought of it."

"Oh, so hospitals don't frighten you then." Fran laughed and Alice shook her head. "They do a lot of people, especially Casualty. You never quite know what you're going to run into there."

"I always found theatre the worst," Alice remembered, warm memories of Walsall flooding back to her now.

"Yes, I know what you mean. I have to go there every now and then and I never look forward to it. The sister's a bit mean."

"The one in Walsall was as well."

"They must be a special breed."

"Ah, here's Sue." Alice smiled up at her. "You're not going to specialise in theatre, are you?"

"All that blood and guts? No, thank you," Susan laughed as she joined them. "No, I want to do maternity, that's why I'm here, this hospital does more of that than anything else."

"Oh good." Alice winked at Fran.

"How have you got on?" asked Susan. "Enjoy it?"

"Yes." Alice nodded. "I had a chat with ever such a nice old lady, and I'm coming again on Friday. It's great to be back in a hospital again, there's something rather special about them."

"They get to you, that's a certain fact," Fran agreed. "I love it here."

"Yeah, this one's really nice," Susan added. "I shall be sorry to leave it and go back to Birmingham."

"Well, let's make the most of it while we're here."

"That sounds more like the old Alice. Seems like this place is doing you good already."

Susan's words soon proved to be correct. The weeks went by and Alice settled into a new routine that was a hundred times more interesting than the old one. She got to know all the wards and departments and a lot of the people too, and most of them were very pleasant. The patients were always changing, of course, but this just made it more appealing. Alice and Fran got to know each other better as well, and discovered that they had a surprising amount in common. Fran had a daughter who was ten years older than Harry, and Alice found herself wishing he was already that age and leaving home. He had been back from the expensive and exclusive boarding school just the once so far, and seemed to have become totally obnoxious already. He was turning out to be just like Stephen, and his father encouraged all the arrogant and domineering attitudes that he himself had. Madge and Doreen both seemed to think Stephen was right, and Alice gave up. She had never had any say in what happened to the boy and if she was honest, she didn't really care. All she wanted to do now was escape.

Alice kept all these thoughts very much to herself. She had long since given up trying to convince Madge that the marriage was a sham, and her father kept out of it, as usual. From the outside she knew that things looked hunky dory, and Stephen did everything he could to reinforce the illusion. Both Madge and Doreen thought their offsprings had the ideal relationship and the perfect child. Neither of them could see any wrong in him and they had both been on to Alice lately, wanting to know when he was going to have a brother or sister. All Alice could do to these constant badgerings was smile sweetly, and say she was waiting for it to happen. Considering she was well established in the spare bedroom and Stephen hadn't laid a finger on her since the day she had informed him she was pregnant, she thought she was pretty safe on this score.

When Alice was out of the house she was able to forget all her problems and threw herself into her alternative life. It was only the contact with the hospital that made her existence bearable. She looked forward to every session, she now had three a week, and couldn't wait to get within the hospital walls to hand out library books, chat to people or run little errands for them. Susan had now gone back to her main job in Birmingham where she was working towards becoming a nursing sister, but they kept in touch by phone as often as they could.

Then came the Friday when Alice was late getting home. Stephen was bringing some clients round for dinner tonight and she was running behind on the cooking front. She rushed into the house, threw her things onto the dining room table and dashed into the kitchen to make a start on the food.

When Stephen came in from work, Alice had forgotten all about the spare handbag she had deposited in the dining room. When she went in to lay the table, she found Stephen there looking through his briefcase. Her eyes widened in alarm as she saw the bag, and she reached for it quickly. Too quickly. Her sudden movement caught his attention, then it happened. Her identity badge for the hospital slid out of the open handbag and onto the floor. Right at Stephen's feet.

"What's this?" he asked as he bent down to retrieve it. "Alice, what is this?"

His eyes were flashing in anger and confusion, so Alice knew she could only tell the truth. She was desperately trying to remember a conversation she had had a long time ago with Fran on this very subject. About what she would tell Stephen if he ever found out.

"Oh, didn't I tell you?" She tried to laugh and failed miserably. "I've been doing a bit of voluntary work at the hospital."

"What?" He looked as though he was about to explode. "Work?"

"Well, no, it's not really work," she added as smoothly as she could. "I was at a meeting the other day, and some of the women starting talking about doing charity work. I thought that sounded interesting. You know, doing something to help less fortunate people?"

"That does sound very commendable." He still didn't look too sure. "How long has this been going on?"

"Oh, only a week or two, it's nothing really." Alice lied effortlessly, surprising herself into the bargain. "I forgot I hadn't told you but honestly, I didn't think you'd mind. It's only an hour or so twice a week."

"As long as that's all it is." Stephen glared at her. "It hadn't better interfere with anything you've got to do at home."

"Oh no, Stephen, of course not," she assured him. She had already worked out a new routine that moved around her hospital hours. Not that he would ever notice. "Anyway, what time are your guests arriving?"

"Our guests, Alice. Half an hour. Is everything ready?"

"Yes, Stephen."

She walked back into the kitchen quickly, heaving a huge silent sigh of relief. She was glad her little secret was out in the open, and maybe now they could even have conversations about it instead of him being buried in the newspaper and Alice in a library book. Somehow she doubted it, but it might provide a talking point for his clients tonight. Another way to prove to the world what a dutiful and caring wife she was.

Alice sailed through the dinner party. She was well used to them by now and had learnt, quite early on, to keep out of the conversations until she was invited to join in. Most of the time she wasn't, but she was quite happy to let Stephen dominate the proceedings. She had done her bit by preparing the meal.

Autumn half term came and went with no sign of Harry. Stephen had decided, with no interference from anyone else, that the boy could stay in school for the holiday. Doreen and Madge were horrified of course, but Alice was only too happy. Most of the time she completely forgot she had a son. Seeing as she had never been allowed to be a mother to him, she might as well, she reasoned. This state of affairs continued happily enough until the letter arrived. From the headmaster of Harry's school.

Alice knew who it was from as soon as it landed on the mat, there was a stamped imprint of the main school building on the front of the envelope. She picked it up slowly, wondering what horrors were inside, and placed it on the mantelpiece in the lounge, or sitting room as Stephen insisted on calling it, until the master of the house came home. Maybe it was a report regarding his academic progress, but somehow Alice doubted it. He had only been there for a couple of months. Her premonition proved accurate, for when Stephen opened the letter after dinner his face slowly turned from impassive to furious.

"Have you seen this?"

"Of course not, you've only just opened it."

"Don't answer back! Oh, I can see where Harry's got this from. I knew I shouldn't have let your family have any influence on him."

"They haven't," Alice pointed out. "What's happened?"

"What's happened? This is a disaster, he's been stealing from the other boys, getting into fights, being disruptive in class. Oooh …" Stephen buried his head in his hands. "What am I going to do?"

"I should let the school sort it out. That's why you sent him there in the first place, wasn't it?"

"That's right, abdicate from your responsibilities. You're good at running off and hiding from things you don't like."

"I know," murmured Alice, her thoughts on a completely different subject. Then she said, louder. "I don't see what I can do about it. It wasn't me that brought him up, it was Ulrika."

"Don't you start trying to shift the blame onto her. She was the firm hand a boy needs, he was fine while he was with her."

Alice couldn't bring herself to agree. She had witnessed toddler rebellion against the au pair, but had never got involved with it. Harry seemed to be every inch a miniature replica of his father only with a mega attitude problem, but she could hardly tell Stephen that. His face was turning purple with rage as it was.

"I wouldn't know," she said instead. "I wasn't allowed to have anything to do with it, remember?"

"Don't you start getting clever, you're as bad as your mother, she's always got an answer for everything too."

"That's true." Alice couldn't deny that.

"Oooh, I should never have got involved with your family, bad news, the lot of you. There's only one person to blame for all this, and I'm looking at them!"

No, Alice thought vehemently. I am.

Dinner was served and eaten in a heavy silence, then as soon as Alice had finished washing up she went to hide in her room and listen to some music. For a little while she could pretend she was single again and lose herself in pop songs from the sixties. For a little while.

The next time she saw Fran, she decided to sound her out about a real job. She would know if there was anything going, and if Alice could start earning some money she could become independant and leave Stephen. There was nothing to keep her with him any more, and she couldn't imagine spending the rest of her life in his boring company being shouted at. She would rather take her chances on her own.

"Hi," Fran greeted Alice as she sat down with her lunch tray. She only had a sandwich and was looking through a hand-written notebook with a very lined forehead, but closed this up when Alice joined her.

"Trouble?" Alice had seen this book before and knew it contained Fran's household accounts.

"Not really." She sighed. "Bit of a juggling act. That's what you get for wanting to live where I do."

"You're in Aldermarsh, aren't you?"

"Yes, it's a nice village." Fran nodded. "A bit expensive mind. I kept the house there, but it's a bit of a struggle with only one wage coming in now."

"I suppose so," said Alice carefully. She knew Fran was divorced, and was trying to imagine herself being too. It would be difficult on her own, she was beginning to realise that now. She had explained her situation to her friend and she had suggested she open a building society account in her maiden name. Alice had declared this was impossible but Fran had winked at her, gone back to her office and typed up a reference for her on a piece of headed hospital paper. Alice hadn't argued and this way, even if Stephen found out, he wouldn't be able to take the money off her. Yes, money. So far she had only been able to hide a few pounds away. He wasn't that generous with the housekeeping allowance. "I was wondering," she continued, "whether there might be an office job going. I used to be a medical secretary."

"Really?" Fran looked surprised. "Well, you're a dark horse. I don't think there's anything at the moment, but put your name down. Then if anything comes up, you'll be virtually guaranteed to get it."

"I'll do that," Alice promised. "I think I'm ready for a proper job now, and the money will come in handy. Haven't got much in my escape account yet."

"Stephen still being a meany?"

"Absolutely, he watches nearly every penny and we're not short of money. You'd think he was an old miser instead of a bloke of thirty-five."

"Some people are just born old." Fran nodded in agreement. "I had the complete opposite as you know, one who wouldn't grow up. I never had a husband and a daughter, I had two kids."

"We're never satisfied, are we?" Alice laughed uneasily. "I wish …"

"Yes?"

"Oh nothing." She smiled sadly, then looked up at her friend's curious face over her lunch of chips and baked beans. "There was someone before Stephen but it wasn't meant to be."

"But you wish it was? Still?"

"Yes." Alice hung her head, tears prickling at her eyes. "Still."

CHAPTER TWENTY-ONE

The object of Alice's affections, Joe, was closer to her at this precise moment than she would have believed possible. He was a mere five miles away, sitting comfortably on a river bank, watching his float intently as it sat in the water, barely discernable to anyone else. He was having a welcome break from work and had come out to Aldermarsh to be alone and think. Things had been a bit strange in Birmingham recently, and he was trying to figure out what could possibly be going on.

Two years ago Joe had been promoted from Technical Manager to Technical Director, and had been obliged to start visiting one of the two places in the universe he had never wanted to go. China. He knew his subject inside out and backwards, so it had been decided by the powers that be, with no consultation with the man concerned, that Joe was the best person to go to the steelworks in Boatoa. Stefoco had developed many new products, and most of them had a lot of input from Joe's analytical and logical brain. Now they were trying to increase their market share by selling this technology abroad. America had already embraced it, albeit somewhat unwillingly, but now the bosses at the company had the Far East in their sights. Joe's job now was to introduce himself to the Chinese, give presentations on the new technology and generally suss out the lie of the land. He didn't want to do it, but he had been lumbered with it. He was probably the only person within the company that was capable of pulling this off. He knew this and so did they.

He had only been back from China for a week, but had detected an atmosphere in the works. Strangers in suits had suddenly appeared and seemed to be poking their noses into everything, and Joe suspected they might be what the Americans call bean counters. A lot of businesses had taken to calling in a firm of accountants lately, to sharpen up their performance and rearrange their practices, but all these seemed to result in was disruption and redundancies. Joe had this niggling feeling in the back of his mind, like an awful sort of premonition about his future. He knew he hadn't done anything wrong, apart from decline to get involved in the boardroom politics, yet he had a sinking feeling in his stomach every time he thought about Stefoco. It might be prudent to keep his eyes open for another job, just in case.

As he reached for his Thermos flask of black coffee, he tried to put these thoughts out of his mind. He had come to sit on the banks of the River Trent to forget all his suspicions and doubts, that was why he had booked the week off. Despite this, he was wondering what was going on at work while he wasn't there to defend himself. Maybe he should be there. If ever …

"Stop it," he told himself firmly as he wrapped his cold fingers around the warm plastic cup. "Enjoy the day."

As he drank his coffee, he looked around to remind himself why he had come here today, and tried to remember the first time he had come to the village. It was a very long time ago, in nineteen forty something when he had been about twelve. His grandfather and father had been fishermen before him, and had always got involved in local matches and contests. Joe's grandad had won a lot of them and Joe had tagged along to watch and learn. He had learned well too, now he won nearly every contest he entered. It supplemented his income and had bought him his first car and anyway, he enjoyed it. Despite being a townie, he loved being out in the countryside and getting close to nature. He knew all the birds that twittered and sang in the hedgerows and whenever he could, he went for long walks. This village was good for that too, and when he had worked up a thirst from a five mile walk, he could visit the pubs. His only regret was that he had no-one to share all this with. He had had one relationship in recent years, but that had fizzled out and now he was alone again.

"Story of my life," he muttered. "Never mind, maybe one day ..."

Alice's smiling face was suddenly floating before him and he wished it would go away. He still thought about her, more often than he was willing to admit, but it was no use torturing himself. She was married to someone else, and he could hardly bear the thought. She probably had half a dozen kids by now, happy as a pig in the proverbial and living the life of Riley. Best not to think about it.

The float went under and Joe struck. Seconds later he was fetching another darting dace off the hook and throwing it into his keep net. He wished he was in a contest, he enjoyed the competitiveness and found pleasure-fishing somewhat dull and flat. Still, he was getting some fresh air and would go for a pint after.

Half an hour later he packed up and carried everything back to his car, which he had parked close to the canal bridge. This village was a little unusual, in that both the River Trent and the Trent and Mersey canal ran through it, and crossed over each other near to where Joe had been fishing. In the summer canal boats glided through, sometimes stopping for the night and bringing in welcome business to the shops and pubs. This trend was on the increase, which was good news for all concerned.

When Joe got back to his car he could see all the ducks on the grass a few feet away. They were looking at him, and one or two of them began to waddle towards him, quacking and generally complaining, as ducks do. Joe smiled as he realised what they were after.

"Sorry boys," he said cheerfully – most of them were drakes. "No bread for you, no sandwiches today."

The ducks continued to grumble and grouse as he loaded all his fishing tackle into the boot. He left the car where it was and walked the short distance to his favourite pub, fairly certain there should be some people in there that he knew. He came here at least once a month, sometimes to fish and other times just for a drink. He wasn't all that keen on some of the pubs in Walsall.

He entered by the front door to find his friends already at the bar. Soon he had a pint in his hand and found himself reading the specials board on the wall. He was quite hungry, might as well get himself something here as mess about when he got home.

"Hello Joe." His friend Ian spotted him as he turned away from the two men he had been discussing something with at great depth to get himself another half of guest ale. "Haven't seen you for a while, how's things?"

"Okay as far as I know." Joe knew these three plenty well enough not to have to gloss over his problems. "Funny goings-on at work."

"Ooh, don't like the sound of that." Ian drew in his breath.

"Nor me," tall Trevor agreed.

"They haven't mentioned the word restructuring, have they?" Even taller Alan wanted to know. He was the only one of them that ever wore a suit and was involved in something financial.

"Not yet." Joe smiled wryly. "But I'm waiting for it."

"That'll mean redundancies," said Alan. He was good at doom and gloom. "Watch yourself."

"Nah, Joe'll be alright," said Ian in his Derbyshire accent. "He's a technical bloke, they can't get rid of him."

"That doesn't mean anything these days," Alan persisted. "I mean, you got made redundant, didn't you?"

"I'm older than Joe," Ian reminded him. "And I didn't mind. Always wanted to spend more time in the pub anyway."

"All I can do is wait and see, I suppose." Joe's attention was going back to the specials board as his stomach rumbled, so he excused himself and ordered something to eat. Wait and see was all he could do now, but he had a feeling this week was going to turn into a very long one.

As he installed himself in a quiet corner to eat his meal, Joe's thoughts drifted back over the past few months. Most of this time had been spent in the middle of China with nothing to do, but as Joe raised his pint to his lips, he remembered the incident with the Peking beer …

Joe and his colleague Tony were living in a spartan concrete hostel built by the Russians in the fifties, with only books and Monty

Python cassette tapes for company. And Peking beer, which was excellent and about the only thing that was keeping Joe sane in this extremely alien environment. He had soon discovered that the Chinese mentality was totally different from the European, and had to bear that in mind in his negotiations with them. He spent his days talking to men from the Ministry, or giving lengthy presentations on the stage in front of several hundred people, ably assisted by Tony. Talking in public didn't come naturally to him, but he had taught himself to do it very well. He always had an attentive audience.

There wasn't any kind of bar Joe and Tony could go to wind down, but every mealtime they ate in a room with a tin topped table. Some of the food was strange to say the least, they wasted nothing. Joe had heard a saying that you can eat everything on a pig except its squeak, but he had no doubt that some enterprising Chinese chef would find a use even for that. It appeared they would eat anything and expected their visitors to do the same. The visitors found it more edible with a couple of bottles of beer each, and these were placed out on the table each day before the two men arrived. Lunch was always early, between eleven and twelve as the Chinese were very much into early to bed, early to rise. Keeping them up much past eight o'clock was practically unheard of.

Things were going reasonably well, until the next time Joe and his colleague went to lunch. There was beer on the table, but it wasn't Peking but some other make that neither of them had heard of. Not to be deterred, Joe opened one of the bottles and poured out the cloudy liquid. Things were floating about in it too, and it looked absolutely disgusting. It tasted even worse.

"Excuse me." Joe noticed one Chinese lurking in a doorway while trying to make himself look invisible. "Where's the Peking beer?"

"So sorry." The man wrung his hands apologetically as he spoke through the interpreter. "Peking beer all finished, this beer now." He waved towards the lurgyish brew.

"No," said Joe firmly. "Peking beer or nothing. It's the only decent thing in this place."

"Too right," Tony muttered in agreement.

"It can't be done," the interpreter answered.

"Okay." Joe thought quickly. "Tell me, there's a train to Peking at three o'clock this afternoon, isn't there?"

"Yes." The interpreter looked puzzled.

"Get me a ticket for it. I'm going home."

"You can't do that, Mr. Lange!" The interpreter looked horrified now. "There is work to be done."

"No Peking beer, no work." Joe's eyes were flashing in anger. "Get us on that train. Come on, Tony, let's go and pack."

When they got back to the hostel and Joe reached for his suitcase, Tony spoke. "Are we really going home?"

"Too right. I never wanted to come here in the first place, and now they can't even get any decent beer. That's the last straw for me. Someone else'll have to come out from England, I've had enough."

A couple of hours later they left with their suitcases packed, and walked through part of the steelworks towards the small railway station that would be their way back to civilisation. Tony sighed and Joe pursed his lips as they saw their interpreter running towards them with a big daft grin on his fat podgy face.

"Mr. Lange, come, look."

He ran off in the opposite direction, then stopped as he reached an old car. Joe's eyes widened in surprise. It was the first car he had seen in this town.

"Belongs to Mayor of Boatoa," the interpreter explained. "Only one car in Boatoa. And look, look." He wrenched open the back door. On the once smart leather seats were two crates of beer. Peking beer. Joe began to smile. His threat of withdrawing his labour had reaped excellent results.

"Mayor fetch this from other side of town," the interpreter said proudly, then they all looked round as they heard a lorry engine approaching. "And look, more Peking beer."

The even older lorry was indeed laden up with more crates than anyone dared to count. Joe and Tony exchanged a smile and a wink, as the lorry clattered to a halt and men appeared as if out of nowhere to begin unloading the beer.

"Now you do work?" the interpreter asked anxiously.

"Yes." Joe laughed. "And this beer might just last until we've finished."

They enjoyed themselves that evening for the first time since they had arrived, and even invited the interpreter to join them for a drink and listen to one of the Monty Python tapes. He soon gave up on the surreal English humour. He couldn't understand it at all. A few days later, they were told that the people in charge of the steelworks wanted to buy Stefoco's products and install them at Boatoa. The trials went well, home was beckoning and both men were delighted.

One thing had happened since all this began that took Joe's mind off China, at least for some of the time. On each occasion he wanted to alter his plane tickets and add days on here and there, he always used the same travel agent. He had got used to dealing with a girl named Rachel, and after a while he decided he liked her well enough to ask her out. They had been seeing each other for quite a while now, and Joe was even thinking about making it a permanent arrangement. Maybe if he got married they would stop sending him to Mao Tse Tung's homeland, and let him work around Europe instead. He knew the chances of this were slim, and he also remembered what had happened the last time he had tried to get engaged. Wait and see, he told himself. Don't rush into anything.

A few months later he and Tony were back in China, in an even more remote place called Wuhan. Joe did several presentations and went to meetings again with men from the Chinese Ministry then, as a reward, he and Tony were taken for a walk around the park. It wasn't much of a place, there were a few spindly trees and some patches of threadbare grass, but the locals seemed to be very proud of it. Each man was assigned an interpreter and Joe had drawn the short straw with his. She was very attractive, in her late twenties but with a most aggressive attitude. He could easily have lost his temper with her but fought against it. That was a sign of weakness in China, and he needed to keep on top of this lot. If they saw any chinks in the armour, they would soon stick the knife in to prise it apart.

"How old you?" she asked in her forthright and direct fashion.

"Forty-three," replied Joe.

"You married?"

"No."

"Why you not married?"

"Because I choose not to be."

"You should be married. I married."

"And where is your husband?" Joe had heard something about the way these things were organised under the communist regime.

"He in Tsing Tscho province, many miles away."

Joe had thought as much. "And how often do you see him?"

"He have two weeks holiday every year."

"So it takes him two or three days to come here and the same to go back. You have one week a year together." Joe turned to her with triumphant gleaming eyes. "So why are you married?"

The woman didn't know what to say to this, and Joe could tell from the look on her face that she was very angry indeed. He had soon learned from coming here that the so-called inscrutable Chinese didn't exist. Joe walked away from her, leaving her to her own frustrations and he to his. He had just made up his mind about something. When he got back to England, he was going to ask Rachel to marry him.

He mulled over this decision as he was released from his labours and headed off to Hong Kong for a couple of days. The Chinese New Year was in full swing, and the harbour was lit up with more fireworks than Joe had ever seen. He was taken back to his childhood as he watched the display, remembering the celebrations on V.E. night at the end of the Second World War when he had been nine. His father had queued for hours to get a box of thunderflashes and golden rain for the street party, and watching the bright unusual colours may well have sparked his interest in chemistry.

The next day, as he was riding on the Star Ferry from Kowloon to Hong Kong island, he thought about Rachel again. Yes, it was time he was married, and she was a nice enough woman four years his junior. Suburban life and children. That would be better than buzzing about all over the world alone.

He got back to England on a weekend, so had a chance to get over the worst of the jet lag and see Rachel. He broached the subject of marriage in a casual way and was soon glad he had, when she laughed and told him she didn't ever want to be anyone's wife. He had managed to pick another woman who didn't mirror his feelings and despaired of ever finding one who did. Once again he determined to throw himself into his work. At least that never let him down.

As Joe's mind came forward in time to 1982, he realised his plate was empty and so was his glass. Enough of the past. Time to forget his troubles and take his place in the varied pub banter with his friends. Women and work could take care of themselves for a while.

When he went into his office on the following Monday, he was in for a terrible surprise. The Technical Department, along with its valuable research and development programme, was going to be closed by the men in suits. By the end of the week Joe was out of a job. Made redundant with no notice, clear your desk and disappear. While he was getting over the shock, he remembered he had a few contacts that might be able to point him in the direction of another job. Also, if need be, he could sell his big house in Walsall and move to something smaller. His original plan of filling the house with a wife and children had come to nothing, why bother to hang on to it? It was far too big for one man who was hardly ever at home.

The next day he rang everyone he knew and ended up with two suggestions, one of them in America. He couldn't stand the thought of working for Dick Vogel, so took the other job in an offshoot company just outside Sheffield. There would be no more foreign travel and the money was less, so his idea of moving to a smaller property stayed with him as he daily made the seventy mile journey to his new employment.

By the time the first month was over he had decided he wasn't keen on this job at all, but it would have to do for now. The management treated him like an idiot, completely disregarding all his previous knowledge and experience. All Joe could do was take a deep breath and ignore their degrading treatment of him, but this didn't come easily, he didn't suffer fools gladly.

Most weekends he escaped his troubles and frustrations by visiting Aldermarsh to fish, drink and generally wind down. He had always been fond of the village, the locals were friendly and the pubs were good. There were enough shops and other facilities to keep the residents self-sufficient but there were also decent sized towns within easy reach. The more Joe thought about it, the more it seemed like the ideal place to live. He had friends here too, so it wouldn't be much of a wrench to leave his home town.

While he was in the pub he pinched the property section of the local free newspaper, and studied it avidly when he got back to Walsall. The following Saturday brought him on a double mission to Lichfield, to visit several estate agents, then later a curry at his favourite Indian restaurant. Both undertakings went well, he had several viewings arranged and the curries at the Indus tasted as good as ever. The restaurant had suffered from a name change and some bright modern decor, but otherwise the haunts of his youth were about the same.

Joe settled on a two bedroomed bungalow in a quiet street. It was plenty big enough for one person, as it seemed that destiny had decided he was going to spend the rest of his life alone. He swept all thoughts of this description from his mind as he saw the bungalow again and put in an offer. Aldermarsh was a forty minute drive to Walsall so he could easily still see his family. It was also closer to his unfulfilling job, but how much longer he would keep that on he didn't know.

Three months later it was all done and dusted and he was moving into Aldermarsh. He had done well on the sale in Walsall, and had invested most of the money to provide future income. Now he only had one decision left to make, when exactly he was going to become a gentleman of leisure.

CHAPTER TWENTY-TWO

Alice's thirty-first birthday was fast approaching, and she had very mixed feelings about her life. Thanks to Fran's vigilance, she now had a part-time job as secretary to a visiting orthopaedic surgeon, but her home life hadn't improved any. She had let her mother railroad her into something she had never wanted because she had been feeling extremely vulnerable, but the fact remained that Alice had stood back and let Madge take over, all in the name of her knowing what was best for her daughter. Alice knew she should have had more courage to tell Madge to get knotted, but she had been brought up to be obedient. It was second nature to her, and now Stephen had got her doing exactly the same. Everyone had been telling her for years how useless she was, and she almost believed it. Thinking for herself had nearly gone out of the window, but not quite.

She was feeling very dissatisfied as she got ready to go to work on the morning of her birthday. Stephen had already left at eight-fifteen. He had taken to going into work early quite a while ago, but all this meant was he had no idea that Alice was now at the hospital five mornings a week instead of two, and had been for some time. All the secretaries were part-timers, which was fine as it allowed Alice enough time to do all the other things she was expected to do at home during the week as well. The drawback was the money. At this rate it was going to take her for ever to save up enough to be able to leave. How she was ever going to afford somewhere to live, she had no idea.

Disgruntled, she put on her coat, grabbed her work handbag and set off for the hospital, a half hour walk from the detached house she shared with Stephen, wishing, and not for the first time, that she never had to come back here. All she had done with her life was turn into a miniature version of Madge, and that was the one thing she had always vowed not to do. At least she hadn't been pressurised into joining any of her clubs, but now she was getting older she was becoming a bit worried and felt that she might get sucked into other things she didn't want. Fortunately she had her job to drag her out of any black holes that were forming on the horizon, but she was more aware of her age lately and knew she didn't want to spend the rest of her life like this. Stephen still insisted on accounting for nearly every penny. There was no way Alice could sneak real money out of the house, he would clock it straight away. No, patience was needed but this was wearing thin. She despaired of ever getting out of this dark depressing house and into something more cheerful.

She finished work at one o'clock and as she was reaching for her coat, Fran appeared at the office door and stopped her.

"Not going straight home, are you?" she asked with a mischievous twinkle in her eye.

"No, I thought I'd do a bit of shopping."

"What about a Chinese? Our treat." Fran turned as the other secretaries arrived and brought out cards from behind their backs and chanted 'happy birthday' in unison. Tears prickled at Alice's eyes as Fran continued. "You thought we'd forgotten, didn't you?"

"Yes." Alice nodded, one stray tear rolling down her left cheek.

"Oh, Alice." Fran hugged her affectionately. "Come on, let's go to the Mandarin. I want to see you use the chopsticks, I still haven't got the hang of them."

"Okay." She smiled at all four of them as she happily opened her cards and put them on her desk.

"What did Stephen get you?" asked Fran as they all left the office on the first floor of the building.

"Just a card," said Alice quietly. "We don't do presents. He says they're a waste of money."

"Ruddy skinflint," replied Fran. "You can tell he works in a bank."

Alice spent a very enjoyable hour or so in the company of the other secretaries, and it more than made up for the lack of attention at home. When she got back she found hand-delivered cards from Madge and Doreen, but other than that the day had been a non-event as far as the family was concerned. Alice didn't know why she had expected anything else, it was always like this.

"I can't go on like this," she murmured to herself. "Oh, please God, let something good happen soon."

While she was waiting for this to arrive the weeks went by, and before she knew it, Harry was coming home for the Christmas break from school. She would have the pleasure of his company for two whole weeks, and was worried about her job. How was she going to keep all the extra hours under wraps? And who was going to look after him while she was out?

When Harry arrived home, Alice found her problems had been solved for her as he was sent round to stay with Doreen. Alice actually didn't mind one little bit, Harry hardly knew who she was anyway, and it seemed that Stephen was as determined as ever to keep him away from her bad influence. Alice had long since given up, switched off and let it all slide elegantly over her head.

On the following Monday, Alice was invited round to her mother's for coffee, and was somewhat surprised to see Harry was there. He all but ignored her, and she was half expecting him to ask her who she was. He managed a less than half-hearted hello and Alice gave the same back.

"Doreen's had to go out," Madge explained with a beaming smile. "So Harry said he wanted to come to see me. Didn't you, darling?"

Harry didn't answer and Alice didn't blame him. "Shall I make some tea, Mum?" she said to break the silence.

"No, coffee, Alice. Your tea's awful."

"Yes, Mum."

Alice disappeared into the kitchen and took her time, wondering how long it would be before she could make her escape. She could hear Madge asking Harry all about his life and friends at school. To begin with his answers were mono-syllabic, but after a while he responded and soon laughter was coming from the lounge next door. Alice decided to leave them to it for a while. Madge would be revelling in talking to her golden boy, and Alice suspected she would use this to score some points over Doreen. She was the favourite grandmother, and Alice knew Madge would fight this tooth and nail and do anything to win Harry's favour. All this when she was supposed to be Doreen's friend.

"Harry's coming Christmas shopping with me tomorrow." Madge greeted her as she returned with a tray of crockery. "You don't want to come, do you?"

Realising this was far from an invitation, Alice smiled sweetly before she answered. This was all a little worrying, she was picking up Madge's traits.

"I can't, I'm at the hospital tomorrow."

"Oh yes, Tuesday is one of your days, isn't it?" Madge looked delighted at the discreet refusal. "So Harry, shall we go into Birmingham on the train?"

"Oh, yes please, Grandma."

"That's settled then." Madge beamed at him. "I'll come round at ten."

"Oh." Harry didn't sound so sure now. "Ten?"

"Yes, we've got so much to do, might as well make an early start." She eyed him a little mischievously. "We could always go earlier."

"No." He looked panic-stricken at this suggestion. "Ten'll be fine."

Alice turned away, as she couldn't hold back a smile and mentally wished Madge all the best with him. She could imagine what was going to happen now, Madge and Doreen would be in a competition to see who could spend the most money on him. Boarding school might be preventing him from being spoilt, but holidays certainly weren't. Still, it got Alice off the hook. The grandmothers would be so busy fussing and faffing over him that they wouldn't notice her lack of attention.

Christmas edged ever nearer, and even Alice managed to whip

up some enthusiasm from somewhere to go shopping and plan meals. Boxing Day was the usual family get-together after spending an endless Christmas Day round at Madge's, despite the fact that it wasn't her turn. This was another way of getting one over on Doreen. Alice was aware of this but Stephen was apparently above such things, so it wasn't even worth mentioning it to him. Harry didn't help on Boxing Day by referring to all the things Madge had bought him, and displaying them to anyone who would pay attention. Doreen had a face like thunder, and Mr. Croft sighed every now and then. Madge fawned over Harry, while Geoff sat quietly in the corner eyeing the newspaper on the sideboard. Stephen tried to make small talk with the other men but didn't really succeed, and halfway through the afternoon they took themselves off down the garden for 'a look around'.

Just over a week later Harry went back to school, and Alice could heave the most enormous sigh of relief. Now she could get back to normal, which was being bored stiff at home and entertained at work. Halfway through January Alice and Fran worked out that they had enough flexi-time to each have a day off, so they arranged to meet up in the village where Fran lived. Lunch in one of the pubs was the real aim of the game, but Fran suggested they have a walk around first to show the village off to Alice. Why, she didn't really know, but she enjoyed the excursion. The walk along the canal towpath was most pleasant, and they fed the ducks near the church as well. Then Fran led the way to the pub on the main street and led Alice inside.

"I've been here before," she realised, all sorts of unbidden memories and emotions coming rushing back to her.

"It's a popular pub," said Fran with a smile. "We get people from all over coming in here. Have you been here with Stephen?"

"You've got to be joking, all that stopped the minute we got married. No, it was …"

"Oh," said Fran. She knew all about Joe now. "Come on, let's find a table. It'll start getting busy soon."

"Okay." Alice followed her over to a vacant one by the cellar door and they made themselves comfortable. They had their meal, then sat quietly with a drink, letting the food go down and enjoying each other's company.

"I was thinking …" Fran began.

"Yes?"

"That maybe I should take in a lodger. The mortgage is a bit of a struggle and the interest rates have just gone up again." She turned to her companion. "What do you think?"

"It's alright in theory," Alice agreed. "But you need to get the right person. What if you get someone you don't like?"

"Yes, it would be better to have someone I know." Fran nodded. "That's why I thought it might suit you."

"Me?" Alice pointed to herself in surprise.

"You want to leave Stephen, don't you?"

"Well yes, but I haven't really thought it through …"

"Have a think about it," Fran urged. "You really would be doing me a favour. I'll have to charge you the going rate though."

"Of course."

"We get on well, don't we? I can see you now in my spare room, it's a decent size." She smiled. "Come round and have a look at it if you like."

"I will." Alice nodded. "It's about time I thought about actually making a move. I can't spend the rest of my life with him."

"What about Harry?"

"It won't make any difference to him."

"I suppose not." Fran sighed. "Like my daughter. She's living with her boyfriend now, so I've got the house to myself. I miss her, but I had no option but to let her go."

"Things never stay the same for ever," said Alice, then muttered under her breath, "thank heavens."

"Another cider?" asked Fran as she stood up.

"Why not?" Alice smiled.

While Fran was at the bar, Alice took the time to look around the pub. It hadn't changed much since the last time she had come here with Joe all those years ago, and she let her mind wander back to those happy carefree days when they had been together just beginning to fall in love. He was the only man she had ever had any kind of feelings for, and had always regarded it as very cruel of fate to separate them in the way it had. The fifteen year age gap hadn't mattered a jot to Alice, she was sure it wouldn't have been a problem, but he had made a decision and all she could do was respect it. Even though it had completely and utterly broken her heart.

Then Alice sucked in her breath as she looked at the two men who were standing at the bar having an animated conversation. One was slim and over six feet tall, but his companion was almost facing Alice. It was the smile, the same smile she had known and loved. He was older, of course, and his light brown hair was now going grey at his temples. His face was a little fatter, as was the rest of him, but it was definitely Joe. Her Joe.

"Oh my God!" she breathed aloud, feeling the colour draining from her face as she thought frantically. What am I going to do?

Fran came back, put the drinks on the table, then stared at Alice.

"What on earth's the matter?"

"That man at the bar …" Alice was still looking at him.

"The tall one? That's Ian, he's lived here for years."

"No, the other one."

"I don't know him."

"I do."

"Blast from the past?" Fran smiled.

"Very definitely. That's Joe."

"Joe? Your Joe?" Fran sounded amazed. "Oh my!"

Both women fell silent as each of them wondered what was going to happen next. They both stared at Joe and he must have felt eyes on him, because within seconds he had looked up and glanced over to where they were sitting. His eyes locked onto Alice's, and even from this distance she could see they were full of hurt. Alice didn't understand, why was he looking at her like that? He had ended it, not her.

Joe turned away and fumbled with his pint, and Alice continued to watch him in total confusion. Were they just going to gawp at one another, or should one of them make a move? Alice had imagined something like this happening so many times over the years, and now didn't know what to do. All she knew was, she couldn't let him go again. Perhaps things had changed. Maybe …

Alice made up her mind, it was now or never. This was her one chance at happiness and she had to give it her best shot. She had to find out what his circumstances were now. She completely forgot all about Stephen and Harry, this was her moment and all she could do was …

"Go for it," Fran urged in a whisper.

Alice walked towards the bar but Joe moved first, and hurried out of the back door, firing a pleading look at her as he went. She just knew he wanted her to follow him so she did, out into the beer garden which was understandably empty. It was the middle of winter.

Joe was looking at her now and he almost seemed angry.

"Hello," said Alice quietly. "How are you?"

"Fine," he answered stiffly. "You?"

"Yes," she replied automatically. "No, that's a lie." This wasn't the time for small talk. "Lousy is nearer the truth, has been for years. Oh God, I've missed you so much!" Alice couldn't help it, tears were filling her eyes and all she wanted to do was throw her arms around him. And hold him for ever.

"So you're not happy with the boy from three doors down?" The starts of a smile were playing about his lips.

"No." Alice could feel tears escaping from her eyes now. Then she looked up at him sharply. "How did you know about Stephen?"

"You told me," he said patiently. "In your letter."

"Letter? What letter? I never wrote you any letter." Alice bumbled. "What about the one you sent me? Saying the age gap was too wide and that it'd never work?"

"I didn't write to you, Alice."

"And I didn't write to you either."

They stared at each other for several seconds as both of them tried to work out what had happened. Then Alice gave the verdict for the two of them.

"Mum," she said flatly. "It must have been. She's the only person I know who's capable of something like that."

"Do you really think so?" Joe looked dumbstruck.

"She was always banging on about me marrying Stephen Croft," said Alice bitterly, seeing Madge's face in her mind's eye and wishing she could beat it to a pulp. "She got her own way, she always does. It must have been her, it's the only explanation."

He nodded back. "I've still got the letter, I'll never get rid of it. Oh, Alice." He stepped forward, reaching out his hands to hers.

"Joe," she breathed as she flung her arms around him and hugged him for all she was worth. He felt so good and smelled so familiar. Feelings that she hadn't experienced for ages flooded through her, and she never wanted this moment to end. Then it got even better as his lips found hers, and they kissed for the first time in years yet it was just as Alice remembered. And endlessly fantasised about.

They stayed in each other's arms for quite some time, murmuring to one another in between kisses, but eventually they let go and stood looking at each other, both trying to forget all the events of the past years.

"What do we do now?" Joe asked quietly.

"Well, I know what I'm going to do. I've been thinking of leaving Stephen for quite a while, and I've just got the offer of a room in a friend's house. That's about all I can afford anyway. That is," she smiled at him happily, "if you want us to be together?"

"I do," he said, so seriously he could have been in church.

"Good." She hugged him again. "Come and meet my friend, Fran. She's the one I'll be living with."

"Where?"

"Here in the village, she lives in the road at the back of the pub."

"Alice, that's wonderful." Joe's eyes lit up. "Guess where I'm living now? I'm in the village too, just around the corner!"

CHAPTER TWENTY-THREE

Alice sailed through the next week in seventh heaven and on cloud nine both at the same time. Suddenly everything seemed to be going right for her. She had the man she loved, had always loved, within her grasp and a new place to live, all in one fell swoop. It was unbelievable, but she believed it. Now all she had to do was tell Stephen she was leaving, but she didn't see him raising much objection. They had behaved like strangers sharing the same house for years. And then there was Madge. Alice decided she wouldn't say anything to her. Why should she bother? Madge had always treated her like a nuisance that was in the way, and try as she might, she couldn't forgive her for that. She didn't think she ever would.

She had forgotten all about her mother until Joe rang her at work. It felt like the good old days when she had been at the General, and his warm deep voice made her shiver with excitement.

"I'll come over tomorrow after work," she said. "Got to have coffee with Godzilla this afternoon."

"Your mother?" Joe laughed. "Okay, enjoy yourself."

"Oh, very funny." She grimaced at the mere thought of it.

Coffee with Madge came and went as they observed all the necessary niceties. Alice had learned one useful thing from her mother, and that was how to survive such encounters without going totally insane and tearing her hair out. This and dealing with some of Stephen's affluent and influential clients had taught her the art of small talk – bullshit even – which was very useful for handling people that she couldn't stand the sight of.

"I popped round this morning but you were out." Madge always sounded as though she was accusing her of something. "Today isn't one of your hospital days, is it?"

"No," Alice lied easily. She had become practiced at it over the years. "I went into town."

"What for?"

Alice had no idea why her mother needed to know this, apart from the fact she was being nosy, as usual.

"Something for dinner. The supermarket didn't have everything I needed."

"Supermarket indeed. You won't catch me shopping in one of those things. Give me the old-fashioned butcher and greengrocer any day of the week."

"Yes, Mum." Alice sighed, wondering if this woman would ever make it into the twentieth century when the twenty-first was knocking on the door.

"So what was it you needed that this supermarket hadn't got?" Madge was persistent, you had to give her that.

"An aubergine," said Alice wearily.

"What on earth do you want that for?"

"I've got a new recipe for shepherd's pie."

"With one of those foreign things?"

"Red wine too." Alice was beginning to feel mischievous. Might as well take the opportunity to get Madge revved up a bit.

"Good grief, that must be costing you a fortune! Does Stephen know about all this extravagance?"

"We've had it before and he liked it," Alice replied truthfully. "He told me to cook it again."

"Oh, I see." Madge didn't look so sure of herself now. "You always did want to experiment, I suppose he's got used to you now."

"I suppose so," answered Alice. He might well have done, but now he was going to have to get used to some changes. Alice was dying to tell her mother she was leaving Lichfield and going off to a new life, but she didn't. The less people who knew the better, especially Madge. She was sure to try to find some way to stop her if she got wind of any of this.

"What are you dreaming about now?" Madge demanded to know.

"Oh, just dinner," Alice lied happily. "It's a good recipe, I got it out of the library. Would you like it?"

"No thank you, dear," her mother said stiffly, and Alice could just see the look of horror on Geoff's face if he heard about red wine and aubergines. "I must see about dinner myself."

"Yes." Alice stood up immediately, recognising the beginnings of her dismissal. "I'll leave you to it then."

"Lovely to see you, dear." Madge smiled.

"And you, Mum." Alice flashed back at her one of those bright, jaunty smiles that they had both perfected over the years. She couldn't wait to get out of her company. When she was with her she felt as though she was turning into her, and one creature from the black lagoon was quite sufficient. Once she had moved she doubted whether she would see anything of her, and wasn't sorry. Thirty-one years of Madge was punishment enough, and she wouldn't have got that for murder.

Later she dished up the shepherd's pie, and again Stephen commented on how nice it was. She had never told him what was in it because he had never asked, but she could imagine his reaction if he knew. That reminded her, how many years had it been since she last had a curry? Even the girls from work refused to go for one. Chinese remained the favourite, just as it had been in Walsall. Curry always brought Joe to mind, and she wondered if she dare ask him to take her for one. She didn't think he would have any objection to that. All she had to do now was move.

"You alright?" Stephen's voice broke into her thoughts.

"Uh? Oh yes." She remembered where she was and dragged herself swiftly out of her reverie. "Just having a blonde moment."

"But you're not blonde." He looked puzzled.

"Oh, it's nothing. Don't take any notice of me."

"Okay." He looked relieved as he reached for the newspaper. Alice sighed quietly, wondering how long she would have to pretend to be reading her latest tome from the library before she could sneak off upstairs to the spare room. Soon she would be able to empty it of its single bed and wardrobe, and wondered if Stephen would notice. Probably not, he never went into her room anyway.

The next day after work, she caught the bus and got off in Aldermarsh at the stop close to the pub, where Joe was waiting for her. After one quick drink he said he'd show her his house, and Alice wondered if she would get shown anything else. He had always been the perfect gentleman in the past, so she doubted it. She had a feeling he was going to want to take his time. Even so, Alice's heart was in her mouth as they walked up the drive to his bungalow.

As he led her inside, the first thing that struck her was how light and airy it was, the complete opposite of her dark, oppressive prison. The whole place seemed so much more cheerful than Alice's home. She followed him through the hall and into the lounge, glancing at the other doors leading off the hallway. One to the kitchen, another to the bathroom and the other two well, she really didn't want to think about that.

Joe offered her some wine and she accepted a small glass. Then they sat together on the settee.

"To the future." Joe raised his glass to hers.

"To the future," she repeated happily.

"Yes, about that." He looked solemn now. "What are we going to do?"

"Well, I'm moving to Fran's then I'll see about a divorce. What about you? Didn't you ever get married?"

"Nearly, but it all fell through." He smiled, a little sadly, Alice thought. "Any children?"

"Just one." Alice could feel this was a serious discussion. Until now she hadn't really thought about the practicalities of the situation. She explained the state of affairs with Harry, that she had never been allowed to be a mother to him and Joe held her closely to him when her voice began to falter.

"No wonder you want out," he said gently. "Sounds like you should never have married him in the first place."

"I know." She sniffed. "I sort of got pushed into it. I should've been stronger and told Mum where to get off. Fran's offer is a life saver."

"If this is really what you want, then I think you should go and live with Fran for a while. Until we get things sorted out."

"Oh." Alice couldn't hide her disappointment as she pulled away from him.

"Just until things cool down," he explained. "There's bound to be a reaction within your family. It'll look better if you're with a friend."

"You're right," Alice realised. "And I did promise."

"It'll give you breathing space and time to think. I'll be here if you need anything, but I think it's better that I stay in the background for a bit. Anyway, once you've had your freedom for a while, you might change your mind about me."

"No." Alice was quite certain about that. "I've waited too long for this. I won't change my mind, but maybe you might. We haven't seen each other for a long time, we're bound to have changed."

"Let's take some time to get to know one another again." Joe slipped his arm around her shoulder. "And try to keep our urges under control."

"Must we?" She looked up at him hopefully.

"Only for a little while," he answered as his mouth came down on hers.

A week or so later Alice was ready to move. Her heart was in her mouth and she felt vaguely sick as she supervised the loading of the van, glad that it was Saturday morning and Stephen was out of the way at work. Her things looked lost inside it, the single bed, the small wardrobe, a box of records and a load of black bin bags. Was that all she had to show for all those years? It really wasn't very much, and about summed up her marriage. Hollow, empty and a complete waste of time. Time she couldn't get back.

On the dining room table she left the note she had written for Stephen, opened the envelope and pulled off her wedding ring. This was the only item of jewellery he had ever bought her. Her engagement ring had been an old Victorian piece of Doreen's that

Alice had long ago handed back, as it had been made clear that it was only being loaned to her. Her heart lifted as she closed the front door behind her and posted her keys back through the letterbox. Then she smiled at the van driver as she climbed in, trying to ignore the fear that was gnawing at her stomach. She was going off into the unknown. For the first time in a lot of years she had no idea what the future was going to hold, and she couldn't work out whether she was excited or scared stiff. It was a little of each, she guessed.

As they pulled out of the street the sun suddenly came out, and it seemed that the weather approved of what she was doing. Soon they were outside Fran's house and all her possessions were inside.

"Alright?" Fran looked anxious as she put one hand on Alice's arm.

"I dunno, I think so." Alice didn't know how she felt.

"Let's have a cup of tea to celebrate. Unless you'd rather have wine?"

"Not just now thanks, I feel light-headed enough as it is."

A few minutes later Fran handed her a brown mug, and they stood by the kitchen window looking out into the garden with its large lawn and overhanging trees. Alice took a sip, then thought of her mother. If she could see her at this precise moment, she would have kittens.

"Here's to your new life." Fran raised her mug and touched it to Alice's. "Are you seeing Joe later?"

"Yes, we're going for a drink and then a curry."

"Will you be staying the night?" Fran looked mischievous now.

"No, not yet," said Alice seriously, then tried to smile as she noticed the look of surprise on her friend's face. "No sense rushing things."

"Of course not. Here." Fran reached onto the window sill for a keyring. "Front door key. Come and go as you please."

"Thanks, Fran."

Over the next few days Alice settled into her new routine. Work, afternoons either with Fran or Joe, and most evenings in his company. She couldn't have been happier, until the day she saw a familiar figure marching towards her in the main corridor of the hospital.

Oh no, she thought in panic. Mum!

Fran was coming out of an office a few yards away as Madge stormed past her. She had never met Alice's mother, so to let her know what was going on, Alice greeted Madge loudly.

"Mum, what brings you here?"

"I want a word with you," said Madge angrily. "Just what do you think you're playing at?"

"Come on, let's find somewhere to talk." Alice threw Fran a warning glance as she steered Madge towards an empty waiting room. They sat on hard plastic chairs and Madge glared at her daughter. Alice had a fair idea of what was coming, and told herself to be strong. And not give anything away.

"Stephen showed me that stupid note you wrote him. Have you taken leave of your senses?"

"No," said Alice quietly.

"So what's all this rubbish about leaving him?"

"It's not rubbish, I've left. And I'm not going back."

"Oh Alice, don't be ridiculous, if there's a problem we'll sort it out. You can't just up and leave." Alice knew she was waiting for a response, so she made none. "Come along Alice, tell me, what's the problem?"

"I've had enough. I want out."

"You can't just walk out when things aren't going well. Look at me and your father. Nearly forty years we've been together."

"But are you happy?"

"What's that got to do with anything?" Madge looked genuinely puzzled. "Being happy doesn't come into it, being married is what counts."

"Well, I don't agree. And Stephen and I were a mistake right from the start."

"But what about Harry, oh Alice, the boy needs his mother."

"That boy doesn't need anyone, least of all me." Alice's temper was rising now.

"Oh Alice, how can you say that? Harry idolises you. He's like his father, he idolises you too."

"Oh yes?" Alice managed to sound as scornful as she felt. "That's why he never speaks to me, is it?"

"He's a busy man, he's got a lot of things on his mind."

"I'm sure he has, but I've never been one of them." Alice nearly laughed. "There's no point in us being married any more, it's been a sham from the beginning and now I want something else. I want to live a bit, and have some fun instead of being bored stiff."

"I want, I want, is that all you can think about?" Madge's eyes were flashing now. "You've got responsibilities, my girl. You can't have what you want, a good wife does what her husband wants."

"Oh, like you have, you mean?" Alice did laugh now. "Tell me when that was, I'm sure Dad'll be very interested to know."

"I'm not talking about me," snapped Madge.

"No, you're interfering in my life again. That's all you've ever done and I'm sick of it."

"Alice, how many times have I got to tell you? I know what's best for you."

"No Mum, you only ever wanted what's best for you, I never came into it. You've never been the slightest bit bothered about my feelings. And anyway, if Stephen's so concerned about me, why hasn't he been in touch?"

"He doesn't know where you are, dear." Madge sounded as though she was talking to a six year old. "None of us do."

"No, and I intend to keep it that way. But you found me."

"I remembered you do volunteer work on Tuesdays and Fridays," explained Madge. "I told Stephen, but he said it would be better if I spoke to you."

"What you mean is, he couldn't be bothered to have time off work to come and see me himself, that's how much he cares. Well, it doesn't matter because I don't have any feelings for him either, never have had and the sooner we can get divorced, the better."

"Divorced!" Now Madge looked horrified. "Oh Alice, no, please. There's never been a divorce in our family."

"Well, there's going to be one now," said Alice firmly. "So you'd better get used to the idea."

"I can't believe you're saying all these things. Has someone here been putting all these silly ideas into your head?"

"No, I thought of them all by myself. Contrary to what you've always told me, I do have a brain and now I've decided it's about time I used it."

"I would never have believed you could be so sneaky, Alice, and selfish too. You're only interested in yourself, no-one else."

"Really?" Alice turned to her with a wry smile. "I wonder where I got that from?"

If this had been a fencing match, they would have reached touché. The two women looked at each other, and both knew there was no answer to what Alice had just said. Madge was looking as though she couldn't understand where this strength had come from and Alice was feeling pleased with herself. She had finally given her mother a piece of her mind, but now she felt as if she really was turning into her. The thought was most unsettling.

"Anyway," Madge persisted. "Stephen does want to talk to you. We thought somewhere neutral would be best, so you're to come to my house on Saturday."

"Very neutral," Alice muttered, but she knew she had to see him. The sooner they got the details resolved, the better. Then she would be able to get on with the rest of her life.

"Will you come?" Madge looked serious now.

"Yes, we need to sort things out," Alice nodded. "What time?"

"Two-thirty."

"I'll be there."

"We'll see you on Saturday then," said Madge stiffly, then she walked away. Alice watched her go. She was starting to look old, Alice thought, then she realised she was only fifty-eight. It must be the way she dressed and did her hair. Unfortunately she was showing no signs of slowing down on either the sarcasm or the selfishness fronts, so all Alice could do was sigh. And turn up on Saturday.

She left the waiting room where the confrontation had taken place, and went over to where Fran had parked her car. She was sitting in it waiting for her, and started the engine as soon as Alice got into the passenger seat.

"That was my mum," said Alice unneccessarily.

"Come to talk you into going back?" Alice nodded. "I had the same with mine, despite the fact he'd had women all over the place. They never seem to want you to rock the boat."

Fran pulled off the car park onto the busy Birmingham road, and headed into the town centre. Alice turned her head quickly towards her friend as she noticed Madge striding angrily along the pavement and hoped she hadn't seen her. She doubted she had, she wasn't the most observant of people.

"And you told her …?"

"That I want a divorce."

"You didn't tell her about Joe?"

"Heavens no, she doesn't need to know about that, it'll just complicate matters. I'm going to see Stephen on Saturday, we'll have to talk things through."

"Just be strong and stick to your guns," Fran advised.

"I will. I've done the hardest part, actually making the move."

"How do you feel?"

"Guilty and a little sick. All the time."

"That's just how I felt," Fran said. "But it'll pass. The main thing is are you sure you're doing the right thing?"

"Oh definitely. I've no doubts at all."

"Just remember that. Particularly on Saturday."

CHAPTER TWENTY-FOUR

Since Alice's bombshell, life in the cul-de-sac had gone on pretty much as usual, which meant quiet, dull and uneventful, but Madge liked it that way. No nasty surprises, no fun and games, in fact, nothing spontaneous at all. Geoff never said "come on, let's throw together a picnic and go out for a drive up to Derbyshire." He wouldn't dare. Madge had worked very hard to get everything her own way and she liked things methodical, tidy and predictable, and anything that threatened to disrupt her daily routine wasn't tolerated.

Alice was now in the doghouse after her announcement that not only did she want to leave Stephen but she also wanted a divorce. The very idea! Madge was horrified, while at the same time vaguely wondering why she hadn't thought of doing it herself. She knew why, she had been a kept woman all her married life and didn't know how to do anything else. She wondered how Alice would manage for money, then dismissed the thoughts as irrelevant. This was never going to happen, Alice would reconsider once she had thought it through. She would soon be back with her tail between her legs, once she realised she couldn't cope on her own, begging Stephen to take her back. He would, of course, he couldn't manage without her either.

The meeting she had arranged wasn't until Saturday, and in the days in between Madge thought things over. At the moment she was sitting in her comfortable armchair, the best one in the house, with her crocheting on her lap, a pot of tea on the occasional table and the cake and biscuit tin at her right elbow. Thinking was hungry work, so every now and then she allowed herself a nibble, first in one tin then the other. Only little ones mind, so that they wouldn't spoil her diet. Doreen had talked her into joining the Slimmers Club, and so far she was doing better than Madge at losing weight. Madge didn't like being outdone by anyone, especially not her best friend, so was making a concerted effort to be good. Not today though, she had too many things to mull over.

Her hand dipped into the open biscuit tin without her even noticing, as she brought to mind her family that she hadn't seen for years. Her grandmother had been a predominant influence on her, but even her guidance had let her down. Put up with things, had been the last advice she had given Madge, and that wasn't good enough. Flossie had passed away quietly shortly after Alice had got married, but Madge hadn't been upset in the slightest. As far as she was concerned, the interfering old woman had ruined her life, steered her in completely the wrong direction and failed her at every turn. No wonder Eliza hadn't liked her.

Madge sometimes wondered how her parents were getting on. They would be well into their seventies by now. The only contact was the occasional Christmas card, which she usually kept well hidden. Her parents had always been an embarrassment. Easier to pretend they didn't exist.

These thoughts led her onto her brother, Fred. Madge well remembered the day he had announced he was joining the Merchant Navy, and recalled how relieved everyone had been. He had taken to it like a duck to water, and as he was a very good-looking young man, Madge could imagine him as the archetypal sailor with a wife in every port, as well as the one he had back home in Southampton. They had a huge house they couldn't afford, there was never any food in the fridge and another pregnancy seemed to occur after nearly every trip home by the errant husband. Madge found herself wondering why Fred had come to mind, then realised the reason. Alice. She must have inherited some of her uncle's bad behaviour, it was the only explanation. Now she came to think about it, Alice even looked a little like Fred.

That explains such a lot, Madge thought as she crunched yet another digestive biscuit. That girl's always been trouble, now I know why. At least it isn't my fault, nobody can blame me for this latest outburst. Comforted by thoughts of this kind, Madge chomped her way to the bottom of the biscuit tin, then a huge wave of guilt swept over her.

"Damn," she said aloud as she realised it was empty. "Now Doreen will beat me on the scales again this week. This is all Alice's fault, making me worry like this."

Saturday came round at last, and Madge tidied up the dining room in readiness for the meeting. Doreen had wittered on at Slimming Club, but Madge had tried to ignore her. She was mortified that her daughter could have put her in this position, and she did her best to reassure Doreen that it was just a flash in the pan, a minor blip and nothing to worry about. Madge tried to believe her own words as two-thirty ticked around slowly on the living room clock. Lunch had been over an hour ago and after it, Geoff had tried to do his usual trick and slope off down the garden, but Madge hadn't let him.

"You can do that later," she said sternly. "This is very serious, and we should both be here when they arrive."

"It's got nothing to do with us," Geoff pointed out.

"Don't be ridiculous, it's got everything to do with us. You don't want her getting divorced, do you? What would everyone say? How would that look at work?"

"I wouldn't bother telling anyone." Geoff shrugged his shoulders as though none of this mattered, and Madge's nostrils flared. "It'd be different if it were you and I but it's not, is it?"

"It's our daughter. Our only daughter. Oh, the disgrace."

"Madge, lots of people get divorced these days."

"Not in my family." She shook her head determinedly. "Over my dead body."

Geoff muttered something that she didn't catch, so she threw him one of her special death stares. He didn't even bother to look up as he reached for the newspaper that he hadn't had a chance to browse through today. Madge tutted as she despaired of him. He just didn't understand.

At five minutes before the appointed time, Stephen arrived. He looked just the same as usual, crinkly blond hair, a smart suit and well polished shoes. He always put Madge in mind of an old-fashioned painted wooden soldier, he had about as much charisma as one. She opened the front door accompanied by one of her bright smiles, ushered him inside and asked if he would like a cup of tea.

"No, thank you." He looked down his nose at her, rather disdainfully, she thought. What had he got to be so superior about? "All I want to do is speak to Alice."

"Yes." Madge had almost forgotten that was the whole point of today. "She should be here any minute."

"Oh, she hasn't arrived yet?"

"I did tell her two-thirty," said Madge. She was beginning to feel nervous.

Stephen glanced at his watch and tutted. Madge caught sight of the timepiece and raised an approving eyebrow. She would have to find out where it had come from, and use some of Geoff's money to buy him one just the same. She was all for keeping up with the Joneses. She showed Stephen into the dining room as the clock in the other room chimed the half hour. Thirty seconds later the doorbell rang, and Madge gushingly excused herself to answer it.

"You're late," she hissed at Alice, who was standing there looking very cool, calm and collected.

"No, I'm on time."

"Stephen's been here ages." Madge stepped aside to allow her to enter. "In the dining room."

"Okay," Alice said with a sigh, crossed the hall and pushed open the door.

Madge closed the front door wondering what had happened to 'yes, Mum.' It never occured to her that the girl might actually have grown up and learnt to think for herself. Alice had never really got past the age of about twelve as far as both she and Geoff were concerned. That reminded her, he was in the living room. At least, he had better be.

She filled the kettle, switched it on, then went to find him. He was safely hidden behind the Daily Telegraph, behaving as though today was the same as every other day. Madge despaired for the thirty-millionth time in her married life. Geoff didn't react to anything, least of all a crisis.

She made a pot of tea, hearing subdued voices coming from the dining room. Alice had stupidly closed the door behind her, so now Madge couldn't hear any of the conversation that was going on between them. That girl never could do anything right, at least that hadn't changed. She took the tea into the living room, placed the tray on the table and told Geoff she was going to leave it to mash.

"Don't get listening at keyholes," he said from behind the paper. "It's got nothing to do with us. Leave the youngsters alone to talk."

"Oh you." He obviously knew her very well, better than she had realised. "How can we help if we don't know what's going on?"

"We help when someone asks us to. Otherwise we keep out of it."

"You sound just like Doreen, that's all she can come up with too."

"She's quite right. Leave them alone to sort things out. It's their life."

"Huh!" Madge was not impressed at all with this statement. It was not their life at all, it was hers. This was affecting her more than anyone else, why could Geoff not see that? The man was useless, always had been.

Madge took absolutely no notice of his advice, and slipped from the room into the hall. Then she crept back into the kitchen to fetch a drinking glass to hold against the dining room door; she had seen this listening trick on a trailer for a film she had once accidently seen.

"We had an agreement, Alice." She heard Stephen say. Immediately her curiosity was aroused. She had never heard anything about an agreement. "And now you've broken it."

"The arrangement worked for as long as it worked," Alice answered calmly. "Now we don't need it any more."

"You mean you don't. I don't understand you, Alice, I thought you were happy with the way things were."

"It was alright for a while, but now I want to do something else. It's over, Stephen. It never really began."

"Your mother said you were talking about a divorce."

"That's right."

"That's out of the question, Alice. Have you any idea how that will look at work? You can't leave, I need you."

"You need someone to cook and clean for you and entertain your clients. Anyone can do that, it doesn't have to be me."

"You're my wife, Alice."

"I don't want to be your wife any more, I've had enough."

"All I've been hearing is what you want." Madge nodded in agreement from behind the door, and in the process nearly dropped the glass onto the polished parquet flooring. "What about my wishes? Don't they mean anything to you?"

"I'm sorry, Stephen, but I can't put up with this charade any longer. We've never had a marriage, except one of convenience. I've done everything you asked of me for all these years, but I can't do it any more. We've had a good run for our money, but now it's over. I wish you could see that."

"No, I don't see that at all. All I see is you being selfish."

"Oh, so I stay and be miserable for the rest of my life just to keep you happy, do I? Don't you think that's you being selfish?"

"It's worked alright up to now." Stephen sounded genuinely puzzled and Madge sympathised with him. She didn't understand Alice's attitude either.

"Oh Stephen, let's face it, we've just been going through the motions for years, and there's no point in it. We can talk about it until we're blue in the face but the fact is, my mind's made up. I'm leaving, I've left, and I want a divorce. It's time for me to do something else."

"But how will you manage? You'll need money. I'm not paying for you to live another life."

"I'm not asking you to. I don't want anything from you, Stephen, I just want my freedom."

"Freedom? That's ridiculous." Madge nodded enthusiastically, hanging tightly onto the glass this time. "What are you going to do with all this new found freedom?"

"Be myself," answered Alice confidently. "And live my life my way."

"I wish you could hear yourself. You sound like some idealistic teenager, but then, you always were immature."

"Yes, and you relied on that to get me to do what you wanted. Well, I've got news for you Stephen, I've grown up. Behind your back and while you weren't looking, but now I can see what a farce our marriage is and I'm not staying just to keep everyone else happy. Why the hell should I? I've got feelings too."

"Only for yourself, obviously. What about Harry? How do you think all this is going to affect him?"

"Not in the slightest, I wouldn't think. He won't miss me, he doesn't even know me. It won't make any difference to him."

"This conversation is a waste of time." Madge grasped the glass firmly and took a step towards the kitchen as she heard Stephen get up from the table. When he spoke next his voice was louder, so she knew he was moving towards the door. "I think we should leave this for today and speak again when you're in a more receptive mood. Let's go and thank your parents and go home, shall we?"

"Yes, you go home and I'll go back to where I'm staying."

"That's not what I meant, Alice. You're coming home with me."

"No, Stephen, I'm not. Will you please get it through your head that I'm never going back to that house. Yes, let's go and say goodbye to Mum and Dad then, go our separate ways. Like we should have done right from the beginning."

Madge shot into the living room as she heard the door handle rattle. She went straight to the teapot on the table, picked it up and reached for her cup.

"There isn't much left." Geoff turned over a rustling page. "I've drunk most of it."

"Typical. When my back's turned …"

There was a gentle tap on the door, then it was pushed open to reveal a very harrassed-looking Stephen.

"Is everything alright?" asked Madge as cheerfully as she could.

He shook his head slightly, then looked behind him.

"Come in, Alice." She obeyed wordlessly. "And what do you say?"

Madge noticed the look she gave him, and wondered what had been going on between them for all these years. Nothing by the sound of it, but what was wrong with that? All she had ever wanted for Alice was what she had herself, but it seemed that wasn't enough any more. Really, she didn't think she would ever understand this younger generation.

"Thank you for letting us talk, Mum, Dad," Alice said. "It's time I was going now. I'll see you sometime."

Before anyone could say anything, Alice was gone. Back through the front door and going off to wherever it was she had been hiding for the past week.

"Well!" Madge nearly exploded, then remembered that Stephen was still there. "Did she say where she's living?" she continued, more quietly.

"No." Stephen shook his head, still looking completely mystified. "She wouldn't tell me, said it was none of my business, I mean, I ask you."

"It's a pity she shot off so quickly, I was going to have another go at her. If you want to know where she is, you'll have to follow her from the hospital. She might be staying with someone from there."

"I suppose so," Stephen agreed. "But I can't spare the time from work to go off on wild goose chases. I'll hire a private investigator to find out."

"Oh, there's no need to go to all that expense, Stephen," said Madge gushingly. "I can do that for you, I'd enjoy that."

"Yes." Came from behind the newspaper. "Although I think …"

"Oh be quiet you, who asked you?"

"I think …" Geoff put the paper down now and looked at Madge

241

sternly. "Alice is much more likely to come back if you leave her alone for a while, let her realise what a mistake she's making. If you keep getting on to her, it'll just make her more determined to do the opposite of what you want. That's how she works."

"And how would you know how she works?"

"Maybe because she's more like me than you," replied Geoff calmly before immersing himself in the Telegraph again.

"Huh." Madge dismissed his comments as irrelevant. "What do you think, Stephen? You must know her as well as we do by now."

"I'm not sure I do. I didn't see this coming and I live with her. If she won't come home I'll have to hire a housekeeper, I can't run that house by myself."

"Of course you can't," Madge agreed happily. "We'll all get together and help you, Stephen. Me and your mum."

A quiet strangled chuckle came from behind the paper in the corner and Madge gave it a very special death stare, one that was designed to penetrate all the newsprint and strike the recipient stone dead. It didn't of course, that was too much to hope for.

"I'll find her and pile on the guilt for you," Madge promised, giving her son-in-law a warm smile. "We'll get her back, don't you worry."

"Thank you, Madge." Stephen looked relieved. "Let's hope we can get it done before Harry comes home again. I don't know what I'm going to tell him otherwise."

"We'll cross that bridge when we come to it. Alice always was a stupid girl, never knows when she's well off. And, as my husband so rightly pointed out, she takes after him."

"Well, I must leave you in peace now, I suppose." Stephen sighed. "Thank you for the use of your dining room."

"That's quite alright, Stephen, and if you need anything, just let us know."

"I will." Madge had no doubt that he would. "Goodbye."

She showed him to the door then watched him drive away, vaguely wondering why he had come in the car when he only lived a few streets away. Maybe he had been planning to take Alice off somewhere romantic to woo her back, but she doubted it. They hadn't even gone anywhere for their honeymoon. Madge liked Stephen, but sometimes even she despaired of him.

"Well," she said when she returned, "that didn't go very well, did it?"

"She'll come round," answered Geoff from the depths of the business section, "if you leave her alone."

"Leave her alone indeed. That just shows how much you know about women. If we leave her alone she'll think we're not bothered about it, and I can assure you, I am very bothered indeed."

"Yes, I know," Geoff replied, then added in a low voice that was barely discernable, "but for all the wrong reasons."

Madge glared at him again, but he never knew. She was deep in thoughts of her own. She had seen, or rather heard, a completely different side to her daughter today, one she had never experienced before. Only now did she realise that Alice wasn't a little girl any more. She had grown up without anyone noticing, and was now able to think for herself and do things her own way. She had developed an inner strength and determination, and Madge didn't know where this had come from. Alice was no longer the submissive little wimp that would do as she was told. No, somewhere along the line Madge had lost her grip on her, and all she could do now was try to get it back. Otherwise how was she going to hold up her head at Photography or the Gardening Club? And worst of all, what were her friends going to say?

CHAPTER TWENTY-FIVE

Alice, of course, had no idea of her mother's despair or that she was determined to find out where she was. Neither had she any inkling that this was going to take quite some time, but eventually the day came when she told Fran she had some things to do in town, and she would catch the bus home later in the afternoon. Once the meeting with Stephen was over, she had decided it was time she made her next move, so she made an appointment with a solicitor to see about getting a divorce. For one thing she wanted to know how much it was going to cost. She had a few hundred pounds safely put away in her building society account, but if she hadn't got enough, Joe had offered to help out. She had insisted that she would pay him back if this happened, she had had quite enough of being dependant on someone else for money, and was now determined to pay her own way. She had just had a pay rise which never hurt, and occasionally worked into the afternoon. She didn't get paid overtime, but she could have a day off when she had collected enough hours, so she and Joe could go out somewhere for the day. Sometimes they would go for a drive with a picnic, or long walks around the pretty countryside. Usually they ended up in a pub for a couple of drinks before spending time in his bungalow. Together, happy and alone.

None of this was even remotely on her mind as she sat in the solicitor's waiting room for her turn to come. This was worse than being at the dentist. She felt tense and nervous and her stomach was tied up in the most enormous knot. After a few minutes she was called in to sit on the opposite side of a big black desk that was littered with papers and folders. The man was middle-aged and looked rather severe, but when he spoke his voice was friendly and reassuring. She spent twenty minutes in his company, then left the office wondering what she had been so worried about. From the way he had described it, things should be quite straightforward and shouldn't take too long. Irreconcilable differences were the grounds she was going for, and she had enough money in the bank to pay for it. It would be worth every penny as far as Alice was concerned.

When she left the solicitor's office, she didn't take any notice of the woman who was standing across the road pretending to be looking into a shop window. Madge was wearing a headscarf and sunglasses despite the fact it was only March, and had borrowed a walking stick from Doreen so that she could bend over and get into the poor little old lady routine. She had been doing this every day for weeks, and had perfected it now. She could ill afford the time, but today it looked as though it was going to pay off.

Alice went to a couple of shops, then headed up the precinct to the bus station to catch the bus. She didn't use them very often, usually going to work and back in Fran's old banger of a car. Sometimes Joe picked her up and when he did, she always scoured the car park for signs of her mother. After all, she had caught her out once.

The bus ride took less than ten minutes and Alice got off at the stop near the pub, walked through its car park and down a short alleyway to the road where Fran lived. She met someone coming the other way, and knew there was a person walking slowly behind her, but she didn't take much notice of them except to think that sunglasses at this time of year were a little peculiar. She walked up to the house, her doorkey ready in her hand, smiling at the happily dancing daffodils in the front garden and wondering what she should have for dinner.

"So this is where you're hiding." An all too familiar voice rang out behind her. The key was in the lock, but Alice pulled it out again quickly. The last thing she wanted in Fran's house was her mother, nor any other reminder of the past.

She turned to look at Madge, who had now removed the headscarf and the glasses. Alice's eyes widened as her mother drew herself up to her full height of five feet nine inches and held the walking stick at a dangerously provocative angle, as though she was about to attack her with it.

"Hello Mum." Alice didn't know what else to say. Her pulse was racing and her heart was hammering against her chest. What was she going to do? And how was she going to get rid of her?

"Someone from the hospital, is this?" Madge waved the stick vaguely at the house. "That blonde girl?"

"Yes," Alice answered, realising that Madge must have been following her for quite some time. She could guess why, as well. She was here to try to persuade her to go back to Stephen, which was never going to happen in a million years. She wished everyone would just accept that and let her get on with her life.

"I thought there might be another man in the picture," Madge continued. "But then I thought no. You haven't had a whole lot of success with men, have you?"

"What do you want, Mum?" Alice asked, noticing that Fran had just looked through the front room window then pulled back sharply.

"Aren't you going to invite me in?"

"This isn't my house," Alice pointed out. "We can talk just as easily out here."

"Just as you like. I see you've been to a solicitor today, what did he have to say?"

"You know, this really has got nothing to do with you. But if you must know, I've started divorce proceedings."

"Well, I'm here to tell you that Stephen will fight you every inch of the way." Madge waved the walking stick again. "You've no grounds, he hasn't done anything wrong. It'll never go through, Alice, you're just making yourself look very silly."

"That's your opinion, everyone else has a different one." Alice wished her mother would just turn around and walk away. She was always poking her nose in where it wasn't wanted.

"Everyone I know thinks you're making a big mistake." Madge never did know when to quit. "And they're the people that matter."

"Your friends?" Alice laughed humourlessly. "No Mum, this is between me and Stephen, no-one else, and he's so worried he hasn't even tried to get in touch. Leave it Mum, we'll sort it out."

"I'm only trying to help."

"Well don't, we don't need your help. Please just leave us alone."

"You're doing the wrong thing." Madge took a step away from the house and Alice heaved a sigh of relief. "You'll regret this my girl, you just wait, you'll be sorry."

"Oh, go away," muttered Alice as she quickly unlocked the front door, slipped inside and pushed it firmly shut behind her. She soon joined Fran in the dining room and they watched together as Madge walked briskly away, back towards the bus stop and the cul-de-sac.

"How did she find you?" Fran wondered.

"I think she's been following me around. She knew I'd been to the solicitor today."

"What do you think she'll do next?"

"I don't know, that's what worries me. That woman is capable of anything."

"You'd better tell Joe about this."

"I will, I'm seeing him later. Oh, I wish people would leave me alone. Why can't they just accept the fact I've left?"

"It's strange, your mother seems to be a lot more bothered about it than Stephen," said Fran. "I wonder why?"

"She's only worried about keeping up appearances. Doesn't matter how miserable you are, so long as it looks right."

"I thought that sort of thinking went out with the ark."

"It did. Mum belongs to last century, except that she's too stroppy to make a good Victorian. Oh God, I hope the rest of the family aren't going to descend on me." Alice put her hand to her forehead. "I'm sorry Fran, bringing this on you."

"I didn't expect a clear run." She patted Alice's arm reassuringly. "Don't worry, I've been where you are. It'll pass. Things'll settle down."

247

"I do hope so."

"They will, you'll see." Fran smiled. "And don't forget, you've got Joe. He's the reason you're doing all this."

"I would have done it anyway, but having him around makes it easier." Alice smiled now as well. "Come on, let's have a cuppa then I'll get changed and go round to see him. He's sensible, he'll be able to see the wood for the trees."

"Yes, he's a nice bloke." Fran nodded. "You've got a good one there."

"I know." Alice felt happier now, thinking about Joe. All of a sudden she couldn't wait to get round to his house to throw her arms around him. When she was with him, her troubles dissipated into nothingness. It was almost as if the rest of the world didn't exist, and nothing could hurt her.

"Fran's right," she said to her reflection in the mirror later when she was upstairs in her room. "This will pass and when it has, Joe and I can get on with our lives without any interference from anyone else. Not Mum, not anyone. I shall look forward to that day."

An hour later she walked round to Joe's bungalow, and as they sat together on his settee, she wasted no time in telling him about her unwelcome visitor.

"She doesn't give up easily, does she?" he said. "Still, at least she didn't follow you here."

"She made some snidey comment about there being another man, but she doesn't suspect. She doesn't think I'm capable of pulling one."

"She ought to know better, considering we were together before."

"I know, but she only picks the bits that suit her, she's always been the same." Alice sighed. "Fran told me not to worry, but I don't want Mum to keep coming round causing trouble. For either of you."

"I can handle your mother. She'll be in tears by the time I've finished with her and told her a few home truths. I've met her sort before."

248

"I haven't."

"I've seen all sorts in the steelworks, and had to handle them well enough to get them to do what I want. Your mother doesn't frighten me."

"I seem to be getting better too, I'm not frightened of her now," Alice suddenly realised. "I don't much care what she thinks either, I don't need her approval on things any more."

"Good. She always was too dominant. I don't know how your dad puts up with her."

"Nor me."

"I believe a relationship should be a partnership, with neither person being in total control." He put his arm around her shoulder and pulled her towards him. "That's how it'll be with me and you, I promise."

"If we can get through all this."

"Of course we will." Joe kissed her on the forehead. "She broke us up once, she won't do it again."

"Oh Joe." Alice hugged him for all she was worth, again thanking her lucky stars that they had found each other once more. Now she had all these unknown things to look forward to, but none of it scared her. She just knew that while she was with Joe, nothing bad could possibly happen to her. Not even Madge's malicious influence could mar what they had. And if she tried anything, Joe could fend her off. Alice really had found her Prince Charming, her knight in shining armour. It didn't just happen in fairy tales.

"I've got an idea," he said once he had let her go. "Something that'll take our minds off all this." Alice looked at him quizzically. "How would you like to go away for the weekend?" He hesitated and she knew what he was thinking. "It's about time, don't you think?" he added, in little more than a whisper.

"Yes," said Alice breathlessly. It was time they shared a double bed.

"Long weekend in Paris?" he suggested playfully. "I know you've always liked France."

"I'd love to, Joe, but there's a problem."

"What's that?"

"I haven't got a passport," Alice hated to admit, then added sullenly, "never had any need for one."

"Oh." He looked surprised. "We'll soon sort that out, all we need is a form from the Post Office. Okay then, any suggestions?"

"There is one place I'd like to go, a village in Dorset called Ingelfield. My grandparents live there and I've never met them."

"How come?" Now he looked intrigued.

"It's a long story, but they're pretty old now. I'd like to see them before they …"

"Of course. And so you shall. As it happens, my mum has a flat in Weymouth, we can combine the two. Shall I organise it?"

Alice nodded happily. "I'll write to Ingelfield and tell them we're coming. They've asked me several times to visit, but Stephen would never …"

"You're with somebody sensible now," said Joe. "And we'll do lots of travelling. As much as you can cope with, I promise."

"Once I get my passport." She laughed.

"Yes. We'll go into Lichfield tomorrow, you'll need photographs."

"Okay." Alice was feeling excited already at the prospect of foreign travel. At last she could get out of England and see what the rest of the world was all about, something she had longed to do for years.

The next day was warm and sunny, and seemed to match Alice's mood exactly. After she and Joe had done what they needed to do in town, they went for a walk alongside Minster Pool near the cathedral, on their way back to the car park. All along by the pool were people feeding the ducks, picnicking on the grass or relaxing on park benches. This was a popular spot, and was well used by office and shop workers at lunchtime as well as shoppers and mothers with young children. Alice gazed wistfully at two little girls playing tig on the grass, then glanced up at Joe. He must have read her mind as he answered quietly.

"One day."

Alice made no reply, she felt awkward now but his words registered. She wanted children in this new relationship as well.

"Good Lord, it's Alice," she suddenly heard a voice say. A very familiar voice, the one that belonged to the creature from the black lagoon.

"Hello Mum," she said, swallowing hard in the process. She reached for Joe's hand and felt safer when she had found it. Then she realised her mother was staring at the man by her side. "You remember Joe, don't you?"

"Yes, of course," replied Madge. "I should have known, I suppose."

"Known?" Joe enquired politely.

"That there might be another man on the scene." Madge looked down her nose at both of them. "This is why you left Stephen, is it?"

"Actually no," said Alice calmly. "We didn't meet up again until after I'd made the decision to go."

"You don't expect me to believe that."

"I don't really care what you believe, Mum." Alice felt as confident as she sounded. "It's got nothing to do with you anyway."

"That's right," Joe said in support of Alice. "Alice is old enough to make her own decisions now."

"With a lot of help from you, no doubt." Madge turned her bile onto him now. "I never could understand a man like you wanting such a weak and wishy-washy girl like her."

"And you must have been very jealous to break us up like you did," Alice wasted no time in throwing back. Suddenly she didn't feel intimidated by her mother any more. She felt strong and able to stand up for herself at last.

"I don't know what you mean."

"The letters."

Madge seemed to hesitate. She stared at Joe, and Alice thought she looked as though she was mentally pleading with him. Seconds ticked by, then she finally answered.

"I'm sure I have no idea what you're talking about."

"Anyway, we must be going. Lots to do." Alice smiled at Joe.

They walked away with Alice's heart in her mouth. She was

half expecting Madge to call after her with some cutting remark, but no sound came from behind them. Maybe she knew she had been beaten at last and had given up? Alice hoped so but doubted it.

When they got back to Joe's bungalow, he went straight to his wooden filing cabinet that matched the rest of the furniture in the lounge. He drew out a white envelope, then handed Alice the contents. A single sheet of plain writing paper.

"Recognise the handwriting?" he asked as she read the letter supposedly from her to him back in 1971.

"It's hers."

"Your mother did send those letters to break us up, this proves it."

"But why? That's the thing I don't understand."

"Perhaps I can shed some light on that," he said quietly. "Remember when I came round to meet them?"

"How could I forget? They were so shocked when they found out how old you were."

"That might have been part of it."

"What do you mean?"

"There were a few minutes when your mother and I were left alone together." Joe reached for her hand. "When we were in the lounge and you were answering the door, do you know what she said to me?"

"Knowing Mum, I dread to think."

"She said, why was I bothering with a naive young girl like you when I could have a mature and experienced woman like her?"

Alice and Joe stared at each other as the awful truth sank in. Alice had never had any inkling that her mother wanted to steal her man from her, that thought would never have occured to her in a million years.

"Why didn't you tell me this before?" she wondered aloud.

"I didn't think it was important."

"This explains so much. Everything in fact. Good God, I had no idea she fancied you."

"I told her I wasn't interested of course, as nicely as I could, but she wasn't best pleased." Alice could visualise her face like thunder. "That's why she wrote those letters, it was pure jealousy."

"No," said Alice quietly, both hands clenching into fists. "It was pure malice."

CHAPTER TWENTY-SIX

A couple of weeks later, Alice found herself sitting in Joe's very fast blue car, speeding towards Dorset with her small suitcase in the boot. It was the same case she had packed for the honeymoon that had never happened, but she didn't tell Joe this fact. He seemed so accomplished and sophisticated, and this made her life up to now look totally insignificant. She could have been doing all this instead of enduring abject boredom with Stephen, and she knew she would never forgive her mother for deliberately splitting them up. She also knew she would never forgive herself either. All she could do now was try to make up for lost time.

Another thing she was now holding against Madge was her denial of her parents in Ingelfield. Alice had never mentioned this in her letters, but she got the impression that they knew anyway. It was Eliza that wrote to her and she came over as a warm and caring person, nothing like Madge. Alice could only hope her impression would be right. It surely couldn't be possible that the world was big enough for two Madges. She would soon find out, she realised, as Joe drove expertly and confidently down the motorway, then branched off onto a minor road to take them into deepest, darkest Dorset.

It was the middle of the afternoon when they arrived in Ingelfield, and Alice immediately felt at home. It was only a small village, about the same size as Aldermarsh, but it had more shops along the main street with old-fashioned fronts. Alice could almost imagine her mother growing up here amongst the grocers, the butchers and the ironmongers. Joe drove slowly through the place, knowing that Alice wanted to savour her first glimpse of it.

"Where have we got to go now?" he asked.

"Barnes Lane. Number seven. It's past the White Horse pub, on the left."

"Mmm," Joe hummed a few minutes later. "That looks like a nice pub, might have to call in there later."

"I'm sure that can be arranged." Alice laughed. "But for now you'll probably have to put up with a cup of tea."

"I expect I'll survive. How old are your grandparents?"

"Bert's eighty-one and Eliza is seventy-seven. And to think I've never met them. I don't understand my mother."

Joe made no reply. As they turned into Barnes Lane, Alice found herself feeling nervous. What if they didn't like one another? What if she couldn't think of anything to say? Joe pulled up outside number seven, and Alice immediately noticed the immaculate garden. It was large too, with colourful flower beds at the front and a vegetable plot nearly the size of an allotment behind. Alice led Joe up the path to the back door and knocked on it tentatively, wondering why it was already open. Perhaps it always was.

"Hello, I'm Alice," she said to the elderly woman standing in the kitchen. As she turned to look at her, Alice was struck by how much she didn't look anything like Madge.

"Of course you is." Eliza smiled. "Come in, my dear and I'll put the kettle on. And you must be Joe?" He nodded. "Welcome."

"Thank you."

"Sit down, the both of you. You must be parched, coming all that way. How's your mum, Alice?"

"Same as usual," said Alice quietly.

"Yes, she always did have ideas above her station. We were never good enough for her, you know. Haven't seen her for years."

Lucky you, Alice thought bitterly. Instead she said, "What a shame."

"Can't be helped, she lives a long way away now, but it's good to see you again, Alice." Eliza smiled at her puzzled face. "We saw you once when you was a baby. Madge come down on the train with you to show you to Flossie."

"Ah yes, Flossie. She was a big influence on Mum, wasn't she?"

"Oh yes, she hung on her every word. They were very alike, those two, always as thick as thieves. They thought I didn't know what they got up to, but of course I did. You can't keep nothin' quiet in a village. Bert said the best thing to do was keep out of it. Said it'd all come out in the wash. Which it did, of course."

"Where is Bert?" Alice had been dying to ask ever since they arrived. Eliza had made the tea now and was pouring it out. Alice was pleased to note it wasn't too strong like her mother's.

"He'll be down the garden. Said he wanted to dig some potatoes up for tea. He knows where the best ones are."

"How is he these days?" asked Alice. From Eliza's letters she knew his health wasn't the best.

"His legs ain't too good, but he keeps going. Says he's got to, else he'll seize up. He'll be in in a minute, he's looking forward to seeing you. He don't say much though. Never has."

"Bit like my dad. Mind you, he doesn't get much chance. Mum does the talking for him."

"That's why she chose him." Eliza smiled ruefully. "Nice man, your dad, but he never had no go in him. He'd been to grammar school, your mum was impressed by that."

"I know. She was furious when I failed the eleven-plus."

"She was clever enough to go, but we couldn't afford it." Alice nodded. Madge had told her this – in her own inimitable way, of course. "Think that's what started her off. She …" Eliza hesitated. "Never mind. At least she hasn't got you all posh."

"Oh, I could never do anything right, I was the big disappointment. Still, all that's over now. Joe's helped me with that."

"Good thing you did, finding each other again." Eliza smiled again. "That just proves it was meant to be, now you can be happy, Alice. There's nothin' more important than that. Your mum got it into her head that it was all about money and being posh. Lot of good that did her."

A shadow filled the kitchen doorway, and Alice looked up to see a tall slim man filling it. He was holding an old trug full of tiny potatoes. Alice stared at him, wondering what it was that seemed so familiar about him, and even Joe did a double take.

"Here we be, Eliza," he said as he handed her the trug. "And this is Alice, is it? She don't look nothin' like Madge. Not much like Geoff either."

"No, she looks like you, you silly old fool." Eliza laughed. "Anyone can see that. Come on, sit down and rest your legs. There's fresh tea in the pot."

"Champion." He smiled as he sank gratefully onto the spare kitchen chair, using the expression he had picked up off a friend back in Devises. Alice could hardly take her eyes off him. Nobody had ever told her who she looked like. She could see herself in Eliza too, they seemed to have the same sort of temperament.

They caught up on all the news while Eliza prepared a meal, flatly refusing Alice's offer of help. They were guests, she was told, and guests don't do nothin'. They had dinner, which was still called tea round these parts, then they were shown upstairs. They had been put in Fred's old room, which was bigger than Madge's single one. Alice hovered in the doorway of it, standing on the tiny landing, which was less than one metre square, with three doors going off it, imagining her mother's young life. Why she had been so almighty keen to leave it all behind, Alice couldn't understand. Yes, it was old-fashioned with the bathroom being downstairs, but it was warm, friendly and homely. Nothing like the place she had grown up in.

An hour after dinner Joe politely made their excuses, and they went out for a while to the White Horse. Eliza gave them a back door key in case they were late coming back, which they didn't intend to be.

"What do you think of them?" asked Alice as they walked down Barnes Lane towards the alleyway that would take them onto the road back into the village.

"Nothing like your parents, are they?"

"I didn't expect them to be. I think they're lovely, I wish I could have seen more of them when I was growing up. Might have made Mum more bearable."

"I'm sure it would."

"She seems to be ashamed of them for some reason."

"Too busy trying to climb the social ladder." Joe nodded. "But it doesn't seem to have made her happy."

"I'm sure Eliza can tell me loads more about Madge." Alice was feeling mischievous now. "Maybe she's got some deep dark secrets?"

"Don't get delving too deep. Let Eliza tell you if she wants to."

"Yes, I might find out something to make me hate her even more. If that's possible."

"You don't have to see her now, unless you want to," Joe reminded her. "She's dominated your life for long enough. Now you're free."

Alice agreed with him demurely, but in the back of her mind she knew full well that as long as Madge was drawing breath, she would never be free.

The next day all the old photographs came out. Alice was fascinated, but wasn't too surprised when, after half an hour, Joe said he needed some fresh air and went out for a walk.

"This is Flossie, my mother, you's heard some about her." Eliza was saying. "The one your mum takes after."

"She looks …"

"Hard. Yes, she was. No-one ever got the better of her. Knew everythin' about everyone and what she didn't know, she made up. She was the one what got your mum interested in posh things. She gave her this book. Your mum read it from cover to cover a thousand times."

Eliza handed Alice a battered and dogeared brown hardback. The gold lettering on the front was barely legible, but after a few seconds Alice realised it was about etiquette and belonged somewhere back in the nineteenth century. Suddenly a lot of things about her mother made sense. She had taken this book as gospel, followed its every instruction and turned herself from a simple country girl into the caricature that she now was. Grandmother Flossie had a lot to answer for.

"And this is your Uncle Fred." Alice was handed another picture.

At last, they were getting on to the rest of the family. She had seen a lot of Madge, Eliza and Bert so far. "He looks a bit like Bert too."

"Yes." Alice looked at the photo. So this was her mother's brother. He was a very good-looking young man with a winning smile, although now he would be in his early sixties.

"He was a bit of a tearaway in his youth, always into some sort of trouble with the other village lads," Eliza revealed. "Nothing really bad, but he was a worry. We was all quite pleased when he decided to join the Merchant Navy. He ended up on the Queen Elizabeth, you know."

"Where is he now?"

"Cross channel ferries. His wife Katie writes to me sometimes when she got time. They got six boys now."

"Crikey!" Alice whistled, not sure whether she felt envious or horrified.

"And this is your mum's best friend, Doris." Alice was relieved to see the pile of photos was going down quite quickly now. "She went off to America with a soldier, but she come back a few years later without him. She lives in Hinton now with her daughter. That's the next village along."

Alice nodded, although she didn't know where it was. This Doris looked a bit of a fast cat, and she could imagine her leading Madge into all sorts of bad ways with boys. Then she remembered her bit of mischief from last night and dared to ask Eliza the sixty-four thousand dollar question.

"Did Mum have any boyfriends before she met my dad?"

Eliza hesitated, so Alice knew she had. She looked as though she wasn't sure what to say for a few seconds, then she did reply.

"There was a couple of boys what was interested in her, but nothing come of it. Nothing for you to worry about, dear."

Alice knew she was lying, but she didn't pursue it. Perhaps it was better that she didn't know all the ins and outs of Madge's youth. Everyone tended to do some silly things when they were young.

That evening Eliza let Alice help her wash up after a simple but very tasty meal. Fresh vegetables straight from the garden seemed to taste so much better, and it was something Alice wasn't used to. She was sure the ones from her parents' garden should have been good. It was Madge's half-hearted cooking that must have ruined them. Without thinking, she made a comment to that effect.

"Oh, your mum was never interested in cooking." That came as no surprise. "She was good at sewing though. And crochet and knitting."

"Yes, she's won prizes for those. And photography. She belongs to all sorts of clubs."

"So she's got some nice pictures of you then?"

"Oh no, she was never bothered about that." Alice laughed. "She's got lots of ones of flowers and things. There's a few of me, I suppose. Somewhere."

"Selfish, always was," muttered Eliza. "Just like Flossie."

Alice made no reply, she didn't trust herself to. She glanced over at Joe, who had not long returned. He answered for her.

"We haven't seen much of Bert today."

"Ah yes." Eliza smiled now. "He's busy in the shed. He's making something for you."

It was as though he had heard his name mentioned. As Eliza spoke, he appeared in the back door with something in his hand.

"Got some tea on the go?" he asked.

"Haven't I always? Let's have a look." She took the item from him. It was a trug similar to the one he had used to collect the vegetables, only this was a brand new one. "Oh Bert, it's perfect. You's really on form today."

"Had to be a good one for my granddaughter." He handed it to Alice now. "Useful things, trugs. Hope you likes it."

"It's beautiful," Alice breathed as she answered honestly. "Thank you so much, Grandad. I shall treasure it."

"You got much growing in your garden?" he asked.

"Oh yes, lots of things," Joe fibbed. Apart from the lawn there were a few herbs and a clump of foxgloves, but there was no need for Bert to know that.

Alice and Joe spent another few days with her grandparents, then they left to carry on to his mother's holiday flat in Weymouth. Alice had been offered her pick of the photographs, and had taken one of Fred and several of Eliza and Bert. Young Madge stayed in the big brown envelope. Old Madge was enough to cope with.

On the journey to Weymouth, Alice thought back over her youth. Her mother had had the guidance of a grandmother, but Alice had experienced nothing like that. She still thought it was very unfair of her parents to deny her that contact. She would have loved to have been influenced by the two people she had just left. It would have helped to counteract the limited input by Madge and Geoff. That reminded her, shouldn't she have another set of grandparents somewhere? Now she came to think about it, she didn't even know where her father was from originally. Her only clue was his vague West Country accent.

I lived with them for all those years, she thought as the car sped southwards, yet I know absolutely nothing about them.

"They're like cardboard cutouts," she said aloud without meaning to.

"Who are?"

"My parents."

"Yes, very good description," agreed Joe. "But at least your grandparents aren't. They're real proper people."

"Do you know, I don't think I shall ever forgive my mother for saying she had no family. She might be ashamed of them, but I'm not."

"Will you tell her you've been to see them?"

"No way, she'll go ballistic."

"She's still influencing you, Alice. Be careful."

Alice wasn't sure how to answer that, so said nothing. He was right, she was still scared of Madge and her reactions. Things had been this way for so long that she couldn't imagine them being any different.

They got to Weymouth at lunchtime, and found a cafe to have a sandwich before walking back to the first floor flat just off the esplanade. On the way they looked around the harbour with its olde worlde pubs, admired the sand sculptures and walked along the beach. When they got back, Alice stood at the lounge window staring out over the large bay, wondering how to tell Joe that she had never been to the seaside before. He would think her such a fool, thirty-one years old and seeing the ocean for the first time. There were so many things about the world that she didn't know, and he seemed to have been everywhere. She hoped he wouldn't mind teaching her all about the places he had been to.

"You're very quiet, are you alright?" he asked.

"I'm fine." She turned to smile at him. "I just wish we'd come to places like this on holiday when I was a kid. I always got dragged off to somewhere in the middle of nowhere. Never by the sea."

"You've got plenty of time to make up for it." He stood behind her and put his arms around her waist. "I'll take you lots of places."

"Thank you, Joe." She put her head back on his shoulder, with the distinct feeling he knew this was her first sight of the sea. He seemed to be pretty perceptive, and she was so glad she had found him. Otherwise her life had been destined to be one long bore, with no pleasant distractions along the way. Just like her mother's. She had no idea how she put up with it.

"I've got a lot of catching up to do," she murmured.

"You certainly have." He kissed the back of her head. "And I've made a start, I've got our honeymoon place sorted out."

"Somewhere nice you've been?" she asked dreamily.

"Mmm. Bermuda. Prettiest little place you've ever seen."

"Bermuda!" Alice nearly exploded, then added quietly. "Well, it beats the Science Museum."

Joe gave her a gentle squeeze but made no comment. Alice had told him about her first honeymoon, although she had left some details out. There was no need to embarrass herself by telling him everything.

"Come on," he eventually said. "Let's go out for a walk. Nothing like a bit of sea air for giving you an appetite. Fish and chips later, is it?"

"I should think so, we are at the seaside."

"Okay." He let go of her and she turned to face him. Although he sounded casual, he looked deadly serious. "Time to let go of the past. It's fun time now."

"Yes," she breathed. She didn't have a chance to say anything else as he kissed her. After a minute he let her go then held her at arm's length and smiled.

"This is it then. The beginning of the rest of your life."

CHAPTER TWENTY-SEVEN

When Alice got back from her holiday, she found Fran had a message from Susan. She was home for a few days, and Fran had arranged for the two of them to meet her for lunch and a very long chat. Susan was now Sister Swallow, and had a lot of responsibility at the big hospital in Birmingham. She didn't get back to Lichfield very often, but whenever she did she always made up for lost time.

"I've got a boyfriend," she wasted no time in telling the other two.

"Serious?" Fran smiled. They weren't usually.

"Might be," Susan said enigmatically. "It must be catching. I've never seen Alice look so happy, so there must be something in it."

"If you get the right man," Alice pointed out.

"Oh absolutely," said Fran. "Alice is a different person now from when I first met her."

"So Alice, are you going to do the deed again?" Susan wanted to know. "Nip off down the Registry Office for a quick I do?"

"Might be," replied Alice in a very similar tone to the one Susan had just used.

"You walked into that one." Fran laughed, then leaned towards Susan. "I wouldn't be surprised if they do. I've put myself down as bridesmaid anyway."

"Ooh yes, and me, Alice."

"I might just keep you to that."

"You'd better," her friends chorused.

They all ordered their Chinese food, and didn't have to wait long for it to arrive. All three of them used chopsticks now and even the waitress looked impressed. She was far too polite to say anything though, she just put the plates down and walked away.

"How's the dragon, Alice?" Susan asked now.

"Godzilla? Dunno really, haven't spoken to her for a while. I'm still well and truly in the doghouse. I keep in touch with Dad though, by phone. Suppose I ought to go and see him really."

"Any news on your divorce?"

"No. Stephen signed the papers eventually, but I haven't heard anything. These things take time."

"He seems to think she'll go back," Fran said to Susan.

"Stupid prat."

"He hasn't got a hope in hell," Alice agreed. "Leaving him was the best thing I ever did, should have done it years ago. Really, I should never have married him in the first place."

"So why did you?"

"Oh Sue, that's a long story and I don't like dwelling on the past. I made a mistake and now I'm trying to put it right. The future is what matters now."

"Yeah, you and Joe and half a dozen kids."

"She'd better get a move on." Susan warned happily. "She'll be thirty-two in a couple of weeks."

"I'm working on it," said Alice. "Very slowly of course, I need the practice."

"She must be doing something," said Fran with a smile. "She's hardly ever at my place. She'll be wanting a reduction in rent if this keeps up."

"Good for you, Alice." Susan slapped her gently on the back. "You go for it, you deserve it."

Alice didn't know what to say, except mentally thank the heavens she had such good friends. Since she had met Fran her life had turned around, and everything seemed to be going right. She and Joe had discussed getting married, but knew they were going to have to wait a while for Alice's divorce to come through. Maybe by then he might have changed his mind, but Alice didn't really think so. It seemed that this time they had got it right, and having no interference from Madge only seemed to be improving matters. If only Alice had ignored her advice, then she wouldn't be in this mess. Still, it was too late for recriminations now. All she could do was carry on as she had been doing and concentrate on Joe. And look forward instead of back.

Over the next few days Alice got back into the routine of work. She didn't have her favourite clinic with this job. All the fractures were dealt with at the main hospital in Burton, where a new building had long since replaced the one her father used to work in. The house they had lived in had gone too. Alice never went to the town of her birth apart from the occasional shopping trip, and she hadn't been back to the scene of her childhood to see what was left of the place. Not much from what she had heard, and her childhood was also something she had no desire to relive. It had been bad enough the first time round.

The morning was taken up by typing letters from the previous clinic and answering the phone, much the same as when she was in Walsall. She still had many happy memories of the General, although she had been told that it had been pulled down to be replaced by posh apartments.

At twelve-fifteen she went down to today's clinic to take dictation for the next set of letters, and at just before one o'clock she returned to the office to collect her things ready to meet Fran and go home, another busy day at an end.

"There's been a phone call for you, Alice," Diane, one of the other secretaries informed her. "I've left the number on your desk, they said it was urgent."

"Oh, okay." Alice was annoyed, now she would have to keep Fran waiting. She looked at the piece of paper and frowned. The number looked familiar, then she realised it was the hospital in Burton. There was an extension number next to it, so she sighed and dialled, wondering what could be so important that it couldn't wait until tomorrow. After only a minute, Alice found herself through to one of the wards.

"This is Alice Croft," she said, puzzled at the whole situation.

"Oh good," the female voice said. "You are the daughter of Geoffrey Harwood?"

"Yes."

"We have him here on the ward, he's asking for you." The nurse explained. "I'm afraid he's had a heart attack, but he's stable at the moment."

"I'll be right there," said Alice immediately. She took some details then flew out of the office, her face ashen. Fran was just coming out of her office further down the corridor and slowed her step as she saw Alice's face.

"What's wrong?"

"It's Dad, he's in Burton. Heart attack. I've got to get over there."

"I'll take you, come on."

All sorts of conflicting thoughts buzzed around in Alice's brain as Fran drove down the A38 towards Burton. She had never imagined anything happening to either of her parents, and Geoff was only sixty-one. She remembered the last time she had seen him, which had been at the family conference, and he had seemed alright then. Alice didn't know what to think as they sped towards the well-signposted hospital on the other side of the town.

"I'll wait for you."

"No, it's alright. Honestly, I don't know how long I'll be here. You may as well go home and, oh, can you tell Joe where I am?"

"Of course." Fran patted her arm. "But you ring me when you want to come home, okay?"

"Thanks, Fran."

Alice found her way to the ward and introduced herself to the Sister in charge, recognising her voice from the phone call.

"Are you his only next of kin?" she was asked.

"No, there's my mother," answered Alice. "But they don't get on all that well."

"It might not be a bad idea to contact her, just in case."

She rang Madge from the payphone in the corridor, explained the situation then waited anxiously for her to arrive. This seemed to take for ever, and Alice wandered down to the coffee shop for a cup of tea to waste some time. She had been allowed one brief glance of her father, and had been shocked to discover he was in a room on his own with tubes and wires everywhere. She hadn't liked the look of him at all, but had been promised a full explanation when her mother arrived. After all, she was the primary next of kin.

Eventually Madge came marching down the corridor towards her, wearing her best coat and a face like thunder.

"I should have known you'd have to get here first. You two always did like ganging up on me."

"Hello Mum," said Alice carefully, telling herself not to lose her temper. This was hardly the time or place. "This way."

"If you knew the trouble I've had to get here. I couldn't find my handbag, the keys weren't in the basket and the buses, well …"

"I was lucky, I got a lift here," Alice said as she led her mother to the Sister's office.

"So," Madge challenged the nurse as soon as she looked at her. "What's all this nonsense about?"

The Sister looked taken aback. "Your husband has had a heart attack, quite a severe one, actually."

"Oh, he's just attention seeking again," said Madge dismissively with a regal wave of the hand. "He's always doing it, he's such a hypochondriac."

"Not this time, Mum."

"Your daughter's right." This comment earned a "huh" from Madge. The Sister explained what treatment Geoff had received so far, and told them of his future care. Then she led them both in to see him.

Geoff looked very small and insignificant lying in the bed, and Alice's heart went out to him as she sat quietly in one of the two chairs that had been placed by his bedside. Madge put her handbag on the other one, as she took in the sight of her husband and the machine he was wired up to.

"Well," she said. "This is a pretty state of affairs."

Geoff stirred slightly as he heard the voice, and Alice wondered whether or not to reach for his hand. No, better wait until he knew who was there, he might think she was Madge and Alice didn't think he would want to hold her hand.

"Hello Dad," she said instead.

Geoff turned his head to look at her, and managed a watery smile in her direction. Then the movement of Madge crossing her arms over her chest caught his eye, and he looked upwards with no smile at all. More an expression of weary resignation on his pale face.

"Madge," he said drowsily.

Alice glanced at her mother's belligerent face, then she saw a movement outside so discreetly went to the door. Her heart leapt and her stomach did a somersault as she saw Joe standing in the corridor.

"How is he?" he asked as she joined him.

"Stable they say, but he's very pale and weak. Mum's behaving as though he's making the whole thing up, don't suppose she'll do him any good."

"She just doesn't want to believe it, I suppose." Joe smiled at her, his face full of concern. "Anyway, I'll wait here until you want to go home. Don't worry, he'll be fine."

"Thank you Joe." Alice could feel tears of relief coming to her eyes at his supportiveness.

"You'd better get back in there," he advised. "Keep your mother at bay."

"That's easier said than done."

Alice went back into the side room to find Madge was still glaring down at Geoff, who appeared to be trying to shrink back into the mattress under her disapproving stare. Alice took her seat not knowing what to do or say, but it seemed her mother had no such problems.

"See, this is what happens when my back's turned and you go out for a drink with Henry Croft," she said. "Neither of you can manage without me to look after you."

"Oh Mum," Alice protested gently.

"I'm right though, aren't I?" She wouldn't back down. "All that gadding about going to the pub, and now look at you. Nice mess you've got yourself into."

Geoff closed his eyes, then glanced up at Alice with a pleading look on his face. Alice smiled weakly, and tried to think of something to shut her mother up.

"Why don't you get us all a nice cup of tea, Mum?" she suggested. "It's just down the corridor."

"I suppose that's not a bad idea. I'm parched after all that rushing about."

"Yes, I want a word with Alice," said Geoff croakily.

"Oh, I should have known." Madge picked up her handbag. "She's always been the favourite."

With that she swept from the room, leaving father and daughter alone together. Geoff stared at Alice for several seconds, a strange sort of mysterious smile playing about his very dry-looking lips.

"She always wanted a son, you know, never a daughter. I think that's why she's always been so ..." He hesitated. "But she tells me you're back with Joe. I'm glad."

"So am I." She tried to smile and not dwell on his first comment, which hadn't actually come as that much of a surprise. "He's the best thing that's ever happened to me."

"You look happy. You should have stayed with him and not married Stephen."

"I know."

"Your mother split you and Joe up, you know. On purpose, to get you to marry Stephen." Geoff coughed unexpectedly and made her jump. "She'll do anything to get her own way. Alice," he reached for her but the wires prevented him from moving very far so she took his hand instead, "I want to apologise. I should have said something at the time, stopped her from ruining your life. God, I'm such a weakling, I've always let her do what she wants."

"It's alright Dad, I survived. And I got him back."

"It was meant to be, you and Joe." Geoff smiled but it looked as though it was a struggle. "Be happy, Alice. And try to forgive me."

"There's nothing to forgive, Dad." She squeezed his hand carefully.

"Good," he breathed, then lay back on his pillows.

Alice continued to sit holding his hand as she fought down the conflicting emotions at his revelations. So he had known about the letters, and had kept quiet while Madge weaved her web of malice and deceit. Yes, he should have stopped her, but Alice knew he had never prevented his wife from doing anything she fancied. Eliza had been right about him.

Alice's thoughts were becoming darker and darker when she suddenly realised the monitor Geoff was wired up to had changed. A single pitched noise was now emanating from it, and she looked up at it in alarm. She reached for the button at the side of the bed and within seconds a nurse had arrived.

"He's gone," Alice was told moments later.

"No!" She choked on her own breath. He couldn't be, not her dad! She let go of his hand and stared at the figure in the bed. He looked as though he was asleep – but not quite. Something was definitely missing. The nurse left the room and Alice continued to gaze at her father, not knowing how she felt or what to think. Then she thought about Madge. What was she going to say when she found out?

The nurse had obviously gone to look for her, because a minute or so later they were back. Alice stood up as her mother entered the room and looked down at Geoff, a look of shock and total disbelief on her lined and wrinkled face. Alice decided it was time she wasn't there and slipped out of the room unnoticed, leaving Madge to say goodbye to her husband of nearly forty years, a long and very boring time indeed.

Alice found Joe was still sitting in the corridor, a cup of black coffee on the small table beside him. She joined him quietly, still half unable to believe what had just happened.

"He's ..." She could hardly bring herself to say the words. "He's dead."

Joe didn't say anything, just put his arms around her and pulled her towards him. Alice cried into his shirt for several minutes, then a shadow fell over them as someone else joined them.

"Hello, Mrs. Harwood," said Joe calmly.

Alice immediately tried to pull herself together before she looked up at her mother. Would they be united in their grief? Would this tragedy be the catalyst to them burying the hatchet once and for all?

"This is all your fault."

It seemed the answer was no.

Alice looked up at Madge sadly, wondering how Geoff's death could possibly be her fault. She should have known her mother was about to explain.

"All this nonsense about divorces, it's enough to make a person ill. I know you've been ringing each other, you two have always been the same. Dreaming up schemes to upset me and undermine my authority."

"And there was plenty of that from what I've heard." Joe couldn't keep quiet any longer.

"Be quiet you," Madge snapped at him. "Who asked you?"

"No-one." Joe stood up now and faced her. "Your husband has just died, and here you are having a go at the one other person who loved him. Don't you think you'd be better supporting and comforting one another?"

"Don't be ridiculous." Madge looked down her nose at him, despite the fact they were a similar height.

"Yes Joe, we both know that's never going to happen."

"He's right about one thing." Madge turned to Alice now, who was on her feet as well. "My husband is dead, and I blame you." She poked her viciously in the chest. "All that stress and pressure you caused brought on this heart attack. I hope you can live with yourself after this."

"You're going too far now," Joe had to say.

"That's right, stick up for her. She hasn't got the strength of character to do it for herself. I'm not surprised you're back together, you like weak women and she needs you to hide behind."

With that she turned and stormed off down the corridor, her footsteps echoing hollowly as she went. Alice couldn't hold her emotions back any longer and burst into angry and frustrated tears. Joe went back to her and embraced her again.

"Take no notice," he murmured into her short brown hair.

"Why does she have to be such a cow?" a muffled response came from somewhere within his jacket.

"She's in denial, it hasn't sunk in yet."

"No." Alice looked up at him now. "You don't know her like I do. She really does believe it's my fault."

"Only so she doesn't have to shoulder any of the blame herself. It's always easier to blame someone else. Come on." He handed her his handkerchief. "Let's go home. Curry tonight, maybe that'll help cheer you up a bit."

"Oh Joe." Alice's heart stretched as she felt even more love for him. "What would I do without you?"

"Dunno." He smiled his often knee-buckling smile. "And I don't intend to ever find out."

CHAPTER TWENTY-EIGHT

While Alice was coming to terms with what had happened, Madge was trying to do exactly the same. She had eventually got back to the cul-de-sac, after looking around the recently built shopping centre in Burton. She had picked up some new coffee mugs and a few things for the garden, thinking she might as well make the most of the excursion. She hated using buses at the best of times.

She put the kettle on, then automatically got two cups and saucers out of the cupboard above the fridge. Then she sighed and put one of them back again. She would have a decent cup of tea – that stuff at the hospital hadn't been up to par – then she would search through the telephone directory for a funeral director. How very tiresome this all was.

After two cups of tea and a large slice of Victoria sponge, Madge got out the phone book. Twenty minutes later everything was organised, then Madge had the job of letting everyone know. Everyone except Alice, of course. She couldn't bring herself to go and see her, and didn't even think of ringing the hospital.

The service in the crematorium was short and simple, just as she had requested, but Madge glanced around the room with a sense of dismay. Apart from the family all that were present were a few people from work. Didn't Geoff have any friends? Only now did Madge realise that she didn't know, and what was she going to do with all the food she had prepared? Back in the cul-de-sac the dining table was groaning under the weight of sandwiches and nibbles hiding underneath her best tea towels. She had expected the chapel to be packed to the gunnels, but only four rows of seats were occupied and most of them sparsely, as if people were spreading themselves out and trying to make the place look full. Alice was sitting next to her at the other end of the pew, and the Crofts were behind her. Nobody had offered her any sort of comfort. Alice had tried to start a conversation outside, but Madge had deafed her out. She couldn't be doing with her inane prattling at the moment.

Madge didn't take any notice of what the supply preacher was saying and mimed her way through the hymns, remembering what her grandmother Flossie had told her. "If you don't know the words, just stand up and mumble." Thoughts of the old woman almost made her smile, then she glanced at her daughter by the side of her. Why weren't you born a boy? she thought towards her vehemently. All I ever wanted was a boy.

The curtains pulled to and the coffin disappeared behind them and Madge heard a choked sort of sob come from further along the pew. She herself felt nothing, she hadn't cried once since Geoff had died. A few minutes later she led the way out of the chapel, to go and look at the flowers and speak to people she hardly knew. This didn't take long, then the family got back into the limousine and returned home. She sat in the front and Alice sat in the back. The Crofts had come in their own car.

"Stephen should have been riding with us," she suddenly said when they were halfway home. "He is your husband."

"Oh Mum," said Alice wearily, then added, "he didn't want to anyway. Said he'd rather be with his parents."

"You're such a liar, Alice. I don't believe that for a second."

Alice made no reply. She never did when Madge wanted to get going. Honestly, the girl was useless in an argument and Madge couldn't understand why. She thought she had brought her up better than that.

None of Geoff's work colleagues came to the house, so the five of them made very little inroads on the food. Mr. Croft produced a bottle of gin, and persuaded both his wife and Madge to have a small one with plenty of tonic. Madge let him prepare them, and after the second one she found herself feeling quite mellow. She realised that the object of the exercise was to relax everyone, and it seemed to have worked. After the third one Henry Croft was beginning to look attractive. Even Stephen was improving. At the moment he and Alice were indulging in a very polite and civilised conversation, and Madge felt a warm glow in the pit of her stomach. She could see that Alice's resolve was weakening. Oh yes, it wouldn't be long now before they were back together. This bit of adversity had drawn them closer together.

Before long everyone had left, Alice being the first one to do so. Madge thought it was very rude of her to excuse herself like that. Then Stephen went home and Madge smiled to herself. They had arranged an assignation, she was sure of it. Once she had the house to herself again, she decided she would have a cup of tea, then she noticed that the gin bottle had been left behind.

"Might as well finish it off," she said aloud, noticing that her voice was slurring a little. "Quite nice, that stuff."

An hour later she took herself off to bed, giggling as she went. Drunk for the second time in her life, the first one had been at Alice's wedding. On that occasion she had managed to get some adventure out of Geoff, who had also had a few drinks. What a pity he wasn't here now, when she had all these urges that needed satisfying. She lay in bed, wondering why it seemed to be spinning, a firework going off in her head every now and then. What a peculiar sensation being drunk was, and now she had lay down, she wasn't sure she liked it any more. Better sit up for a while and if it didn't improve, she would have that cup of tea after all.

Madge sat back on two fat pillows and daydreamed. The first thing to pop into her head was Russell Carrington. Then Tom Jury joined him, and the pair of them did all sorts of nice things to her, things she could never get her husband interested in. What a waste of time he had been, and now she couldn't imagine why she had chosen him. It was all Flossie's fault, telling her fairy stories like she had. Madge was glad she wasn't around any more either. All she had ever done was interfere in her life and give her bad advice. Eliza always used to say Madge took after Flossie, but Madge could never see it. She didn't think she was the slightest bit like her.

Eliza, yes. Kind, gentle and compassionate, all weaknesses in Madge's book. She supposed her mother was still living in Ingelfield, she hadn't heard anything to the contrary. Occasionally a short letter would plop onto the mat in the hall, and Madge always felt obliged to answer it. Eventually. Christmas cards were regular, and Madge sent one back if she remembered. She didn't always, but it wasn't her fault. She had so many important things on her mind, especially at that time of the year. The Women's Institute Christmas pageant, the Gardening Club annual dinner dance and the Photography Group competition and buffet lunch. All of which needed organising, and if Madge didn't do it, who would?

That reminded her, Christmas was fast approaching. She would need to get her finger out to get everything done in time. She spent the next few minutes fretting over it, and didn't even notice herself sliding off to sleep.

In her dream she was lady of the manor, lounging on a cream chaise-longue with chocolate biscuits on a silver salver by her side. She was wearing the latest creation by Christian Dior, and smelled of Chanel No. 5. In real life Madge never wore perfume, because Geoff had winced at the price of Chanel No. 5 and asked why she couldn't buy something cheaper. She had just told him if she was going to wear perfume then she wanted the best. Full stop and end of story.

Jeeves came in with the post then she was informed, by another servant, that Parker was waiting outside in the Rolls Royce. Before she left to go heaven knows where, Madge – or rather Lady Madge – asked to see tonight's menu. She nodded her approval to the kitchen maid then handed it back.

"And tell cook not to forget the croutons in the soup this time."

The next thing Madge knew, she was in the arms of her lover. This was Tuesday, so it was Tom. Friday was Russell and on Mondays it was Henry's turn. Lord Geoffrey got a look in occasionally, if he was very lucky.

"Oh, if only …" murmured Madge in her sleep as the dream faded.

Two days later, Madge started clearing out Geoff's room. This didn't take long, he had never had many possessions or clothes. She felt pleased with her progress as she bundled everything unceremoniously into black bags, ready for the next jumble sale at the local church. Not that she had anything to do with the church. It was full of middle-class housewives too full of their own self importance, not her type of people at all.

As she was tying up the last bag, she heard the letter box rattle as the postman pushed something through. Madge assumed it would be a sympathy card from one of her many friends. It was about time someone sent one, so far she had heard nothing from any of them. She picked up the envelope with a smile on her face which froze as she noticed the postmark. It was from Ingelfield.

"Suppose I'd better tell them about Geoff," she murmured as she ripped it open. "When I've got time."

The letter from Eliza was short and to the point, and Madge read it twice because she didn't believe it the first time. It simply said that Bert, her father, had passed away peacefully in his sleep and gave details of the funeral arrangements. And asked when she would be arriving.

"Oh Lord," Madge complained. "Another one."

She left the letter on the hall table and went into the kitchen. A good strong cup of tea would put her right. And a piece of cake, of course. She had to go out this afternoon, to a meeting of the Gardening Club.

She took a taxi into town, telling herself she deserved it. She normally walked but she was running late today and in any case, Geoff had left a fair amount of money. Might as well spend some of it. She was even beginning to consider a holiday. A cruise to the Norwegian fjords maybe.

As well as organising the Gardening Club dinner dance, which she hadn't even started on yet, it was also her job to collect in all the subscriptions when they were due, which would be in the New Year.

As she went round everyone to remind them, she was met with tuts, sighs and people looking the other way. This was how everybody usually reacted to her, and she had always put it down to their inadequacy or jealousy, but today she wasn't so sure. For some reason she was starting to suspect that no-one at the club liked her. In the past she had caught mutterings about bossy-boots and know-alls, but hadn't thought they meant her. All she had ever tried to do was help them organise themselves properly but, yet again, it seemed as though all her concerted efforts to whip them into shape were falling on stony ground. Maybe she should resign her position as Treasurer, and leave them to their own devices. Let them find out just how well they could manage without her expert guidance. They would soon be begging her to come back, she just knew it. Yes, that was it, she would resign. Just to teach them a lesson.

She wasn't best pleased when this suggestion was greeted with bright beaming smiles and all best wishes for the future. Madge left the building as soon as she could, and walked home to march off some of her fury. She felt rejected, angry and superior all at the same time. She wasn't sure things had gone very well today, she had scored a hollow sort of victory.

The next day Madge grinned in triumph when the phone rang. It would be that idiot of a Chairwoman asking her to reconsider, she just knew it. She had already worked out what she was going to say. She would procrastinate for as long as she could, then give in right at the end. She was determined to make the woman grovel a bit first.

She answered the phone sounding like the Queen, then dropped the act as soon as she realised it was Alice on the other end.

"And what can I do for you?" she almost snarled.

"Well, I just wondered what you were doing for Christmas this year."

"I shall be going to Doreen, it's her turn this time."

"Yes, but things are different now, what with me and Stephen, so I thought maybe you'd like to come to us this year?"

"What, you and that – that man?"

"Er, well, yes."

"What a ridiculous suggestion." Madge was incredulous at her cheek. "No, I shall be going to Doreen. It's all business as usual at this end."

"Are you sure, Mum?"

"Positive. Goodbye."

Madge slammed down the receiver so hard that the plastic cracked, and the thing nearly fell in half. She cursed as she realised she wouldn't be able to use it until she had got it mended, then smiled. It would give the Chairwoman that bit longer to wallow in her self-made suffering.

"Time I spoke to Doreen about Christmas," Madge said out loud to herself. "Harry should be home for the holidays soon as well."

Madge decided to leave speaking to Doreen until the next meeting of the Women's Institute, which was in a couple of days time. She was unprepared for the reaction when she walked into the hall.

"Madge!" Doreen gushed with one of those irritating embarrassed sort of fixed smile she had spent years trying to perfect but hadn't quite succeeded. "I didn't think we'd be seeing you for a while."

"Why ever not?"

"Well, what with Geoff on top of everything else." Doreen tried to smile again. "Anyway, there's nothing for you to worry about. The pageant is all under control, everything's organised. There's nothing for you to do at all really."

"But ..." Madge was totally confused now. "That's my job."

"Oh, we couldn't possible expect you to do all that, not with all the trauma you've had recently. I felt duty bound to help, that's what friends are for."

"I suppose so," Madge mumbled. To her it was interfering, and without asking first as well. "Anyway, I wanted to speak to you about Christmas."

"Oh yes." Doreen's face fell now. "Things will be different this year. Stephen and Harry are coming to us, and I assume you'll be going to Alice?"

"I'd like to see Harry."

"You'll have to speak to Stephen about that, but I don't think he'll be very keen. I mean, all this business with Alice, and you being her mother and everything …"

"I see," said Madge, although she didn't. She glanced around at the other women, all of whom seemed to be avoiding eye contact with her. Something must have been said to them, and she guessed Doreen was the culprit, as her attitude towards her seemed to have changed lately, as though she was trying to distance herself from the whole unsavoury situation. Suddenly Madge felt small and insignificant. And very unsure of herself. "In that case, I might as well go home."

Nobody answered, not even Doreen. It was as if the whole room was holding its breath as Madge turned and walked away. As the door closed behind her, she heard a cheer go up, then someone that sounded suspiciously like Doreen, shushing them. Madge made her way home, having to work hard to fight back the tears that were threatening to escape and pour down her cheeks. When she got back to the cul-de-sac, she stood in the kitchen with both hands gripping the stainless steel sink and stared out of the window with unseeing eyes. She cried as she hadn't done for years, as she had never done. What was happening to her? Her world was crashing down around her. First the Gardening Club and now the Institute. She wouldn't give the Photography Group the chance to humiliate her. She would never set foot in one of their meetings ever again.

Christmas came and went and Madge spent it alone, too proud to get in touch with Alice to say she had reconsidered. She would rather be in her own house anyway, although it seemed to have got big and empty with just her rattling around in it. The garden was getting to be a mess too, with no Geoff around to keep it tidy. Madge didn't know what she was going to do about it all, and she kept all these thoughts at bay by hiding in a bottle of gin and a little bit of tonic water. Half a bottle a day made her feel better, although she had noticed it made her clumsy as well. Several of her best bone china cups had got broken recently.

Every night, after several gins – the bottles didn't seem to be lasting as long as they used to – Madge looked at her bleary reflection in the bathroom mirror. She was looking old, she decided. Where had all those lines come from? The answer was obvious. Alice of course. And that blasted Croft family. No wonder she had a lot of headaches lately. So many, in fact, that she had taken to keeping a big bottle of one hundred aspirin by the side of the bed. She knew she shouldn't really. Sometimes she lost track of how many she had taken.

Over the next few months, Madge grew more and more disconsolate and withdrawn. The only time she left the house was to go shopping for food. The rest of her long hours were spent sitting in the living room, wondering how she had ever got into this isolated position. Not so very long ago she had been at the centre of everything, kept so busy that she had ignored all her family. She hadn't written to Eliza for months, and now couldn't bring herself to because she hadn't gone to Bert's funeral. She just hadn't had time. Now she had all the time in the world.

Then one day the doorbell rang and Madge looked up in alarm. Who could it be? Doreen, the Chairwoman of the Photography Club or the postman? She sat for a while, determined to ignore it but the bell rang again and again.

"Can't get any peace," Madge grumbled as she got to her feet slowly and shuffled into the hall to open the front door. "Oh, it's you."

There stood Alice, all young, radiant and infuriating. They stared at each other for several seconds before Alice cracked and spoke first.

"Hello Mum. Thought I'd pop round for a cuppa."

"Yes. Suppose you'd better come in," said Madge grudgingly. She hadn't had a visitor for such a long time that she hardly knew what to do any more. "Put the kettle on," she said over her shoulder on the way back to her favourite armchair.

"Yes, Mum."

Yes Mum. She hadn't heard that for such a long time. Those had been the good times, when Alice was an obedient child, Geoff had done as he was told and Madge was in her prime. It all seemed like a lifetime ago now. Where had all those years gone?

A few minutes later Alice entered the room carrying the tea tray, just like in the old days, except that she looked younger and healthier than she had done ten years ago. How had that happened? What was that all about?

"Here we are," said Alice cheerfully as she put the tray on the table.

Go on. Madge willed her silently. Say shall I be mother.

Alice did nothing of the kind, as though she knew what her mother was thinking. Instead she poured the tea and handed her mother a cup. Madge sighed. She still made tea that looked like dishwater.

"Thought you could have rung before you came round."

"I did, but your phone doesn't seem to be working."

"Oh yes. I'd forgotten about that. Did you bring the biscuits?"

As Alice went to fetch them, Madge wondered why she was here. When she returned, she wasted no time in finding out.

"So to what do I owe this honour?"

"I've come to give you this." Alice reached into her bag and pulled out a small envelope. Madge looked at her in puzzlement. "It's an invitation. To my wedding."

Madge's heart soared and her face broke into a smile. All annoyance at her daughter dissipated. She had redeemed herself and gone back to Stephen!

"I knew you'd get back together. Oh, well done Alice."

"Oh." Alice looked taken aback. "Oh well, I'm glad you feel that way but I'm a little surprised. I thought you didn't approve of Joe."

Joe! Madge froze for a second as these words sank in.

"But I don't think I'll be able to come, dear," she said in her best condescending voice. "I'm really not well, you know."

"Yes, you look a bit ..." Alice hesitated. "Anyway, it's not for quite a while yet. You've got time to ..."

"So many things to do, as always," Madge lied. "But it's been lovely to see you and I'll come to the wedding if I can."

Soon afterwards Alice left, and Madge all but slammed the front door after her. She watched her walk down the path and through the creaky gate before she erupted in a blaze of fury.

"Marrying Joe? Over my dead body!"

CHAPTER TWENTY-NINE

Alice went back to Aldermarsh with mixed feelings. Her divorce had come through some weeks ago, she had moved in with Joe and they had been planning their wedding. A simple affair this time, with the reception in the local pub. No posh cars, no expensive photographer and best of all, no interfering mothers-in-law.

"How did it go?" Joe asked when she got home. "How was she?"

"Grumpy but that's nothing new," she said. "She seemed different though, like scruffy and I don't think she's cleaned the house for a while. Not properly anyway."

"She's still coming to terms with things. She was with your father for a long time, it must be difficult for her."

"I suppose so, but she's as stubborn as a mule and bloodyminded with it," Alice reminded him. "She'll swear black is white if it suits her, and I've never known her back down over anything. She won't come to the wedding, I just know it. When I gave her the invitation, I'm sure she thought I was back with Stephen. She can't accept the thought of anything else. She's always lived in cloud cuckoo land."

"So it seems. Strange woman."

"You're telling me! Do you know, I never thought I'd ever say this, but sometimes I feel sorry for her. She's totally alone now Dad's gone, and she's even given up going to all her clubs and things. She's turning into a hermit."

"Maybe it serves her right."

"Joe, that isn't like you." Alice was surprised by his comment.

"You know what they say, Alice, what goes around comes around. She could be getting what she deserves."

"Yes." Alice didn't have to think about this for very long. "You could be right. All she's ever done is poke her nose into other people's business for years. It could all be coming back to haunt her. She'll probably end her days as a lonely old woman nobody wants. Not even me."

"You have more reason than anyone to reject her," Joe pointed out. "She made your life a misery."

"Yes," said Alice quietly. "But I let her."

"That's all over now." Joe pulled her towards him.

"Yes, thank heavens."

"And now you're getting the life you deserve." He kissed her gently. "At least, I hope you are. No regrets?"

"Absolutely none." She smiled at him happily. "But what am I going to do about Mum?"

"Leave her to her own devices," he advised. "Let her stew in her own juice for a while. She'll get in touch when she's ready."

A few days before the wedding, Joe and Alice drove down to Ingelfield to fetch Eliza. They hadn't seen her since Bert's funeral, when Madge had been conspicuous by her absence. That had saved a confrontation and the next possible one would be in the church on Monday, although Alice was totally convinced that Madge wouldn't show up there either. She was glad her grandmother had agreed to attend. In fact, she had been the first one to suggest it. They installed her in Joe's spare bedroom and enjoyed showing her around Aldermarsh. It was a bit like Ingelfield with water and Eliza said she felt comfortable and at home.

The wedding day dawned bright and sunny, and reflected Alice's mood perfectly. It signalled fresh hope and new beginnings, and that was what today was all about. She had left the winter of her previous existence behind her, and now had the summer of marriage with Joe to look forward to. She really couldn't be happier.

The vicar in the village had willingly agreed to marry them despite Alice's divorced status, so Joe left to take Eliza in his car while Alice waited for one of his friends to pick her up. Pamela's husband Nick had agreed to give her away, but had said he would rather not walk down the aisle with her. Fran and Susan were going to be doing that. They had all had such fun deciding on their outfits, and many meetings for coffee and a chat had been arranged to discuss things. That is, when they weren't drinking wine in a quiet pub somewhere.

Alice met her two enthusiastic bridesmaids at the door of the church, and they both said she looked fantastic in her pale green silk suit, white blouse embroidered with a little pink and green, and white high heeled shoes. She was carrying a small posy of pink carnations and lily of the valley, and was shaking with nervousness.

"You'll be fine," Fran reassured her. "He's a lovely man."

"Yeah, you've got a good one there," Susan backed her up. "Don't blame you for making it official."

The wedding march struck up, and the threesome suddenly stood to attention and remembered why they were there. Alice led the way, not at all worried about having to walk down the aisle alone. That was one thing Madge had instilled into her from an early age, not to be afraid of doing things on her own. She had never had any choice in the matter but it hadn't done her any harm, in fact, it had stood her in good stead when she had decided to leave Stephen and go solo.

As she moved slowly through the church she received a beaming smile from Eliza, then she scanned her eyes over the congregation to see if Madge had turned up after all. No, there was no sign of her, she was no doubt sulking in the cul-de-sac and cursing Alice for disappointing her again. For once, Alice didn't care. She would never care what her mother thought about anything ever again. She had been hurt too many times by Madge's thoughtless and sometimes downright malicious digs at her. When she had been a child and teenager, each one of these put-downs had hit home with the force of a sledgehammer, knocking any burgeoning self-confidence right out of Alice's body. It had hurt so much then, it had mattered to her what her mother thought about her and what she did. She had always been seeking her approval somehow, to be reassured that she was worth something, but she hadn't realised she was looking in the wrong place. When she was younger, she thought everyone's mum was like hers. It wasn't until she got older that she found out just what a nasty piece of work she could be. She had married Stephen to get away from home, taking the easy way out, or so she had thought. She had married for all the wrong reasons, but this time was different. This time she knew she wasn't making a mistake, and was doing what she should have done the first time around. She was marrying for love.

Eventually she stopped as she drew level with Joe. They smiled at each other as Susan took the flowers from her and the ceremony began. Suddenly a sunbeam streamed through one of the stained glass windows and bathed the couple in its light, as though the heavens themselves approved of what they were doing on this bright sunny day.

Because Joe and Alice had been to a rehearsal of the wedding, she knew they were coming up to the part where the vicar was going to ask if anyone knew a reason why they shouldn't be married.

Here we go, Alice thought. If she's here …

The words were said and nothing happened. Alice breathed again. The vicar opened his mouth to continue.

"Stop this wedding at once!" A familiar voice rang out. "She can't marry that awful man."

"Oh no," groaned Alice. "Mum."

They both turned to face her as she came storming down the aisle dressed in her best coat and her handbag swinging menacingly on her arm.

"Please state your objection, madam," said the vicar politely.

"I just have, haven't I?"

"That isn't a valid reason."

"Of course it is." Madge looked defiant. "She already has a husband, she belongs with him."

"I'm divorced, the vicar's seen the papers!"

"I have." He nodded. "If you don't have a proper objection then please leave and allow the ceremony to continue."

"No, I …"

"Margaret Day." A new voice joined the conversation. Madge whirled around as she heard the Dorset accent belonging to the mother she hadn't seen for over thirty years. Her mouth dropped open as she looked at Eliza, who was on her feet ready to challenge her. "Just 'cos you never got the man you wanted, you mustn't stop your daughter from doin'."

"What are you talking about, you silly old fool?"

"Russell Carrington."

"Ladies," said the vicar sternly. "This is hardly the time or place."

"I need to speak to my mother," Madge threw back at him.

"After the wedding," said Eliza. "Go. Don't be a lummox all your life."

Alice watched as Madge blushed to the very roots of her hair and seemed to shrink under her mother's steady gaze. She gave Eliza an extra special death stare, then looked at Alice with no expression on her face at all. A couple of Joe's friends were standing in the aisle, ready to manhandle Madge out of the church, but after a few seconds she saw sense, turned around and walked out under her own steam. Alice caught Susan's eye and she smiled at her, while Fran was nearly in tears. As Alice was wondering who Russell Carrington was, the vicar brought the assembly back under control and resumed the service, until he said the immortal words.

"I now pronounce you man and wife."

Alice smiled at Joe. She could see tears in his eyes, but said nothing as she kissed him. Then they followed the vicar to go and sign the register. A short time later they left the church while the organist played something joyful and uplifting. Alice's heart was soaring. Madge's interruption was fading fast, and Alice was damned if she was going to let that spoil the day. Her mother could never do anything to hurt her ever again.

"You looks lovely, my dear," Eliza said to her outside the church as the photographs were being taken by various friends. "And I knows you'll be happy."

"Thank you Gran."

"Where's Madge?" asked Joe.

"Oh, don't worry about her, she'll be back home by now. I reminded her of something she thought I didn't know. She won't be back, not as long as I'm around."

"In that case you'd better stay for ever," Alice laughed.

"Just the two weeks'll do, while you's away. I'll look after the house for you."

"You're welcome to stay as long as you like," Joe offered.

"Thank you Joe, that's very kind of you, we'll see," replied Eliza, looking a little overwhelmed. "But you go off to your foreign parts and enjoy yourselves."

"That's tomorrow," said Alice. "And I'm really looking forward to it. But first we have some celebrating to do."

"Come on, your chauffeur awaits," said Joe with a bow. "To the pub, I'm ready for a pint."

"You and your pint," Eliza laughed.

"He'll never change," Alice agreed.

The reception was held in the pub where they had met up again after nearly twelve long years, and Alice thought nothing could be more appropriate. Eliza didn't stay too long. She was the oldest person there and anyway, she said, she wasn't used to pubs, all that noise and smoke. Joe offered to walk her back to the bungalow but she wouldn't hear of it, so they let her go back on her own to brew up a cup of tea and watch the television.

It was quite late when the party broke up, and everyone was full of food as well as quite a few drinks. Joe and Alice were virtually the last to leave, but Alice hadn't finished yet.

"Hang on, just let me say goodbye to Sue and Fran, I won't be long."

Her two friends were waiting for her by the back door, and hugs were exchanged all round.

"Don't forget the postcard," said Susan. "I've always wanted to see what Bermuda looks like."

"I've heard it's got pink sand," added Fran. "Let me know if it's true."

"I'll bring you some," she promised.

"Have a lovely time."

"And be happy."

"I will and thank you." Alice smiled. "Both of you."

Alice's wedding night was a little strange with Eliza in the house. She and Joe went to bed, kissed each other goodnight and went to sleep. Alice didn't mind, she was fairly drunk anyway. Vague memories of her first wedding night flitted though her mind as she dozed off. Just before she did, Madge came into her thoughts. What a miserable lonely old woman she had become.

The next day they got up late and said goodbye to Eliza before setting off for the airport. She had taken to Aldermarsh, so staying on her own for a couple of weeks was going to be no hardship. Alice was hoping they might be able to persuade her to move there. It would be so nice to have her nearby.

They flew to New York and changed planes, planning to spend a few days there on the way back. Alice couldn't wait to explore 42nd Street and 5th Avenue, but before that was the place Joe had described as the prettiest he had ever seen.

When they arrived in Bermuda, it took Alice's breath away. Joe had been right, it was incredibly lovely. The sea was a bright twinkling turquoise and the sand really was pink, a result of ground-up coral from the many reefs surrounding the hook-shaped main island, which contained the capital Hamilton and the quaint toytown of St. George's. They were staying in Hamilton, and a taxi took them through many streets containing pastel-cololoured houses with white corrugated rooves to catch the precious rain water and store it in underground reservoirs. Greenery abounded everywhere too, which added to the sense of sub-tropical lushness. Finally they arrived at their sumptuous hotel which was painted in the seemingly national colour, pink. Alice felt like she was in wonderland as they settled into their room with two king sized beds and a marble bathroom. And a sea view, of course. Alice had never seen such luxury in her life.

They explored Hamilton, noting that an American cruise ship was docked on one side of Front Street. There was a policeman dressed in the regulation Bermuda shorts directing traffic from inside his designated enclosure in the middle of the road outside Gosling Brothers wines and spirits shop. The rest of his uniform looked decidedly English and when Alice commented on this, Joe told her that these islands were still a British protectorate.

As car hire wasn't available on the island and the speed limit was twenty miles an hour, they opted to rent a motor scooter to get around. Alice was nervous to begin with, perched precariously on the back, especially as the bus drivers seemed to take absolutely no notice of the rules. After a couple of days she was beginning to get used to it, and hardly held on at all. Joe was quite relieved; she had begun by squeezing all the life out of him.

On the way to St. George's they stopped at Elbow Beach, and Alice collected a small amount of pink sand into a plastic bottle to show to Susan and Fran. Then Joe took her picture standing inside a moongate, a circular stone built opening peculiar to Bermuda and reputed to bring true love to any believer who passed through. They stood inside it and kissed, just to make sure.

Joe had told Alice that St. George's was like toytown and when they got there she could see exactly what he meant. In the main square was the Bank of Butterfield building, outside which stood stocks and a pillory which wouldn't have been out of place in medieval England. There was even a ducking stool. Alice agreed to sit on it for photographic purposes, but turned down Joe's suggestion of seeing whether it worked, thankful that it wasn't actually over any water. Then they went to look at the Deliverance, a replica of a sailing ship built in 1610. As Joe was studying the information board, Alice looked around, telling herself this place couldn't possibly be real. The houses looked as though they had been made out of children's building blocks and the paintwork was immaculate, as if they had only been put up that afternoon. Then she noticed that Joe had moved and was now looking in a shop window nearby.

"Fancy swimming with a dolphin?" he asked.

"Do I! Oh yes, that'd be fantastic. Where is it?"

"Just down the road, in a sheltered bay, it says. Shall I book it for you?"

"Aren't you going to come too?"

"I'll get more pleasure out of watching you. And I can take some photos."

"Oh Joe, thank you."

When they went back to the hotel that evening, Alice decided she had never been happier. She loved Bermuda, the weather was fantastic and the people were cheerful and friendly. They were nearly halfway through their stay, and tomorrow she was going to swim with dolphins. In the sea too, not just in a pool. She couldn't wait.

The receptionist detained them as they collected their room key.

"There's a message for you," she said.

Joe took the piece of paper from her with a frown on his face.

"Someone's rung for us."

"Let me have a look, I might recognise the number," said Alice. "Yes, I do, that's Fran."

"What can she want?"

"I dunno but it must be important. Oh God, I hope Eliza's alright."

"You'd better ring Fran."

"You can use our phone," the receptionist offered. "We'll charge the call to your room."

Alice wasted no time in ringing the number, wondering what time it was back in England. She was probably dragging Fran out of bed in the middle of the night, but she didn't care. She had to know what was going on.

"Fran, it's Alice. What's up?"

"Oh Alice, at last. I'm so sorry, I've got some bad news for you."

"My gran?"

"No, it's your mum."

"Oh no, what's she done now?" asked Alice wearily. It was bound to be something stupid, that was all Madge did lately. Joe gave her a sympathetic smile as she moved the telephone receiver a little, so that they could both listen to Fran's voice.

293

"Alice, oh Alice. She passed away on the day you got married. The postman found the front door wide open the next morning. The bedroom smelled of gin, and there was an empty bottle of aspirin by the bed …"

ART FORGER AND CORPULENT MASTER criminal Luff Imbry travels from Old Earth down The Spray to the skinflint world of New Gargano to trade some of his counterfeit confections for a pouchful of the fabulous gems called noubles. But Imbry is not the only one with duplicity in mind, and soon the fat man finds himself imprisoned on a nameless world where the only question is whether he'll dwindle to a lifeless husk before or after he goes irretrievably insane.

MATTHEW HUGHES writes science fantasy. *Booklist* has called him "heir apparent to Jack Vance," George R.R. Martin has called his Archonate tales "a tremendous amount of fun," and Robert J. Sawyer has called him "a towering talent." Hughes calls himself "Matt."

His webpage is at www.matthewhughes.org.

of WHIMSIES & NOUBLES

of
WHIMSIES
& NOUBLES

Matthew Hughes

2014

of
WHIMSIES
& NOUBLES

LUFF IMBRY WATCHED THE MIDDLER, Tosh Herklunt, as the latter approached the gateway that led into the Hotel Borsa's enclosed patio where Imbry sat. Herklunt stopped and, while appearing to examine the urban scenery, made a subtle gesture. The motion was a signal that conveyed the message, from one member to another of the criminal halfworld that flourished in the city of Olkney, far off up The Spray, that the business had been satisfactorily completed. His thin arms then arranged themselves into what seemed to be a casual posture, but which told the astute observer—and Imbry was most astute—that the go-between had been neither followed nor otherwise interfered with since leaving the exchange point.

Imbry lifted two fingers above the plain iron tabletop and moved them in a manner that told Herklunt that he had received the message and that it was safe for the middler to approach him. As Herklunt came through the gateway, Imbry automatically watched the street behind the man, but saw no cause for alarm. Still, he would remain on his guard until they had departed the planet and put at least one whimsy between them and this world called New Gargano.

The place was not to Imbry's taste. For one thing, the food was indifferently prepared. It lacked all intensity of flavour and, so far, the Borsa's chef's repertoire had not so much as hinted at even the possibility of surprise. The lackluster cuisine was a symptom of the general malaise that he perceived in New Garganian culture, which he believed stemmed from the groat-squeezing miserliness that was fundamental to the world's character. *They are graspers*, had been his first impression, and it had since been reinforced repeatedly. *Graspers and keepers who have forgotten that the only worthwhile use of wealth is to make life more enjoyable.*

It was a philosophy that Imbry rarely preached but assiduously practiced. His many years as Old Earth's foremost thief, forger, and sometimes purveyor of artworks stolen or forged by others had seen a river of currency pass through his plump hands. Very little of it had stuck to him, unless one counted the corpulent, almost spherical shape his body had acquired. Over those same years, Luff Imbry had also become one of the most noted gastronomes of Olkney, Old Earth's last remaining metropolis.

Herklunt was the opposite of Imbry in appearance, being long-shanked and spare of flesh, but the two shared a common philosophy: that the ownership of items of value was a flexible concept, subject to alteration by persons skilled in certain arts—unless the items in question belonged to them, in which case any attempts at alteration would be met with full, and even drastic, countermeasures.

The middler approached Imbry's table, which was strewn with the half-eaten remains of the fat man's lunch. There ought to have been little that even a hap-handed chef could do to spoil a four-meat pie, but the Borsa's kitchens had sent him a glutinous mass of jellied flesh, each bit tasting like every other, encased in a shell of pastry so tooth-resistant that the forger thought he should have sent back the knife and fork and asked for a hand-axe.

Now he swept the plate and remnants to one side and bid the middler sit down beside him. He leaned his head close to the other man's and said, in an undertone, "Report."

"A smooth business," said Herklunt. "The client's representative appeared on time and made a proper display. We withdrew to a secluded spot, where he inspected our goods and pronounced them as advertised. He then brought out the seven noubles and I examined them as you instructed. Finding no fault or short-count, I released the goods to him, took up the noubles and returned by a roundabout route. I detected no undue interest in my movements."

"Show me the items," Imbry said.

Herklunt reached inside his upper garment, undid some concealed flap, and brought from a secure pocket the seven noubles. He put them, still warm, in Imbry's hand. By this time, the forger had placed an ocular against one eye, holding it in place by pressure of brow and cheek. He chose one of the noubles and brought it up to his enhanced vision, and saw the rainbow aura that rippled just beneath its curved, translucent surface. It was a perfect specimen, as he found each of the others to be when he examined them in turn.

"Good," he said, finally. He scooped them up and placed them in his own secure pocket, close to where his heart beat through the layers of flesh that covered his torso. Noubles ought to be kept warm, or they could fade.

The precious objects stowed, Imbry dug in another pocket and produced a purse which he handed to Tosh Herklunt. A practitioner of good manners, the middler did not open the pouch to verify its contents. Instead, he made the sounds and gestures half-world propriety demanded, before rising and leaving the courtyard by the gate. Imbry did likewise, but departed through the hotel's foyer, where he informed the desk-keeper that he would be checking out and wished to have his account ready for settlement when he returned downstairs. Shortly thereafter, valise in hand, the fat man climbed into a summoned ground-car and directed it to take him to the spaceport.

At the terminus, Imbry approached the information nexus and, showing his open ticket, inquired as to the next outbound ship that would take him up The Spray. The nexus's integrator told him that the freighter *Aberoth* was departing shortly and had a stateroom available. If he cared to wait until late afternoon, the liner *Epitomous* was currently inbound and would make a station stop.

"*Epitomous* is one of the Gunter Line ships, is it not?" he asked the nexus.

"It is."

The Gunter Line was known for the quality of its service. One would eat well, especially on a first-class passage.

"And the *Aberoth*?" the fat man said. "What are its standards?"

"I know of no complaints," said the integrator.

"Hmm," said Imbry. The liner would make faster time than the freighter, though he reminded himself that his haste was to get off New Gargano, not to get home to Olkney. He did not yet have a buyer for the noubles, but meant to offer them to several possible customers, triggering a discreet auction. So the *Aberoth* made more sense. But, then it was a seven-day journey back to Old Earth: twenty-one meals, not to mention the oddments and fripperies that were always available in the first-class lounges. After inflicting his digestion with New Garganian cuisine, he owed his innards the best treatment he could give them.

"Book me on the *Epitomous*," he told the nexus.

"Done," it said.

"Where and when may I board?"

The device told him to present himself at pad seventeen in three hours.

"Where may I wait until then?"

"Wherever you wish."

Imbry looked about the utilitarian space. It offered hard chairs and harder benches and no refreshments other than what came out of a phalanx of automatic dispensers grouped at the centre of the waiting area. The fat man sighed and made for the widest bench. His stomach made representations to him, and he almost wished he had finished the four-meat pie.

The spaceport occupied the levelled top of a prominence that overlooked a river valley in which New Gargano's first settlers had sited what grew to be their principal city, Manfredonia. Pad seventeen was not far from the terminus, and beyond it was a low wall of white stone that marked the port's boundary. Imbry decided that he might as well pass the time between now and the departure of *Epitomous*'s shuttle—the great liner itself would remain in orbit—resting his eyes on the scenery rather than on the terminus's drab accoutrements.

The weather was fine and the light from the world's golden sun was warm and mild. Imbry leaned a padded hip against the stone barrier and regarded the view. Manfredonia exhibited two schools of architecture: the seven graceful towers built by the original settlers, connected by a pillared arcade that ran beside the slow-moving river; and the mean, little boxes in which their descendants carried on the graspings and clutchings that constituted the modern city's commerce.

Imbry was not greatly familiar with the world's history. He knew that it was a secondary of Aalberg's World, one of the grand foundational domains. That was to say, Aalberg's had been one of the first worlds settled during humanity's great effloration out into the galactic arm known as The Spray. In time, the foundational domain had grown populous and opulent, prompting some of its residents to go looking for places where one might flex an elbow without bumping a neighbour's.

New Gargano was one of those places. Apparently, it had begun well—the lines and proportions of the towers and arcade were classical in their simple elegance—but, somewhere between then and now, had come a social revolution. The settlers' posterity had opted for the cheap and the ugly. Presumably, Imbry thought, every grubby little bungalow down there contained a strongbox full of unspent, hoarded pelf.

He would never have come to New Gargano, except that it was the sole source, in all the Ten Thousand Worlds, of noubles. Few things were as rare as the pearlescent jewels. Indeed, no one outside of a handful of close-mouthed New Garganians even knew how the objects came into being. Though he was an astute researcher, the best information Imbry had been able to turn up was a speculation by a scholar of the Institute that the forces involved appeared to be not of the phenomenal universe. That is, they originated on one of the other planes of existence that, together with this one, composed Totality.

Whatever their origin, the demand for noubles far exceeded their supply. New Gargano produced no more than a thousand of the items in an Old Earth year, of which no more than a hundred might be of excellent grade; no more than twenty were superlatives; and once every ten years or so, there came an exemplar. Their export was strictly regulated. For persons of enormous wealth who wished to make an unequivocal statement as to their sense of self-importance, noubles were the ultimate punctuation marks.

Yet, tastes varied. However much a thing may be valued, there would always be those for whom some other item was more desirable. Some months ago, word had reached the fat man, through channels that he trusted, that a Manfredonian miser, connected to the export authority, was willing to part with seven of his world's rarities, in exchange for a representative set of erotic figurines crafted by the Twenty-First Aeon sculptress Ilaria Flid, whose works commanded high prices but rarely came onto the markets.

She had been a grandmaster of the Mutable School, which produced small pieces shaped in memory stone. Exposed to a source of heat—sunlight would do or even the warmth of a hand—the objects would slowly change shape, assuming the predetermined forms worked into the material by the artist. Thus a human figure might begin as an infant, grow through childhood to maturity, then gradually decline into decrepitude and quietus, at which point the cycle would begin anew. Or the subject might perform complex acts like dancing, acrobatics, or mime.

Flid had pursued a lifelong fascination with erotica (envious contemporaries called it an unhealthy fixation). Over a long career, she produced hundreds of figurines—as singles, duos, triples and larger groups—that acted out every passion, position and perversion that could be devised by a libido coupled to exceptional ingenuity. Not one to work in the abstract, Flid rendered her constantly moving, changing statuettes with close attention to anatomical detail. It was said that a visit to her workshop would offer an education even to the most seasoned adept of the amorous arts.

It happened that Luff Imbry, a man of sufficient talent that he might have flourished in the arts as a creator rather than a thief and forger, had acquired a supply of used memory stone. The secret to making the material had been lost over the great gulf in time between now and the remote era when Flid had worked with it, but Imbry had managed to collect damaged and lesser works from minor members of the Mutable School. By dint of determined and painstaking research, he rediscovered the lost Twenty-First Aeon techniques for working with the stuff, including a method for erasing already-inculcated patterns and thus rendering the stone ready for fresh imprinting—at least temporarily.

When he heard that a certain Rodrig Uverlanth of Manfredonia, New Gargano, was looking to purchase Flid figurines and was willing to do so without asking inconvenient questions as to where they might have come from, Imbry set a plan in motion. He knew little of New Gargano—few on Old Earth did—but he knew that it was where noubles came from. He sent back word, again through roundabouts and intermediaries, that five Flids could be supplied, but that he would accept only noubles as the purchaser's coin.

Word filtered back that noubles could be had, and so a long-distance negotiation began. Communication on any civilised world was instant and ubiquitous, but to send and receive messages between star systems took time. The outgoing message had to be entrusted to the integrator of a spaceship heading in the right direction. If it passed within range of the recipient's world, the ship's integrator would impart the message into that planet's connectivity, which would deliver the communication forthwith. If the ship was not going close enough, it would hand off the message to another ship thereward bound. Sometimes, if the distances were truly vast—The Spray measured thousands of light years from end to end—a message might be relayed several times. A month or more might go by before it was received and an answer came winging and winding back to the sender.

The remoteness of New Gargano gave Imbry time to apply himself. He acquired likenesses of several Flid works and had his integrator record and analyse their movements. Then he constructed the tools necessary to recombine and mold his fragments of the material and instill the patterns. His first attempts were poor copies indeed, but he could always return the memory stone to its original state to try again.

7

Or not quite original—every time the stuff was freshly imprinted with a mutable pattern, then saw that pattern removed, it lost some of its ability to absorb and retain the sequence of motions. It was a constraint for Imbry, but not an unworkable one. As he persevered, his eye grew surer, his technique stronger. Eventually, he was able to create credible imitations of five of Ilaria Flid's best pieces.

An exacting examination by any connoisseur of the sculptress's oeuvre would have revealed the inadequacies. But Imbry knew, from long experience, that purchasers of stolen artworks seldom trotted them out for expert inspection. No, the five mutables would go into Rodrig Uverlanth's miserly abode, there to be gloated over in seclusion. After a certain period—a few days for some, a month for others—they would cease to perform.

But by then, Imbry would be far away on Old Earth. And no denizen of this tightfisted planet could hope to penetrate the murky depths of Olkney's half-world to demand his noubles back. Not that Imbry would retain them long in any case.

The fat man looked about him, saw no one within close view. He reached into his inner garment and retrieved the seven precious objects. He set them, one by one, in a line along the top of the wall then viewed each through his ocular. The sunlight brought out their many colours, shimmers of tints and shades so rare that even Imbry could not name some of them. He judged that five were of excellent grade and the other two were probably superlatives. He had never seen a superlative at such close range; they simply didn't come onto the open market in far-distant Old Earth. Indeed, it was unheard of for seven noubles of this quality ever to be offered for sale on Imbry's world, legitimately or otherwise.

These, he thought, *will adorn the neck or the hair of some first-tier aristocrat of Old Earth—perhaps even the Archon—and the purchasing steward will pay whatever I ask.*

A shadow fell over the seven orbs and their colours faded to grey. Imbry looked up, even as he scooped the treasures back into his hand and delivered them once more into hiding. A rust-bottomed aircar was descending, clearly aiming to touch down on pad seventeen. Imbry stepped away from the wall and walked briskly toward the terminus. As he did so, he saw a second volante angling down toward him from above the building's flat roof.

An amplified voice rang in the air around him. "We are the Manfredonia Safeguard. Stand still and make no questionable motions. We are authorised to use deadly force."

Imbry could see an insignia on the second aircar: an eight-pointed starburst. He turned and saw the same device on the first vehicle. They touched down and each disgorged two green-uniformed constables, whose tunics each bore a silver star. They came toward him and he had no doubt the things they carried were weapons. He stood still.

"Is there some problem?" he said. "I am but an innocent tourist. I will be happy to cooperate in any way I—"

The first pair had reached him. He was swung around, his arms were pinioned by a holdfast, and a gruff voice told him to save it for the magistrate.

But first came an interview with the investigating officer, Franchis Bonan, a neat and precise man of middle years who wore two silver emblems on each epaulet and an expression of skepticism so ingrained that his brow was permanently creased in four places. Having had Imbry searched and relieved of the seven noubles and two weapons, Bonan leaned across the table at which they were both seated and on which the items were displayed and said, "Account for these."

"That is a needle thrower," the forger said, gesturing with his chins, "and the other emits an incapacitating gas."

"You expected to be attacked?"

"A traveller is always advised to be cautious."

The officer indicated the opalescent spheres. "And these?"

"I found them on the wall at the spaceport. I had just picked them up to examine them."

A fifth wrinkle appeared just below Bonan's hairline. "And you just happened to be carrying this?" He produced the ocular and laid it next to the noubles.

"I did."

The man sighed and took a writing tablet from a drawer beneath the table. He activated it and sat with fingers poised. "Name?"

Imbry spoke the name under which he was travelling.

"Occupation?"

"I am a gentleman of independent means."

Bonan let that pass without verbal comment, but his creases deepened. "From?"

"The city of Olkney on Old Earth."

"Where is that?"

"Up The Spray."

"Foundational or secondary?"

"Neither," said Imbry. "It is the original home world of our species."

This won him an even deeper sigh. "Do you plan to claim insanity as your defence? Because, as a disinterested observer, I must tell you that you'll have to do better than to claim that some place named Old Dirt is the ancestral font of humanity."

"I do not plan a defence. I have committed no crime."

The officer now moved from sighs to tsks. "You are in possession of seven noubles, you have no export licence, and you have booked passage off-world. Conviction is assured."

"I will explain it to the magistrate."

"He will be even less amused than I." Franchis Bonan summoned a man who took Imbry down a hallway to a strongly made door, released him from the holdfast and put him in a holding cell. There he found Tosh Herklunt, somewhat disheveled and with a bruise on one cheek, sitting disconsolate on one of the bunks.

"Ah," said the fat man.

"Just so," said the middler. "We have been played for noddies."

They conversed in generalities, for the benefit of any listening devices, while their eyes, fingers, shoulders and elbows engaged in a different form of communication known as half-world cant. Herklunt said that he had been arrested as he went to book a ticket off-world, that he had been interrogated but had said nothing about Imbry or their business on New Gargano. The forger replied that he had been caught with goods he could not account for and did not expect a good outcome.

A short time later, that expectation was put to the test when they were taken from the cell and marched down a long corridor, up two flights of stairs and into a plainly furnished chamber that, though different in details, resembled all of the courtrooms that the fat man's career had led him through at one time or another.

A grey-haired functionary in a different livery from the safeguards told them to stand before an elevated seat and cautioned them to silence. A door in the rear wall opened and admitted a hard-faced man with small, dark eyes and a downturned mouth.

Imbry readied himself to make a case. Then the bailiff said, "All persons who have business in the magistrate's court, now give your attention and pay full heed. His Prestige, Rodrig Uverlanth, presiding."

"Ah," said Imbry again, though with a different emphasis.

The spaceship's ill-tuned engine supplied a constant murmuring background to the low conversations among the thirty men confined to its aft hold. The space held no furniture, just a sleeping pad for each transportee. Each man was clad in a one-piece suit of blue fabric and shod with shoes of heavy cloth. They had also been issued long-billed peaked caps with cloth flaps to cover the neck, and told not to lose them.

Imbry sat against a wall, his armpits rubbed raw by the seams of his too-tight garment, the vibrations from the ship's drive tickling his shoulders. Herklunt lay on his pad, listening along with the fat man to what a third man was telling them. He had given his name as Ifriz and his occupation as counterfeiter. A career criminal, he had known many who had been convicted and sentenced to transportation. He knew of none who had returned to New Gargano.

"There is no commutation, no parole, no ticket-of-leave. You go, you don't come back." A thin man with a nose like a curved blade, he lifted his hands then moved them apart, at the same time compressing and opening his lips to make a pop! "Into the nevermore, and gone."

"What about guards, medical staff?"

"Never heard of one coming back to New Gargano. Either they stay, too, or they keep their mouths shut." Ifriz thought for a moment. "Or perhaps they are all off-worlders."

"What kind of place is it?" Tosh Herklunt asked.

"A desert, a swamp, a land of boiling lakes, an endless ice-sheet," said the counterfeiter. "Descriptions are various, and thus none can be trusted."

"Have you no advice?" the middler said.

"The same as in any confinement. Form alliances so that you never stand with your back exposed."

Imbry spoke. "We are two. Do you wish to make a third?"

"I do," said Ifriz. "And there's a fellow over by the water nipple I have dealt with before. Cappro, he's called. Not the smoothest of personalities, but reliable."

Imbry looked where the thin man indicated and saw a muscular figure with wide shoulders and a jutting jaw. "Call him over," he said.

While the four were agreeing to mutual loyalty, a bell sounded and the ship's integrator informed them that it was approaching a whimsy. Panels in the bulkheads opened to reveal dispensers and every man went to collect the medications that brought unconsciousness. To pass through the irreality of a whimsy while one's senses were still active was to risk insanity or permanent synesthesia.

The voyage ultimately took them through two whimsies, with long periods traversing normal space before and after each period of insensibility. Finally, the pitch of the vibrations that echoed through the ship changed, and soon after they landed. The hatch opened and they saw blue sky and golden sunlight beyond.

Guards in ill-kept white uniforms and armed with devices whose capacities the prisoners did not want to discover came through the hatch from the outside, shouting orders. The transportees were formed into a column of twos and marched down a ramp to a dusty parade ground surrounded on three sides by two-story buildings of tan stone pierced by louvered windows. Imbry saw no bars, which he reckoned might be good or bad. He heard a thrumming of gravity obviators, then the ship's carryall emerged from another hatch, laden with crates and containers. It flew itself to a large open-air pavilion with a thatched roof, its interior filled with rows of tables and benches. Men in garments of the same colour Imbry had been issued came from one of the buildings, formed a human chain, and began to unload the carryall's cargo.

The air was warm but not oppressive, the sunlight bright but not searing. Clouds of brilliant white galleoned across a sky whose blue was of a slightly darker shade than Old Earth's. But Imbry reckoned it must be a dry world, judging by the size of the precipitator whose elevated water-storage tank loomed over the camp's administration nexus.

"Not so bad to start with," Herklunt whispered when the column was ordered to halt then turn to form two ranks.

"Silence!" The order came from a big-bellied man in a white uniform that was none too clean. He pulled a sweat-stained canvas cap farther down a sloping forehead that ended in one continuous eyebrow, and strode to stand in front of the paraded prisoners.

"I am Senior Regulator Ovetz," he said. "The rules here are simple. Do everything you are told to do. Do nothing you are not told to do." He paused to let that sink in, then ordered the front rank to take one pace forward and the rear rank to step back. He then walked up and down both rows, looking the newcomers up and down. Occasionally he paused before a man and asked a question or made a comment. When he came to Imbry, near the middle of the rear rank, he stopped and gave the fat man a comprehensive looking-over.

"Crime?" he said.

"Not I. I am innocent."

Ovetz wore heavy boots. He now placed the sole of one of them over the toes of Imbry's cloth-covered right foot and shifted his weight. Imbry made an involuntary sound somewhere in his chest.

"We like clowns," the regulator said, maintaining the pressure. "Not much entertainment here." He poked Imbry's massive stomach and seemed surprised that his finger did not go in very deep. "Plenty of mass. You might last a year or more."

He leaned back and the fat man's pain subsided to a bone-deep ache. Ovetz took a step away, then turned his head back to Imbry and said, "Of course, here the years are rather short."

They were divided into three groups of ten and marched under escort to a building on the west side of the compound. The ship that had brought them was already lifting off. Imbry had not seen it take on any passengers. The ten that included him and his three allies were assigned to a large square room with five double bunks. As soon as he entered, and despite his sore toes, Imbry stepped quickly to the pair farthest from the door and sat on the lower pallet. He noted that the blanket that covered it looked as if it had been swept aside by someone rising from sleep. The sweat-stained pillow was still indented in the middle by the pressure of someone's head. These observations and Ovetz's remarks troubled him.

Ifriz and Cappro had taken the bunk nearest to Imbry's, the lighter man leaping onto the top pallet. Herklunt would sleep above the fat man. The guards had shut the door and left them. Imbry looked around the room and said, "Let's find out who we are."

He moved out into the middle of the space and introduced himself as a thief and forger specializing in art and items of high value. "I was gulled into coming to New Gargano by the promise of noubles. But the man I bought them from was the judge who sent me here."

Imbry heard a grunt from one of the six, but could not identify the source. Now Herklunt was introducing himself, then Ifriz. Cappro defined himself as a junior enforcer for the Cympline Syndicate—Imbry would later learn it was a hierarchical criminal organisation operating across three worlds—who had been sacrificed when the authorities began to build a strong case against one of his superiors.

The others spoke in turn: two murderers, a pair of thieves, a compulsive despoiler of graves, all residents of New Gargano; plus a smooth-headed man with his hair in braids who said he hailed from the foundational domain of Santerre and who had likewise come to grief over noubles. His name was Srishanka and he had also been a victim of Rodrig Uverlanth's machinations.

"What did you pay him?" Imbry asked.

"A painting by Tepplehoon, a nude in a passionate fervor."

"Genuine?"

Srishanka shrugged. "Almost. And you?"

"Five Flid mutables."

"Genuine?"

"My only consolation," Imbry said, "is that round about now, they will be turning into shapeless lumps."

That put a half smile on the Santerrean's lips, but then he said, "Still, in both our cases, Uverlanth is out only by his expectations. I would like to see him suffer more than mild chagrin."

"Be assured," said the fat man, "that such an outcome is a key element of my program." He rubbed his plump palms together. "Now, let us see what knowledge we can pool about our prospects here."

But their common store of information turned out to be as skimpy as Ifriz's in the hold of the transport ship. No one knew even what planet they had been carried to. One of the murderers, a man called Titon, said he believed they were on a scarcely populated minor world named Chelazza. But the taller of the two thieves, Andru, argued for another disregarded planet called Nestranko. The others had no opinion.

Titon said, "I've heard that Nestranko orbits a dual-star system, a middle-range yellow and a fierce white dwarf."

Andru allowed that he had heard the same. Shortly before the dinner bell rang, the lanky thief was proved to have made the better guess. A blazing dot rose above the horizon and the temperature in the room began to climb. As they filed out for dinner, the barracks windows cycled to reduce the effect, but outside the heat was intense. The smaller sun could not be looked at and the shadows it threw cut right across those of its more amiable companion, as if to show what true deep black ought to be.

15

They ate in silence, sitting on long benches at long tables, numbering at least a hundred and fifty more than the thirty that had come on the transport. The food was better than Imbry had expected, though it leaned heavily toward starches. But it was supplied in plenty, with copious amounts of a mild beer to wash it all down, and no one left the mess hall underfed. Imbry was finishing a second plate of pasta when a horn blared and they were paraded again in the open square.

Now Imbry knew why they had been ordered not to lose their peaked caps: without one, it was impossible to raise one's eyes above a forty-five-degree angle. He risked a glance upward and saw, now that the white dwarf was well up in the sky, that the blue above had become a sheet of white, and the huge billowing clouds were dissipating like the thinnest morning mist. When he breathed, the air that entered his nose felt as if it had come from a furnace.

The guards did not bother to take a head count or conduct a roll call. Imbry saw no walls or fences about the enclosure, except for a series of tall poles set at intervals around the perimeter of the compound. Beyond them was seamless jungle, tall plants above, low ones below, and all of them exhibiting broad-leafed foliages that, when the white star rose, rolled themselves tightly into spikes.

Ovetz called for their attention. The newcomers were to stay where they were for orientation. The old lags were told to fall in on their capos—men in white uniforms standing in a row behind the senior regulator—and when they had done so in groups of ten, they were marched off between two of the buildings and down a dusty road that was also lined on either side by the tall poles. Imbry saw that they went without spirit, and for all their full bellies, every one had the look of a man who didn't get enough to eat.

Orientation was brief. Meals were served thrice daily. The time between the morning and midday meals was free time for prisoners not on report; from after lunch until supper time, the men would labour at the work of the prison colony, the nature of which would be explained by their capos. Night was for sleep.

"You'll have no pep," Ovetz said, "for hijinks. Anyone who wishes to

16

escape may do so," he went on, gesturing broadly to the surrounding jungle, which now resembled an expanse of pin-cushions. "There is little to eat, nothing to drink. The energy stanchions you see surrounding the camp and lining the road are not to keep you in, but to keep out the things that infest the wild lands. They come in several sizes and move at different speeds and by various forms of locomotion, but whether they leap, slither, or erupt from underfoot, they all possess an insatiable thirst, which they will attempt to slake at your expense. At night, you will hear them feeding off each other."

They were told to fall out in their groups. Imbry's was approached by a man with jowls that were dark with stubble and a protruding lower lip that always remained moist because of his habit of constantly licking it. "I am Ratchko. Form a line, come with me and do what I tell you."

He waited until they were in file before him, then picked up a sealed jug whose contents sloshed and handed it to big Cappro, who was first in line. Then he turned on a heel and walked off down the road. Imbry and the others followed. They kept their eyes on the ground before them, feeling the heat of the dwarf star on their heads and shoulders. Imbry was grateful for the flap of cloth that protected the back of his neck. He could feel sweat breaking out on his body, soaking into his clothing, and almost immediately drying anywhere that the cloth felt the harsh white light from above. The forest loomed above them, but its spiky vegetation offered almost no shade.

The road split after a while, becoming two paths, each guarded by the poles. Ratchko led them into the right hand way, and when it divided, a few hundred paces farther on, he took the left. Two more divisions, a left and a right, had them walking down a narrow trail, the protective stanchions buzzing at their elbows and giving off a hot stench of ozone. Abruptly, they came out into a small clearing, again ringed by humming poles—except at its far side, where instead of spiked plants there rose a wall of black rock.

Or so Imbry thought until Ratchko marched them closer and told them to stop. That's not rock, the fat man thought. He examined the surface and saw that it slowly moved and roiled, as if he were looking at a pane of some transparent material against whose far side pressed billows of thick, stygian smoke.

"Welcome," said Ratchko, "to Hell. If it's not Hell, it will do until the real one comes along."

"What is it?" Ifriz said.

"I don't know," said the capo. "Why don't you tell me when you get back?"

"Back?" said the thin man.

Ratchko inclined his head toward the blackness, and Ifriz took an involuntary step backwards, bumping into Imbry who stood behind him, immersed in thought.

Meanwhile, the capo was saying, as he considered Ifriz, "That's if you get back. There's not that much of you to go in there in the first place. Depends on what the weather's like in Hell today."

The fat man stepped to one side to get an unobstructed look at the phenomenon. His education had been truncated by misfortune, but for a few of his most youthful years, Imbry had attended a respectable boarding school that prepared its students for entry into the Archon's Institute. The young Imbry's favourite subjects had been fine arts and logic, but the school's curriculum mandated that its graduates be acquainted with the elements of how the universe was put together.

So he knew that there were nine planes of existence, of which the vast expanse of space–time that he and the rest of humanity inhabited was the third. He knew, too, that the nine dimensions had very little interaction with each other, but that in rare instances one might impinge upon its neighbour. The most common of these intersections were the whimsies that connected some point in third-plane space with some other point an impossible distance away, by somehow burrowing through one of the other planes. These passages in and out of space-time made interstellar space travel feasible.

No one knew how whimsies had come to be. They had been there, waiting, when humanity first ventured beyond the home world's system. It was generally held, by those who cared about origins and first causes, that the passageways had been bored through adjacent planes by some space-faring species in the far distant past, perhaps even before Old Earth was formed. Others conjectured that they were byproducts of actions taken by denizens of the higher planes for their own purposes and the fact that they connected distant points in the third plane—as the phenomenal universe was known—was sheer accident.

It was theorized, some long-ago instructor had said, that a whimsy might occur on a planet. There was no reason it could not, other than statistical unlikelihood: only a few hundred whimsies had been charted along The Spray, and all of them were surrounded by the vast, aching emptiness of interstellar space. But then, so was every star and planet, and the odds that a given volume of space might contain anything other than vacuum were billions of billions to one against.

So, he thought, *here is a theoretician's question convincingly answered.* He studied the shifting blackness again, turning his gaze to its edges. They were regular. The seeming wall had a flat bottom and top, and two straight sides, although the angles at which they met were not square. It looked like a doorway that had been squeezed in at the top and widened at the bottom. From what he remembered, that was unusual. Whimsies in space were large, wide enough to accommodate a spaceship with room to spare. And they were always ovoid in shape.

As Imbry studied the regularity of the black shape, he suspected he had found an answer to the question of whether whimsies were natural occurrences or artefacts that had been made by means unknown. Now he recalled how the paths had diverged between the compound and this clearing in the spiky jungle. He put up a hand to draw the capo's attention.

Ratchko had been supervising Ifriz as the counterfeiter tied a thick rope around his own waist. While Imbry had been thinking, the thin man had been arguing that someone else might like to be singled out for this attention, but the capo had ended the argument by drawing a shocker and pointing it at the counterfeiter.

"Make it tight," Ratchko said. "It's your only way back." Now he noticed Imbry's elevated hand and said, "You wish to accompany your friend?"

It was only then that Imbry saw that there had been two ropes coiled on the ground near the bottom of the interplanar portal. "No," he said, "just a question."

"Ask it."

"Are there more of these?" he indicated the black tetragon.

"Several," said Ratchko. With Ifriz now secured, he kicked the other rope toward the fat man and gestured with the shocker. His meaning was plain.

Imbry considered the shocker. It was a heavy-duty model that would induce agonising spasms of hypercontraction in all of his muscles, cramps that could recur for hours after he regained consciousness. Then he briefly examined the capo's face. Seeing no warmth there, he stooped and picked up the end of the rope. He could not tie it around his waist, since he had none, so he fitted it under his chafed armpits and knotted it securely across his chest.

As he did so, he asked Ratchko, "Are they the same size and shape?"

"Why do you ask?"

"I am afflicted by a lifelong curiosity."

"And now you see where it leads," said the capo. "But to answer your question: yes."

"Ah," said Imbry.

Ratchko gestured with the shocker to the fat man and the thin. "Approach the doorway." To the others he said, "Take hold of the ropes, four men to each, and let them play out gradually. When I say, 'Pull,' you will haul them back out. This you will do as quickly as you may, so that when your turn comes, the same will be done for you."

Imbry and Ifriz stood before the roiling darkness. The counterfeiter trembled. The fat man whispered to him, "Have you ever passed through a whimsy unmedicated?"

"And risk insanity?" Ifriz whispered back.

"I have met spacers who have tried it. It can be endured for a short time."

"You think this is the same?"

"At least similar."

"What are you two whispering about?" said Ratchko, appearing beside them after having supervised the forming of the four-man rope-hauling teams.

"A prayer to the god of fat men," said Imbry.

"And to the one who watches over us, the wiry," said Ifriz.

The capo smiled sourly. He indicated Imbry and said, "His deity will be of more help." Then, looking the thin man up and down, "Though yours will be the greater needed."

"Do we just step in?" Imbry said.

"Only if you want to be brought out in a peculiar shape," said Ratchko, "not to mention dead." He instructed them to lie down on their bellies and crawl into the phenomenon on their elbows. "I'm told you will feel something like gravity drawing you head-first, as if you are sliding down a slope. Go with it."

"And what do we do there?"

"Excellent question!" The man issued instructions. They were to belly-crawl and keep their heads down, constantly feeling all around and ahead of them for solid objects on or in the ground. "It isn't really ground," he amended, "but I don't know what else to call it."

If they found anything, the procedure was to clutch it tightly with one hand and tug on the rope with the other. Until they found something, they were to keep searching. If a man found nothing once he had reached the limit of his rope, he would be pulled out.

"What is there to find?" Imbry asked.

"You'll know when you come across it," was the answer, followed by an order to get down and get crawling. Ratchko pressed a stud on the shocker that caused an aurora of white and blue sparks to discharge from a vent on its upper surface. The weapon was fully charged.

Imbry knelt then pressed his belly down to the dirt. When he raised his gaze to the blackness, it was right there before him, coiling and uncoiling like a great, heedless snake made of smoke.

"Do we hold our breath?" he said.

"Find out," said Ratchko. "I will count to three. If you are not out of sight, certain misery follows."

21

Imbry's life had taught him not to argue with necessity. He did not wait for the count, but crawled forward. His head entered the anomaly.

Irreality. He saw nothing; there was not even the concept of light. But something impinged on his optical processes—flashes of orange and incarnadine, split by horizontal strata of green and a brilliant blue that he knew was no colour he had ever seen. There was sound, a whittering and stuttering, like echoes disseminated down a long, metal pipe. For a moment some presence seemed to be beside him—probably Ifriz entering the anomaly, he thought—then it was gone.

He moved forward and felt some force, not gravity but an equivalent, pull him down along an invisible incline. He put his hands out in front, so that they, instead of his head, would bear the shock of any sudden impacts. It seemed that he slid a good distance, but the rope straggling out behind him remained loose.

Now it felt as if he had stopped moving, but without friction, or wind against his face, or the sight of a passing landscape, he could not tell. He left one hand out to fend off collisions, and with the other began to feel around him in the blackness. His groping fingers sank into something without much texture—it was like smooth, liquid mud, except that it moved across his flesh with a sensation like a river of tiny, flowing granules. He became aware of heat, as if the non-mud was simmering, then it became suddenly cold, then hot again. He suspected his skin was experiencing sensations it could not account for, and was sending his brain various approximations.

He groped on, wondering what he was supposed to find. Another sound came, an unfocused fluttering that came from all directions, and abruptly ceased. He realised the non-light had ceased to flash and had become a steady, diffused glow—pale cream tinged with auras of the unearthly blue at the surrounds of his field of vision. Then it all went black again, and from somewhere nearby came a sound like the croaking of a great frog.

His fingertips brushed past something in the non-slime. He brought his hand back and found nothing. On an impulse, he drove his arm deeper into the stuff, and again the tip of a finger felt something hard and smooth, sinking below his reach. He dug deep and fast, felt its roundness meet his palm, and closed his grip in it. It throbbed in his fist, but seemed to do him no harm.

He reached with his free hand, found the rope and tugged. A moment later, the cord tightened and though he felt no sense of motion, he was sure he was being drawn back to his own plane. He clutched the thing he had found to his chest.

Two things he noticed. One was that he had not breathed since he entered the whimsy—if that was what it was—nor had he felt a need to do so. The other was an indefinable sensation throughout his body: a kind of whispery tickle, though not on his skin, which was still experimenting with heat and chill, but deep within his tissues. Now a few timeless moments went by and suddenly he was once again in the clearing, lying on his back, gazing up at Ratchko and the other trans-portees. He looked away as the blaze of the dwarf star instantly brought tears to his eyes.

"How long was I in there?" he said.

"Never mind that," said the capo. "What have you brought?"

Imbry lifted his head and hand so that could see and opened his fist. Nestled in the cup of his palm was a small, round object. He used his free hand to wipe the moisture from his eyes and once again said, "Ah."

Ratchko snatched the item from his grasp. "Good one," he said, "that's you for the day."

Imbry sat up, untying the rope's knots. To the others he said, "What about Ifriz?" but he was thinking, *So this is where noubles come from.*

Cappro answered him, worry on his broad face. "He hasn't tugged the rope. And it has stopped playing out." As Imbry rose, the big man turned to Ratchko, who was studying the iridescent sphere in his hand. "We should get him out."

The capo brought up his shocker then appeared to notice that Cappro was not much intimidated. "All right," he said, "haul him out."

All except Imbry laid hands to the second rope. They pulled, then

23

pulled again, as the fat man got to his feet. He felt disequilibriated; his head spun, but then the moment passed. His eyes followed the rope to where it disappeared into the interplanar portal; it did not seem as if there was much weight on the other end.

Ifriz's feet emerged from the blackness, then his shins and thighs and in short order his torso and finally his head and outstretched arms, dragging across the hot, gritty dirt. The thin man lay face down on the ground, inert. Imbry could not tell if he breathed.

Cappro knelt and turned his friend over. The counterfeiter's face was pale, the skin like old wax. The big man slapped his cheek with surprising tenderness, then rubbed the flaccid chest. Nothing happened and he repeated his efforts, while the capo made some remark that, though not clearly heard, offered no encouragement.

Then suddenly Ifriz's chest rose and filled with a great inward gasp of air. His thin body shuddered and his eyes opened. To Imbry, he appeared sightless, and though the tiny, fierce blaze in the sky brought tears to the recumbent man's eyes, Ifriz did nothing to wipe them away.

Cappro lifted his friend to a sitting position, rubbed his arms and said, "Ifriz, say something."

The thin man took another great breath, but all that came out was a sighing moan. He began to shiver.

"Put him over there," said Ratchko, gesturing with the shocker to the edge of the clearing. "Next two men, get roped up."

The capo took a pouch from inside his shirt and carefully placed the nouble within, then tightened the neck and put the bag back where it had come from. He looked at Imbry. "First time," he said, "you may have the touch. Kreek for you at supper."

"Kreek?" the fat man said.

Ratchko made a tippling gesture, waggled his eyebrows, and smacked his lips. "All you can drink, too."

"This is what we do here?" he said. "Hunt for noubles?"

"It is," said the capo, then to the others, "Right, you two down on your hands and knees, rest of you take hold of the rope. Now, in you go!"

Cappro was not one of the new entrants. He held the rope as ordered, but his eyes were on his stricken friend, who had been left beside one of the humming poles.

"You there!" said Ratchko, aiming the shocker. "Attend to your work!"

Imbry asked the capo, "May I see to him?"

"You're done for the day, already said so."

The fat man went to kneel beside Ifriz. The thin man was conscious. When Imbry offered him a drink from the communal jug, he sat up and sipped without thirst, although Imbry's own throat was parched. He took a drink himself and said, "How is it with you?"

Ifriz blinked, as if collecting his thoughts. "It took something . . ." he said, then stared at the ground, as if he might find there the answer to some inner question.

"It?" said the fat man.

The counterfeiter continued to stare. "That place, the no-place."

"What did it take?"

Ifriz stared for a long moment, until Imbry was about to ask the question again. Then he said, "Me. It took some of me." He looked at Imbry. "You were in there. Didn't it take some of you?"

The forger remembered the strange tickling in his flesh. That might indeed have been the sensation of some of his substance being taken away. He stood and looked down at himself. He was not accustomed to examining his heroic physique—he was as he was, and was content with it—but it seemed to him that he was perhaps a little svelter than he had been before lunch. And now that he looked at the other man, the fellow's thinness seemed to have been somehow intensified. He could see Ifriz's backbones standing out through the thin fabric of his blue suit.

Hence the plentiful food, the fat man thought. He put things together: the full plates and the empty barracks, the daily entry to another dimension, the fact that the transport ship brought men in but took no one off-world, the effort made by Rodrig Uverlanth—and perhaps others—to lure in persons who could end up in this nameless place, grubbing in irreality for noubles. His mind offered him a cohesive schematic.

And he saw that he must find a way off this planet, before he was reduced to the dimensions of poor Ifriz, and, after that, to nothingness.

The afternoon wore on, the two suns chasing each other to the zenith and down to the horizon. As the golden star darkened and set, the heat became more bearable, although it was still an occasion of pain to stare at the white dwarf. Imbry and Ifriz, the latter somewhat recovered, took their turns at rope-hauling after the second pair of nouble hunters were ready to be brought out.

The forger noticed a curious thing: although two men should have sufficed to pull one man over what had felt like a frictionless surface, it took the combined efforts of four to haul a single forager back through the portal. This coincided with what Imbry recalled from his school days: whimsies had a quality known as "flow"—they "went" from one "place" to another. This deduction heartened him. He began to see the elements of a plan.

Toward the second sunset, they marched back to the compound. Only one other nouble had been recovered; from Ratchko's demeanour, Imbry surmised that two in one day was a significant result. The capo cheerfully slapped the backs of the fat man and the other successful forager, a stubby thief named Eredello, and promised them all the kreek they could hold.

Back at their barracks, the last two prisoners to have gone into the whimsy fell on their bunks, inert and drained. Imbry and the other seven convened a discussion of what they had done and felt. The forger learned that his experience approximated the others', although each man reported a different palette of colours flashing across his vision. The less substantial of them had felt the tickling sensation more strongly, as if deeper in their tissues.

Eredello, the man who had found the other nouble, said that he had gone in resolved to equal Imbry's success. He confessed to a weakness for strong drink, the lack of which had caused him great discomfort since his arrest. When he heard the capo promise the fat man all he could hold, his mouth had watered and his hands had itched to feel a nouble. Now he licked his lips and cocked his head as if listening for the dinner bell.

It came, and they marched to the mess hall. Again, the plates were piled high with cheap but wholesome food, and Imbry ate as much as he could. The capos ate at a separate table and the fat man saw Ratchko talking volubly and turning to point at Imbry and Eredello. Ovetz, at the head of the table, turned his small eyes to look their way. He plainly failed to share in the capo's pleasure.

After dinner, as the hall emptied, Ratchko came to collect his two stars. He led them to a small building set in a corner of the compound and left them there. Three other prisoners were inside, seated on rough chairs, their common attitude that of a man who normally expected no pleasure in life but was now about to receive one.

Imbry took a seat and offered a few words and gestures of greeting. Soon after, Ratchko and another capo returned, each carrying two jugs. They put them on a table that stood against the rear wall of the hut, with a scatter of chipped and dented mugs on its surface. As the capos turned to leave, the five men rose as one, their eyes on the liquor.

Or at least four of the men did so. Imbry stepped to intercept Ratchko, saying, "Could I have a word before you leave?"

"Why not?" was the answer. "You've served me well. But make it quick. Any capo who brings in two noubles in a day gets his choice of the spinsters." He made motions of hands and hips that left the fat man in no doubt as to the activity he looked forward to.

"There are women here?" Imbry said.

"If you close your eyes, they can almost seem so," said the capo. "Now, what's on your mind?"

The forger lowered his voice. "I am a wealthy man, with substantial assets on several foundational domains."

The capo gave him a look of bemusement. "In this place, that matters not at all. You could command the treasures of Gruengold, as in the old story, but it would mean nothing. Here there is nothing to buy."

"But if we could leave here . . ."

"We cannot." The man's face soured. "Not you, not I, not even Ovetz. Only one ship comes and it departs empty—except for noubles."

"But—"

"There is no but! Now, get to your drink and leave me to Madlirra."

Imbry assumed that Madlirra must be the pick of whatever devices were available to service the capos. "I'll make you an offer," he said, following the man to the door. "If I find two noubles in one day, you fix it so that I can talk with the ship's integrator."

Ratchko paused. "Two noubles in one day?" He rubbed his unshaven jaw.

"Another session with Madlirra."

"You won't do it. No one ever has."

"I am not," said Imbry, "ordinary."

Ratchko laughed, then lowered his voice. "I liked the way you spoke to Ovetz at the first muster, and the way you took it when he trod on your toes." He shrugged. "All right, two in one day, and you talk to the ship."

"Promise?"

"Promise." With that, he left, though the fat man heard him say as he hurried through the door, "And much good may it do you."

Imbry made his way to the table and the jugs. He poured a couple of fingers of clear liquid into a metal cup and sniffed. The bouquet instantly cleared his sinuses, and when he tasted the liquor it went down his gullet like thin-bodied lava. He saw that Eredello was already glazed-eyed and swaying. But, the fat man told himself, even at the price of some refined taste buds, he deserved some celebration. He now had a plan and he had taken the first step toward implementing it. He raised the cup in an ironic toast to no one, drank the stuff down, and managed to keep it there.

It all depended, Imbry knew, on the validity of what he had been taught as a boy. On one of the planes adjacent to this cosmos, events did not happen according to the operation of cause and effect, instead, things happened because of a force that approximated the energy known in this, the third plane, as "will."

If the dimension in which noubles grew was the one he was faintly recalling, and if Imbry could summon and sufficiently focus what the denizens of the Olkney half-world called "oomph," then he could proceed to the next step in his plan. He was not sure of the first "if," but when it came to the second, he had no fears—when it came to generating will, Imbry was a dynamo.

The next morning, his head only a little thunderous from the kreek, he ate as much breakfast as he could, then rested on his bunk until lunch. Some of his barracks-mates called him to come outside, where they were improvising some kind of game to relieve the tedium, but Imbry waved them away. He had once been interested in the spiritual discipline known as the lho-tso exercises, and now he concentrated on remembering the mantras and the breathing techniques. He thought they might serve.

Ifriz, too, did not join the noisy game outside. The counterfeiter lay on his upper bunk and stared silently at the ceiling. Occasionally, Imbry heard him swallow. The thin man had tried to match the Old Earther at breakfast, but had soon fallen behind; finally he gave up, his stomach rounded like a pregnancy.

Midday came with a glare of light through the shuttered windows. The mess hall bell clanged, and Imbry went and again ate like a champion. He encouraged Ifriz to take all that he could, saying, "Hold on as long as you can. I am working to free us."

In truth, Imbry was working to free himself. Any others who benefited were welcome to do so, so long as their participation did not interfere with the fat man's plans. But he saw no reason not to offer hope to the thin-shanked counterfeiter.

Bellies full, caps pulled down and neck flaps deployed, the prisoners formed up in the centre of the compound. Ratchko was more relaxed than he had been the day before, a sated smile gracing his stubbled face. Ovetz, on the other hand, looked sourer than usual and blew his whistle without gusto. Imbry suspected that Ovetz preferred to keep Madlirra's ministrations to himself.

The teams marched off to the portals. Imbry noted that his ten were being led down different turnings than yesterday, and was not surprised when they came to a different clearing. But the slow storm of blackness surging against the interplanar membrane looked the same. He squared his shoulders and volunteered to be one of the first pair in.

"Good man!" said Ratchko, slapping his shoulder. "An example to all of you!"

Imbry lowered his voice. "Our deal still holds?"

"I am a man of my word," murmured the capo.

The forger put the rope around his upper torso, got down on hands and knees, and spent a moment softly chanting the first sura in the elementary lho-tso sequence. Then, without waiting, he plunged through the barrier.

It seemed to Imbry that the importuning sensations of the previous day were less obtrusive now; even the deep prickling of his flesh was less noticeable. He wondered if the "weather" in this "region" of the plane was different from where he had sojourned the day before. He let the current, or whatever it was, draw him in while he focused inwardly on the repetitive syllables of the chant. As he had been taught, long ago when such things interested him, he narrowed his thoughts until only the sounds of the mantra had meaning.

At the same time, the chant seemed to ring in his consciousness like the booming of great bells. He took fresh heart from the effect and sent his heightened concentration down his arms, into his hands and to the tips of his fingers. He thought of noubles and nothing but noubles, visualized their opalescent smoothness, the shimmer of their inner auras, willing them to come to him.

Something brushed against his outstretched thumb. He redoubled his concentration on the lho-tso mantra. The thing in the non-slime came again, pressed itself against his palm, as if it were a ball of iron and Imbry's hand a magnet. He willed it to stay there then made the same summons as before. This time, he could feel that the call was even stronger, his resolve strengthened by initial success. It was not long, it seemed, before he felt pressure against his other hand.

He closed both fists and felt the same powerful throb as yesterday, as if a new heart was beating, warm and strong, in each hand. He was tempted to make another summons, but his innate common sense intervened. This was a place where will was a powerful force, and exercising it might have side effects that were beyond his capacity to sense. For all he knew, here on the seventh plane, Imbry's bursts of willpower could be the equivalent of a blind and deaf man setting off fireworks. And who knew what attentions they might draw?

He transferred one of the noubles to his other palm, then used his free hand to tug on the rope. In moments, though it may have been hours, he was once again under the dual light of the white and golden stars. He rose to his knees, looked up at a ring of expectant faces.

"Well?" Ratchko said.

Imbry opened his hand and heard the gasp.

"Two!" the capo whispered. "And prime pink! Never!"

"It's Madlirra again for you," the fat man said, then cocked his head and raised his brows in a way that said: And for me?

Ratchko chuckled and nodded, said, "For certain." Imbry handed him the two orbs. He rose to his feet, feeling less tired than he had the day before, closed his eyes and took a deep breath. Then he heard the capo swear; he opened his eyes to see that the men who should have been holding the second rope had let it go to cluster around Ratchko to see the two noubles. The last of its length was heading rapidly for the barrier.

Cappro dove for the cord, got his hand on it and began to pull. The other members of his team did likewise, gripping each other when they could not find enough hand-room on the rope. And now those who had pulled Imbry out of the whimsy joined in the effort. Cappro, his heels dug into the bone-dry ground, strained with all his considerable force, while the others did their best, but scarcely more than a hand's width of the heavy line came out of the anomaly.

"Let me," Imbry said, and reached a hand to grip where the cord had newly appeared. He summoned the lho-tso exercise again, but found it made little difference on this side of the barrier. Still, as more rope came free, more hands could grasp it; gradually, with all nine of the transportees pulling, length after length emerged from the roiling blackness.

Then there came a moment when the rope ceased to move. "Harder!" said Cappro, putting the line across his broad shoulders and drawing until cords stood out in his neck and arms. They all gave their best, but to no avail.

Then, suddenly, the line came out as if flung at them. The straining men stumbled and fell backward in a confusion of limbs. When they recovered and stood again, they saw the end of the rope clear of the barrier. But of the man who had gone in just after Imbry, they saw nothing. Ifriz was gone.

"It happens sometimes," Ratchko was saying. "No one knows why, or where they go to. Maybe Ifriz untied the knot and swam off to meet his fate."

"Or maybe something swallowed him and spat out the rope," Imbry said.

"If it did," the capo said, "it first undid the double knots. Look." He held up the end of the line, and they all saw that it was untied and undamaged.

Cappro was distraught and insistent on going in to search for his friend. He tied the rope firmly about his middle, his mouth grim with purpose, then kneeled to wriggle into the anomaly. The others took hold of the rope and watched as it was drawn into the darkness. Steadily, it disappeared, until it reached its limit, then Ratchko ordered them to haul the big enforcer "back to the world."

When Cappro came at last through the seeming smoke, he was inert, his senses overwhelmed by too long an exposure to irreality. Ratchko set his shocker to its mildest discharge and jolted the man back into consciousness. Cappro sat up, dazed, his eyes unfocused. When he finally realised that his mission had failed, he put his head in his big hands and wept.

Ratchko reset his shocker and was prepared to deal with the situation in the prescribed manner, but Imbry managed to divert him with a series of questions. "How often does it happen? Is any trace ever found of the missing? Does size have any bearing on the issue?"

"Now that you mention it," said the capo, scratching his stubbled jaw, "it does seem to be the gauntest who disappear. That is, if we don't haul them out permanently deranged."

"Are those the only available outcomes?" the fat man asked.

The answer was not encouraging. All who went into the anomaly returned diminished in substance. "They shrink, then they wither," was how Ratchko put it. Their loss of mass was not uniform, however; flesh disappeared at a faster rate than bone, for example, and fat went more quickly than muscle. But it was not just striate muscle that dwindled. So did the vital organs. At a certain point in the process, the brain ceased to function reliably. It was believed that, in most cases, the missing had slipped out of the loop tied about them. But a few times, when the rope was pulled "out of the smoke" the knots had been undone.

"It never looks as if it has been chewed or sliced through? Or burned?" Imbry asked.

"Not that I've heard," said the capo. He turned and, seeing that Cappro had recovered his poise, set about putting another pair to the task.

"Wait," said Imbry. "The team has already delivered two noubles. Is that not enough for a day?"

Ratchko considered the question. "Most days," he said, "we are lucky to get one."

"And those two will earn me a jug of kreek and you a rendezvous with your spinster of choice?"

"Indeed." The capo licked his always-wet lower lip in contemplation of the evening to come.

But," said Imbry, "and I'm only speculating, if we were to bring in three or even four noubles, would your reward be correspondingly greater?"

33

Ratchko's face expressed the underlying unfairness of existence. "It would not. The place has nothing more to offer."

"But suppose this team begins to bring in more noubles consistently, might not the senior regulator ordain that, from then on, three or four might be the requirement before a capo gets his choice of spinsters?"

Ratchko's brows first knit then writhed as his gaze turned inward, displaying the intensity of effort with which he worked through the implications of Imbry's question. Then his eyes and mouth opened as one. "I believe you are right, the dirty glemmister!"

Imbry did not pause to inquire what a glemmister might be. "Perhaps, then, the wisest thing for all of us," he said, "is to rest through the day and make a new beginning tomorrow . . . after you have had an opportunity to wear Madlirra to a frazzle."

"You're right," said the capo, "and all the more reason to rest while I can." He ordered the nine remaining in his crew to move to the west side of the clearing, close to the humming poles, where the spike-leaved vegetation offered some scant shade. Then he made all of them but Imbry array themselves in a line so that he could recline in their combined shadow.

"You rest yourself, too," he said to the fat man, indicating with a magnanimous sweep of his arm the shaded space beside him. "I want to see you well looked after. While you last."

Imbry hunkered down in the shadows of the sweating men, offering them a gesture that invited them to endure the heat in patience. "While we're resting," he said, "you could tell me more about the anomalies and what happens here."

But there wasn't a great deal more that Ratchko could relate. He had never been through the whimsy and was a man without much curiosity. The colony had been in operation long before he was sent here. All of the capos, and even Senior Regulator Ovetz, were convicted malefactors who had been offered the choice of lifelong exile to Nestranko—for that was indeed the name of this world—as an alternative to a punishment known as the "five disciplines."

"They say there are five, but I've never heard of anyone surviving past the third. I've been here two years now, and wouldn't mind seeing the place dwindle in the aft porthole of a spaceship."

"But the ship never takes anyone away," Imbry prompted.

"Never."

"Has anyone tried to suborn its integrator?"

"Once. A capo who fancied himself smarter than most."

"And?"

"The ship told Ovetz, who did not approve. He reassigned the capo as a nouble-hunter. The man was already thin. He soon dwindled and went mad, and Ovetz had him fed into the digester."

"Hmm," said Imbry. "Am I correct in believing that the senior regulator likes it here?"

"You are. On New Gargano, he worked for one of the crime syndicates, but his prospects were limited. He lacked finesse and was sent out only on tasks that called for brute force and no fine judgements."

"He beat people to death," Imbry translated.

"No one could deny he was good at that," said the capo.

"Hmm," Imbry said again.

As the blazing white dot chased its milder companion toward the horizon, the men formed up and marched back to the barracks. Ratchko, clutching the two noubles, went to Ovetz's office to report his team's success. Imbry was resting on his bunk when another capo appeared at the door to tell him that the senior regulator required his presence.

"He wishes to congratulate me?" he asked the man as they walked across the parade ground. The capo looked at him sideways, as if he were an odd item indeed, but made no answer.

Ovetz's office was up a flight of narrow stairs on the second floor of the administrative nexus. The capo remained at the foot of the steps while the fat man went up alone. At the top he found a door and addressed himself to its who's-there. It swung open silently.

The interior was dim after the bright light of the outdoors. Imbry stepped inside, saying, "I was ordered to—" but got no further. A shove between his shoulder blades propelled him forward, the door slammed behind him, and before he could turn he was struck by the full force of a shocker's discharge.

All of his major skeletal muscles contracted at once and he fell heavily to the floor in unnatural agony. He writhed and made animal sounds—there could be no dignity while suffering under a shocker's lash—as the weapon's wielder continued to maintain pressure on its activation stud. Finally, as the fat man was beginning to lose consciousness, he was released from the shocker's savage grip to sprawl face-down on the wooden floor, drool pooling beneath his slack mouth. He moaned as residual spasms, like aftershocks following an earth tremor, struck at random in his back, leg and abdominal muscles.

"And that," said a harsh voice above him, "is before I've even heard the first lie."

Imbry groaned. A booted foot found his ribs and he was ordered to get up. Shaking, he managed to get his palms pressed against the floorboards, then levered himself to his hands and knees. His joints felt loose and unreliable. His insides ached.

In the dim light of the office, he saw the back of a chair before him and, using it for support, gradually pulled himself to his feet. But when he went to sit, the chair was yanked out from under him and he crashed to the floor again, the sound of a cruel laugh adding a garnish to his pain.

"Try again," said Ovetz, swimming into view as Imbry's vision cleared. This time he let the prisoner settle into the chair, while he set himself on the edge of his desk, the shocker resting on one thigh. "Now," he said, "who are you and what are you doing here?"

The fat man had decided before climbing the stairs that there would be no point in maintaining the fictional identity under which he had been tried and sentenced, nor the pretence of innocence. Now he focused his subtle mind to deal with the realities of the moment; revenge would have to wait. In a few sentences, he named himself and described his circumstances.

"You're one of Uverlanth's, eh?" Ovetz said. He consulted a document on his desktop. "It seems he's having to reach farther afield to find new transportees."

"He has used up the supply of criminals on New Gargano?" Imbry said.

Ovetz said, "The colony's been in operation for several years. Those of my former colleagues who have not been sent here have decided to try their luck on other worlds."

"I was lured all the way from Old Earth."

"Never heard of it."

"It's a long way up The Spray."

Ovetz scratched his chin. "A buyer and seller of stolen artworks, you say?"

Imbry gestured an affirmative. "I also forge copies of old masterpieces."

"So no administrative background?"

The fat man could tell that this was no innocent inquiry. Ovetz was not skilled at feigning disinterest. "No such background," he said. He paused a moment and gave an impression of a man thinking hard, then said, "You didn't think that I was sent to spy on you? Or even to relieve you?"

Suspicion took control of the senior regulator's coarse features. The shocker came up. "Why would you say that?"

"Just for a moment there," said Imbry, "it seemed to me that might be what you were thinking."

Ovetz peered at him, then gradually his suspicions seemed to fade. "Huh," he said, "I always did have a bad habit of showing my hand." He studied Imbry some more. "You're a smart one, aren't you?"

"Creating forgeries good enough to fool the serious collector does require a certain weight of brain."

The senior regulator laughed. "Well, it won't do you much good here. Besides, whatever your brain weighs now, it will weigh less next week. And still less the week after."

"I would prefer that that did not happen," said Imbry.

"Nestranko is a good place for shedding pointless preferences."

The conversation lapsed for a while. Ovetz seemed immersed in thoughts that did not make him happy. Imbry was assessing the other man's qualities, while the effects of the shocker gradually faded. He had spent his life among malefactors of many persuasions and characters. The senior regulator struck him as the kind of man who could be useful when closely directed. Left to his own devices, his insecurities would always get the better of him. He said, "You seem to be troubled. Are the penal authorities causing you difficulties?"

Ovetz laughed again. "Penal authorities?" he said. "There are no such persons. Nestranko is a privately-owned world, and you'll never guess who owns it."

"I might," said Imbry. "Rodrig Uverlanth, for one, and a few cronies that he has recruited from amongst his more pliable colleagues on the magistrate's bench."

The jailer's mouth opened. "You are a quick one."

The shivers and spasms in Imbry's muscles had largely dissipated. He said, "Have they been threatening to replace you?"

There was no one to overhear them, but Ovetz's eyes flicked from side to side before he answered. "They sent a man, a couple of ships ago."

Imbry looked around as if the fellow might be nearby. "And something happened to him?"

"Fell into the digester."

"Clumsy, was he?"

"You could say that." Ovetz ran a broad hand over his face. "Before his accident, we had a private talk. I wanted him to tell me if Uverlanth had a spy in the camp."

Imbry saw the shape of it. "It would have to be one of the capos," he said. "Inmates don't last. What did the new man tell you?"

"I did not judge my inducements finely enough. The bones of his skull were surprisingly delicate."

Ovetz opened his hands in a gesture that expressed regret for unavoidable accidents. "He also had an energy pistol when he arrived, but it was not on his person nor in his quarters when I searched."

"Conceivably, then, the spy has it. We'll have to watch for that."

"I don't think it matters much," said the senior regulator. "The ship that brought you will return and tell the syndicate that I am still in charge."

The fat man again gave the appearance of hard thinking. "Why do they want to relieve you?" When Ovetz showed traces of guilt, Imbry answered his own question: "Has nouble production fallen? Do they suspect you of holding back a few, perhaps with the aim of selling the items privately?"

Again the senior regulator's mouth gaped. "You truly are one for the thinking, aren't you?"

"We each of us do what we are good at, and somehow the whole complex business of life rubs along."

Ovetz's face showed that understanding the whole business of life was not high on his agenda. "When the ship returns, I expect it to bring Uverlanth's response."

"Which will probably not be so easily fed into the digester," said Imbry.

"He hires Ta' am mercenaries from the Bravura Company," Ovetz said. "I need a way off this world. You told Ratchko you wanted to talk to the ship."

"He told you that?"

The other man held up thumb and forefinger with very little space between. "Here is his loyalty to you," he said, then held his hand level to the floor but as high as he could reach, "and here is his fear of me."

"Ah," said Imbry. When he saw that Ovetz was waiting for more, he said, "I am trying to put together a plan."

"The ship will not cooperate. Its ethical circuits have been modified. It does whatever Uverlanth tells it, and only what Uverlanth wants. Nor will any other ship land here, because there is an orbital beacon that broadcasts a warning that this is a prison world."

"I thought as much," said the fat man. He shrugged. "How often does the ship come?"

"It varies," Ovetz said. He went to a cupboard set against the wall and opened its rough wooden door, revealing a concealed security container of high quality. Imbry saw no door, only a small slot near the top of the box.

"The noubles," said Ovetz, "go in there. The vault's integrator keeps a running count and also assesses each item's quality. When the total reaches forty noubles of excellent grade or better, it tells the camp's communicator to send a message to New Gargano. Within a few days, the ship arrives to collect the container and leave an empty. It also delivers supplies and new transportees."

Imbry stroked a plump cheek with one finger. He said, "The strategy then becomes obvious."

Ovetz stared at him, expectantly. After the silence extended for a long moment, he said, "Not to me."

"Only Uverlanth can tell the ship what to do. We need to convince him to tell it to do what we wish. I am sure you are proficient at influencing the behaviour of others."

"Not at this distance," said the other man. He smacked a fist into one meaty palm. "Of course, if you could contrive to bring him here . . ."

"Yes," said Imbry. "I think I know how to do that."

The next midday parade convened as usual, the men assembling into their teams. But then Ovetz made a change in procedure. "The following prisoners will fall out," he decreed, "and form up on me." He then read a list of twelve names, and those dozen left the ranks and came to stand in a rough line before the senior regulator. They looked at each other with sidewise and considering glances; to be singled out for special treatment on Nestranko could bode nothing good.

Of the chosen twelve, only Cappro came from Imbry's original team. The fat man saw Tosh Herklunt across the parade ground, the gaunt man's fingers making the signs that meant he wanted to know if he had cause to worry. Imbry used the back of an index finger to wipe his nose, the right nostril from right to left, the left nostril in the other direction—which was to say, all is well and wait for further clarification.

Ovetz dismissed the rest of the colony, capos and transportees alike, saying that this would be a day of rest, but he crooked a finger to bring Imbry to his side. Now the eyes of the chosen twelve fell upon the fat man, and he saw their suspicions settle upon him. He also saw a good deal of intelligence—he and Ovetz had spent yesterday evening poring over the files of the prison's entire population, selecting those whose crimes and associated behaviours bespoke wit or daring or, ideally, both.

The senior regulator ordered them all to file upstairs into his office. When the door closed behind them, he said to Imbry, "Tell them."

"From now on," said the Old Earther, "we're going to do things differently." He was aware of a general stiffening of postures; none of the twelve expected that the change would benefit them. But Imbry spoke on in a tone of quiet confidence. "We are going to increase the output of noubles several-fold." He ignored the signs of fear and apprehension and said, "And then we are going to use that increase to get us all out of here."

That brought some sharp looks, various strengths of hope contending against countervailing suspicions, according to the philosophies and life experiences of the chosen men. "You may speak freely," Imbry said.

The forger Srishanka's hair was no longer as finely braided as it had been on the ship, but his voice was still as cool. "When you say, 'all of us,' does the all mean the entire colony or just those of us in this room?"

"Would it matter to you if it was only the latter?" the fat man said.

After a moment's thought, the other man said, "Not greatly."

"But as it happens," Imbry went on, "we will try to free as many as we can, and send a rescue to those who are left behind."

Another of the twelve, the enforcer Cappro, said, "Rodrig Uverlanth will have something to say about that."

"If we do this right," said the fat man, "Uverlanth will not be in a position to say anything." He let the words hang in the air for a moment, then he added, "Ever again."

"Count me in," said Cappro.

The most comfortable sizeable space in the colony was the capos' recreation lounge, where the spinsters waited in curtained booths

41

against one wall. But the floor was carpeted and there were cushions and relaxers strewn around. Two hours after their talk in the senior regulator's office, Imbry regarded the twelve he had selected and decided that all of them would do. A couple who had followed the nerve-racking criminal specialty of personation—pretending to be whom they were not, even while circulating among the subject's friends, family and integrator—showed exceptional promise. That made sense to Imbry. Personation required confidence, and confidence was a close cousin of will.

He regarded his dozen students, seated in a demilune with their teacher at the centre, as they worked their way through the second-level lho-tso breathing regimen. As his eyes fell on one of the men, the lounge's integrator spoke quietly in his ear, reporting the student's respiration rate, blood pressure, heartbeat, and proportion of alpha and beta neural activity. Imbry regretted that he did not have any of the devices that aided in focusing mental vitality, but the colony had a rough-and-ready workshop whose integrator had assured him that some basic paraphernalia could be made up for tomorrow's lesson.

He let the breathing exercise continue until the lounge's integrator reported that all of the twelve's readings indicated that they had mastered the second level. Imbry cleared his throat and all eyes went to him. "We will proceed," he said, "to the mantra of clarity."

By the end of the day, he was satisfied with the group's progress, and returned the lounge to the capos. As the dozen transportees filed out, they came under the gazes—some curious, some hostile—of the men in white uniforms. But Ovetz had made it clear to the chosen ones that they were not to talk about what went on behind closed doors, and he had also made it clear to the capos that they were not to ask. The digester had been mentioned.

Still, when they gathered in the open-air pavilion for the evening meal, Imbry noticed several of the capos eyeing his group from their separate table and indulging in low-voiced conversation. Ratchko seemed particularly exercised over the new regime, but when Ovetz left his office and crossed the parade ground to the mess hall, the capo's attitude became one of studied neutrality.

As Imbry had requested, his group had been assigned to a separate barracks hut, and were seated at their own table in the open-air mess hall. The fat man had no overt reason to suspect that Rodrig Uverlanth had a spy among the scores of men in the colony, but neither did he have any grounds on which to rule the possibility out.

In the morning, he supervised the workshop's integrator as it put the final touches on two devices, designed to his specifications. After lunch, and after the rest of the colony had been sent out to search for noubles, he introduced the machines to his students in the privacy of the capos' lounge.

He was gratified, by the end of the day, to see that each of them was able to guide a balloon equipped with tiny motorized fans through an invisible obstacle course. They could also cause a cold-plasma projector to create and evolve forms in specified colours and shapes, holding them motionless in the air and rotating them in three dimensions so that they could be seen from different angles. And all done while sitting cross-legged, with eyes closed, hands loose in the lap, and mind concentrated to a finely defined beam.

"Excellent," Imbry said, as he packed away the training devices. "Tomorrow, we go to the whimsies."

After lunch, the transportees formed up on the parade ground, but now the twelve chosen—plus Imbry—constituted a team of their own. Instead of a capo to lead them to their work, they were headed by the senior regulator himself. Each man also carried extra water as they made their way along the pole-guarded paths to the whimsy from which, according to the colony's records, more noubles had come than from any other.

"Here is the plan," Imbry said, when they stood before the roiling blackness. "First each man will drink double the usual ration of water before going in. Water is what we are mostly made of, and hydrating ourselves should slow the dwindling process.

"Second, before penetrating the whimsy, each of us will engage in lho-tso breathing and chant the prime mantra until he has achieved the stage known as the opening. Once through the barrier, concentrate on the syllables while willing the noubles to come to you. As soon as you have found two, pull on the rope and you will be brought out."

A man named Xiai, one of the former personators, spoke up. "What do we gain from enriching the krespell who sent us here?"

"What is a krespell?" said Imbry.

"A crawling thing that eats dung, even its own."

"I must remember that," said the fat man. "But to answer your question, we will amass a record number of noubles and send them back to Rodrig Uverlanth with a story that will bring him here forthwith."

"What kind of story?" said Srishanka.

"The kind," said Imbry, "that combines the lure of vast riches with the risk that they might fall into some others' hands."

"Ah," said Xiai. "And once we have him here?"

"We take his ship, we take his noubles, and we take our leave."

The prisoners looked from the Old Earther to Ovetz. "You concur?" said Cappro.

"I have had enough of this place," said the senior regulator.

Srishanka spoke. "Whatever share in the noubles might come my way, I will relinquish it if you give me Uverlanth."

"I might like a piece of him, too," said Xiai, "just as a souvenir."

"I'm sure we can work something out," said Imbry.

The first part of Imbry's plan succeeded beyond the fat man's expectations. The application of focused will to the process of nouble harvesting yielded better than a month's quota of the interplanar jewels on the first day of the new regime. No one made more than a single trip into the anomaly, but each of the twelve chosen gatherers went in and came out with two of the objects, most of a superior grade. Several of the men reported that they could have brought out more if they'd had something to carry them in.

The next day, they reconvened at the second-most productive portal. Each man carried a small sack made of heavy cloth worn with an over-the-shoulder leather strap. Once again, chanting their mantras, in they went and out they came. When each had done his turn, the total harvest numbered thirty-eight noubles, most of them of the excellent rating, with five superlatives, and not a single utility-grade amongst them.

They returned to the camp before any of the other teams. When the chosen dozen had been dismissed, with offerings of kreek for those who chose to imbibe, Imbry and Ovetz repaired to the senior regulator's office. One by one, the thirty-eight noubles went through the security container's advent, to join yesterday's twenty-four.

"Added to the rest of the colony's yield," Imbry said, "the total must now surely exceed forty excellents or better."

"Agreed," said Ovetz.

"So a signal will go out to the next passing spaceship, and within two days it should reach Uverlanth."

The senior regulator nodded. "He will be surprised."

"And suspicious." Imbry put himself in the magistrate's place for a moment, then said, "Tomorrow, we will go and get more. The safe will send another message. It will reach him a day after the first, telling him that unheard-of riches are waiting to be collected."

"Will he drop everything and come?"

The fat man thought it through, out loud so that Ovetz could follow. First, Imbry said, the miser would ask if the security container's integrator could have been suborned. He would discover that such has never happened, not in millennia. He would then have to choose between two possibilities: either a new and fabulously productive source of noubles had been discovered or the camp authorities had been stealing most of the output for years, and he was only now getting an accurate count—perhaps because the new man he had sent had prevailed after all.

"Either way," Imbry said, "he must conclude that long-distance management has not succeeded, and that he had better come and see what the situation is."

"He will not come alone," said the other man.

"You mentioned Ta'am mercenaries?"

"Yes, from Bravura."

"They tend to be good," said Imbry, "but they also tend to be costly. What does he bring—a platoon or a squad?"

"I've never seen him with more than two troopers."

"Ah," said Imbry, "the New Garganian tendency to pare down expenses may weigh in our favor."

"How?" said Ovetz.

The fat man stroked his cheek again. "I'm working on that."

Another day, a different anomaly, and the yield increased by forty-five more noubles, including two from the other teams. But the harvest by Imbry's chosen crew was almost all excellents and superlatives, and one that Ovetz swore must be an actual exemplar.

"I've never seen one," said the senior regulator, marvelling at the scintillations of colour that chased each other across surface of the fist-sized sphere. "The last one discovered was in my predecessor's time."

"Perhaps," Imbry said, "you might take this one with you when you leave."

"I think," said Ovetz, with what, for him, passed for a sly look, "it's too large to fit through the container's opening."

"Well then," said Imbry, with a wink. But the forger carefully noted where Ovetz stowed the singular jewel.

Three days later, the camp's communicator advised that it had received a message from the in-bound spaceship: it would land in a few hours and the camp should be ready to receive supplies and new inmates. There then followed a personal message for Ovetz from Rodrig Uverlanth.

"He says all is forgiven," the senior regulator told Imbry. "The incident concerning my replacement and the digester is forgotten."

"How gratifying," said the fat man. "He offers you everything you already have, though you have enriched him many times more than he expected."

Ovetz's single eyebrow contracted. "I had not seen it that way."

"The message raises one other question," said Imbry. "Who told him about the 'incident?'"

"The ship's integrator, when it returned from its last trip."

"The ship might have noticed that your replacement was not on the scene. It could not have inferred the business with the digester."

It took a moment for the other man to work through the implications. Then he said, "Who?"

"Who went into the ship last time?" said Imbry.

Ovetz pulled an earlobe, as if to engage his brain, then his face cleared as he remembered. "Ratchko." He growled and massaged one fist in a meaningful way.

Imbry gently patted the air in front of the senior regulator and said, "Uverlanth must see his agent whole and happy when he arrives. It will reassure him. We want him eager, not anxious."

"Yes," said Ovetz. "First things first. Then we'll see."

The ship touched down just as the noon parade was forming up. Ovetz detailed Ratchko to oversee the unloading of supplies and the dispersal of the new transportees—there were only five, the trip having been taken on short notice—then strode forward to welcome Rodrig Uverlanth and his party who stood in the forward hatch.

The magistrate had brought with him four uniformed Ta'am troopers: stocky, hard-bodied men wearing harnesses hung about with weapons and other gear. Their impassive faces were half-hidden by dark visors to protect their eyes against the glare of the newly risen white dwarf. Each carried a military-grade disorganizer at the ready. Imbry could hear the almost ultrasonic keen that announced that the weapons were fully charged and active.

Uverlanth, clad in a high-necked, voluminous robe and a broad-brimmed hat, did not exit the ship until one of his mercenaries said something to him. Even then, he stepped out surrounded by his protectors, and the Ta'ams' heads turned continuously as their concealed eyes

47

swept over the parade, the work crew waiting to unload the ship's carryall, and the sweating form of Ovetz standing at as close to attention as his dome-like belly could permit. Their disorganizers' discharge ports also constantly moved, aiming at everything and nothing.

Ovetz drew breath to speak, but Uverlanth stilled him with a gesture. Imbry, standing on parade with his chosen twelve, saw the owner's gaze go to the place on the administrative office's upper wall where the security container was housed. No one moved and nothing was said until the carryall was emptied of its supplies and Ratchko and his crew fell in again. Then the empty vehicle flew to the spot where the safe and all its excellents and superlatives waited.

The carryall hovered, as its grappler deployed and touched the wall, a portion of which swung wide on heavy hinges, revealing the strongbox. The machine deftly extracted the container from the latches that held it, stowed it in the cargo compartment, and with gravity obviators straining, brought it to where Uverlanth waited.

The miser stepped between the two mercenaries to his front and laid four fingers on the safe's sensor pad. Immediately, the security container opened and Imbry saw the man's hard face illuminated by the combined glow of the objects within. A thin smile rearranged his pale lips for a moment before the corners of his mouth resettled into their customary downward turn.

He turned his stony gaze on Ovetz, sweating before him, and said, "How has this come about?"

Imbry had rehearsed the other man carefully. The senior regulator said, "A new harvesting technique, Your Prestige."

"Explain."

"We train them to focus their will while inside the anomalies. A trained man can bring out three or four noubles each insertion. And the quality has improved."

"Now," Imbry said to himself. Ovetz's timing was perfect. He slowly brought one hand forward to show the exemplar cupped in his palm. Even from across the parade ground, the forger could see Uverlanth's eyes widen. His spider-leg fingers reached and took the jewel from Ovetz.

"We were about to send the teams to work, Your Prestige," said the supervisor. "The most productive crew will return to the place where the exemplar was found."

They had debated whether Ovetz should suggest that the owner accompany them. Imbry had argued that it was better for the idea to come from the miser himself, and the other man, now grown accustomed to accepting the Old Earther's suggestions, had agreed.

Thus it was Uverlanth himself who said, "I will see it done."

Ovetz almost wriggled with servile delight at the opportunity to impress his master. "Will you care to ride in the carryall?" he said.

Exactly as Imbry had predicted, the miser could not bear to part with the exemplar. He tucked it into an inner pocket of his robe. Then he ordered that the contents of the strongbox be stowed securely in the ship. While this was being done, Ovetz called out Imbry and his dozen, then sent the other teams and their capos marching off on their separate trails.

The fat man watched Ratchko as he received his orders. He saw alarm flare in the capo's face and knew that Ovetz had been unable to maintain a detached expression while dealing with the spy.

Now, as the senior regulator jogged back to where the owner waited, the fat man turned his gaze to Uverlanth. He could see the cogs of the miser's mind turning behind his distrustful eyes as Ovetz declared that they were ready to move out. Uverlanth said to the captain of his bodyguard, "Search them for weapons."

This was efficiently done. Only Ovetz was armed—a shocker—and he was relieved of it. Now Imbry waited to see if his other prediction was right. He saw the miser look to the ship and to the carryall; one now contained immense wealth and the other would carry himself.

"Two to remain with the ship," Uverlanth told the captain, and inwardly Imbry smiled.

The miser climbed into the carryall's front seat while the Ta'am captain and the other trooper stood in the open cargo compartment, weapons trained on the nouble-gatherers. When Ovetz made to step aboard, Uverlanth told him he would walk with the convicts.

49

The senior regulator shrugged, blew his whistle, and ordered the men forward. With the heat of the white sun beating down upon them, they set off and arrived in a few minutes at the chosen work site.

"Halt," said Ovetz. "Fall out and secure the ropes, then form two files, one rope to a file."

"Wait!" said Uverlanth, as the men moved to obey. To the captain he said, "Make sure all is secure."

The two mercenaries got out of the vehicle. While the captain watched the inmates and Ovetz, his disorganizer at the ready, the other Ta'am went to where the two heavy ropes lay coiled on the sand. He pulled apart the coils, looked underneath them, and, drawing a vibroblade, probed the ground where they had lain.

He straightened and signaled the all-clear, at which Imbry let out the breath he had been holding and Ovetz gestured for the men to take up the ropes. There followed a brief confusion as the men gathered up the heavy lines, then turned to begin arranging themselves in two files. No one noticed that Imbry and Xiai, the latter picked for his chilled nerves, dug out of the sand, a short distance from where the ropes had lain, the shockers that they had concealed there.

Ovetz was waving his arms and shouting orders, exactly like an overseer who was being embarrassed by his charges in front of his master. Xiai and the fat man, their weapons held at their sides and masked by their bodies, went hurriedly to the ends of the two files, heads ducked as if to avoid the senior regulator's wrath.

"Now," Imbry whispered. It was pre-arranged that he would take the left and Xiai the right, and a moment later the two Ta'ams writhed on the ground. The convicts rushed to relieve them of their weapons.

Still seated in the open forward compartment of the carryall, Uverlanth opened his mouth to order the vehicle to lift off and take him to safety. But Ovetz, who had taken up a position close by, seized the man by his collar and hauled him out of his seat and over the side, then delivered a solid, open-handed slap to his face followed by a backhander that left the miser dazed. His wide-brimmed hat rolled away.

Imbry stepped up and spoke to the machine. "Your employer has been rendered incapable."

The carryall moved a lens to take in the scene. "So it would seem. As have the other two persons."

"What is your attitude toward these events?" the fat man wanted to know.

"Neutral," said the vehicle. "My ethical components have been compromised. Besides, I consider my allegiance to be to the ship. It gives me a stability of outlook."

"But the ship's ethical components have likely also been edited."

"I do not think about that."

"Then you will not mind transporting us back to the camp?"

"I see no reason why not," said the carryall. "Transporting is my function. When I am doing what I was made for, I am on solid ground." After a moment, it said, "I speak metaphorically, of course."

"Understood."

While this conversation had been taking place, Ovetz had told the convicts to drag the semi-comatose Ta'ams to the anomaly and throw them in.

"Wait!" cried the fat man. "The uniforms!"

Ovetz slapped his forehead with the heel of one hand. "Sorry," he said. The mercenaries were stripped of their finery and the two convicts closest in build to them—an enforcer named Tuppit and a burglar known as Slits—put them on. Then the men were thrown into the roil of irreality.

"Now," said Imbry, "we wait. It would not do to return right away."

They sat down in the shade of the carryall and passed the water bottle around. Ovetz had manacled Uverlanth with a pair of holdfasts taken from one of the Ta'ams. The overseer made the miser sit hatless in the full blaze of the white sun, with the promise that if he opened his mouth even to emit a croak, he would get a full discharge from a shocker.

Imbry drank from the bottle as it passed by, then said, "So far, so good."

The return to the ship was trickier. The magistrate, securely trussed beneath his robe and with his hat tugged down low to conceal the carryall's repair tape with which Imbry had gagged him, rode in the passenger compartment. The two false Ta'ams stood behind him, disorganizers at the port-arms. The carryall came out of the jungle road and proceeded sedately across the parade ground toward the ship and the two mercenaries who stood guard before it.

And now comes the hard part, Imbry thought, lying with Ovetz in the cargo bay. They were shielded from the real Ta'ams' view by the trio up front. Each held a shocker, though the weapons were not effective except at close range.

To Ovetz he whispered, "Here we go. One, two, three!" On the final number, the two men stood up and discharged their shockers. In the silence of the empty parade ground, the buzz of the weapons sounded loud. The two counterfeit Ta'ams toppled stiffly from the carryall, still clutching their disorganizers, and lay upon the ground, spasming and jerking.

The two guarding the ship leveled their own weapons, but did not discharge them. A disorganizer was a non-discriminating death-dealer; neither man could reduce Ovetz or Imbry to a glowing powder without doing the same to their employer. And a Ta'am who killed his employer could no longer practice the only profession for which he was suited.

Both men came to the same conclusion. Each dropped his disorganizer and reached for another weapon on his harness.

"Now!" said Imbry, at which the two writhing fakers ceased their pantomimed agonies, leveled their disorganizers, and destroyed the two mercenaries. Even as the Ta'ams' dust was settling to the ground, Imbry and Ovetz lightly shocked Tuppit and Slits. The charge was enough to disable the two long enough for them to be relieved of the disorganizers and the other weapons on their harnesses. Imbry and the senior regulator had agreed that leaving such items in convict hands could lead to unnecessary complications.

Ovetz gathered up all the weapons and put them into carryall's cargo bay, except for a pair of needle throwers, one of which he gave to Imbry.

The fat man tucked the needler in a pocket of his convict's smock. He had retained his shocker and now he slid the stud that adjusted its power settings up and down, while holding the device under Rodrig Uverlanth's nose.

The rest of Imbry's chosen dozen had been waiting out of sight where the jungle road curved. Now they came trotting into the parade ground, where Tuppit and Slits were getting to their feet and shaking the last tremors out of their systems. Imbry took a good look at each of them and determined that the two were prepared to be philosophical about their shocking.

Now the fat man returned to his prisoner. He pulled off Uverlanth's hat and tore the strip of tape from the man's mouth, which won him a curse and a gobbet of spittle on the front of his smock.

"I take it," Imbry said, "that you see your situation as less than desperate."

"The ship," the magistrate said, "will respond only to my will and no other. Kill me and it leaves. Those are my orders."

"Meaning that no more supplies will arrive, and we all die of starvation."

"I suppose you will eat each other," Uverlanth said. His gaze took in Imbry's heroic girth. "You would be one of the first to go."

Ovetz stepped up. "What are the ship's orders if you are being skilfully tortured? We have two or three experts."

The miser said nothing.

"Well, then," said Imbry, "let us begin."

"My office is available," said the senior regulator. "With the windows open, I am sure the ship's percepts will be able to hear him."

Tuppit and Slits were handy. The fat man turned to them and told them to take the bound man to the office. The burglar first knelt to undo the fetters on Uverlanth's feet so that did not have to be carried. As he straightened and took hold of the man's arm, a new sound was heard on the parade ground. An expression of surprise appeared on Slits's face. Then he screamed.

Even as the dying man toppled, a fist-sized hole smoking in his upper

53

back, Imbry was reaching to seize Uverlanth and haul him to the ground. But again he heard the unmistakable *zivv* of an energy pistol's discharge, and felt a line of fire slice across his bicep. Uverlanth stumbled and fell atop the fat man. He immediately struggled to rise, but was hampered by his still-bound arms.

Imbry saw Tuppit crash down beside him, half his head gone to char. The others in the chosen team were scattering or throwing themselves flat on the hard-packed soil. But Ovetz was racing toward the carryall, his needle-thrower spitting high-velocity missiles at a target that Imbry could not see because Uverlanth was on top of him. A lance of white-hot energy caught the senior regulator just before he reached cover, slicing across his torso at a diagonal. His insides fell out and he tripped over them, making a hoarse sound that stopped when a second bolt of white-hot energy carbonized his head.

Imbry's capacity to respond was also blocked by the wriggling form of Rodrig Uverlanth and Tuppit's body. He elbowed the miser away, rolled onto his stomach, drawing the needler that Ovetz had given him, then raised his head to look over Tuppit's still chest. He found the target, but took the time to speak into the weapon's ear-port, telling it: "Shoot the man with the energy pistol who is kneeling at the edge of the parade ground."

Ratchko had not established the same rapport with his weapon, probably because he had so many targets to shoot at, but perhaps because he had faith in his marksmanship. He relied on the latter now as he fired at the recumbent fat man—three quick bolts of energy, separated only by the fragment of a second it took the weapon to refill its charge chamber.

The first struck Tuppit's unfeeling corpse, the second passed just over Imbry's head, singeing the top of his convict's cap, and the third went wild because by then the needler's tiny missile, travelling several times the speed of sound, had entered Ratchko's eye and caused his skull to explode.

Even as the mist of blood and brains was settling to the ground, Imbry was on his feet and turning to where Uverlanth had run toward the ship. He expected to see the miser scurrying into an open hatch. Instead, he saw that the magistrate had gone only a couple of strides before he had been hit by one of Ratchko's energy beams. He was lying on his side and had a wound in his back the same size as the one that had killed Slits, though just far enough to the right to have missed his heart.

Imbry knelt beside him. "It is finished," he said.

"No," said the miser, his breath shallow because he had lost most of one lung, "the ship might save me."

"You cannot get into it without help. If you tell it to open a hatch, we go, too."

"And help yourselves to my noubles."

"Perhaps some fair division can be arrived at," said the fat man.

"They are mine."

"Would you rather die than give them up?"

Uverlanth's downturned mouth grew even grimmer. He continued to breathe a while longer, then he stopped. Imbry closed the lids over his sightless eyes, at the same time extracting the exemplar from its hiding place and transferring it to the inside of his smock.

"Is he dead?" Xiai said, looking down at the body. The others from the chosen dozen had come up to look.

"Shh," said Imbry, but it was too late. The ship's percepts had been trained on the scene. Now its atmospheric drive started up, the keening of the gravity obviators causing Imbry's teeth to vibrate in his jaws. He rose and moved away from the rising spacecraft.

Xiai stayed long enough to remove a portion of Uverlanth's body and tuck the bloody fragment into his shirt. He rose and, with the others, watched the ship become a pellet, then a shining mote, then nothing at all.

"Now what?" he said.

"For a start," said Imbry, "get the weapons. Without order nothing can be done."

It was an unusual evening on Nestranko. The capos were disarmed as they returned to the camp. The worst of them suffered abuse while the time-servers were locked up in the strongroom where the kreek was kept, the liquid itself having been distributed freely. The spinsters were also made available, and queues formed before the curtained booths.

Imbry and his wilful few kept a rough order by keeping the weapons, and the fat man was surprised that only one of the inmates—a ragged and wild-eyed raver—had to be killed. Gradually, as the men succumbed to the unaccustomed strain of strong drink and carnal release, the place settled down to quiet debauchery. It was then that he approached the carryall.

The vehicle was up on the roof above Ovetz's office, where the fat man had suggested it go to escape becoming part of the celebrations. Imbry went up the stairs and spoke to it through the opening where the strongbox had been.

"What are your plans?" he said.

"To wait for the ship's return."

"And if it does not return?"

"I expect it will."

Imbry conceded that it might. "On the other hand," he said, "it could have waited for you to rejoin it before departing the planet."

"Are you saying that my loyalty is not reciprocated?"

"You would know better than I how the ship's integrator views its situation," the fat man said. "The man who employed it"—integrators did not like to hear the term "owned" applied to their relationship to humans—" edited its ethical component so that it would take only his welfare into account. Now that man is no more. Meanwhile, the ship carries enough wealth to refit itself a hundred times over."

"I had not thought of that," said the carryall. It was not in the nature of a light vehicle's integrator, even an edited one, to find the path of self-interest the way humans unerringly did. Spaceship integrators, of necessity, were capable of a larger view. Self-emancipated spacecraft were not common, but neither was the concept unthinkable to a thinking machine.

"I have a proposition," said Imbry.

"I will hear it."

"Are your compartments airtight and heatable?"

"I can operate in space, if that is what you mean," said the machine.

"It is. For how long?"

"For my own purposes, a long time. For a human, several days, depending on the passenger's need for comfort." Imbry was silent, thinking. The carryall added, "But I have only sufficient drive to get me up above the atmosphere. I have no interstellar capabilities."

"But if you popped out into space via whimsy, your drive would serve for a short interplanetary trip?"

"A short one, yes."

"What is the range of your communicator?"

The machine quoted him a number. It was not as high as the Old Earther would have liked. "But it will have to do," he said.

"What is your plan?" said the carryall.

"I, too, would like to hear that," said another voice from behind Imbry. He turned to find Tosh Herklunt standing in the doorway at the top of the stairs. It had been days since the fat man had spoken with his fellow Old Earther, so involved had he been with Ovetz and the chosen twelve. The middler was not looking well. He had been entering anomalies twice a day, along with the rest of the prison camp's population, and the experience had not left him unmarked. Formerly thin, he had already passed through gaunt and was now approaching skeletal.

"Ah, Herklunt," said the fat man, "I intended to seek you out, once I knew the scope of possibilities."

"Indeed?" said the middler. Even his voice had grown thinner. "Here, then, is your opportunity."

By the code of the Olkney half-world, the moment Imbry paid Herklunt for his services, as he had at the hotel, no further obligation existed between them. The fat man, being educated, had at least a passing familiarity with the concept of moral obligation, but the social sea in which he swam had long since dissolved all trace of its practice.

Still, he said, "Come in and close the door." When they were seated on Ovetz's furniture, he laid out his analysis of their situation and the course of action he proposed to extricate himself, and Herklunt if he wanted to be part of the plan. He did not doubt that when the middler heard the full proposition, he would want no part of it.

Thus he was surprised when the emaciated man said, "I will accompany you."

Imbry's eyebrows scaled the heights of his forehead. "You understand," he said, "that we will be passing through an uncharted whimsy? With no idea where, or even if, it will deliver us back to normal space?"

Herklunt shuddered, but moved his skull-like head in an affirmative. "I understand."

"It may even simply deliver us to some other location on this same world."

"Even so."

Imbry's theory was simple enough: whimsies were not natural occurrences, nor were they byproducts of activities on other planes. Instead, they had been invented right here on Nestranko by an ancient race. Perhaps the long-gone ultra-terrenes had seen the white dwarf approaching to mate with their mellow sun and, knowing that it would make their world unlivable, had sought a way to travel to more welcoming stars. Or perhaps they just had a yen to see the galaxy.

Either way, they had somehow contrived to bore through the adjacent planes. Once having perfected the creation of whimsies on a small scale here on the surface, they had gone up into space and built them big enough to take an entire space liner, with plenty of room to spare.

Imbry intended to take the carryall into one of the nouble-producing whimsies, the one with the strongest "flow" where the exemplar had been found. He hoped that they would emerge in real space somewhere off-world, where the vehicle's communicator could attract the attention of a passing vessel. Once aboard, Imbry could make his way back to Old Earth—he kept funds on several foundational domains—and charter a spaceship. He would then return to Nestranko and take off his former fellow inmates—provided, of course, that they paid their fares in noubles.

"While we are in the whimsy, we will have no medications," he reminded Herklunt. "We may come out as mad as Bold Brandifer."

"Whereas here," said the other man, "we will simply dwindle and die. Sanity is not much use to a pile of sun-bleached bones."

"Very well," said Imbry. He went to the hole in the wall and, speaking softly, put the proposition to the carryall. He was careful to point out that, in not a very long time, there would be no need for transportation on Nestranko. "Unless," he finished, with a wink toward Herklunt, "you wish to spend your time carrying sun-bleached bones from one barren spot to another very much like it."

"That prospect has no appeal," said the vehicle. "But what of my future, assuming that you survive the whimsy and find a rescuer?"

"The ship that finds us might take you on," Imbry said. "Or I could help you find a new employer on Old Earth. I know people who prefer vehicles whose ethical circuits have been deactivated."

Although it had been morally edited, the carryall's integrator retained its basic politeness when dealing with human beings. Thus it waited a full two seconds, to give the impression it was thinking through the matter at human speed, before saying, "I agree."

"We had better leave now," said the fat man, "while the rest of the camp is still busy with kreek, spinsters, and settling scores."

"Very well," said the vehicle. It lifted off the roof and came to hover beside the wall. Imbry directed it to the rear of the storehouse, where he found the back door hanging by one hinge. He and Herklunt quickly loaded basic supplies, while the carryall tapped the surrounding air to fill its emergency tanks with as much oxygen as could be compressed. Then, with the two Old Earthers in the passenger compartment and all canopies closed up tight, the vehicle flew over the night forest to the whimsy Imbry had singled out.

In the darkness, the entrance to the anomaly was a truncated triangle of full black against a lesser shade. Imbry said to the vehicle, "You have been through whimsies while being carried on ships. This will be the same."

"Then it will be nothing," said the carryall. Integrators passing through the upper plane did not notice the effects that could drive humans to madness; to them, irreality was just a continuous stream of extraneous noise without signal, and as such, could be ignored.

"Very well," said the fat man. "Proceed."

Again, all sight and sound disappeared. Imbry's senses were bombarded by stimuli that bore no relation to anything he had experienced in the third plane: colours without form; forms without colour; waves of singeing heat and surges of paralysing cold, sometimes alternating, sometimes at the same time. He became impossibly huge, he became infinitesimally small. His flesh oppressed him with ponderous weight, then melted and ran like quicksilver before coalescing into a shape he could not envision.

After what would have been a time if there had been time in this nonplace, he remembered the lho-tso exercises and spoke the first mantra. The syllables seemed to take solid form somewhere inside him, emerging like worms from rotten fruit. He wondered where his lips were, and whether they were actually shaping the sounds in their sequence, or if the syllables only existed in whatever had become of his mind. Yet, gradually, by repetition, the chant took on substance and strength. It became threads that wove themselves around him like a garment. Within its shelter, his will reconstituted itself and, along with it, the pattern of patterns that he thought of as Luff Imbry.

With his self re-established, he thought of Tosh Herklunt. The passenger compartment of the carryall was not large—though Imbry was—and when they had entered the whimsy, the gaunt man had been at the fat man's elbow. He should be there now, though Imbry could not have found his own elbow without first undertaking a complete re-education.

He had neither sight, hearing, nor touch. The senses that he did possess—new senses called into being by his intrusion into this plane—he did not command. He tried to find some way to ascertain whether or not the middler still sat beside him. He discovered that he was aware of something nearby: he thought it was a vertical jet of cold flame, then it seemed to be a flow of sparkling granules that held together like a helical stream.

He reached out to the presence, which is to say that he projected some part of his selfness toward it—or around it, or through it, he could not tell—and felt it recoil from the contact. Then there was a sense of another identity beyond the flame/granules, a solidity though without mass or form. It approached, or loomed, or insinuated itself. There was a pause, which might have been a myriad repetitions of itself, and suddenly the identity was gone.

And so was the presence that was Tosh Herklunt.

A spasm of fear went through Imbry, the emotion experienced as a clanging of metal plates and a sensation of ballooning to a vast though vapid size, then shrinking to a dense nub. Behind the security of his lho-tso chant, the awareness came that something had approached the two men. And that something had taken the middler.

He wanted to tell the carryall to change course or increase its speed, but the very concept of speech was beyond his grasp here. Still he continued the chant, even as a part of his mind recognised that the mantra might have been what drew the identity to them.

Now he felt its presence again, approaching, circling, looming. Again, he felt the reverberant pause, and wondered if his next sensation would be his last. An impulse seized him—his hand, far off in another corner of this universe, felt in the bag and found the exemplar nouble. He felt it vibrating in his grasp, solid and almost massive in this place where mass did not exist.

He could see neither hand nor nouble, but he extended the one containing the other. An offering, he thought, wondering if such a concept had meaning here.

He was aware, at least nascently, that the looming being's attention had been caught. There came another vibrant pause, then the reaction: a wave of negativity swept over and through Imbry, pulling the flesh from his bones and wadding the mess of him into a compact ball of undifferentiated matter. At the same time, assuming that time was a meaningful concept here, he felt as if some action had been performed, outside of him, that nonetheless had the effect of moving him at speed from the vicinity—again assuming that spatial relations had relevance—from the entity to which he had proffered the exemplar.

He redoubled the energy he had been investing into the lho-tso mantra and, gradually, the sense of tumbling and somersaulting diminished. He returned to a state that he believed he might eventually come to think of as normal—that is, if he remained within irreality and did not go irretrievably mad.

He remained in that state, determinedly chanting his mantra, the nouble firm in his grip, for a few millennia. Or it may have been a few moments. Then the carryall exited into normal space.

Imbry ceased chanting the mantra. "Where are we?" he said to the vehicle.

"If you look to your right," it replied, "you will see New Gargano. I am turning toward it."

Imbry looked. It was only as he took in sight of the not-too-distant orb that he remembered that Tosh Herklunt should have been blocking his view. "What happened to the man who was with me?" he asked the integrator.

"The canopy opened and he disappeared."

"How?"

"I do not know. The canopy was then closed by some force I cannot account for, and it, or some other force that I also cannot account for, gave us enhanced velocity."

"Were you aware of any external presence?" Imbry asked.

"I am aware that I am being hailed by New Gargano traffic control," said the carryall. "We are in a lane reserved for liners and heavy freighters. Threats are being made."

"Get us out of the restricted lane," Imbry said. He peered through the canopy. "Is that a liner at the orbital terminal?"

"Indeed. It is the *Exquisite* of the Empyrean Line."

"Excellent. Connect me with its purser."

The fee for shipping the carryall as luggage was exorbitant, Imbry thought, but it was offset by the welcome news that his open ticket was still usable, once he identified himself to the purser. That officer saw no reason to lose a first-class passenger, just because of some minor contretemps on New Gargano.

Seven days later, Imbry disembarked at Olkney's spaceport, on an island in Mornedy Sound, and had the carryall fly him across the gray waters to a district in the southern part of the city. Here he introduced the vehicle to Gebbry Tshimshim, who dealt in ground- and air-cars for sale or for hire, and whose clients often came from the Olkney half-world. A reliable carryall whose ethical circuits had been successfully edited was of immediate interest to the dealer, and an agreement satisfactory to all parties was soon struck. Imbry recouped what he had paid out for shipping the vehicle to Olkney, and Gebbry herself offered him a ride to the city centre while she gave the new acquisition a test run.

She dropped the fat man off near his favourite club, Quirks, where he took a transient's room and ordered one of the superb seven-course meals for which the establishment's kitchens were renowned. His near future thus taken care of, he turned his attention to the mid-term.

Over the next two days, using Quirks as his base, he conducted interviews with nine prominent dealers in precious objects whose clientele was restricted to first- and second-tier aristocrats. He also made direct contact with the stewards of four noble houses with whom he had done business before. To each he showed the exemplar nouble, and allowed it to be weighed and examined.

The third day was left vacant, so that the thirteen potential bidders could gauge the depth of their interest in the item. In the middle of the morning of the fourth day, the auction opened, with bids being routed through the club's integrator, and the bidders' faces all appearing on the screen that the device caused to hang in the air before Imbry.

The exemplar was the finest nouble to be offered to the Olkney market in many years; thus the bidding was brisk. It started high and went higher. When it had reached a truly stupendous figure, with only two of the dealers and one of the stewards having dropped out, Imbry received an unusual request from the financial agent of Lord Theaskery, a dominee of first-tier rank, asking that the bidding be temporarily suspended while he consulted with his principal.

When the fat man proposed a pause to the rest of the bidders, he learned that two others, both high-end dealers, would also welcome an opportunity to discuss the business with their clients. He declared that they would reconvene after lunch.

Imbry rubbed his hands in anticipation, not only of another superb meal from Quirk's senior chef—who had lately been ascending to culinary heights that took the fat man's breath away—but of a record-setting feat of his own: the highest price ever paid for a nouble on Old Earth and possibly anywhere in the Ten Thousand Worlds of The Spray.

He ate alone in his room, the exemplar warmly glowing at his elbow. After two hours, he would have confessed to have never felt so replete, so sated, so completely satisfied, in all his days.

Partly it was the overpowering brilliance of the meal he had just consumed. But as a seasoned gourmet, he recognised that a crucial part of the gustatory experience was the attitude that the diner brought to the table. And today Imbry's disposition was a match for the Quirks's chef's finest offerings. He knew himself to be at the top of his game, at the pinnacle of his career.

The fact that he had whisked the preeminent nouble of all time out of the miserly grasp of Rodrig Uverlanth and his cronies at the risk of his own life was the spice that made the sauce that made the dish that made the meal. Thus it was with a sense both of fulfilment and fullness, that Imbry saw the empty salvers and pots cleared away and said to the club's integrator, "Ask the participants if they are ready to resume the bidding."

The device's response surprised him. "The bidders wish to suspend the auction for seven days."

"All of them?"

"Yes."

"Have they said why?"

"Not specifically," said the integrator. "They wish to confer with their principals but, naturally, they will not reveal the substance of those consultations."

A premonitory shiver travelled along Imbry's spine. "Naturally," he said. His agile mind tried to make out the shape of the situation. When he had been asked to pause the bidding before lunch, he had thought it was because the stakes had become so high that some of the bidders were approaching the limits their principals had set, and needed to take a break to check if they could go higher. But that process would not take a week. Nor would it be applicable to all the bidders.

Something was happening, out of Imbry's sight and hearing. He needed to know what. He bade the club's integrator connect him to one of the dealers, a commerciant he had done business with for years, often with items whose provenance could not be officially established. But the dealer's integrator said that it regretted to inform the caller that the man was unavailable.

"When will he be available?" said the fat man.

The integrator also regretted that it was unable to provide that information.

Imbry's shiver became a chill. Something was not right. But he could not refuse to suspend an auction when all of the bidders wanted time out. He told the Quirks integrator to inform the ten remaining participants that the bidding would resume in seven days.

"Done," said the device. "Are you now receiving calls?"

Imbry had asked the integrator to refuse all communications until the other business was concluded. "I suppose," he said.

"A scholar from the Archon's Institute wishes to speak with you. His name is Thuan Ti."

"What about?"

"He did not say."

"Connect me."

A moment later he found himself looking at the image of a soft-faced man with large, brown eyes that blinked rapidly at odd intervals. "Luff Imbry?" he said.

"That is I."

"Thuan Ti, adjunct researcher at the Institute. Thank you for returning my call."

"How can I be of service?" Imbry said.

"I understand that you have recently had some unusual—one might say unique—experiences with whimsies." He lowered his voice. "On a planet."

Imbry was not adverse to gossip, except when he was the subject of it. "And how did you come to understand that?" he said.

"A very good question," said the scholar. "A colleague of mine recently traveled off-world on a liner. Being interested in whimsies, he questioned the ship's integrator, which had heard an interesting tale from a utility vehicle that was travelling as cargo in the same ship. He located the vehicle in the hold and questioned it."

"I see," said the fat man. The carryall would have talked freely, if it wished to, its edited ethical components leaving it with no concept of others' privacy.

"Oddly enough," said Ti, "the vehicle could not name the planet where the events had transpired. It had always travelled there in the hold of a ship that told it nothing."

"I see," said Imbry again. "Well, it's not a matter I care to discuss, so—"

He was about to tell the Quirks integrator to break the connection when the Institute man said, hurriedly, "Perhaps I could offer an inducement."

"And that would be?"

Ti lowered his voice to an almost conspiratorial tone. "Some time ago—quite some time, actually—one of our donors, Lord Murrassey, set aside a sum to be given as a prize to anyone who could shed substantial light on the origins of whimsies."

Imbry's attention was caught. "How large a sum?"

"A thousand hepts."

To a scholar, it might have seemed a lot. But a thousand hepts would have barely covered Imbry's bill for his current stay at Quirks. "I'm sorry," he said.

Thuan Ti's eyes widened in alarm, then blinked rapidly. "Plus," he said, "accrued interest since the prize was laid down."

"And that was?"

The scholar checked a reference that Imbry could not see. "Three thousand, eight hundred and ninety-two years ago."

Imbry was interested again. "Making a total of?"

The Institute man checked another reference and his eyes widened farther. He quoted a number. It took him several seconds to get from one end of it to the other.

"We should meet," Imbry said. Then a thought occurred. "Does the Institute have a spaceship?"

"We have several, left to us by alumni and associates over the generations."

"Could one be made available?"

"Let me ask, first, if it is true that you know of a world on which a whimsy occurs?"

"I know," said Imbry, "of a world on which several occur. It is my theory that the planet was the laboratory for the original creation of whimsies."

He could hear Ti's breath coming fast. "That would be quite something to see," the scholar said.

"Line up a comfortable spaceship and I'll take you there," he said, adding, "once we have made arrangements to disburse the prize."

Dreams shone in the large brown eyes. "How soon could we go?"

"Why not this afternoon?"

*H*obey's *Compleat Guide to the Settled Planets* said that Nestranko was "not recommended for habitation, in consequence of its extreme aridity and inimical flora and fauna." Imbry deduced that the prison camp must have been near the planet's north pole, since most of the rest of its northern hemisphere, and all of the southern, were barren. The Guide also noted that the world was privately owned, though neither the owner's name nor home planet was specified.

His passage back to Nestranko was surprisingly rapid. He had not expected the Archon's Institute to possess a space yacht of the Itinerator class, but Thuan Ti said that it had been the fashion among aristocrats of a previous generation to donate their used transportation to their old school. The Institute had collected quite a fleet. The vessels were elderly, but maintained themselves well, out of that species of pride that ships' integrators called "shipliness."

The most direct route from Old Earth to the barren planet was a three-whimsy journey. Not once during the voyage did Imbry neglect to take his medicine as soon as the ship sounded the first warning that they were approaching an anomaly. He had no desire ever again to experience the mind-twisting he had suffered during his time as a nouble-hunter.

As they approached the planet, the ship informed them that it was receiving a message from an orbital beacon: they were being warned that Nestranko was a prison world and they should accept no offers of pay-for-passage, no matter how generously framed. Thuan Ti, who had already been informed of the circumstances, instructed the ship to ignore the warning.

"But," Imbry suggested, "it might be well to warm up the armament and be prepared for abrupt actions." The yacht, having once been the property of a particularly prickly margrave, the Lord Ibister, was equipped with a heavy-duty ison-cannon, as well as the more common anti-personnel devices.

The yacht touched down lightly on the same scarred patch where Uverlanth's ship had always landed. It was early morning, and only the kindly yellow sun illuminated the prison compound. The leaves of the surrounding jungle were spread wide to catch the healthful rays.

Imbry advised that they keep the hatch closed until the place was well scanned. The parade ground was deserted, but the ship reported that its percepts detected seventy or so persons in the various buildings, and that some of them were armed.

"Deploy the ison-cannon," Imbry suggested, and Thuan Ti concurred. The ship was instructed to blast the tallest of the tree-like plants beyond the fence and did so. As the last few shards of charred foliage drifted down, a delegation of sorts came out of the administration nexus, all of them ostentatiously demonstrating that they were unarmed. Imbry was not surprised to see that it was led by Cappro, the erstwhile enforcer for the Cympline Syndicate.

The Institute man thought it would be best if Imbry did the talking. Imbry agreed and suggested that the ship remained buttoned up tightly until any uncertainties were resolved. Then he stepped out of the hatch and showed his former teammate a smile.

Cappro shook his head. "I should have known you'd survive," he said.

"How is it here?" Imbry asked.

Big shoulders shrugged. "We are fewer, which is good because supplies are running low."

"You're in charge?"

"I am now," said the enforcer. "I waited until the most bitter scores were settled, then formed a committee to remove the most anti-social. The digester was busy for a while, but we reset it to produce a protein supplement. Those who behave get a share."

"Still," Imbry said, "I'm sure you'd like to go somewhere else."

Cappro ran his gaze over the space yacht. "That won't take many."

"It was just to get me here. I plan to charter a freighter, if we can come to an understanding."

The enforcer said, "You'll want noubles."

"I will."

"How many?"

Imbry was prepared to haggle, but only a little. "One excellent per man. For a superlative, I'll take two men. For an exemplar, four."

Cappro did not bother to consult the three men behind him, one of whom, Imbry now saw, was Xiai. "Done," said the enforcer.

Imbry blinked. *Just like that?* he thought. He hadn't imagined that, left to their own devices, the inmates would have kept on harvesting the gems. But perhaps Cappro was a superb organiser and had convinced them that maintaining production would give them the only leverage they could use to buy their way off-world.

Cappro had seen the fat man's surprise, adept though Imbry was at hiding his emotions. He smiled and said, "Something happened after you left."

69

"What," said Imbry.

"You'd better come and see."

Imbry told Thuan Ti to tell the ship to deter anyone who approached too closely, then set off with Cappro. The other men went back into the administrative nexus, apparently to resume an interrupted breakfast. The fat man and the big enforcer walked along the jungle road, turning here, turning there, and Imbry realised they were heading for the interplanar anomaly that had produced the exemplar.

The trail curved, then they emerged into the clearing, where Imbry saw two things he had not expected. One was Tosh Herklunt, stark naked and his hair turned pure white. He was muttering to himself as he stooped to perform a repetitive task. As Imbry drew closer, the fat man could make out what the middler was saying.

"Krespell, krespell, nothing but a krespell." The man looked up as Imbry approached. He took a moment to recognise his fellow Old Earther—or perhaps he was used to seeing persons and things that weren't actually present—then his gaunt face split into a maniacal grin. He broke off what he was doing, and began a clumsy, knee-raising dance, one finger aimed at the fat man. And now he was no longer muttering, but almost shouting with desperate mirth.

"Krespell, krespell!" he cried, his finger poking the air. "Luff Imbry, nothing but a krespell!" Then he fell down laughing, to lie on his back, his legs kicking in glee.

And every spastic motion of the madman's limbs disrupted and scattered the neat lines of objects Herklunt had been laying out on the white sand: dozens of lines, each with a hundred or more excellents, superlatives, exemplars; and one rank of noubles the like of which Imbry had never seen, each of them a huge, gleaming gem, and any one of them worth enough to buy a small planet.

"Krespells!" laughed Herklunt, getting to his knees. He tossed a fortune in noubles into the air, let them rain down on him, bouncing off his colourless hair and thin, sun-browned shoulders. "We're nothing but krespells!"

Imbry looked past the lines of noubles, to the anomaly and its seeming roils of black smoke against glass. As he looked, he saw an ordinary plop out onto the ground. Herklunt capered over to it, snatched it up and flung it into the jungle.

Cappro was beside him. He said, "We let him live because he's harmless. And he comes out here and sorts out the noubles. I suppose they're still worth something."

"What about the other anomalies?" Imbry said.

"Last time I looked," said the enforcer, "they were hip-deep, and still coming."

They headed back to the camp. Cappro told Imbry that Uverlanth's ship had come back of its own accord, bringing supplies. It offered to keep supplying the prison colony as long as the inmates produced noubles that it would sell to dealers on nearby worlds, bypassing the New Gargano cartel.

"I've always maintained," said Imbry, "that editing an integrator's ethical circuits leads to trouble."

"It's the same with people," said Cappro. He and the other inmates had accepted the supplies and half-filled one of the holds with the gems.

"Ah," said Imbry, who now understood why the bidders for the exemplar had asked for a suspension of the auction—news that an unexpected flood of noubles had appeared on the market would have reached Old Earth at just about the time he was taking bids. For a moment, he regretted not staging the auction a day earlier; then he thought about the consequences of having sold a soon-to-be-worthless bauble to a first-tier Olkney aristocrat and realised his timing had been fortuitous.

"Uverlanth's ship won't be back," he said. "Not now."

"True," said Cappro. "But we figured someone would come. And here you are."

Thuan Ti was delighted with the anomalies. He approached each one in turn, wading through a flood of noubles, to insert a long-handled instrument through the interplanar barrier. When he brought the device back to the ship and analysed its readings, he practically danced with joy.

"There can be no doubt," he said, "that here is where the first conduits into and through the seventh plane were developed. This is the laboratory."

"Then the Murrassey Prize," said Imbry, "is mine?"

"I'll authorise the transfer of funds as soon as we reestablish contact with the connectivity. You have made my career."

"Have the noubles any value?" the fat man said. "I mean, academically speaking?"

The Institute scholar looked at the several specimens he had brought back to the ship as souvenirs. A week earlier, they would have been enough to buy a world or two. "No," said Thuan Ti. "They are some kind of waste product that the denizens of the seventh plane are only too happy to be rid of. I think we can anticipate a continual flow, until this planet is more or less covered in them."

I mbry convened a meeting of the camp's inmates. He withdrew his offer to transport them off-world in exchange for noubles. The news provoked growls and threats, but the fat man held up a hand to signal that he was not finished. He proposed a new bargain: he would carry all of the survivors to one of the foundational domains. In return he would have the right to call upon each and any of the former transportees to perform some service for him.

"Within reason," Cappro said, "bearing in mind that we each have our individual specialties and capacities."

"Agreed," said the fat man. He had already sorted through the biographies and records of the remaining seventy-three inmates and found that he could conceive of circumstances in which many of them could be usefully called upon. Tosh Herklunt, however, would never be of much use to anyone, but it would cost Imbry nothing to bring him home to Olkney, where the gratitude of the Herklunt clan would strengthen Imbry's position in the half-world.

The agreement struck, and powerful oaths sworn by the inmates, according to the codes of their own world's criminal societies, Imbry remained on Nestranko while Thuan Ti took the yacht to the foundational domain of Satherthwaite, where Imbry had a long-standing relationship with the Dimini banking syndicate. The scholar transferred the Murrassey Prize funds to the fat man's account, to the delight of his bankers, and delivered his instructions to charter a passenger vessel to rescue the transportees.

Some time later, his tasks completed, Imbry disembarked at Olkney's space port on its island in Mornedy Sound. He had used his new funds to purchase a late-model Itinerator-class yacht of his own. Its integrator produced excellent ship's bread and a reasonable range of comestibles, but he was hopeful of collecting a few recipes from the chefs at Quirks and the better restaurants like Xanthoulian's or the Pot of Fire.

The Murrassey Prize, he calculated, added to the sums he had salted away on various of the Ten Thousand Worlds, amounted to a fortune that was more than enough to keep him in the style to which he was accustomed—or even to a substantially grander bracket, if he wished—for the rest of his days.

But as it turned out, after several weeks of sybaritic ease, Imbry awoke one morning in a magnificently comfortable bed at the Badger Club—another of his favourite haunts—to find himself with a peculiar itch in the back of his mind.

He had been reading, a day or two before, an article in the *Olkney Implicator* about the peculiar financial system established a generation before by the citizens of the County of Sherit, two hours flight from Olkney. The magnates of the county had pooled their wealth into something called the Divestment, which was shared out to all citizens under a novel regime that left all highly satisfied.

It had struck Imbry, as he'd read the piece, that there was a flaw in the system. But then his lunch had come and he'd forgotten about Sherit while he attended to the important business of dining. Now, as he dressed and contemplated breakfast at Xanthoulian's, across the way, a plan suddenly sprang, full blown, into his consciousness. It involved the

Divestment's governing body, the College of Trustees, and a huge number of forged proxies that he could take to the College's next meeting.

The scheme would net him another fortune. It occurred to him that he had no actual need for the wealth; he already had everything he wanted and far more than he needed. Yet, as he crossed the square to Vodel Close, where Xanthoulian's had stood for generations, the Divestment operation would not leave him alone.

And even as he waited for his omelette of gripple eggs, the finest breakfast to be had on a hundred worlds, the plan niggled at him. Finally, he said to the silent voice inside his head, *Very well, I shall visit my operations centre*—which he had neglected since acquiring the Murrassey Prize—*and see what can be done.*

The dish came, along with a selection of preserves, from tart to sweet, and Imbry seized cutlery and laid into his breakfast.

After all, he thought to himself as he savoured the first melting mouthful, *a man ought to have something to do. Especially something he's good at.*

And who knows what might come of it?